Also By Alice Ewens

Fear Country – A Journey from Lost to Mostly Found
(modern poetry)

WHISPERS & WILD THINGS

THINGS

Short Stories & Modern Folktales

by

ALICE EWENS

Cover designed by Alice Ewens utilising royalty free stock photography and fonts.

Cover images – @jr-korpa via Unsplash

Cover font – Horros

Internal font - Garamond

First Printing, 2019

ISBN 9781694264534

For more, see www.alicewroteit.com / @alicewroteit

For Mum,

This one's for you.

Contents

Introduction

For as long as I can remember, I've been captivated by folktales, myths, legends, fairy tales, all that good stuff. My paternal grandmother had several heavy books full of them that she'd leave piled under the bedside table to read to me when I stayed at her house. Often, she'd fall asleep first, resulting in my nudging her with a, "Wake *up* Grandma!" I'm still delighted with the somewhat fairy-tale like image of little me tucked up in the massive bed covered in chintz while my grandmother read into oblivion. My mum would tell me made-up stories of Herne the Hunter, lord of the wild wood, largely inspired by stories she loved. I grew bigger and began collecting my own tales, shepherding in stories around the little campfire of my mind, realising that this story was like *that* one, which was in turn so very similar to *this* story over here. The connections, the tendrils that wove and linked these old stories together fascinated me almost as much as the tales themselves did.

The Portuguese have a word - Cantadora - which means 'she who collects and passes on myths and stories to others', and though the closest lineage I can claim is Maltese, the word felt like a settling of my bones on the porch of a house I didn't know I'd been looking for. I can't claim the title of Cantadora; I'm not a linguist or even an academic scholar of folk and myth. But I do love a good folk story. I do know I've always collected well-worn tales caked in time and moss, refurbished them and passed them on, and that I like to do it in unexpected ways. It's a path left lit for me by many bolder, braver minds than mine, the keepers of worlds infinitely more imaginative than I could ever hope to dream up. Neil Gaiman, Terry Pratchett, Dr. Clarissa Pinkola Estes, Angela Carter, Ray Bradbury, to name a few.

I could dissolve into an academic essay here on the importance of myth, legend and folklore within history and evolution, our sense of cultural identity, of symbolism and psychology... but that's all been done a thousand times over by others. It's not really all that important to us everyday folk, just going about our business as the supporting cast in these vast weaving tales, is it? No. Nor does it really matter to us where they came from (although, again, that's a whole wonderfully complex map of human interaction and movement). What is important is that these stories exist at all, nurtured, folded, patched and passed down through generations. These are our inheritance.

Myths, legends, folktales - they *are* important. They serve a purpose, even if only to make us smile, though often they help us feel connected to something much bigger and older than ourselves. Humans have always told stories, as a way to make sense of the unknown, to learn and grow, to entertain, to build community. We still do it now, even though the world is so much bigger than it once was, even though we now know what lies beyond the campfire, the cave, the dark wood, the next hill. These old stories are symbols, and clues, and maps to where we came from, but also, I believe, inwards to where we can go. I love that. To paraphrase both G.K Chesterton and Neil Gaiman, stories are important not because they teach us that the bad stuff is out there, but because they teach us the bad stuff can be defeated.

This book houses some updated versions and new takes of those old stories in one place. Everything here is inspired by the rich tapestry of myths, legends and folktales specifically from the British Isles (England, Ireland, Scotland, Wales, Cornwall, the Hebrides, Orkneys and Isle of Man). Go back far enough here and the edges of history blur into myth and legend. Story is nestled in the roots and rocks and bones of these islands. There are many common threads weaving through them.

Apart from opening up the world of short stories to me (where fully formed characters and worlds exist for us to dip in and out of, though we know in our hearts we will never truly belong within them, like glimpses caught through windows as we shuttle past), Neil Gaiman and Stephen King's writings have also left me with the unerring conviction that every book must have an introduction. The how and where and why of the author. Honestly, I always feel a little disappointed now when there isn't one to pore over, in the same way that I pore over the behind the scenes and directors' commentaries on movies I love. So I'm including some extra little thoughts and titbits on the contents of this book here for you to entirely ignore if you wish - the stories will stand up just fine without you having read these extra bits, although I can't promise they won't hold a bit of a grudge...

The Price Of Success

Dragons are the ultimate mythical beast. Before there were giants, there were dragons. Dragons, wyrms, wyverns, serpents – they decorate cave walls. They are some of the oldest myths in the history of the British Isles, and what's a dragon story without some treasure to horde? There are so, *so* many stories of dragons and treasure scattered all over our little collection of islands, and I thought it would be interesting to take all those really recognisable tropes and sink them beneath the Nation's financial sector, and the heart of our modern non-stop business world where money is all, and the fear of losing it can make people do crazy things. Though this tale is first in the collection, it was the last to be written, and I kind of like that symmetry.

Changelings

Celtic folklore teaches us about the small folk, the Fey, and there have been tales of fairies whisking away human children and replacing them with something *else*, something inhuman, for many hundreds of years. In the old stories, the Changelings were seen as evil, or at the very least, ugly problem-children. The very bare bones of this story were scribbled in a notebook in a Bristol coffee shop overlooking the river Avon when I was eighteen and studying creative writing, in 2004. It has been through a lot, has this story. Originally, the *Them* in the story were pure villains, stealing away susceptible youths and replacing them with their dark reflections. But, I've been a dispossessed youth, and music saved me. The tribes and subcultures that erupt around music scenes give many people, especially the lost and lonely, a family, a sense of belonging. So what if the *Them* were helping, not hurting? What if, in the same way all these subcultures get vilified as dangerous and subversive, the *Them* weren't the bad guys? Somewhere along the line, that scribble in a notebook became this. This is written for my dad and his legacy to me of music. He listened to me read chunks of this to him when he was still alive, and it was his suggestion that the pub jukebox should be playing The House of The Rising Sun on repeat. This is also dedicated to my beautiful soul-saving Goths, Kit and Spider.

Huck, Shuck, Howl

A poem, sort of, that's great fun to read aloud. When I was researching common folklore specific to the British Isles for the book, one of the stories that got the most mentions was of Old Shuck, the Black Dog. There are lots of different local versions of this story, and the dog has lots of different names, but there are common themes. The 'black dog' crops up all over Europe, and even in India. That the black dog has also become an analogy for depression gave it this whole other flavour of how the myth, made real, would survive in our modern world.

The Odd Uneven Time

I started knocking around with the characters and ideas in this back around 2008, in the strange no-man's land between leaving University in Bath and moving back to Bath for work. It was meant to be a very different story. I'd envisaged it being much shorter, with both elemental characters of Winter and Summer being far less humanised; a shot of their battle across the world in various locations, culminating in a shopping centre all decked out for Halloween. Winter was far more Jack Frost-ish, mischievous and impish. But it got shelved in the brain-bank. I then read the story of The Holly King and The Ivy King, brothers that battle every year to reign for their own six months. I unboxed this story and finished it in 2014. Then finished it again in 2016... before re-finishing it for this collection in 2019. I think it's done now...

Some of the stories in this collection deal with where British Isles folktales come from; about the constant flux of people coming to these lands from elsewhere and bringing their own tales that morphed and shifted. This one is about where our stories might go afterwards.

Fee Fi Fo Fum

Giants feature a lot in British Isles folklore and mythology. Giants carved out much of our landscape. Giants ate wayward beanstalk-climbers, were slain by giant killers. I wanted to try and tell a story we know in a different way. I don't mean the giant story.

Hoof And Horn

We inherited a lot of ancient stories from the people that came here from elsewhere. Cernnunos is one of my favourite immigrant myths. His character is so woven into the fabric of the green spaces and forests of Britain now that people forget he didn't originate here. He's come to symbolise the pagan 'Horned God' of fertility, virility, seasons and cycles, and can be thought of as an aspect or face of the archetypal Green Man, along with similar counterparts of Pan and Herne the Hunter. The details in this story about the Pillar of the Boatmen in Paris are true. I wrote this very quickly in the early summer of 2019, sitting in my overgrown garden because my husband had broken the lawnmower by running over its power cord. It's also possibly the most personal piece of fiction I've ever written, though it *is* a fiction. It took me a while to get over the writing of this one, which probably means I needed to write it.

And I Shall Go Into A Hare

This story came into being while on holiday in Cornwall after wandering around the Museum of Witchcraft and Magic in Boscastle. Hares have always had a hugely important role within folklore, holding a mystical place throughout much of the world from Japan to Mexico, Indonesia and here in the British Isles. The hare is often a symbol of the feminine and of fertility, associated with the Moon and lunar cycles (and therefore often associated with witches), as well as being adopted as a symbol for post-Christian spring festivities at Easter. In some cultures, Hare is a messenger from the gods; in others, Hare is a trickster god himself. But always, Hare has been fleet of foot, a shifting shadow dwelling in twilight, a keeper of secrets. This particular story is inspired not just by that vast lineage but by a few tales specific to Britain – that of the 17th Century witch Isobel Gowdie who allegedly confessed to being able to transform into a hare using a chant, and of another alleged witchcraft confession from 1662 of Julian Cox, who apparently was chased, in her hare form, by the local hunt. She ended up exhausted and afraid, forced to transform back to her human form in a hedge, only to be discovered naked and wounded by a huntsman that recognised her. This story is sort of a companion piece to Hoof And Horn, although I can't quite put my finger on why – something about the tone, perhaps. All I know is, they're meant to sit beside one another in the running order.

Once Upon A Meeting

I knew that this collection would not really be complete without Robin Hood or King Arthur making an appearance. The problem is having anything original to say about them, and in a modern context, too. Through my research, it became apparent how similar the two sets of legends were, and it occurred to me that they may have somewhat of a rivalry. That was the seed of this story. I then decided to throw as many characters as I could into it and see what they did. It was great fun to weave this one into the now almost mythical memories I have of corporate events with agendas where nothing really, actually, when you get right down to it... happens...

This is a story about stories, and about people. It's a little bit silly, it's a little bit Monty Python-esque, a little Goon Show-ish. It's also my gift of thanks to Sir Terry Pratchett, who taught me that there's not a lot a determined story can't do if he finds his courage, and that a hedgehog can never be buggered. It is dedicated to my friend and proofreader, Phil.

The Man Who Went Up A Mountain And Came Down a Poet

Through my collecting, reading and research, one tale that grabbed me and wouldn't let go was that of the mountain Cader Idris, to the south of the Snowdonia National Park. It has a whole host of folklore tales about its own Giant, but my absolute favourite was this odd little throwaway story that if you fall asleep on the mountain, you'll wake up a poet, or a madman, or else not wake up at all. What would it be like to wake up after accidentally falling asleep up there, unable to form thoughts or sentences that weren't poetry? And, having written a great deal of poetry myself, I can tell you the line between metaphors and madness is an ever-shifting sandbank.

Ursilla's Coat

When I first got the idea for this book, I started planning a story about selkies - seal people. They feature hugely in Scottish, especially Orcadian, folklore (although they crop up in Irish and Cornish tales too, as well as within other cultures that grew up around water in Canada and Alaska). I read a bunch of these stories, looking for threads I could weave into something new. I found the story of Ursilla, a human on the Orkney Islands who is rumoured to have had children with a male selkie and had to try and hide the webbed horn-like growths between her children's fingers and toes. I loved Ursilla - fierce, feisty, not waiting around to be proposed to. She knew her mind. I also found the story of Undine/Ondine, a water elemental often depicted as being trapped on land. Throw into this the symbolic elements of the sealskin story, especially for women - the notion of giving up a part of yourself and then struggling to regain your wild essence, a concept found in countless folktales all over the world - and I had a solid idea. I knew I wanted this to be a story about women being their own heroes. Angela Carter's ghost loomed over me. I was scared of buggering this up. Instead of writing the story, I finished off several others, then asked a bunch of people what their favourite folktales and myths were, in case I could conveniently forget the selkie tale and focus on something easier to write. Of course, ninety percent of the people I asked mentioned selkies, so I really had to write the thing, didn't I? It took a while to find the women at the heart of this, but I'm very glad I stuck with it. This story is written for Lainey and Lisa who embody the very essence of the 'mad' woman rising up in her power. This is also dedicated to Matt, who helped me shape Spencer and Sam, and 'Georgie's Place'. Matt and his husband also own a cat called Georgie...

Lamp Light, Marsh Light

Marsh lights, Will O' the Wisps, Friar's Lanterns, Hinkypunks, Hobby Lanterns, Fool's Fire or Ignis Fatuus... these ethereal, disembodied lights have made their way into many folktales, taking on local names and flavours throughout the Isles (and across the World). My favourite is the story of the Lantern Man that haunts the marshy Fens of East Anglia. In the traditional stories, the Lantern Man is drawn to whistling, but doesn't it make it so much creepier if he is the one to whistle?

Between A Rock And A Hard Place

This is an amalgam of a couple of different folk stories and locations. Kits Coty is a real megalithic dolmen/quoit, but it's located in Medway, in a field on a hill close to where I grew up. It does indeed carry the folktale that something of value placed upon it acts as a sort of sacrifice that grants you something in return. My dad took me to find Kits Coty once, and we got lost in the woods on the way, and it snowed. The story of the iron horse nails belongs to another similar ancient stone structure of Wayland the Smith's Forge in Berkshire. Wistman's Wood is also real and is located in Dartmoor. It's a gorgeously twisted short forest with its own ghost stories. It, however, does not have a hill with some ancient standing stones at its centre. Remember kids, please don't ever just jump up on top of ancient monuments for a photograph opportunity! Unless, of course, you want to run the risk of being a sacrificial offering to the stones...

Final Thoughts

It's important to point out that, though there are very real places mentioned in this collection, this is a work of fiction. All people, places, names and incidents therein are fictitious and any similarities to any real persons or places is purely coincidental. Some places and ideas have been melded together; others created solely for the purpose of the story.

Some of the stories in here are long, some are short, and some are (shhhhh, don't tell anyone) more like poems. But though you'll find here stories that you think you know; though there are all manner of familiar beasts, creatures, old gods and ancient ideas, the stories don't always go how you think they should. These stories bridge a gap; they haunt the in-between places. Old stories woven into modern times, for modern folk just minding their business, folk who can't help but feel the tug of something deeper, something older, something creeping around the edges of the world, whispering and wild...

"The most we can do is dream the myth onward and give it a modern dress."

- Carl Jung

The Price Of Success

It is so incredibly, unbelievably hot in the office. The middle of August and the air con has been busted since the start of the week. I'm wiping a sheen of sweat from my face when Luke stalks towards me, on his way back from a cigarette break. I can smell it clinging to him even before I see him. Three years since I quit and I still want to beg him to give me a smoke. He leans on the blue felt-covered partition between my desk and the walkway. He's got his shirt sleeves rolled to the elbows and his hair is limp. I look up from my spreadsheet and he gestures at the desk to the right of mine.

"Seen Jacob today?" he mutters.

Now that he mentions it, I haven't. I stare at the desk. Still has its stack of paperwork, the file from the Ashton project, that weird clay pot his kid had made and covered in glitter stuffed with all his pens. The photo of said kid and wife and he in Paris pinned to his partition. I look at the clock, huge and foreboding, hanging on the wall above the coffee machine like a great eye. It's 10.30. Jacob's never late. None of us are. I get that sinking feeling in the pit of my stomach.

"Maybe he's got a doctor's appointment," I offer, quietly, "Maybe his kid's not well...?"

Luke is looking at Jake's desk, but flicks his eyes to me once. Doesn't make a face, doesn't say anything, just looks at me.

"Yeah... maybe..." He shrugs, after a beat. "Maybe he'll be in later."

But Karen and Steve are bustling down the office talking loudly, throwing words and business talk around like confetti in the otherwise quiet space. So Luke slips away to his own desk and I go back to my spreadsheet, slide down into my chair, try to make myself small.

"Ah, Jesse." Karen stops beside me. "Just the person I needed to see."

Shit. I don't believe 'Karen' is her name. It's a rank she's earned. She's taken on this mantle, this 'Partner in a Power Suit' thing, and the name arrived over night with that hairdo and that 'I demand to speak to your manager' way of standing.

I smile back at her, widely. "What can I do for you?"

"I was running over the Ashton figures, wondered if you can give an update on where things stand on the timeline?"

I swallow. "Ashton is Jacob's project, so I..."

"I'm asking you, *love*, aren't I?" Karen grins again, tightly.

Steve is hovering at her elbow, has the decided look of a mobster's goon, the way he leans on the partition nonchalantly with his cool blue eyes and lack of neck.

"Look into it and get me an update by close of play, OK?" Karen does that head-twitchy thing I've noticed that she does when she's strung out on caffeine and nerves.

I give her my winning can-do smile and nod. "Sure thing, Karen."

She nods with a little nose wrinkle and walks away. Steve raises a singular eyebrow at me, with not quite a smirk, and follows. I sigh. Luke, over the way, catches my eye, points at Jake's desk and makes a cutting, slicing motion to his throat. Yep. Looks like Jake's been booted. I sigh. The Ashton project is huge, and I don't know if I physically have the time to take it on with all the other projects and clients I have. But. I get paid well. We got five-figure bonuses at Christmas and another couple of grand at Easter. We get a heap of corporate social things where there's always an open bar. There's the gym memberships and the dental... We might not dare to be late, but I'm not sure I can really complain, can I? So what if they get rid of people for underperforming? Isn't that what all businesses do? If you can't stand the heat, you shouldn't get in the water, right? Right?! Yeah it might be tough, but work hard, play hard, right? To be part of a hugely successful corporation like Wormlow and Wyvern is something other people dream of, right? We get amazing holiday allowances, decent maternity packages, a ton of perks and the pay-check rewards are impressive. That's why we do it, right? The stress, the sleepless nights, the deadlines upon deadlines, the being shouted at, being threatened by a single raised eyebrow from Steve, the sixty-plus hour weeks, the looming fear of being one of the ones who doesn't turn up at their desk one morning, throwing in the odd weekend, picking up the projects from others who get fired with no warning... well, that's just the price we pay.

Except... I glance back at Jacob's desk. Except Jacob was a nice bloke. He worked really hard. He secured the Branning report which led to the Ashton project. He'd been invited to represent W&W at the industry awards, the big black-tie thing in Canary Wharf. And now, apparently, he is just gone. Like Phoebe. Like Jack. Like the entire support team, and that girl from accounts last year, and the guy from the front desk who supported Aston Villa.

I wheeled my chair over to grab the Ashton file from Jake's desk. I guess, in a fast-paced internationally recognised financial environment like W&W, everyone is at risk when they have to hit their KPIs and their margins, and secure each new stage of investment funding. I sigh. It's a shame though. I really did like Jake.

That afternoon, I take my sandwich out and sit in the sunshine on the concrete steps up to the office. Our office is snazzy, all chrome and glass, but I always think, sitting on these hard, cold steps, that it must have been built on something much older, like a bank or a church or something. The city is roiling, snarling cars, groaning buses and hot city workers striding around avoiding eye contact with everyone. I swear, if I listen and concentrate, I can hear the tube trains rumbling along beneath me.

There's something about London in the summer. So much concrete and glass, everything reflects heat back on itself. My skin feels tight out here. The air feels tight.

I'm tucking into my chicken club when I see Luke. He's staring at his phone, pacing up and down, fidgeting, trailing a cigarette around, having a full conversation with himself, hand with the cigarette making little spasmodic gestures. I think at first that he must be having a hands-free business call with someone, but no. He's talking to himself. His eyes are wild, his hair is damp with sweat and sticking up at strange angles. It's not unusual to see people out here having little breakdowns while they try to sort shit out and get stuff done to schedule, but there was something frantic in Luke's eyes. He catches me watching him, glances around to, I guess, see if anyone else has noticed his Walter Mitty impression, and comes over.

"I'm screwed. This is it, Jess." He's still mumbling and muttering like he was upstairs, glancing around wildly.

"Did you do a 'reply all' on your last email?" I try to jest, but he just absently shakes his head.

"No... no, I got a meeting invite just now. With Karen and Steve and the Ops Board at one thirty..." he checks his phone. "That's ten minutes away."

I feel that same weird sinking feeling in my stomach as earlier but, like while looking at Jacob's unoccupied desk this morning, I force it down with a huge bite of chicken and mayo. "Quarterly review?" I splutter, around a mouthful.

"Oh, don't be a moron all your life, Jess. Have a day off." Luke rolls his head back on his shoulders and stares up at the cloudless, accusing sky. "I'm up for redundancy. I know it."

I wipe my mouth. "You're indispensable! No way they'd get rid of you! Your clients love you, you're bringing in the big bucks. They need you!"

"Yeah?" Luke is still staring at the sky. "That's what we said to Jacob too. What *they* said to him in his last review. But there's Nicole and Fabian in my team now. They don't need all three of us. They can pick up my pile, just like they'll get you to pick up all Jake's accounts."

I screw up the paper bag that my sandwich came in, form it into a little ball between my palms. "Well, look, 'WW' operate like this, on the fly, right? They always have. We knew the risks when they offered us the jobs. But so what if they make you redundant? You'll get another position within a week, I guarantee it. What with this on your CV, half of the Square Mile would snap you up!"

Luke shoves his hands in his pockets. He looks resigned, defeated, forlorn. "You don't understand, do you? You're just like the rest of them, so brainwashed, thinking this place is the dog's doughnuts." He's looking about him again as if afraid of being overheard. "You don't *get* to leave WW, you don't *get* to quit, you don't get to go somewhere else. Once you sign the contract, that's it. They've got you to do with as you please." He sighs and it's like the paper bag I just crumpled between my hands. He sags, becomes less. "They're bidding for the new H-Spec Capital Markets venture, means they'll need funding. Lots of it. So they're feeding the beast, and I'm next..." His phone is ringing and he looks at it like he's going to cry. I can see the display; it's his girlfriend. He cancels the call, avoids my eyes, says, "Just... just tell Michelle I honestly did love her."

He looks up at the award-winning W&W offices like a man going to the gallows, steels himself, and darts up the steps into the atrium. I am afraid for him, a little afraid *of* him, too, if I'm honest. A man on the edge. Too many late nights. The seat-of-your-pants lifestyle Wormlow and Wyvern cultivates and thrives on can burn you out. I look at the crumpled sandwich bag in my hand, recall the look on Luke's face, the "tell Michelle

I loved her..." Jesus, is he going to throw himself off the roof or something?! I rise and sprint into the building, ask Tom on the desk if he saw where Luke went, feeling a dread growing that I just can't swallow down this time.

"Steve and someone from Ops Board were waiting for him and took him up in the lift. He's got a meeting with them," Tom says.

I feel relieved; at least I can see him on the way out of the meeting, get him a coffee, take him home if I need to. Maybe I can find Michelle on Facebook or something and get her to come pick him up...? His face, the glistening tears in his eyes, the resigned terror. If the job had gotten to him that much, why was he so afraid of them telling him to leave? Maybe it's a pride thing? Maybe getting made redundant from W&W is a failure he doesn't think he can come back from. Whatever. I think a break would do him good, let him get a little perspective. I've swiped through the security barrier and am waiting for the lift to take me back up to the 5th floor where my desk is. Got to crack on with the Ashton stuff for Karen if I've got any hope in hell of getting home before ten tonight. The lift arrives, the door opens with a ping and I step in, and am heading up, thinking about Luke and everything he said.

He sounded like a crazy person. But... if he is having 'the' meeting, the 'escorted from the premises' meeting, like Jacob must've had yesterday evening, that'll be the fourth one in two weeks. The company is doing great – we've all seen the stats. Champagne receptions and summer BBQs on the roof. So why the sudden spate of redundancies? Of good, hard-working staff? In the lift, with the stupid plinky music, watching the numbers of the floors tick past, I, for once, admit that it just doesn't make any sense. I feel guilty, like I'm somehow betraying W&W just by thinking this; like somehow I'm defecating on their good reputation and corporate values just by wondering what the Board's deal is. I think it's that which makes me realise Luke was right – I am brainwashed. We all are. It doesn't make any sense at all. Why get rid of these people? Why so many? Why so frequently?

The lift reaches the fifth floor, pings, and the doors open. I look across the open-plan office, can taste that frantic electric energy up here just like always. Then I reach out and press the button again, drop down a floor to HR, where the conference rooms are, and walk into the hallway. It's so quiet here, no strange frenetic energy. I look around. I'm not sure I've been on this floor since my first day when I signed the contract in Karen's big office that looks towards Bank and Monument. It's all narrow corridors and strip lighting. Sure, it's all in the corporate colours, looks fancy, but there's something sinister about the grey carpet with the deep pile that doesn't have a single mark on it; not one coffee drip or leaf walked in on someone's shoe or anything. It's too immaculate. I walk along the corridor towards Karen's office, suspecting that Luke will be having his meeting in the conference room next door. No way Karen would hold it in her office – that was for welcomes only, not goodbyes.

I feel like I should be creeping along, sliding against the wall. I feel like I shouldn't be here, though there's no real reason for that. I can see the conference room, with its slit of glass panel like a vertical pupil in the thick door. I can see Luke sits side-on to the door. Karen's in there, and Steve, and a couple of others in suits that I guess must be Ops Board. Luke is sweating profusely, I can see it from here, making his sandy hair dark, his shirt armpits stained. Karen's leaning over the desk towards him, hands braced either side of a pile of paperwork and her laptop. She's smiling, in a very condescending politician kind of way. It's a smile that says, "yes, I really do understand how terribly unfortunate this all is, but really, it's out of my hands."

Luke is shouting, rising to his feet. I can't hear him, can only see the redness of his face, the sweat and the spittle and the fear as his mouth works. Then Steve, big old Steve – Steve that goes big on a night out, likes the brandy, likes the ladies, likes the cocaine, big Steve with no neck and the Armani suits, Steve is there behind him injecting him with something. I see him do it, casual as you like, sticking a needle into Luke's neck. I feel sick. My knees feel weak. I wish I had my phone so I could've filmed it, but it's in my bag under my desk because I'd only meant to nip out to eat my sandwich quickly and see the sky briefly. I watch Luke buckle and slide gracefully into Steve's strong arms. Steve picks him up in a fireman's lift, tosses him over one shoulder and I know I've got to not be seen, so I duck into the mail room. The mail room on this floor is dark and cool and barely used since we all have mail rooms on our own floors, and the fourth floor seems used solely for the hiring and firing, or whatever the fuck that was I just saw. I heard that Will Stevens and Emily were caught in here once. Thinking about it, Will got fired not long after that...

I'm willing myself to meld into the shadows here as I hear the conference room door open. Karen's chatting and laughing about something. Steve tells her to get a coffee before the bid presentation, that Jen's got it all set up and ready to go, that Mike has got some great graphics and H-Spec are really going to love it, he can tell. There's another voice chiming in, too, all hearty laughs. They're walking along the corridor, past the mail room. I hold my breath, but they probably wouldn't have heard me anyway, so wrapped up in the presentation chat. I expect to hear the lift ping, but it doesn't. Instead I hear a loud click and thunk, the definite *waaaahhhump* of a heavy fire door being opened. Fire escape.

"Right, well, excellent, I'll see you at two-forty-five for the pre-meeting briefing? We'll need to have the funding secured by then ready to hand over," Karen says, in that officious way of talking she has when she's mildly concerned or nervous. I can imagine her doing the head twitch thing.

"Everything's under control, don't worry, get coffee. You deserve it," Steve is almost cooing at her. Sycophantic dickhead.

I'd actually forgotten for a moment there that Steve the Sycophant has an unconscious-possibly-dead friend of mine draped over his shoulder. When I remember, I feel sick to my stomach. Their small talk. Their laughing. Luke knowing something terrible was going to happen to him. I consider barging out right then, but, no. There might be more of whatever was in that needle. Better to get the evidence and live to whistle-blow another day.

I hear Karen walk back to her office, hear her shut her door, hear Steve and whoever he's with walking down the concrete fire escape stairs, hear the fire door sliding shut across the deep pile carpet. I wait a pause then dart out of the mail room, around the corner, and just manage to catch the door before it shuts completely. I listen. Steve and Luke and, I think I can hear a woman's voice, are quite a way down the stairs already, moving fast, so I slip into the stairwell and begin to follow them.

The fire escape coils around the centre of the building, around the central core of the elevator shafts. It's filled with a murky, dim green light from the emergency exit signs that glow on each floor. When we have fire drills and all have to pile down here, with the sirens blaring, it echoes and you're turning in a seemingly endless spiral to spill out on to the street around the back of the office and it always makes me feel dizzy.

Now I'm taking off my shoes to walk on the cold concrete in my socks, so they don't hear me. The steps are sharp-edged. Steve and the woman from Ops Board are chatting but I can't really tell what they're saying; their voices are distorted by the echoes and their distance, and the hum of the elevators and electrics and security lights. I can hear Luke, too, groaning. At least I know he's alive. We go down, second floor, first floor, ground floor, basement level where the car park is. I expect them to head out here onto the street, like we all do during fire drills, but they haven't, they've kept going. Down to basement level 2, where the gym is. I hear another door open. I always thought this was an access hatch to under the elevators, but they keep going down and I follow, at least two levels behind them at all times, sticking to the shadows.

Down, down, down.

The green emergency exit security lights have stopped, but there's a glow from below. Orangey. Fire, maybe? Lanterns? The stairs become smooth, crumbling at the edges, worn down in the centres. They become damp. I'm afraid I'm going to lose my footing and slip, but am more afraid that they'll hear my footsteps if I put my shoes back on. The walls are damp. This is not, I realise, W&W's offices. It can't be. This is too old. Ancient.

Down, down... the walls become ragged and glistening. I can hear water trickling and dripping. There are burning torches in brackets on the wall. I can still hear Luke's semi-conscious moans, but these are followed by a meaty slapping sound and I guess Steve must've knocked him out cold. All the echoes are sounding different now and levelling out so that I intuitively know I must be nearing the bottom. I reach the last step.

I press my back against the inside of the curved stairway and peer around.

It's a cavern.

A really huge cavern. It's vast. The ceiling vaults high above. Steve and the woman's voices reverberate. The cavern walls seem both natural and man-made; here and there, amongst the cold rugged rock, brick-work arches and parts of buttresses. I hear a rumble above us. The Central line.

Steve's got a torch in his hand and he's flashing it around the cave. I keep hearing this clinking, shifting sound, like chains or like coins. Then, there's a roar of flame. It's like, I imagine, standing behind a fighter jet. The sound presses in on my eardrums and my chest, the flare of heat and air makes me drop to my knee and cover my face, ducking back up onto the steps. When the roaring flame dies away into the ghost of an echo, I peer around once again and see the cavern is now lit by several small fires in these little metal fire-pit pyre things. I can now see that the cavern beneath the office, beneath the underground lines, beneath London, is filled with treasure. Gold coins, chests overflowing with jewels and gems and strands of pearls. I can see ruby-encrusted swords, tiaras, I don't even know what else. It all just glistens and gleams in the firelight. And then, from the darkness at the far end of the cavern, I hear it. The shifting of treasure, the tinkling tumbling of so many coins moving beneath a very big something coming towards us. I can hear its breathing; a huffing grunt. I can smell a sour, rancid smell of rotten meat and burnt hair. I don't want to look. I don't want to see it, but I force myself to. I need to, for Luke.

It's a dragon.

The dragon is mud coloured. Brownish-reddish-greenish. There's no gold, no glitter or sparkle here. It's all wild beast. It's leathery looking. Maybe it has scales, but from back here, I can't see. It has huge bat-like wings folded back against its spine, and its tail whips around, dragging through the horde of treasure that makes it ripple and shift like sand drifting on dunes. I can feel a pressure in my bowels like I might empty myself right there on the cold stone floor. I have never known a fear so consuming. To look on this thing, with its snout and its huge yellow eyes and the dirt and grime caked on its legs and in its claws – centuries, millennia maybe, of our capital's detritus smeared upon it – to look upon this is to look into the void at the centre of terror. I push my fist into my mouth to stop from yelling out. I'm not sure a sound would've even escaped, but I'm not going to risk it.

Steve takes the limp, unconscious body of Luke from his shoulder and holds him out like a baby in his arms. The dragon is filling the space in front of them and it leans its huge slab of face and snout down, inhales. The fires flicker. Then the dragon lifts a single toe and filthy talon in a gesture I recognise as an arrogant, pompous acceptance. He's accepted Steve's offering.

I have a moment to rake in a breath before Luke, my buddy, my late-night pizza and deadline pal, my panic presentations and six a.m. coffee on trains comrade, is tossed into the air and snatched in the suddenly gaping and razor-teeth-filled maw of this monster.

Luke's gone.

Eaten by the dragon.

I dry-heave, have to slither onto the bottom step and press the heels of my palms into my eyes. I can hear the wet crunching. When I look again, the dragon is coiling itself into a pile, resting its chin on its front feet, blinking slowly. The woman from Ops Board has a bankers' sack in her hands and Steve is filling it with gold, scooping up armfuls of the treasure in an efficient and clinical manner. Neither Steve nor the woman seem afraid. I suppose they must have done this often enough. All these redundancies, all these sacrificial offerings to secure the funds they need to float Wormlow and Wyvern's business ventures. Any time they needed funding, any time there was a recession to weather or a rocky stock exchange. All they needed to do was bring a tribute or seven, and take what they needed. That's why they treat us so well, to ease their guilt, or to keep their supply store of flesh full. When the sack is full, Steve looks at the dragon, gives it a funny little salute.

The dragon blinks, lazily, snorts out a cloud of smoke. Then it speaks, and I can feel its voice in my nerve endings.

"What of the other one?" It swivels that huge head and its feral yellow eyes, and looks at me.

I feel the heat and wetness of hot piss spreading from my crotch, dribbling down my legs. I can't breathe. Steve is snarling, striding towards me, slipping and sliding on the coins that carpet the floor, and it's like a jolt of adrenaline. My limbs begin to function. I am up and running up the stairs. All I need to do is get to the basement, then into the lift. I can do it! I can make it. Steve might be big and strong, but he's not fast, and the dragon sure as hell isn't chasing me. It didn't seem to care one way or the other. I'm glancing back over my shoulder as I climb, can hear Steve yelling and cursing below me.

But then there's a hand, grabbing me by my shoulder.

Manicured nails digging into me.

It's Karen, in her heels and dark suit and her severe chignon and her too-wide grin.

"This, my love," she states with that politician's smile, "Is just the price of success. That's all."

And with a simple thrust of her strong and corrupted hand, she pushes me backwards. My feet leave the floor and I'm falling.

Down.

Falling.

Towards the fire and the waiting beast.

* * *

Changelings

Come away, O human child!
To the waters and the wild
With a faery, hand in hand,
For the world's more full of weeping than you can understand.
(W.B. Yeats - The Stolen Child)

(When the Levee Breaks)

Jonathan was eighteen when he was offered a place at the University of Bristol to study history. It was the first time he'd ever moved away from home and he was a quiet, entirely unassuming lad. He came from a quiet, entirely unassuming village where they could count the number of kids that had gone to University on one hand. But then, this was 1972. University wasn't like it is today. Then again, a lot of things are still the same. Jonathan, Jon, went off to University with seventy pounds from his mum, which was a lot of money back then, and a grant from the government that was to see him through to his second year. He'd never seen so much money in his life and he wondered how the hell he was ever going to spend it. Don't be mistaken into thinking that, because he was quiet, he was weedy and shy. Jon was tall, brawny and broad, laughed easily and made friends fast. He'd played in the village rugby team since he was fourteen, and he was smart, sensible, logical and he wasn't loud. Maybe it was something to do with growing up on a farm, because he was also great with dogs.

Through some mix up at the Admittance office, he'd not been allocated a room in the huge halls of residence with the rest of the first years and they'd found him, last minute, a room in a flat above a pawn brokers in Portland Street, Clifton. He didn't mind particularly, as long as he had somewhere to eat and sleep, so he dragged his duffel bag and his suitcase to the address on the piece of paper they'd given him and stood outside the red door beside the pawn brokers and knocked. And knocked. And knocked again. And then he dropped his bags and lifted the letter box. A dark, narrow staircase cluttered with piles of post, a push bike, jackets, coats and shoes, and Jon understood why his knocks had gone unanswered. Led Zeppelin blared from the flat, beyond the second door at the top of the dark and narrow stairs.

Jon hammered, called, yelled, and in the end, sat on the step and ate the sandwich he'd made before leaving his parents' house that morning. During the next half an hour, Jon ate his sandwich and crisps, listened second-hand to the remainder of the Led Zeppelin IV album and took careful note of the street around him. He clocked the pub down the hill and the newsagents three doors up, a greengrocer and a collection of antiques shops. And an already-tall girl in yellow knee-high stacked platform boots, with a shock of ginger hair striding towards him. She wore a rainbow-striped T-shirt under dungarees, the legs of which were tucked into her boots like glam-rock plus fours. She had rounded the corner with a purposeful march, rummaging through an oversized carpet bag that was various shades of browns and purples, never once looking where she was walking. She had a roll of what looked like wallpaper, almost as long as she was tall, tucked under her arm. It kept slipping and she kept hitching it as she marched and rummaged and shook her bag, her halo of orange hair bouncing around her head. Jon stared, impressed. He'd never seen that many colours on one person before. She, inevitably, slowed to a stop in front of him as a bunch of keys were triumphantly snatched from the bag. She looked down at Jon. Jon looked up at her. Robert Plant wailed behind the door.

"I'm Jonathan," Jon said, and stood up.

"Right...?" Scottish. The girl with all the colours was Scottish and she raised an orange eyebrow.

"First year. New flatmate." Jon held out the letter he'd been given by Administration. The girl gave it a cursory glance, peered back at his face and nodded.

"Anita." She kicked open the door, the music washing over them, stepped over his bags and disappeared up the stairs. "Are ye coming or no'?!"

He struggled and tripped his way up the stairs behind her, sure she was speaking but unable to hear a word. She led him into the flat – all narrow corridors and high ceilings, as if the building were on its side, and dumped her roll of wallpaper in the hall. She gestured to her left and showed him an empty room barely larger than a broom cupboard. A single bed rammed against the wall, a window at the foot of the bed. A cupboard built into the wall above the bed, and a chest of drawers with a knob missing. That was it. This space was to contain all his worldly possessions for the next year, at least. He appraised it with his 'son of a farmer' expression, the blank 'make do and don't complain' face his own father had worn most days of his life. At least it was light, and there didn't seem to be any damp spots.

"Cosy," he said, eventually, and plopped his bags on the bare mattress. The rusty bed springs groaned in reply.

Anita leant against the doorframe, watching him with an unreadable expression. Maybe she came from a family of farmers, too. Then she turned, "Kitchen's this way!" and disappeared.

Jon followed. The music was emanating from behind a closed door opposite Jon's new room. There were two other bedrooms in the hall, one clearly Anita's – silk scarves draped over lamps; sketches, masks and black-and-white photographs of kids mid-performance on various stages were stuck to the walls. The other was occupied by a tall and lean young black man, more big hair than face, who was folded in behind a tiny desk writing. The hairy man saw Jon, rose to fill most of the room, and held out a hand.

"Derek!" the hairy man shouted.

He wore a Steppenwolf T-Shirt under a cut-off denim jacket. Jon shook his hand and continued to follow Anita past a bathroom and through a living room with one lumpy-looking ripped sofa, a couple of large floor cushions and beanbags, full ashtrays everywhere, a single bookcase crammed to overflowing.

"We're all third years. Derek is Geology, I'm English an' Theatre," Anita was shouting over her shoulder as she scooped up some empty mugs and headed through a door into a kitchen that was so vividly yellow, it filled the beige living room with a faint buttercup-under-chin glow. It was the same colour as Anita's boots. Jon wondered if she'd painted it.

"Vic is Classics an' Philosophy."

"Right," Jon replied, looking at the various posters that were plastered over the peeling wallpaper. Gigs, plays and band posters torn from the centrefolds of NME magazine, rag week, poetry jams. "History," he added, following her into the too-yellow, too-small kitchen. There was, ridiculously given the size of the room, a square wooden table with two chairs at the far end, jammed up under the eaves. The table sported a butter dish, a teapot with knitted tea-cosy, and was draped with drying laundry.

Anita opened the fridge, pointed. "Milk an' tea is shared. If ye finish either withoot replacin' them, ah will hurt ye. Top shelf is yours. Ye buy yer ain food, ye eat yer ain food, an' if you're smart, you'll pit yer name on yer food, reit?"

"Right," Jon said again. Anita appraised him, that orange, cynical eyebrow raised again, retrieved a bowl of what looked like cold spaghetti from the fridge and disappeared, leaving him standing alone in the kitchen with the fridge door still open. He heard thumping and Anita's voice shouting:

"Oi! Prick! Turn it doon!"

Jon stood unsure what to do with himself, read a leaflet pinned to the notice board about the Student Union's folk night next Tuesday.

"Oi! Prick!" *Thump, thump.*

The music stopped and the sudden silence was followed by the sound of a door opening.

"Dickheid..." He heard Anita snarl, then another door slammed.

When it became evident that Anita would not be coming back, Jon shut the fridge, washed out one of the mugs she had deposited in the sink, found some tea bags and made himself a cup of tea. When he made his way back to his room with his mug, Derek looked up, smiled amiably and went back to whatever he'd been working on. Anita's door was shut. The door opposite Jon's was now open a crack, but dark inside. The strong scent of marijuana wafted out. Jon had smoked a few sneaky joints behind the rugby club with some pals from school, but that stuff had smelled (and tasted) bitter and cloying. This stuff smelled smooth as honey, clearly the good stuff. Jon went into his new phone-box bedroom and started to unpack. After about ten minutes, he became aware that he was being watched. He turned his head and found himself under the gaze of a skinny youth with dirty blonde hair that brushed his shoulders and drifted over his eyes, eyes that were grey and far-off and stoned. He was barefoot, in flares that were so faded the knees were almost see-through, and a white cheesecloth shirt; some sort of dangly pendant hung around his neck. He was draped in the doorway opposite like a rakish urchin. A lit cigarette dangled from between his middle and index finger. He stared at Jon until Jon began to feel uncomfortable. Jon wasn't given to feeling uncomfortable; he was generally pretty calm and just sort of got on with things. Now, he felt awkward and held to the spot by those grey eyes.

"Are you lost?" the stoned young man asked, eventually, with a lazy sort of smirk in his voice. He had a soft voice, well-spoken. London or the home counties. Slightly drawled; maybe that was the weed.

Jon shook his head. "I just moved in. I'm Jonath–"

"Got any biscuits?" the man interrupted. Jon shook his head again.

The man shrugged and dance-walk-stumbled across the hall; drummed his hands on Anita's door.

"NEETA! Biscuits!"

And that was how Jon first met Vic.

Over the next few weeks, Jon learnt a lot. Some of it was during lectures. Much of it was within the walls of that flat. He learnt how many sugars they all took in their tea (two for everyone, except Anita who took three); exactly how long he could peacefully spend in the bathroom before someone hammered on the door (approximately three and a half minutes); that Anita was from a town outside of Glasgow and loved Thin Lizzy and T-Rex and sometimes, when she was sad, Janis Joplin; that Derek was from Burnley and loved Hawkwind and Steppenwolf and Pink Floyd. He learnt that Vic was from the better part of Surrey, that his parents had expected him to read at Oxford, but he'd chosen Bristol because the 'scene' was better and, he would smugly explain, because it appalled his parents. Jon learnt that Vic's choice of music won out, every time, and so it was Vic's music, in the main, that provided the soundtrack to their lives from the jerry-rigged cassette deck and vinyl player in the living room. Mismatched speakers everywhere, wires taped together. Vic's music was anything and everything, from classical through blues and mo-town, rock, and strange instrumental stuff full of cowbells which, he announced, was Uruguayan farmers music. Jon learnt that sometimes Vic loved his course with a frenzied passion, talking long into the night about Chomsky, Orwell, Nietzsche, and sometimes he loathed it, skulking into the flat and throwing textbooks into the oven. It was Vic's music that threaded its way through their lives like a refrain and Jon learnt to recognise Vic's moods by what was playing when they woke up in the mornings. If Vic was out when they woke up, they learnt to guess what music would be chosen by his entrance, either loud and laughing or explosive and aggressive. But always, with Vic, it was big.

Jon learnt all this by not saying much and listening a lot. Anita was surprisingly easy to win over – he made her breakfast one morning when she was suffering from a particularly bad hangover. Derek seemed to just be happy to have someone normal living with them. Vic on the other hand never spoke directly to Jon, only around him if he happened to be in the same room. Jon also discovered Vic was quite unashamedly stealing his food on a regular basis. Jon mentioned this to Anita over a beer in the Student Union, unsure of how to deal with it and quite sure that Vic hated him.

"Don't take it personal," she told him. "He did it tae all of us. We got through seven different flatmates before you. I think he thinks it's a test. Just tell him he's a prick and he'll stop."

"Why didn't you and Derek kick him out?" Jon asked.

Anita shrugged, smoked, looked at the ceiling. "He's Vic."

It was the only explanation she offered. Jon nodded. Vic wove this strange peculiar magic around all of them. He was a pain in the arse and, as Anita constantly reminded him, a prick, but he had this gravity about him, a magnitude, a glamour. Jon had watched him in the Student Union, in the pub, in the shop. People just wanted to be near him and wanted him to like them. Even Anita. If Vic held you in his favour, even for ten

42

minutes, before his attention was caught by something else, it made you feel just a little bit special.

Shortly after that, Jon received a package from an old school friend. It included a letter and an early Yardbirds bootleg. After some careful consideration, Jon walked across the hall, knocked on Vic's door and gave him the cassette without a word.

An hour later, Vic barged into his room, thrust a carrot cake and three joints at Jon, saying "You need to be stoned to appreciate this properly," and beckoned Jon to follow.

They then spent the afternoon sitting cross-legged on the floor in the living room, playing the bootleg tape over and over again whilst they talked about everything and anything, and got so stoned their sides hurt from laughing.

"I think... probably... I could be yellow. If I had to pick a colour..." Vic gesticulated vaguely, trailing thick smoke from his elegant hand. "Jonny... Jonny... it's not a happy colour, you understand, but it makes do, you know?"

Jonny. He'd never been a Jonny. But now, he'd been Christened, and he knew it would stick. He'd been enveloped in that hazy glow that surrounded Vic wherever he went.

Jon appraised Vic. "You do talk some bollocks."

"I do," Vic asserted, nodding his mop of dirty blonde hair, "But pick a colour anyway."

"Green. It was my favourite crayon in the box."

Vic squinted as he passed the joint. "Fucking predictable."

Jon inhaled deeply. "All right then, I'll be... Persian Blue."

Vic grinned a crooked-toothed smile. "That's more like it! I'm Ultramarine!"

"Tangerine Dream," Jon added.

"Purple Haze!"

"Yellow Submarine!"

"...Lily The Pink..." Jon snorted.

And then they collapsed in hysterics, holding onto each other and wheezing out laughter. They held out until Anita and Derek were home, then shared the last joint and the carrot cake between the four of them, eating without plates or forks.

When they drifted out of the living room to their beds, Anita said "'Night, Jonny," with a sleepy, stoned smile.

"Good night John-Boy!" Vic called from somewhere down the hall.

(Man of the World)

Sometimes, like when Derek had used the bath for an experiment on sedimentary deposits, or when Anita had insisted they all read lines with her for a week before she played Katherine in Taming of the Shrew, or when Vic had come home at stupid o'clock, drunk and signing rugby songs at the foot of Jon's bed, Jon honestly thought he was the only sane one there. But they gave him life outside of the boy he had once been, moulding him into a real person with likes and dislikes. He became a person Who Liked Bread Pudding and a person that Preferred Revolver To Sergeant Pepper's, and someone that Used The Brown Mug. In turn, Jon gave them stability and someone who would make mugs of tea calmly during any calamity, crisis, bad trip, hangover or busted relationship.

Jon was sitting at the tiny rickety kitchen table working on an essay, because Derek had a half-finished scale model of Krakatoa drying in the living room. He'd made it out of papier-mâché with Anita's help, but it had grown enormously and now took up most of the room. Jon chewed the end of his biro whilst Anita made tea. It was the last week of October. The front door banged open, then slammed shut.

"Fuck. Fucking fuck!" Vic snarled from the hallway. "When the fuck is he going to move this fucking Christmas tree out of my living room?"

"Oh, it's a Jonny Cash day, is it?" Anita reached for a third mug.

"No, it'll be Cream..." Jon replied absently.

Presently, the bluesy, guitar-heavy opening to Born Under a Bad Sign filled the flat, and Jon held out a hand. Anita took a Digestive biscuit from the packet and gave it to him. Jon grinned smugly at her and she stuck her middle finger up at him in return. He pushed the biscuit into his mouth and swept up two mugs, before steeling himself for whatever lurked in the living room. He found Vic sprawled on the floor beside the model volcano, with a hand draped over his eyes, a burning cigarette between his fingers. Jon rolled his eyes and swallowed his mouthful of biscuit.

"Tea..." he said over the music, setting the mug on the floor beside Vic's prone body.

"I've got half a mind to set fire to this thing..." Vic didn't open his eyes but prodded his cigarette against the paper wall of the volcano, raining sparks onto the carpet.

"Last week you were in here at three in the morning, sticking bits of newspaper to it and singing that Arthur Brown song," Jon replied calmly and sipped his own tea.

"That was before it became the size of a small country." Vic's violent grey eyes snapped open and he scowled. "Piss off. I'm trying to sulk."

Jon shrugged. "You can't sulk properly without a flight of stairs to sit halfway up," and he turned to go back to his books.

"Jonny, am I OK?" Vic asked suddenly, and ripped the needle from the record, filling the room with silence. Jon stopped and glanced back at him.

Vic was propped on his elbows, eyes wide. "Tell me I'm OK? Tell me I'm all right, and I'll believe you. Lie if you have to, but just tell me..." He blinked too quickly, looked away. "Am I real?"

Jon peered at him. He wasn't sure he was up for dousing an existential crisis when he really needed to get his head around feudalism during the Italian Renaissance, but there was something a lot like fear in Vic's voice that unnerved Jonny. Vic wasn't ever scared of anything.

"Yes, Vic, you're OK." Jon squatted beside him and poked him in the chest. "You're in fine working order. All components present and correct. You're real."

Vic's expression was distant as he rubbed a hand absently where Jon had jabbed him, but he mumbled a, "Thanks."

Jon stood up to leave him to his artistic brooding, but Vic scrambled to his feet. "Come to the pub with me."

Jon shook his head. "I have a paper due on Friday."

"Come to the pub!" Vic insisted, hovering at his elbow.

Jonny swatted at him. "I can't. What the hell is wrong?"

Vic's expression narrowed to sour, sullen and storm ridden. "My brother took me out for lunch."

"And you don't get on?"

"Ha!" Vic exploded, tossing his head. "It's not a case of getting on... it's a case of me being a total disappointment, and *oh* how he loves to tell me that. Fucking homophobic bureaucratic white collar tosser, a genetic throwback to the fifties."

Jonny rose his eyebrows. "Nothing like brotherly love."

Vic hunched his shoulders, looking waif-like with that petulant mouth. "Geoffrey's a lawyer. He was married by my age, kid number two is on the way. PhD and suits from Saville Row. He's... well, my parents *like* him." He said this as if it was the defining aspect of a person. He scraped his shock of unkempt hair back from his face. "Let's go get pissed."

And with that undefinable gravity that sucked everyone in and held them there, Jon found he couldn't refuse.

Vic dragged him round the four or five pubs in Clifton that they used frequently, stopping in each one for a pint before Vic got annoyed with the beer, or the other customers, or with the carpet or something equally idiotic. Finally they ended up in a smoke filled pub not far from the river, tucked up in a side street. Jon could see Brunel's suspension bridge hanging across the Avon Gorge from here, if he twisted his neck and pressed his face to the window. They'd consumed enough alcohol by this point to ignore the faint smell of urine and stale spilt beer, and the smog of cigarette smoke swirling across the ceiling, or the fact that the jukebox only seemed to play 'House Of The Rising Sun' on repeat. Vic brooded, hunched over his pints, swirling patterns on the sticky table top and chain smoking, insisting on buying round after round but making Jon go up to the bar each time to order. On the plus side, the more they drank, the more life returned to Vic, the more he smiled, the more he talked. By the time Jon stood up to go to the toilet, they were both, he realised, utterly drunk.

"My legs are pissed..." Jon staggered slightly, returning to their table and sitting down heavily.

Vic laughed. "You shameless lush!"

"Shameless like you." Jon grinned but Vic's grey eyes turned intent.

"No..." Vic shook his head once and drained his pint. "You are nothing like me."

Jon knew he had no reason to feel disappointed, and yet that was exactly the emotion that clanged in his stomach. He hid it behind the rim of his glass. "I guess not."

Vic smiled his sad half-smile. "You're still in one piece. Me, I've been broken for years."

They drank until the pub closed and the landlord ushered them out into the dark, stumbling and giggling and hanging onto each other. They were singing, or at least attempting to sing, a folk song Jonny had taught Vic, a song he'd learnt in the pub back home, where they didn't have jukeboxes and the landlady kept a shotgun under the counter.

"And there was Brown... WHERE?"

"UPSIDE DOWN!"

"Shhhh!"

"...hang on... lost my shoe..."

"What's the next bit?"

"No idea..." Vic hopped on one foot, trying to get his shoe back on, then threw his head back into the night, "Somebody shouted Macintyre!"

"MACINTYRE!" Jon howled.

"Shut *up*! And we all got absolutely shitfaced drunk..."

"When the old Dun Cow caught fire... I think we missed a bit."

"MACINTYRE!"

"MAC... fuck..." Jon slipped off the kerb and gracefully sank onto his rear with his feet in the gutter.

Vic was giggling helplessly, trying to pull him to his feet. A group of people emerged around the corner and glided towards them, carrying an air of decidedly un-drunk superiority. They slowed, watching Vic and Jonny flail around like drunken fish. Young men and women, five of them, all tall, all slender. Velvet and lace, furs, long hair. They flowed. They shimmered. Skirts and corduroy trousers, soft shirts unbuttoned one button too low, knowing eyes that suggested mystery and that feeling of cool fingers lightly brushing skin. They oozed sex. They all wore jewellery, all jangled as they walked. Androgynous, ethereal, beautiful and eerily quiet as they turned their attention from Jon to Vic, who was still tugging at Jon's elbow.

"Do you need some help?" one of the women asked. She spoke softly, musically.

"Nah, 'm fine... Drunk legs..." Jonny explained, wafting a hand at the group to shoo them away.

The woman who'd spoken was an indiscernible age, somewhere between seventeen and forty. She had long straight black hair that fell past her waist. Her eyes were made up with bronze and gold and her slim wrists were piled with bangles. Her whole body seemed to make its own secret music. She was dwarfed in an oversized afghan, which she clutched at her throat, and her mouth was full and sensual.

Vic sniggered, still trying to tug Jon to his feet. "I fear we've needed help since birth but..." He looked fully at the woman, then at the rest of the group – these impossibly graceful, quiet, decorated and made-up people, these magic-and-moonlight people – and seemed to grind to a halt. He dropped Jon's arm as he stared at them, blinked. "We're... um ... fine..."

The woman who'd spoken smiled.

"Thanks..." Vic added as she nodded once, slowly, her eyes lingering on Vic's face.

The group drifted away, leaving behind the sound of their jangling jewellery, the glitter of their eyes, the echo of the soft billowing clothes they wore, and the smell of incense – smoky, earthy, woody. The group moved away up the street, a few of them glancing back before they disappeared around another corner. Jon clambered to his feet by hanging onto Vic's elbow. Vic was still standing dazed in the street, staring after the group.

"Her eyes..." Vic muttered.

Jon looked at him, looked down the street, then back to Vic. "I thought you were gay?!" Jon shoved him, incredulous.

Vic shrugged absently, still not looking at Jon. "Sometimes I am..."

"Victor, you fancied her!" Jon grinned, swung wildly and pointed in the direction the strange group had gone.

"What?" Vic finally looked at him. "Not really... she just... they all looked so... don't call me Victor! It's awful. Stop clinging to my arm like some old housewife, will you?" Vic shook himself out of Jon's grasp, angry now.

Jon looked at him strangely, not knowing what he'd said to piss Vic off. He just knew he didn't like Vic being angry with him. It was like a light suddenly being switched off.

He held up a hand, placating. "I'm sorry, OK? Let's go get some chips?"

Vic staggered on the spot, still staring off into the distance. "Like stars..." he murmured. "Like... dark stars..."

"Come on, Vic, let's get some chips, yeah? You're being weird. Making me nervous..." Jon shook him, suddenly feeling a lot less drunk and a lot more concerned. Vic seemed to steady himself, found some kind of inner anchor and blinked a few times at Jon.

"Jon... Jonny... I'm sorry. I'm drunk. I'm a fucking prick, aren't I? Neeta's right. I'm absolute worst. Let's go get chips. On me...." he stopped abruptly, frowned, then leant over and threw up into the gutter.

The next morning, they reconvened in the living room. Jon's hangover was immense. His ears were ringing. He felt it was quite possible something had struck him around the back of the head with a sledgehammer some time during the night. He found Vic sitting very upright on the sofa, hands resting on his knees, dressed in his shirt from the night before and his boxers, and a pair of dark sunglasses. Jon sunk down onto the seat beside him slowly and felt Vic stiffen, his breath catch in an inwards wince.

"Don't!" Vic snapped, raising his fingertips from his knee.

"...what...?" Jon was struggling to pull the squashy cushion from behind him so that he could lean back in the seat.

"Don't... move... I've only just got the room to stop spinning...." Vic spoke very softly, his back still very rigid. Jon glanced at him and the peculiar shade of oatmeal grey of his skin and grinned, couldn't help but laugh.

"Fuck off and find me a cigarette!" Vic snapped again.

And much to his own amazement, Jon did. He pulled himself to his feet and went in search of cigarettes. Because it was Vic and... because it seemed like everything was OK again, and the relief of that was a surprise to Jon, but not something he wanted to undo. He found cigarettes and Anita made them bacon butties and strong tea with too much sugar, and Derek came home from his shift at Woolworths and laughed at them. They spent the day lounging around the living room, talking, laughing, eating, listening to the radio until Vic felt well enough to get sick of the cricket and drag out some LPs to play. It was Elton John and ELO and The Supremes. It was pop music and it really, really did seem like everything was OK. Until it got late and people started to yawn, and Vic didn't want to let any of them go to bed. A strange sense of worry reared in the pit of Jon's stomach. A vague alarm of wrongness.

"I've got another early shift in the morning." Derek shrugged, apologetically, sidling out of the room.

Vic threw up his middle fingers at Derek's departing back, turned to the others. "Well sod him, we don't need him, do we? Shall we crack open a bottle of wine?"

"Ugh, Vic, how can ye think of drinkin' after the state of ye this morn? I need tae sleep." Anita dragged herself to her feet, yawning. "It's gone eleven, I've got a lecture at nine."

"No, stay, come on, the night is young. We could go out!" Vic pleaded. Anita rolled her eyes, patted him on the head and helped Jon to his feet.

"Sorry mate, I've really got to get that paper finished for Friday. Another time, yeah?" Jon squeezed past them both and escaped to his room, relieved yet guilt ridden.

Jon got into bed and heard Vic plead with Anita again, offer her a joint and a biscuit and a nice cup of tea. Jon heard her bedroom door shut with a very deliberate sound. Jon heard the music stop, the toilet flush, heard Vic moving around in the living room, heard him pause in the corridor outside their rooms. Jon stared at the ceiling in the dark, listened to Vic standing out there in the corridor, alone. Heard the raked breath and sniff of stifled tears. And still, Jon didn't get up, open the door, comfort him. He hoped Anita might. He could hear Derek snoring already. Jon knew something was wrong, had been wrong since Vic had come home from lunch with his brother the day before, and still, he was afraid to comfort the boy. The door of the flat opened, closed. Then the front door out onto the street. Vic had gone out into the night. He didn't come home for three days.

It wasn't entirely unusual for Vic to stay out or go away for a few days without mentioning it, taking spontaneous trips to see friends or family, getting caught up with some boy or some girl and their beds, but this time when he came back, sliding into the flat silently, sheepishly, drenched head to toe and shivering, Jon knew something irrevocable had happened.

Vic had shut himself in the bathroom without saying a word to any of them almost an hour ago. Anita leant against the hallway wall. Derek sat on the end of his bed, peering out from his room. Jon leant in the doorway to his own bedroom. They silently studied the shut bathroom door, listening to the water and clattered noises from within. When the bathroom door finally opened, Vic emerged in a cloud of steam, wearing a blue cotton bathrobe. He stopped abruptly, looking at them all looking at him,

"Don't tell me," he raised an eyebrow at them, "Lou Reed's dead." He followed it with a laugh but swallowed it when none of them returned it. "Christ, what's the matter?"

"You... all right, are you?" Derek asked carefully.

"Peachy keen, jelly bean!" Vic smiled. "What is this, Women's Institute meeting?" He looked from one to the other of them, dripping on the hallway carpet.

"Where were ye?" Anita asked.

"Out," Vic responded. "You know, the opposite of being *in*."

Anita folded her arms at his tetchy tone, a clear signal to the rest of them that she was about to break into one of her tirades.

Vic spotted the warning signs and held up a hand. "I'm sorry." The tetchiness was gone, replaced with contriteness. "I didn't mean to worry you. Didn't think I'd be out that long but I bumped into some people. Don't be angry, OK? I hate it when you're angry with me." He pulled

Anita into a hug and planted a wet sloppy kiss on her forehead, his wet hair smooshing into her face.

"Ah, gie up, would ye? Yer fair drippin' on me." She shoved him away, but she laughed, mollified, clubbed him on the shoulder. "Ye scunner, ya had us worried."

Vic laughed, shook his hair at Anita, who squealed and retreated to the living room. Derek grinned and flopped back onto his bed, reaching for his newspaper.

Jon watched all this and had the sneaking suspicion Vic was playing them all, buttering them up, throwing them off the scent. Who '*bumps into people*' for three days? Vic opened the door to his own room; always shaded, always cool and dark in there.

"Who were you with?" Jon asked him, quietly.

"I just met some people..."

"What people?"

"Just *people*. Jesus Jon! You know, those people we met the other night when you fell down."

"The weird ones with all the jewellery and the patchouli?" Jon raised his eyebrows incredulously.

Vic's face lit up. "Ah Jon, they're great. Artists, poets, musicians. So... alive! I think you'd love them!"

"You were with them for three whole days?!"

"It was just so intense, Jonny, they're so far out. Politics, music, art, they have so many *ideas*... I guess I lost track of time. They introduced me to new people, new things, new food, new drinks... have you ever tried absinthe, Jonny?" Vic wasn't even looking at him anymore, he wore a fevered expression. "It's like drinking dreams."

Jon felt the wrongness in his gut, knew he should say something, *do* something, but remembered the empty, haunted look Vic's eyes had that afternoon after Vic had met his brother; the palpable throb of Vic's loneliness that night they'd all gone to bed and left him, and Jon decided that this, whatever this frenzied excitement was, was infinitely better than that.

"You're all right, then?" he asked, finally.

Vic threw one of those too-dazzling smiles at him. "Never better!"

As Vic slid into his room, Jon had enough time to notice the almost imperceptible tremor running through Vic's body, the slight shake or shiver or whatever it was in the hand that shut the door.

(Green Manalishi)

Over the course of November, Vic was hardly in one place long enough to speak to. He'd run in, dump his bag, spend too long in the bath singing, and then run around half naked, deciding what to wear, before slamming out of the flat. They all noticed it, the changes. He seemed to be existing on fumes – he barely ate when he was with them, smoked too much. He'd lost weight, and he'd always been slim to begin with. He stopped shaving, dirty blonde stubble only accentuating the hollows of his cheeks, the darkness of the circles beneath his eyes. The way he dressed began to shift. The way he spoke was different. He seemed stoned all the time – that, or jittering and bouncing off the walls. Sometimes he brought *them* back with him, his new crowd. The flatmates started to simply refer to them as *Them*. *They'd* fill the tiny kitchen with their patchouli and fancy cigarette smoke, laughing knowingly, talking in low voices, until Jon or Derek or Anita wandered in to get a drink or something to eat, and *They* would fall silent and watch. Always smiling, always courteous, always passing utensils or plates before they'd been asked, jangling their jewellery, all pressed up and draped over each other, with Vic in the centre, laughing too loudly, everything striking a strange discordant note.

"Predatory," Derek had said decisively, over a pint and a shared packet of crisps. Jon and Anita had nodded sadly. The flatmates didn't go home as much themselves these days, choosing instead the sticky floors and lukewarm beer or shitty coffee of the Student Union bar over another night in the flat with *Them*.

One cold, dark, damp evening, Jon and Anita came back from the Student Union to the smell of that strong incense, bitter and woody, wafting down the stairs to the street. Jon tensed, keys still in the lock, and glanced at Anita. It was a strange smell that the flatmates now associated with *Them*. It made you feel a little dizzy and disorientated after a while. Anita's face had hardened into anger.

"I've had enough o' this…" she muttered. "This bullshit has got tae stop, They're goin' tae be the end o' him…" She thrust her carpet bag into Jon's arms and took the stairs at a run – two, three steps at a time.

Jon rushed after her as she flew into the flat, red hair flying. *They* were crammed into the kitchen smoking and drinking and draped over the counter tops, while strange psychedelica played in the living room, and there was Vic sprawled on the chair by the table. He was wearing jeans – not even flares, these were dark and skinny right down to the brown Cuban heels on his feet – and a black shirt that hung off him, so thin it was more of a suggestion. Dishevelled and unkempt, tarnished silver pendant around his neck, and smiling. Anita took a deep breath, grit her teeth and stomped into the kitchen, pushing her way into the room.

"Ahh, would ye wheesht?!" she shouted, "Oot of ma kitchen! This is ma home and I'd like tae cook in peace!"

They tittered, shared knowing smirks, began to stand up, floating around her in all their flowing finery.

"Get oot!" she stamped her foot.

They danced slowly around her, all arms and mystical fingers reaching for her, stroking at her. Someone opened up a palm towards her, revealing a pile of what looked like cinnamon and sand and dry leaves, blew it at her. She bristled, closed her eyes, shook her head as the shimmery what-ever-it-was settled in her hair and on her shoulders.

"Get out!" *They* whispered, laughed. "Get out..."

"Come with us, love... we'll make you feel real good..."

"It's a wild ride..."

"Join the dance... fire in your hair and in your heart... come with us..."

They trailed hands over Anita's shoulders, through her hair. It seemed both sensuous and yet threatening.

"Get off of her!" Jon yelled, from where he stood in the living room. "Get out! Out!" It almost became a howl.

They looked from Anita to Jon, laughed, began drifting out of the room, down the hall, out of the flat.

"Ah wait, Oona, Angus... they don't mean it..." Vic was up and placating, pleading, but his group of strange ethereal companions were drifting along the hall already.

Jon watched *Them* and realised he couldn't really tell them apart. They all looked alike, as if they all drifted together and merged then separated like the fog on the shoreline, as if *They* were all made of the same insubstantial stuff.

"Maeve? Wait!" Vic reached for a girl with long black hair who might, Jon suspected, have been the same woman that spoke to them that first night. She placed a hand covered in silver rings against Vic's unshaven cheek, but said nothing, gliding from the kitchen with one final appraising look at Anita. Anita still stood rigid in the centre of the kitchen, shoulders raised, fists clenched and eyes clamped shut.

Vic watched the departing backs disappear through the front door of the flat and down the stairs, hand still outstretched, then glared at Anita. She turned to him, her eyes wide, afraid, but unable to speak.

"Look what you've done!" Vic bellowed, swept up a black leather jacket from the back of the chair he'd been sitting on, and made after the retreating group.

Jon realised he was still holding Anita's bag, threw it aside. "Vic..." he called, "wait, Vic!"

Jon caught him between the living room and the bathroom, pulling him around.

"Get off!" Vic shrugged himself free but Jon pinned him against the wall with one hand.

"What is wrong with you?" Jon demanded.

"Nothing's wrong with me!" Vic snarled back, squirming.

Jon grabbed the front of his shirt. "Yeah? Looked in the mirror lately? How's the shakes? Huh? What are you on?"

Vic laughed, threw his head back against the wall and flashed him that winning crooked smile. "Jonny, what are you..."

"Acid? Mushrooms? That new stuff Reggie was selling?"

Vic flinched under the glare of Jon's uncharacteristic severity and seriousness, looked down at the fist gripping his shirt, looked away, around, anywhere but at Jon directly.

"I'm fine..." That flash of a smile again, eyes darting around, fingers picking at the ripped skin on a thumb.

"You're not," Jon told him.

Vic rolled his eyes. "I'm going out..." pushed Jon's hand away and strode towards the door.

"Don't." Jon stepped after him. Vic paused. "Don't go with them. They're not... not good for you. Stay here," Jon added. "...Please..."

Vic turned slightly in the narrow hallway, met Jon's gaze, and for a moment looked open and bottomless and unfathomably afraid. "But... they're my friends..."

" *We're* your friends," Jon replied flatly. "You know they're not. I... I'm not even sure what *They* are."

Vic raked in a breath, seemed to flounder.

Jon reached out a hand towards him. "We can get you help..."

But then Derek was bundling in through the door of the flat. "Guys, why is the front door ope-" he was gesturing back over his shoulder down the stairs, but stopped short, surprised by the scene in front of him, somehow understanding it all at once, growing serious.

Derek's arrival seemed to break something. Jon felt it shattering into a thousand pieces, saw Vic's face shift and solidify into something hard and sharp.

"They're my friends," Vic said quietly, but firmly, and he left. The door to the street banged shut behind him like a full stop.

There was a void. Then Jon remembered, turned, found Anita standing in the kitchen doorway, one hand holding her elbow, the other wrapped around herself. She held herself awkwardly, like something had been taken from her. She was trembling. Poor Anita. Fiery, lanky, fierce, stroppy, terrified Anita. He reached for her.

She turned huge, watery eyes to him. "Oh... ohhh Jonny..."

She began to cry as he pulled her into his arms.

Derek entered the living room, met Jon's worried expression over the mass of Anita's hair, slumped against the wall and wiped his face with his big hand, aghast, stunned. They all were.

Vic didn't come back. Not after three nights. Not after two weeks. It was December now and though the streets, shop windows, cafes, pubs and the University were draped in streamers, tinsel and lights, though John Lennon was telling the world that War was over, the flat on Portland Street remained unadorned. Anita and Jon huddled around the kitchen table, silently, grimly holding hands around an untouched plate of toast. Anita had been having these awful dreams since *They'd* blown that handful of stuff at her. Nightmares that she woke screaming and drenched in sweat from. She could never seem to remember much of them, save the notion of faces forming in mist, watching her. Jon had taken to just sleeping in her room to hold her through the night, and somewhere along the way, they'd restlessly, miserably, fallen into a relationship.

Derek burst into the room. "He's dropped out of the University!"

"What?!" Jon sat up. "Since when?"

"Last Wednesday, apparently." Derek took his bag off from over his shoulder, tossed it into the living room. "No one's seen him around campus. He's not been to lectures or groups. So I asked at the admittance office. They said he'd withdrawn from his course. He's got exams, he's graduating in the spring!"

"Fuck..." Anita pushed her head into her hands. "Fuck!"

Jon flopped back on his chair. "Did you tell them? Explain he's not been home? That the police don't care? That they said if he left willingly there's nothing they can do? That he's... different now?"

Derek nodded, slid out of his coat and threw that, too, into the living room. He reached for the kettle, turned on the tap to fill it.

"I said we were concerned for his welfare, that he'd not come home... but they knew Vic. Everyone knows Vic, y'know? They all think he's an upper class rich kid parading his eccentric little posh boy self around. The woman in the office, you know, the one with the hair that doesn't move? She said everyone knows he's a 'character'," he pulled a face, "But he'd seemed just fine when he'd had a meeting with the head of Classics and withdrawn from the course. Mollie on the front desk said she saw him. He was fine, she said. Usual barmy self. Laughing, joking..."

Derek placed the kettle on the hob, looked at the other two sitting in worried silence, read the unspoken things on their faces. "What happened? Did you find something out?"

"His mam... I spoke tae her," Anita sighed, "asked the shop doonstairs if I could use their phone, said it was an emergency. His mother was reit pissed, sour, dusty hag that she is, but he's been home to her. Says he wis there yesterday. Rattled up in a... a, what did she call it?" she looked to Jon.

"A hippy wagon," Jon replied quietly.

"Aye, a hippy wagon. Said he'd strolled in bold as buggery, told her he wanted to go away with his pals, and asked her fae his trust fund details."

Derek gaped at her. "Oh shit..."

"Oh aye, an' it gets better. Dear mumsy says she told him no, that he wis a disgrace and a sodomiser and no son of hers an' all that, but then he did something to the brother, ol' fuckface... what's-is-name. Geoffrey. Says Geoffrey was there visitin' with his wife and bairns, and Vic said something to the wife, obscene, the mother says, said something to her and she fair near creams her knickers, and *They* came in and took her aff. Then Vic looks at Geoffrey, whispers somethin' tae *him* and, she says, the man gets this dreamy look on his face like he wis smoking the devil's grass, she says, then just tells Vic straight off all the trust fund details, whit attorney to speak to, all of it. *Geoffrey?! Can* ye believe it? And off Vic strolls to Christ knows where!"

Derek looked from Anita to Jon, who nodded his validation of the story. "...what the actual fuck?" Derek leaned heavily against the slither of countertop beside them. "Now what? He's just gone, is he? Gone and no one cares. Gone off with... with the fucking fairies?"

It was the first time any of them had referred to *Them* as something supernatural. But they all knew. The story Vic's mother had told Anita seemed ridiculous, outlandish, and yet... the flatmates had all seen the way that group were, how *They* drifted and floated, jangled and confused you. The way *They'd* danced mockingly around Anita, blew that stuff in her face. The only thing worse than knowing no one else would believe them – not when kids were dropping LSD at house parties – was the guilt. If they'd done something sooner, helped him sooner, reacted to all those gut feelings, maybe their friend would still be here, sprawled in the living room swapping out LPs, moaning about Ted Heath and the squares in parliament. And so Vic had gone. *They* had taken him. *They'd* found him at his weakest, his lowest, his most lost, and they'd fed off that. Fed off his pain, stole him away. And now he was becoming like *Them*. Or maybe the thing that visited the University and frightened his mother wasn't even Vic at all.

What followed was a strange, messed up time for all of them. Anita went home to Scotland in the April of 1973. The nightmares wouldn't stop. Jon called her most weeks from the phone in the pawn shop beneath the flat, paying them in pennies and odd jobs, until the Christmas of 1974, when she told him she was going out with some lad from her hometown. They'd not spoken since. Jon and Derek carried on in the Portland Street flat for as long as they could. Derek had graduated in '73 and started work full-time at Woolworths. Jon was awarded a Second-Class degree in 1975. He didn't tell his parents. He didn't attend the award ceremony, so the University posted his certificate. It fell, unceremoniously, onto the doormat at the bottom of the stairs to the flat and stayed there, unnoticed for almost a month. The two men rattled around that flat, drifting from one shit job to the next. They were waiting, in an unspoken pact, for the others to come back. For Vic to wander in with a cigarette and a grin and throw on a record, for Anita to stomp in behind in those ridiculous yellow boots and call him a prick. They didn't, of course, and the two young men wilted, languishing in the memories imprinted within their home. In the end, in '76, they moved out. The yellow kitchen was sour. The flat was faded and worn around the edges. Derek got a job in London working the doors on the nightclubs, and Jon got hired to do security work for factories, ended up in Swindon. They'd catch up occasionally, over a pint in some crap-hole pub somewhere in suburbia along the M4 corridor, but eventually even those meetings began to dwindle. But then, when he'd almost started to pretend he'd forgotten it all, Jon saw Vic again.

(Because the Night)

It was in a punk club in Reading in 1979. Jon was working nights there, pulling pints. He'd shaved his head, wore Doc Martens boots everywhere. There was something comforting in the nihilism of punk, of grotty clubs in shitty towns at night when he couldn't ever seem to find his sea legs in the daytime. Jon had been serving a customer, looked up across the club, and there Vic was. He hadn't aged a day. He was all in black – black jeans, bovver boots, fitted black T-shirt. His face was just the same. He was leaning against a wall, coolly watching the crowd.

The Sex Pistols had been blaring. It was as if the whole room was moving at a different speed to Vic. These kids, they pogoed, bounced, thrashed around to the music. Vic seemed perfectly still, perfectly separate. The room seemed to ripple around him and, Jon noticed, he wasn't alone. There were three others with him. *Them.* Fairies, though that name caught and felt absurd. Vic, another male, two women. Gone were the floaty, hippie clothes. Now it was all tighter; sleek black denim and dark glasses, boots and braces but still a lot of hair. And *They* were hunting, Jon knew it. That predatory look of sex and mystery, like *They* could just lay a hand on anyone in that room and make them do anything. It made all the hairs on the back of Jon's neck stand on end. He remembered that weird magnetism Vic used to have back at Uni, in the pubs, in lectures – the way people wanted to be near him, like he was the Sun. Now, Vic was the Moon. Cold, distant, shimmering, but with just as much gravity.

Girls and boys stole glances at *Them.* A young lass with her hair in an array of chunky spikes and wearing tartan trousers bravely snaked over to them and tried to speak to Vic as Johnny Rotten shouted about Anarchy in the UK. One of the women Vic was with, maybe it was Maeve with the long black hair, draped herself over the lass's shoulder, stroked her cheek with the back of a long finger. Vic stepped too close to her, and Jon felt it, the pulse, the magic, whatever it was, the god-damn spell Vic was weaving, just as Jon had seen *Them* do to Vic all those years back.

Jon didn't remember dropping the pint of beer he'd been passing to a customer, but the other bar staff later told him that it had slid from his hand as he vaulted over the bar and launched himself across the club at *Them.* He got almost close enough to grab Vic before Vic tore his eyes from the punk girl and saw Jon barrelling towards him. Those grey eyes, too unnatural now, too faceted, too bright in the club's darkness, they widened. And then he vanished. It wasn't a disappearing in a puff of smoke, but one second Vic's face showed horrified recognition, then a glut of people pushed between the two men and Vic was gone. The others he'd been with were gone, too. The punk girl with the mohawk was swaying on the spot, staring vacantly into the space where Vic had been standing. Jon shook her. Her eyes rolled and her knees buckled.

The manager got the girl an ambulance, told the paramedics she'd just drunk too much, maybe taken something. If she'd come to the club with friends, none of them hung around for her. But then, Jon guessed, that's why *They'd* chosen her. She'd been lost and alone. She wouldn't be missed.

Later, back at his one-bed flat, Jon found his address book, thumbed through it, picked up the phone and called Anita. He wasn't even sure the number he had for her was still good. It rang for five rings, ten, and just as he was about to hang up, he heard a click, and a muffled voice say

"...hullo?"

Her sweet, rolling voice.

"Anita?" he asked, stupidly.

Silence for a moment, then "Who's this?"

"It's Jon... Jonny."

"Jonny?" she sounded fuzzy, quiet, confused. "Jesus, it's four-thirty in tha mornin'!"

He glanced at the clock on his bedside table. She was right. He had no real comprehension of time these days.

"Ah, fuck, I'm sorry. Really. But I just got off work and, well, there's something- I had to- I saw him, Neeta. I saw Vic."

There was silence down the phone.

"He was there, in this club I work at. With *Them*. He hasn't changed, hasn't aged, but he's different. He's like *Them* now. He nearly... I dunno," he struggled to find the words for what he'd seen, "*Bewitched* some girl and I thought it was all going to happen again. I mean, it *is* all happening again, *still* happening. But I stopped him. And he vanished before I could speak to him, and the ambulance took the girl. But it was him, Neeta. It was Vic!" Jon stopped, breathing hard, felt his heart hammering. She said nothing. "Neeta?"

"I heard ye," she said quietly.

Jon waited but when she said nothing more, he snapped "Aren't you... I don't know, *concerned*? Shouldn't we *do* something?" he was wrapping the phone chord around his wrist, gripping and tugging at it.

"Do what?!" she said, rushed, almost whispering. "So what if it's him? So what?! It's been seven years, Jon. He hasn't given a single thought tae us. I'm done whi' all that. It's... it's no' real. Faeries an' snatchin' people awa'. Magic spells and... and the dreams that..." She trailed off, drew in a breath. "Jon, I can't let it be real any mair. First Derek callin' on me, now you. I cannae... I cannae get back intae this with you. I've got a life here. A home. A family. I'm tryin', ya ken? Go tae sleep Jon... Goodbye."

She hung up and Jon sat in stunned silence. Didn't she want to stop *Them* from doing this? Didn't she care about these lost kids falling through the cracks into this dark other place? He placed the phone's handset back in its cradle.

A family? Was that why she'd been whispering? Was someone laying beside her? Were there children breathing softly in another room? Well, good for her. He squashed the disappointment and regret down into his stomach. He pictured her pale, long body, her flame hair, spread beneath him, holding him tight inside her. Gone now. Lost to him as sure as Vic was, as sure as the concept of sleep. Something else she'd said suddenly registered; he snatched up the phone again, flicked through the address book and punched in another number.

Derek was up when Jon called. Derek had seen Vic more than once, throughout London while he worked security or door detail. At first Derek had thought he'd imagined it – night work and not sleeping great, probably too much drink, he'd said, maybe he was just seeing people who looked like him. Like *Them*. But no – it was Vic, Derek was certain. He asked Jon to meet him halfway between their two places and hung up.

When Jon walked into the greasy spoon café in Slough that Derek had named, Jon saw the tall, black man at once. Derek was clean shaven, his afro shorter, but his face was lined, aged. He looked tired, in faded jeans and a grey stained sweatshirt. He smelt faintly of booze and stale cigarettes. It was six a.m. The night crowd hadn't gone to sleep yet, the day commuters and city lot were just getting going. The men huddled over bad coffee in tiny cups, ate greasy sausage rolls that tasted of disappointment, to compare notes. Derek had a photo of Vic taken at a Queen gig in Hammersmith.

And that's how they started researching, investigating the *Them*. They followed up on missing persons reports and picked up on common threads, areas that Jon and Derek had seen *Them* and the sort of people *They* looked for. The men collected evidence – accounts from people who'd seen *Them*, photos, newspaper clippings, even the old folktales about the dark Fey, the Unseelie. Historical accounts. Disappearances. Reappearances where the person seemed utterly changed. Unexplained abilities. Jon sent an envelope of the cuttings, their notes, the photo of Vic that Derek had taken, to Anita.

In the spring of 1980, the doorbell of Jon's flat rang. Derek had moved in and was sleeping on his couch, dramatically decreasing the number of visitors, so Jon was cautious, opened the door slowly. It was Anita. Dishevelled, sloppy brown cardigan hanging off one shoulder, backpack slung over the other with a busted zip, what looked like a blue vinyl anorak poking out of it. Skinny strap of a handbag caught in the crook of her arm. She wore a crumpled moss-green dress belted at her waist, the laces on her tennis shoes were snaking loose. Her hair was long now and wild around her pale, angular face. Gone was the fierce girl with all the colours, the purposeful stride. She looked pinched, pale, the tip of her nose red, like she'd had a cold for the last decade.

"I lied." she sighed. "I havnae slept reit for years now. Ron... he left me. Said I was a ghost hauntin' ma own life."

Derek had woken, propped himself up on his elbows to blearily peer at her. Anita glanced at him then back to Jon.

"The dreams." She pushed her hair out of her face absently. "The dreams never stopped."

She shrugged her bag from her shoulder and let it and her handbag drop wearily to the floor. Jon opened his arms and she capitulated into them.

The reunited flatmates wholly, entirely blamed the *Them, The Fey Ones* for this unravelled, bedraggled life they found themselves living. All those times *They* had been in the flat at Portland Street with their incense, their music, their strange eyes – *They* had, it was quite apparent to the flatmates, stolen something vital not just from Vic but from the other flatmates also. Since Vic had gone, everything was cast in half-light. So, huddled around the evidence that the flatmates had collected so far, poring over the photos and the notes and the fairy-tale books in the frowsty stale air of the shaded bedsit, Derek said what they had all been thinking –

"We have to stop *Them*."

It was the only thing any of the flatmates could do now – try and stop *Them* from spreading this misery to others.

(London Calling)

Over the months that followed, that somehow flowed into years without them noticing, the flatmates tracked *Them, The Fey Ones*. Across the night-time places of London, Reading, the South-West, and further. Juggling part time jobs to pay bills with their research and investigations, the flatmates figured out the places *They* liked to frequent. Music seemed to gather the sort of people *They* hunted. Gigs, clubs, bars – but also solitary, poetic spots. Museums, libraries, wistful places. Lakes. Rivers. Windswept hills and beaches. The darker places, too. Crack houses. Dark bridges where homeless people huddled. Hospital waiting rooms. Cold places. The threshold places. Lonely places. All the places where the hopeless and the lost wandered.

Sometimes the flatmates found *The Fey Ones* lurking, drifting, waiting, luring people in with their promise of dark delights, and though they could never catch *Them*, they could spook *The Fey* into disappearing, fading back into the gloom. Sometimes Vic was with *Them*, often he was not. Sometimes the flatmates arrived too late, with nothing but whispers and wild things clinging to the air, another lost soul gone.

Jon decided that *The Fey Ones* were like Vampires, but rather than blood, *They* fed off the sadness and emptiness of these kids. On the occasions that the flatmates could stop *Them* from stealing away more of these haunted, empty kids, keep those kids here and get them home, get them the help they needed, it was catharsis, a kind of redemption. It was their crusade.

1984 was a year of bleak disquiet, not just for the flatmates but for the country. For the whole world, it seemed. The miners were on strike. Dole queues stretched. The working week was three days long. The power went off after six in the evening. Riots and protests and bombs and closures. Stomachs were empty. Shoulder pads were wide. Hair was big. Hearts were angry. Greed was good. Punk was splitting, dividing into new things – punk-metal, post-punk, new wave, goth-rock. Henry Rollins raged poetry and politics, Robert Smith dreamily sang about desolation. Anthony Keidis sang about heroin and fucking. The flatmates folded themselves into that tiny one-bedroom flat in Swindon. They didn't own much. They drank too much coffee and ate when they remembered. They smoked weed that Anita brought home from somewhere.

Derek slept on the couch, though sleep would only ever come fitfully to him after strangled hours spent tossing, turning and drinking until the glass would slip from his hands.

Anita shared Jon's bed and their sex was urgent. Cold flesh and arched backs, but silent, a kind of shared suffering. The nights were too long, too full of shadows.

Through some connections, the flatmates had tracked a group of *Them* to a particular part of Brixton in London. Over the years, the flatmates had built quite a network of others that knew about *Them*. This network swapped sightings, stories, helped to localise *Them* in certain areas, places, or upcoming events. On the 7th December 1984, after careful planning with Jon and Anita, Derek was going to drive to Brixton and see if he could attempt an interception. Jon watched Derek pack up a messenger bag with some maps, a flashlight, snacks.

"You're going to be all right, yeah?" Jon shadowed Derek around the flat. Jon had to work that night, a shift in a warehouse for a supermarket. Anita was following up on a lead back in Bristol. So Derek was going alone.

"I'll be fine! Tim from the Nags Head is going to meet me."

After so many years living in the south, Derek's Burnley accent had softened. Anita's broad accent had too, come to think of it, except when she got angry. Derek kicked aside a pile of empty wine and gin bottles that had piled up on the floor by the end of the sofa. He'd been drinking a lot. More than usual. Anita said she thought she'd heard him crying in the night. Jon drifted around behind him. Derek's afro was unkempt, parts of it had twisted into dreadlocks. He'd not been looking after it. His face was pock-marked and sallow, covered in unkempt beard. Sweat coated his forehead and upper lip. Had Jon just slept through the last decade while Derek turned into an alcoholic? That weird pit-of-the-stomach claxon was sounding inside Jon.

"Don't go. Stay here, Dez. I'll skip work. Let's cook up a steak and chips and watch the footie."

Derek halted, straightened from where he'd been pulling a musty sweatshirt from a pile by the washing machine.

He looked at Jon. "Thanks... but... It's too late. I think."

"What do you mean? I'll call in sick, I'll –"

"No." Derek pushed the sweatshirt into his bag, pulled the strap over his head so it sat across his body, wiped his face. "This whole thing..." He gestured round the flat. "Us. Anita. Vic. It's a lie. Maybe you don't want to see it yet. Maybe I hope you never will. But, the thing is," he grabbed up his keys from the shelf by the door, "I know now. You peer into the cracks enough, Jonny, sooner or later, you end up in an in-between place yourself."

He was out of the front door, striding along the dank hallway towards the stairs.

Jon ran after him in bare feet. "Derek, stop, don't drive like this!"

Derek didn't stop, didn't slow. "I'm fine, Jonny. Sober. Can't remember the last time I was. If I find *Them*, I'll get to the bottom of all this."

Derek bounded down the concrete steps to his car with a fierce determination that Jon hadn't seen for years. Jon ran to the top of the steps feeling desperate. It was exactly like the time Vic had last walked out of the flat in Portland Street... except... *They* hadn't been here to climb inside Derek's head. *Had They?* He watched helplessly as Derek reversed out of his parking spot, threw his battered Honda Civic into a three-point turn and disappeared up the street. Jon watched the taillights round the corner, listened to the sound of the engine fade into the background sound of traffic, then sank onto the top step in his bare feet, and sighed.

Derek never came back.

(Maybe Someday)

In 1990, in a goth club in Soho, Vic came to find Jon. Anita had an inkling *They'd* show up in this place sooner or later, so they'd been taking it in turns to stake it out. Jon was wedged in a corner by the bar, keeping himself to himself and feeling too old, too done, too weary to be surrounded by all these youngsters. But these were exactly the kids *They* liked. So Jon slowly drank his cider and lager with a dash of blackcurrant – he'd been reliably informed by the plump goth barmaid that this was called a Snakebite – and watched the crowds. Bauhaus and The Cure mixed with newer stuff that Jon realised he didn't know.

Over the years, *The Fey Ones* adapted and shifted. New Romantic had been big for *Them*, but Goth was even bigger. Though *They* had haunted the edges of raves in their neon and baggy trousers, and had adopted Grunge, *They* seemed to have found a comfortable fit in the dark romance of the Goth scene that would last. The soft black lace leather and velvet, from the 80s Siouxsie Sioux look to the Victoriana vibe – it just sat well with *Them*.

Jon spotted one of *The Fey Ones* on the dancefloor, a billowing gothic beauty with mesmerising, too-bright green eyes made up like an Egyptian goddess. Her auburn hair was swept artistically into a perfect death-hawk. Jon was trying to place his pint down without losing sight of her or the captivated, black-haired urchin that was approaching her, when Vic appeared beside him. Vic's hair was still that same dirty-blonde hair, but he wore it longer now, teased and messy. He wore leather trousers that hugged his hips, ankle boots with pointed toes and silver buckles, and a ripped Bauhaus shirt that skimmed his midriff and hung off his collar bones. Jon was greying at the temples and thinning on the top, his gut going soft, and Vic didn't look a day older than the first time Jon had seen him, aged twenty, stoned and draped in the bedroom doorway at Portland Street. Vic seemed younger now, somehow, with those strange luminous grey eyes lined and smudged in kohl. He was there so suddenly, too close, staring at – into – Jon with those inhuman eyes, that Jon stepped back, startled.

"Stop following us, Jonny," Vic said.

His voice! The same and yet, not. It reverberated through Jon like several voices speaking at once.

"You know I can't, Vic," Jon answered.

"You've no business here. Let us help them."

Jon's eyebrows shot up. "Help *who*?!" Though Vic's voice had been quiet and easily heard, Jon found he had to raise his own voice over the music. "Those poor, lost kids you steal away?! We're trying to save them, Vic! Trying to save *you*! After all these years! We... we've been trying to find you!"

Vic smiled faintly, a sad smile, put his hand on Jon's arm. "You don't understand. You're not ready to yet."

Vic was a pocket of stillness, like he absorbed everything around him, sucked the air out of Jon's lungs. "You could never see... you've never been broken enough, not lost enough. We don't look for the kids and steal them. They find us. We save them. You thought my friends were poisoning me, but they got me straight and sober. There'd been heroine, Jon, and too much acid. They got me clean and then they gave me this life. It's my fault you're here, like this, afraid and living this half-life, caught between worlds, between sleep and awake, and I'm sorry. But I promise, it won't last forever. One day, it'll be time. And I'll see you then, OK?"

Jon was forty, a past-it punk in a 90s kids' goth club, and tears filled his eyes then, choking him. Nothing Vic said made any sense. Jon reached for him, desperate. "Come home, Vic!"

Vic gently removed Jon's hands from his bare, pale arms then pulled something from his pocket – a drawstring pouch made of soft black leather – and pressed it into Jon's palm.

"A gift. Stop now. Go home to Anita, love her. Sleep. Derek says hi. I'll see you."

Vic was gone as suddenly as he'd appeared, leaving nothing but the pouch in Jon's hand and that woody, smoky incense taste in the back of Jon's throat, like burning sage and cloves.

Jon stumbled out into the night. London never slept, and Soho buzzed around him as he walked. His whole body felt electrified. His skin crawled. Vic had done something to him, hadn't he? Once, the bright-eyed, bushy-tailed village rugby champion and eager student he had been, the tall sensible farmer's son with the easy smile, had wanted desperately to come to Soho, where all the cool kids were. Now he was here, it seemed grubby and tarnished. He could see the figurative man behind the curtain operating the magic show of it all. Had it always been like this? Was this what Derek had meant about staring into the cracks for long enough? How much had Jon just been sleepwalking through? He was nothing more than a smudge, a blur against the bright lights. He drove his rental car home in a hazy stupor, knowing somewhere in the back of his brain that he probably shouldn't be behind the wheel, but going through the motions nonetheless. He drove, motorway lights flashing overhead in a dull pulsing *whoomp whoomp.*

For so long, Jon had been buoyed along by the sense that he was doing some good, snuffing out the misery that *The Fey Ones* spread. But had he actually ever seen *Them* take a human? Actually seen one of *Them* reach out and pluck an unsuspecting victim? No. All the lost kids approached *Them* first. The kids sought *Them* out. *They* were just in the right place to be found. What did Vic mean Jon wasn't broken enough? Not lost enough? What the fuck had this half-life for the last twenty years been, if not broken and lost? Jon glanced at the leather pouch Vic had given him, discarded on the passenger seat, and felt chastised, like all this time he'd somehow been missing the mark, missing the point.

The flat was dark. Anita was in bed, all her hair spread around her across the pillows, but she opened her eyes and looked at him when he sat down on the edge of the bed. He doubted that she had slept at all.

"How'd it go?" she asked quietly.

Jon dropped his head forward, sighed, and carefully placed the black leather pouch on the bed covers where she could see it. "Saw Vic. He gave me this."

Anita sat up, the covers pooling in her lap, her naked body pale in the dark room. "What is it?"

Jon had looked already, of course he had. "The truth."

She reached out to take it, recoiled, scooted over to him and placed her head on his shoulder.

"Look in it," he told her.

Slowly, cautiously, she picked up the pouch and pulled the drawstrings apart. She peered inside, then poked a finger into it. Jon felt her body stiffen.

"Jesus..." she whispered. "Jonny it's..."

"I know." He placed his hand over hers. "It's the same stuff, right?"

The pouch was filled with what looked like sand and cinnamon, dead leaves, nutmeg, salt. It shimmered and glittered. It smelt like *They* had always smelt – cloves and sage and woodsmoke, like spices and night-time and a deep knowing. It was alive. It was hot summers and rain on bare skin and freedom.

Anita began to cry.

"They weren't ever nightmares," she muttered, tears dropping onto the bedsheets, nose running. "They were peace. They were home and hope and – I just didnae ever want to believe it. I used tae scream when I woke up not because I wis afraid, but because the dreams wisnae real. All this time I've... we've... been fooling ourselves that we were tryin' to dae the right thing, but it's a lie."

"I know." Jon squeezed her hand.

When he'd looked into the pouch, sat in the car, pulled over on the side of the motorway; when he'd poured some of that old deep magic into his palm and sniffed at it, he knew. They'd spent these years desperately chasing this, not letting themselves see that they were desperate only to claim it and possess it, never understanding that *The Fey* could not be possessed, you had to find them when you were ready, and only then would they enfold you.

"I didnae want to believe." Anita drew her knees up to her chin. "I could've had it, back then, in the kitchen. They invited me, but I said no..." She pressed her wet cheek into her bare knees. "I said no. And then I didnae know how to be free of the hunger for it, so I fought it."

"Not broken enough..." Jon sighed. He understood now. The sort of broken and lost that led you to the lands of *The Fey Ones* was when you'd utterly fallen through the cracks, unseen. He had never wanted to destroy himself, had never hated himself, had never stood in a crowd and felt utterly, entirely unnecessary. Tonight, perhaps, walking and feeling the city stream past him, he'd had a taste of it. *The Fey Ones* offered a home for the lost, a place to belong.

"What now?" Anita asked.

He looked at her, beautiful bedraggled Anita, and at the leather pouch between them, felt their reality peeling like damp wallpaper all around them. He plucked up a pinch of the shimmering dust, rubbed it between his thumb and forefinger, blew it at her.

"We wait," he said.

* * *

Huck, Shuck, Howl

There is a dog,

With paws as big as shovels and eyes as large as fire pits,

Breath as frowsty as the crypt,

Fur as black as if the Devil tipped ink on the darkest moor,

Claws like razors, and teeth like knives,

With a howl to send shivers down your spine.

As big as a pony, as big as a truck,

Black Shuck, Old Shuck, prowls the night.

The Black Dog is a story every person I know knows.

Where the Black Dog goes, the midnight chill will follow.

The Black Dog is a hellhound,

Or bound to the Baskervilles or perhaps it's the Grim.

The Black Dog is known across all the country and in

Every rain-battered country inn,

There'll be that one odd old fella who'll draw you close

With a pint and a wink and an open fire and begin

To tell his version of the tale and the name

The Dog wears in these parts.

He'll start to tell you he, maybe his mother,

Or his brother down the lane

Saw the Dog once and was never the same –

A ghost upon the hill and a shadow in the night,

Echoing through darkness and smothering the brightest light.

The Black Dog stands with banshees

Beyond your window to let you know

He is the harbinger of doom,

To tell you that Death will visit soon

And stalk these hills or that hospital wing.

The Black Dog sings at the moon and those who see him are

Lost in a puff of smoke or else gone mad.
The Black Dog brings you 'sad' like a dug-up-bone,
Makes a home in your muddled-up mind,
Climbs upon your back and drags you to
The deepest darkest depths of bleakest hell.
The Black Dog, then, will tell you he's
The hollow sound of your soul scraping
Along the bottom of a sigh.
The Black Dog rides the night with the Wild Hunt and
The Black Dog guards the entrance to the Underworld,
And the Black Dog is the thunder rumbling like a threat
As you count the beats between his paws.
The Black Dog is in the land and of the land,
Hewn from soil and chalk,
Stalks amongst the standing stones,
Makes a home in the deep dark caves,
Sprung forth from mines
Along the spine of this country's dark satanic mills,
And still he will protect by tooth and jowl.
Howl of soot and coal and dying embers of the fire.
The Black Dog is ancient, old and wise.
The Black Dog knows the world is not too bright nor
Too full of 24-hour-convenience lights;
He doesn't mind.
He pads on tarmac, claws click-clack on driveways,
He navigates the crooked miles and byways
To hide beneath the sculptured begonia patch.
His growl catches you in flickering streetlights,
And in the creaking rusted swing set at midnight.
He is in the rustles of the leaves at the lonely bus stop
And the bristle that creeps along the top of your head

As you take the groaning darkened stairway to bed.
He is the fear that lurks in the deserted car park.
Is that barking you hear as you fumble for your keys?
Is that shape in the shadows some kind of beast?
Old Shuck, Black Shuck, is close by
When your heartbeat starts to increase,
And he'll still be here, in the wind, the rain
And the bloodstains on the barricaded doors and
In the moonless nights upon the moors and
The battered cliffs and twisted trees and the shifting
Listless
Mournful country lanes
Long after the earth has forgotten my name.
He'll still be here in all the fear,
Haunting the dark nights of their souls,
That Old Black Dog curled up upon their porch,
The whip-crack of his tail a caution,
Eyes like burning torches, big as saucers, full of fire
And old,
As old as time.

* * *

The Odd Uneven Time

I

There is a moment of stillness - then with a lurch, I feel my heart hammering in my chest. I'm not dead. I can still feel the blood clinging to my skin, dried and tight; can taste the wind and snow on my lips... But when my eyes open, the sky is clear and blue. How long have I been laying here? There is blind panic as I try to establish how I came to be sprawled beneath an apple tree, covered in blood...

I remember; I'd been in a corn field south of Humboldt, Iowa. I'd been sitting on the hood of my pick-up, one dusty boot hooked on the fender, the denim of my tired jeans just starting to go see-through on the knee. The sun was a hazy thumb-smudge on the horizon, reflected in the lazy Des Moines river, but already hot. I wiped my face with the bottom edge of my T-shirt and lit a cigarette. Gnats hummed and, somewhere up the road, a dog barked. I just sat and watched the world unfolding, feeling the morning heat on my bare arms, getting drunk on it all like a hornet full of fermented fruit. And then, from nowhere, I got this feeling in my guts. An awareness tinged with nerves; butterflies flipping somersaults in my stomach. I rubbed one finger across the stubble dusting my top lip, and exhaled smoke down my nose. I knew the feeling; it was always the same. I tried not to panic - it wouldn't do me any good to panic - but there was a sudden jolt of adrenaline anyway. I realised I was holding my breath as I waited to be sure. Had to be sure that it had really started. But it was there, alright, a buzzing in my mind louder than the gnats and yet silent. It was as though a fishing line were caught in my head and suddenly being tugged.

Shit! I bristled with a sudden chill, the first this year. *Not now. Not yet.*

I checked the date on my smartwatch. Checked it again, incredulously. How could it possibly be late September already? The summer had flown by. But, I supposed, with a sigh, he was right on time. It's funny how it always catches me unawares. I'll sit and strain myself till I get a migraine, listening for it, and when it does come, the knowledge that he's after me again, it shocks me. I stared out over the corn field, golden, heavy and ready for reaping.

"Not yet," I whispered.

The buzz in my head strengthened for a second. A sharp reminder. I couldn't put it off any longer. Sliding from the hood, my leg twinged and I absently rubbed at the joint.

Getting old, I thought. *Getting too old for this.*

I hauled myself into the driver's seat of the truck and glanced at myself in the rear-view mirror. Flecks of grey and white in my auburn hair now. I scratched my chin - yep, in the beard too. They used to call me 'Red' when I worked in the lumber yards in Oregon. They thought I was Irish. Maybe I was. I was Big Red. Now they'd call me Old Red. There were lines around my eyes. My eyes - hadn't they once been vivid green? Hadn't women swum in my eyes? Hadn't they called me handsome? Now my eyes were stagnant. When did I get old? Where did the time go? Again, the pull in my mind. If I didn't get going, he'd be on me in a cornfield feeling sorry for myself. No place for a fight. I slammed the door and started the engine.

He'd track me down eventually, I knew that, he always managed to, but I was pretty sure I could make it difficult for him. I had a hankering for trees, mountains, water. Might as well try to get some big sky, some nature back in my blood, maybe shake him off my tail for a bit. Wisconsin. Camp up in the Black River State Forest, maybe make it out to Lake Michigan, that sounded just fine to me. It'd been a long time since I'd hiked or fished or spent any time in the real wilderness. The big dark forests always felt like home to me. Let him come find me in the shadows of the pine trees.

The decision made me calmer. The calmness after the surge of panic made me hungry. As salt 'n' pepper as my hair was getting, I was still a big man. Couldn't drive all that way on an empty stomach. I looked up the nearest place I could grab breakfast and wondered whether they'd have pancakes.

By the time I pushed open the door of a 24-hour truck stop an hour up the highway from Humbolt, it was just gone nine and I was fantasizing about a whole mountain of those pancakes, swimming in syrup. The girl behind the counter, young and freckled with her strawberry-blonde hair pulled back into a ponytail, saw me as I walked in. I saw her eyes travel up over the height and size of me as I clumped my way over to a table. A couple of guys sitting at the counter turned and stared. I sat and stared right back until their gazes flinched and they went back to their plates. The only other customers were a middle-aged couple, silently eating, who never once looked up.

The waitress wandered over to me, eyeing me. "Hey there fella. What can I get ya?"

"You got pancakes?" I asked, hopefully.

She nodded awkwardly. "Sure we do." She nervously shifted from one sneakered foot to the other. My size has always made people nervous. "We got 'em with fruit, we got 'em-"

"Bacon, syrup, the works," I interrupted with a reassuring smile.

Her face and body relaxed as she nodded again and allowed herself to smile back at me properly. I nudged at her thoughts. She didn't think I seemed dangerous. Dangerous guys didn't order a stack of pancakes and syrup. Didn't seem like I'd give her trouble. Just some big guy out on the road. Trucker, maybe. Divorced, she thought, but she didn't think I looked like anyone's daddy.

"You want coffee?" She scribbled on her pad but paused to glance at me. I looked kinda sad, she thought. Sad eyes.

"Yes, ma'am," I replied. She nodded once more.

She wondered what I was like in bed. The thought popped into her brain and I couldn't help smiling a little as the blush rose across her throat. She could only have been twenty-two at most. She went away back to the counter, called my order through the hatch to some unseen cook, filled a coffee mug from the pot and brought it back to me, all the while stealing peaks at me. Her cornflower-blue eyes flittered across my face, my chest, my arms, through her long bangs. I let her look, sitting back in my seat, wondering if my eyes looked a little greener. Once, if she would've had me, I'd have taken her out into the night, filled her with stars. I wouldn't do anything now, didn't have the time to, but I liked the way her eyes crawled over me. It warmed me a little.

The pancakes were just as I'd imagined. A tall stack of fluffy, syrupy goodness that almost made me want to go declare love for the still-unseen chef out back. The coffee was strong and velvety. Who said road-side truck stop food couldn't be culinary art? I'd almost cleared my plate, folding another forkful of deliciousness into my mouth and closing my eyes in appreciation, when I heard the door open. The hairs on my arms and the nape of my neck bristled and my mind wheeled. Vertigo and nausea and a rush of ice in my blood. I froze, fork still in my mouth. My eyes snapped open.

Shit, I was thinking, *shit, shit, shit.*

He wasn't meant to catch up so fast. He wasn't meant to catch me unawares. I was meant to get to Wisconsin. I was meant to get to the forest at least! I wasn't ready. Not even remotely.

84

I didn't turn. I lowered my fork and waited, as the noise in the diner, the tinny radio, the waitress chatting to the chef through the hatch, it all faded away into the squeaking of his feet on the linoleum. He stopped at my elbow.

"Hey," he said softly.

"Hey," I replied.

He slid himself into the chair opposite me, resting his chin on his small hands. I glanced at him. He was so young. I was struck with that, every time. His youth. He swung his feet under the table; they didn't reach the floor. Anyone else'd say he was a cute kid, with clear pale eyes like mountain water, thin sloping shoulders, his hair like white unbleached silk cut short. One piece stuck up, bobbing. He wore a little pair of jeans with the bottoms rolled up, revealing scuffed yellow Velcro sneakers, and a blue T-shirt with a dinosaur on it. He was the very picture of innocence. I suppressed the urge to shiver.

"Been a while," he said, his voice unnerving me. All that time and knowledge held in that high sing song child's voice. The kid sitting opposite me looked seven years old at most.

"Not long enough," I said, then pushed the last forkful into my mouth and chewed carefully. The Kid looked around the diner, tracing patterns on the table top with his stubby fingers.

"How was your summer?" he asked.

I frowned. "Condescending shit."

His eyes flicked back to mine and there was a slight smile on his soft unformed face. "Always."

I laid my fork neatly on the plate and looked at the girl behind the counter sadly. She had forgotten I was here, that I'd ever arrived. She didn't see me now, or the Kid sitting opposite. She was wondering what Denny was doing tonight.

"Well then," I said, stretching.

"Well," he answered.

I got to my feet, took a note from the bundle in my pocket and let it flutter to the table, ambled towards the door. I got as far as the last table before the Kid grabbed my shirt and yanked me around, flinging me backwards over the table. My head cracked against the floor and my eyes clouded for a moment. The guys at the counter didn't see us. They didn't see the 230-pound, six-foot-nine man and the seven-year-old boy fighting. The Kid straddled me, his tiny legs pinning my arms, and rammed my head back by shoving a clammy hand into my throat. I gagged once, had forgotten how strong he could be, grunted, pulled my fist up and landed a punch in his stomach. He toppled sideways, eyes wide. He'd forgotten my strength too. I flipped onto my feet as he threw a roundhouse kick at me. I caught his foot and flipped him over backwards. He somersaulted right over, back onto his feet, grinning. We eyed each other, anticipated each other, shifted on the balls of our feet.

"I missed you, old man," he said, with a small smile.

My chest was tight. I wasn't fast enough for this. I hadn't been prepared. I needed to get away and regroup, plan my defence. He came at me then, ducking under my arm and swiping my feet from under me. We fell with a crash into the middle of a table where the middle-aged couple sat, still eating. They reached around us and over us even as we squirmed and rolled. I needed to get on top. Get the higher ground.

"George, pass the salt," the woman said.

The Kid giggled. I pulled all my energy into the centre of my body, then with a grunt of effort, pushed all my limbs out straight, sending him sailing over my head. I heard him land, heard him swear, but I was already running. I jumped into the truck and fumbled with the keys, lurched forward and spun out of the parking lot, tires squealing. I saw him standing in the window. He raised his hand and waved. Creepy child.

On the road, I let myself shake. I rubbed my mouth with my fingers and studied the road. He was so strong. I glanced at myself in the mirror. My hair was shaggier. Thinner. The flecks of grey I'd noticed earlier were now more like solid iron-grey streaks. My forehead was furrowed with deep lines, my back ached where I had hit the floor and the edge of the table. He was so young and *so* strong, and he wouldn't stay that young, that little, for long. He would change, age, as quickly as I was.

"Fuck," I whispered.

I knew it would be like this, but it was my nature to strive for survival. I had to try. I pressed my foot down on the gas, feeling him fading in my mind to a dull distant presence.

I crossed into North Dakota sometime in the mid-afternoon. Though the lure of the forests and mountains was still there, somehow putting a whole country border between us suddenly seemed more appealing, and straight up seemed the most direct route into Canada. I drove towards the huge artery of the Missouri River. Another town, the houses rising alongside the road, churches, antiques stores, and an honest-to-goodness hardware store. I thought those had been left in the 80s. It was a regular Baptist-Church-on-Sundays, town-meetings and homemade-apple-pie kind of small town. I thought these had all been left in the 80s, too. I drove past, seeing and not really seeing. Banners hung over the street to announce the annual Harvest Festival Fun-Fayre, spelt in that pseudo-'Olde Worlde' way that made me grimace. Not as much as those goddamn 'Renaissance Faires', but still. It made my skin itch. I wondered if any of these people, excited by the lights and roller coasters and Ferris wheel;

ready to eat their candy apples and drink hot cider and watch fireworks, had any idea what they were celebrating. I doubted it. I remembered with a sudden lurch a field nearly four thousand miles away. A field in darkness, dotted with fires. The smell of smoke and burning rosemary came to me so strongly there in the truck, it made my eyes water...

The air had been crisp, the moon a raven's eye in its hazy ring. The sounds of people in the darkness, whispering, waiting. Once, people had come to see us fight, had sensed us as much as we sensed each other. I had stood, the firelight throwing my face into strong angles and shadows, flexing my fingers on the hilt of my sword. That sword had been magnificent. Long and broad, I used two hands to lift it. No one else could lift my sword. In those days, my size was a good thing. I had stood there, in the circle of fire, waiting. I cast my eyes back to where Cate had stood, arms wrapped around herself, her eyes flickering with firelight and unease. Frail as she was by then, she was still strong, still fierce, even with the worry in her eyes, and her beauty still caught in my throat, just as it had the day we'd jumped the besom and wed in a summer long before; just as it had the day we'd met. The wind had whipped at her dress and hair, lifting and folding it all around her – I couldn't tell you now what colour that dress was – had it been red or maybe green? She had met my gaze and tried to smile. He came then, striding towards me, and the crowd hushed. He shimmered with his own strange light, pale hair falling to his shoulders. He stood, resting his hand on the hilt of his own thin blade.

"Evening," he had said. "How was your summer?"

I'd grunted, refusing to look him in the eye, hefted my sword instead. I could be an arrogant posturing bastard in my earlier days.

He'd pouted, arrogant and foppish, quite the noble Lord-ling himself back then, looked about, breathed into the night. His breath curled and steamed although the night until then had been quite mild.

"Suit yourself." He offered his hand and bowed in a magnanimous gesture, inviting me to lead us out into the field. We had walked out into the darkness. We had fought, steel against steel, his will against mine. I had lost. And Cate had died...

I pulled the truck over and braced my hands against the steering wheel, clamping my jaw down on old hurts. Ah, Cate. Beautiful as a May morning. I'd fallen helplessly in love with her, though I should have known better than to let her have me as a husband. At first, I'd thought the sting of her death would never fade but over the years it had, until moments like this brought the ache of it flowing back, slipping through my fingers like fine sand. Many women have had me since, some have even said they loved me, all beautiful in their own ways but none have shone as brightly as my Cathryn. I never married again. I don't think I could stand the pain of it.

II

I drove up through North Dakota, the farmland giving way to flat billowing wheat fields and the occasional silo. It got dark. My head and eyes ached; I needed to stop. I found myself in Portal, a shell of a town. One main street, gas station and a café. The railway tracks intersected the road, and a small complex of buildings marked the border control – on this side, the US, on the other side of the tracks, Canada. Three hundred feet or less and I'd be in another country. I slowed to let a uniformed border agent cross the street and saw an Americana Motel. I felt my body sag. I'd been driving for hours. More than 700 miles. From *him*. Was it far enough? I could keep going, over the border... and then what? He'd find me anyway, and I was so tired. I pulled into the dusty parking lot and somehow muttered my way through, asking for a room. The middle-aged paunch-bellied man at the desk eyed me sceptically but handed me a key. Once alone, I stripped off to my underwear and fell onto the bed.

I must have slept, because I opened my eyes with a start to the sound of arguing from another room. The motel's neon sign was throwing my room alternately into stark red and pitch black. It didn't stay either long enough for my eyes to become accustomed to it. I lay there, on my side, one arm up under the thin pillow, staring at the wall and listening to the arguing couple somewhere down the hall. Red, black, red, black, red, black, twenty-four-hour service, pay per night T.V and telephone. The 'roaches, clanking pipes and domestic disputes you get for free. They were shouting in Portuguese or maybe Spanish. I could only hear the shrillness of her voice and his thunderous replies. I could've nudged their thoughts, picked out the shape of their words and understood, but I didn't want to. I didn't want to hear about his drug problem, or her gambling debts, or that he never stacked the dishwasher the right way, or that she couldn't sing for shit, or where they should bury the bodies of nosy eavesdroppers. Red, black, red, black. Give me the vast open Van-Gogh summer sky and a symphony of crickets any night over this. But it was too cold to sleep outside now, and I needed to rest. Rest.

"Ha!" The incredulous noise escaped from my dry lips like a small choke.

I wondered where he was. Again, if I thought about that for more than a second, I would know. I didn't want to know. I deliberately avoided focussing on the incessant pull of his presence.

"You must rest." Her voice, cool as rain. Her hand trailing whorls up my bare chest. "You never seem to sleep."

Cate, or the ghost of her, dredged up from the dark memories of the day. She was almost real to me then, almost solid. I could almost feel the weight of her against me. I rolled over and stared at the wall, remembering another restless night like this, years back, when we had both been young and strong and sunburnt...

That night, the real one when Cate had really been there folded in around me like a promise, she had startled me. I'd thought she'd been asleep. She constantly surprised me, something I was unused to; something that had made my appreciation of her flow and shift into something more. I hadn't known how to reply.

I settled on a non-committal, "No, I never seem to sleep."

She tutted, raised herself up onto her elbow, long hair falling across her shoulder and pooling onto my chest. "You're waiting for him, aren't you?"

I'd winced in the dark of our bed. I didn't like it when she spoke about him. It was like walking across thin ice. Any minute it might crack, and she would be sucked in further than she was already. She rarely brought up the subject of my fight with him, knowing how it made me squirm, but when she did, it was with cautious persistence. She quietly demanded answers I wasn't sure she could comprehend, and then listened so intently to my reluctant responses, storing it all away in that vast mind of hers. When she did this, I could hear the ice creaking. Underneath was a rip tide. I was waiting for him, yes, even though it was far too early, not even Midsummer yet, and I didn't have the slightest inkling of him in my mind. I didn't like that she read me so well... I loved that she could read me so well.

"Yes," I admitted finally, pulling her broad, sun-reddened body closer, "I am. I'm always waiting."

"And him?" she'd asked, whispering feathery kisses on my chest. "Does he wait for you like this?"

I looked down at her, tried to make out her brown eyes. Unflinching and honest. There was never any lie in Cate's eyes. She stroked my face, settling against my shoulder.

"I suppose he does," I'd answered eventually. "Come Imbolc, when the lambing starts, he'll already be waiting for me to bring the fight back to him."

"What would happen if you didn't fight?" she had asked, as our room began to lighten with the smoky-salmon light of dawn.

What would happen if we didn't fight? How could I ever answer that? Somehow, she had known the answer anyway and had held me all the more tightly.

"I'll be here waiting for you, after you've fought, just like always."

But it was impossible for you to wait, Cate. No one lives forever. Except maybe him and I.

I blinked. Maybe I'd slept again. Her scent lingered in the motel room. The arguing couple had fallen silent. I pulled my arm from beneath the pillow, fumbled with my watch, twisting the face towards me, tapped the little inky black screen. Red, black, red, black, sudden luminous electrical blue-light. It was just gone two in the morning. I flipped onto my back and looked at the water-stained ceiling, listened to the clank of the pipes. I was restless, agitated. Fine, I was nervous, afraid even, after the speed at which he'd found me earlier and the ferocity of his attack. I didn't want it to be over so soon; there were more sunrises to watch, more pancakes to eat, more cold beers to drink and I still hadn't made it to the mountains and the forests and the big sky yet. I was running out of time. I'd wasted so much of it already, and I wasn't sure how long I'd hold out with him getting stronger. It was no use. I *did* want to know where he was. How long did I have before he'd catch up again? I took a deep breath, closed my eyes for a second. Felt for his presence in the great vastness of space, like a beacon in the dark, then felt my mind empty to a clear white point, like a dot of light that hangs in the centre of old T.V sets. I focussed on that point and felt myself slipping forwards into it. It was like plunging myself into a tunnel of white light so cold it burnt. With a lurch I felt contained again.

"...and..."

I looked around me. I was surrounded by bright lights and strange smells, sickly sweet. Shrieks and thumping music and lights going round and down and over and through. Thumping music that made my chest heave. I floundered for a minute, getting my bearings, finding my legs. I felt a little seasick. Using this way of transporting myself from my body, which was probably still lying on a motel bed somewhere in Portal (or perhaps it wasn't – I could never be sure), was convenient. I don't think I'd ever taught myself how to do it, it just happened when I wanted it to; when I focussed. But it did take my breath away, throwing myself into someone else's mind and inhabiting their body. A Creole witch I'd courted down in New Orleans in the 60s once called it 'corporeal possession', but that felt clunky and vaguely distasteful to me. She said I could call it 'body hopping' if I was a hoppity frog-boy scared of calling shit what it was. She had also hated that I referred to our very physical arrangement as 'courting'. Now, I felt myself spreading into a body significantly smaller than the one I usually inhabited. I looked down at small, slender hands, a silver ring with a large amethyst stone sitting on my left middle finger. I was holding a stick of cotton candy; I could taste the itchy sugar coating on my teeth. Ah yes, a fairground. A collective scream whirled past me as a roller coaster spun along its track. It was warm, the air humid with adrenaline and lust. I was suddenly aware that this was the town I had passed through earlier, the one with the banners across the street. I was leaning against a metal barricade, one consciously naïve leg hooked into the railings. I was wearing denim shorts just long enough to not be hot pants and a T-shirt that said 'Namas-Stay-in-bed' over a 'Hamsa' palm. I was Alison Maddison and I was seventeen. I was suddenly aware that Alison had been in the middle of a sentence when I had flung myself into her body. I jostled in her mind, finding her memories, her voice and picking up her last train of thought before I'd gate-crashed: *The boy with the silver hair. He's staring at me like I'm made of starlight.*

Oh. Jesus... Really?!

"...and," I continued, struggling to pick up the nuance of her voice, "...I was really scared but we did it anyway and Marcy said we coulda got hurt but we didn't and Jack Hailer, Kim's older brother, who's like, twenty-one, was steering anyway so we were ok."

The boy with the silver hair smiled, his ice-blue eyes lingering on Alison's neck, on the thin silver chain she was wearing.

"I love boats," the Kid said. "They're so graceful. You were lucky Kim's brother could take you out."

His hair hung into his eyes as he smiled at Alison Maddison. Alison had been wanting to touch his hair from the moment she had seen him and I stopped her hand from twitching. She thought his smile was mesmerising; she thought it was a good-weed-and-good-sex kind of smile. I, cramped within her body, felt sick. I stared at this boy, this young man, with horror at how much he had grown in so short a time. His voice was on the deeper side of youth; it rippled with self-assurance and all the unsaid things that pulsed between these two kids. He really was looking at Alison like she was made of starlight. I remembered Cate then, the way she would look at me with heat in her eyes. It made me stumble, even as I tried to form a response that would distract him long enough to let me slip away unnoticed from here, out of Alison's body,

"But I don't think he'll take us again, he says we screamed too much..."

Then I laughed, but my discomfort made it too high and too loud. Something in her voice, in *my* voice coming from her vocal cords, must have slipped and the Kid frowned, that smooth face puckering downwards, sharp as an arrow. His eyes hardened as he stared at me, *me*, inside Alison, seeing me for the first time.

"Get out, old man," he whispered, and his breath curled from his lips.

I shivered. He started forward, hands raised as a final warning. If he attacked me there, I would only have Alison's strength to fight back with. He would kill her, and with me separate from my body, my mind inside hers, I wasn't sure what would happen. Would I die too? Or just be flung back into the body that might or not might not be laid empty and waiting on a lumpy motel bed? I didn't want to find out. Fortunately for me, the Kid hesitated, and that gave me the second I needed to pull myself out and dive for safety, plunging through the cold whiteness.

I pulled into the first available body with a jolt. It wasn't my body, but it was open to me. Safe. I felt myself unfolding from Alison's girlish, slender five-feet-four into a beefy thick six-foot-three. My arms were covered in coarse black hair, roped with veins and swirled with tattoos. I felt the metal bunk digging into my thighs and saw dust motes spinning in the shaft of light that spilled from the only window high in the wall. Prison cell. I picked at the knee of my washed-out orange jump suit. I was incarcerated in the maximum-security wing of Montana State Prison. Michael Millar. Mickey Ink. Mickey boy here had shot Ruth Freeman in the head and now he was condemned to death. They didn't call it 'Death Row', but that's where he was, and had been for fifteen years. But the bitch had it coming. Had it coming, the bitch. Damn fuckin' whore... I pushed all his rage, all the gory slow-motion replay memories down inside him, knowing that if I let it, Mickey Ink's soul would begin to imprint itself on mine. I had chosen Mickey because of his strength and his anger, knowing the Kid couldn't be far behind me. I needed to be able to handle the next round that I'd inevitably brought upon myself prematurely. If I had just left the Kid alone; let him come to me instead... I'd pissed him off. Peeked into his existence where I should not have been. But damn it, the Kid had done it often enough to me. How often had I caught him staring out at me from the eyes of some bank teller, or street bum or businesswoman in the car next to me at a red light? Shit, even the odd alley cat or crow.

The sound of approaching footsteps on the hard floor made Mickey's stomach writhe – I did not have complete control over this body, he was too raw, too angry. I needed to be careful I didn't get lost here. I pulled myself up onto the murderer's thick legs and found myself running a finger over the tattoos on my right arm, a tick I couldn't get Mickey to shift. I looked up at the steel door with its single porthole window and waited. The shoes clicked and squeaked, and Mickey's memories provided the picture in my mind – shiny black Oxfords, lace up. So shiny you can see your face in 'em.

A shadow across the port hole in the door. The sound of fingers punching in numbers on the electronic lock, and I had to really concentrate to keep Mickey's urge to burst forward with a fist under check. The door slid open with a mechanical whir and the guard stepped in. A man shorter than Jonny Ink, but thick set. He removed his cap and held it by its peak in one hand. Square-ish face, close-cropped dull brown hair. His uniform sharp, ironed creases in the pant legs, navy shirt pressed and buttoned to the neck. A proud man. How fitting, I thought, that the Kid would choose this guard out of all on duty this evening. Stewart Jennings. Thirty-eight years old. Wife at home, baby on the way, enjoyed a laugh with the guys. Streak in him meaner than an angry skunk. Mr. Jennings put the cap on the floor, then turned to me, almost a Nazi heel click, and his plain brown eyes flashed, for just a second, with ice-blue coldness. Mr. Jennings pulled at his cuffs and flicked some fluff from his shoulder, then pulled his fist back and landed a punch to my guts. I let him. The first hit was his; he deserved it, I guessed, for my spying on him. I doubled over with a grunt but didn't fall. Then I straightened up and looked into Mr. Jennings' angry eyes.

"You shoulda stayed in your motel, old man," he said.

So he had known where I was. He had known and had still chosen to stop at the fair. How long would he have stayed there, leaving me alone, if I hadn't been curious?

"Yeah, I guess I should've," I replied.

He hit me again and this time it winded me. I staggered backwards and hit the metal bunk, twisting round to keep him in sight.

"You cheated." He stepped forwards. "You know the rules."

My outrage blossomed into a laugh, Mickey's voice thick and heavy like cigar smoke. "Rules? Since when do you play by the rules?"

Mr. Jennings' eyebrow rose; for a minute I thought the Kid might laugh too, but he didn't. Stewart Jennings glowered.

"I wanted to know where you were," I told him.

He swung at me, but I caught his shoulders and spun him away, following it with an elbow crack to his ribs.

He grunted, bracing his arms on his knees, studying me. "You don't need to know where I am. I'll find you when I need to. This is my turn. My attack. You don't come looking for me until it's your turn. That's the way it works."

He flung himself into a roundhouse kick that sent me sprawling to the floor.

"It only works that way when you say so, huh?" I muttered, scrambling to my feet, wiping the blood from the corner of Mickey Ink's mouth.

"You had no right to do it," he spat.

No right? How could he talk about rights? He did the same to me often enough. Peeking into my life, checking up on me. Sometimes, I thought he did it for the fun of it, simply to freak me out and piss me off; just because he could. He had no right to be angry! He couldn't have it both ways! Fucking punk-ass kid. *'How was your summer?'* Damn fucking punk. He's got it coming... I clenched my jaw and pushed Mickey Ink deep down. Contained him in a ball behind the solar plexus. I needed this guy, but I didn't need to become him.

"I know," I said, calmly, dodged a punch.

"You were spying." Mr. Jennings ground his heel into my foot and as I went to push him away, he brought his knee up into my face. Black spots danced in front of my eyes.

Mr. Jennings drew his night-stick from his belt, a dull silver telescopic thing that sprang to a half-metre long when he flicked it. He brought it round towards my neck. I twisted away and tangled my booted feet between his legs, bringing him down with a thud.

"'S'fine to spy on me when you want to?" I was trying to hold back his hand as he struggled to bring the metal stick into contact with me.

The Kid looked at me through Mr. Jennings' eyes, a flash of ice in the hazel eyes. "I had enough decency to pick my targets."

"*Decency?* Fuck you!" I shouted back, jamming my hand under his chin, trying to force his head away.

Mr. Jennings was deceptively strong. I knew now why the Kid had really chosen him. To try and catch me out.

"I never jumped into *her.*" he gulped, eyes narrow and fierce.

"Who?"

"Her. Your precious Cathryn."

My hand lost its strength for a moment. Hearing him say her name, even in Jennings' voice, threw me. He used that moment to bring the night-stick around to my temple. White light exploded with the pain, and I reeled. It took me a moment to realise the shock had sent me spiralling out of Michael Millar and back into the cold void.

I let myself glide for a while, numb. Cate. No, he had never jumped into her. What would I have done if I had turned to her, in the bright English sunshine, or over the table while we ate, or while I was moving inside of her in bed, and seen his arctic stare within her honest eyes? It was the hardest blow he dealt me all day. I plummeted like a stone.

I was Colin McKenzie and I was fifty-two. I was a Geography teacher in Putney, London, and I was standing on the side of the M25 beside a red Vauxhaul Corsa, which currently had a silver Mercedes C Class embedded into its rear. Both were spewing smoke. The woman opposite me was dressed in some kind of expensive power suit, black hair scraped back into a severe chignon, red lips pursed in annoyance. She was scribbling down her details on the back of an envelope, red nails pressing together around a pen.

"...when you just stopped dead in front of me," she was saying.

Colin McKenzie's memory filled my mind. He had been completely stationary for at least two minutes, as had the rest of the traffic in front of him. I nudged the mind of the woman standing opposite me. Karen Grey, senior partner of a large London financial services firm, the one with a whole lot of skeletons and secrets in its basement. She had been oblivious to anything other than the board meeting she had been conducting via her mobile phone. Colin McKenzie would have argued with her, would have wanted to take her insurance for everything it was worth. I said nothing. I stared at the curlicues of smoke, the crumpled bumper. I was waiting for him to follow me. I felt the Kid drop into the woman's body a few seconds later with a shudder. I then allowed myself to look at him. Her. Face pinched and down turned.

"You think you can just body-hop?" he said, in the woman's clipped British accent. "Sooner or later you'll have to return to your own body, and it'll be too old for you to fight at all!"

She seized my shirt in her hands and tried to push me. She wasn't strong enough. The Kid hadn't thought about this, and his eyes, behind the woman's heavy mascara and shadow, widened. He raised her hand and slapped me around the face instead. I still staggered involuntarily. Colin wasn't used to any kind of violent act.

"I didn't know," I mumbled, pressing a fleshy pale hand to stinging cheek.

The Kid threw the woman at me, her high heels sliding on the tarmac, trying to shove me backwards. "Didn't know what?"

Colin McKenzie didn't move despite all efforts being made to shove him.

I looked at the Kid inside the woman. "Didn't know the girl was special to you."

The woman's body went slack and her face stared up into mine. An articulated truck thundered past. The road trembled.

"I just dropped into the person nearest to you. I shouldn't have, but you do it all the time. I didn't know the girl was important to you..."

The Kid turned Karen Grey's expertly made-up face to watch the traffic for a moment, "She... wasn't. Not really. Not yet. But – I thought maybe she could've been."

When she turned back to me, the eyes that stared out of the woman's face were sad and alone.

"To hell with it," he said.

And then he was gone. Karen Grey stood, hollow for a second while her real self struggled to surface. I was shocked and found myself trembling a little, inside Colin's body. I shoved his hands into the pockets of his jeans. I watched Lin's face assimilate itself into a vaguely apologetic expression.

"I'm sorry," she half-laughed. "Do you know, I completely zoned out for a minute, there."

She handed me the envelope still clutched in her hand, slightly confused as to why it was now so screwed up. I took it from her.

"I'll... um... I'll phone the AA." She turned and absently rummaged in her handbag for her phone.

When her back was turned, I slipped from Colin McKenzie's body.

III

Back in the Motel, I lay on my back and felt myself spread out like honey into all the cells and capillaries and nerves. My hands made a few spasmodic twitches. I lay there, letting my mind reacquaint itself with the body, and tried to figure out what was going to happen now. The Kid had gone. He hadn't just left to resume the hunt. He'd run away. He'd ceased the fight. I knew it, with that same deep certainty I'd had in Iowa when I'd realised he was coming for me again. He wasn't supposed to run from me. He was supposed to chase me. It was his turn, his attack. He had said so himself. And once this round was over, it would be my turn; I would go and hunt him, return the favour. That's the way it had always been. Until now. I shivered. It meant that I could move now and be in control of all my muscles and ligaments. It also meant I was freezing. I pulled myself upright and lurched across the room to the plywood closet, pulled a thick mohair blanket from the top. I checked my reflection in the long mirror on the closet door. The Kid had been right. The body-hopping had drained me. I looked awful. Lank, greasy, hollow. I looked like I was on the wrong side of sixty and on the worse side of some kind of addiction. My body yielded to the understanding, back clicking then chest tightening with the onset of a wracking cough. I pressed my hand to the closet while I coughed, hocking up a vile glob of something that I spat into the waste bin. When I was done, I wrapped the blanket around myself, and took a steadying breath. I fumbled in the pocket of my jeans and pulled out my Marlboro's, flicked the end of the pack and slid one between my teeth, lit it with a match. Coughed again. Dragged in a breath. I stood at the window, in my boxer shorts and blanket, smoking. I watched the sun rise over the still-sleeping town, watched it set the metal roofs of the warehouses on fire with little dancing flames.

It was a tug-of-war fight between me and him, never ending. A fight borne out of necessity and survival. A fight I had been fighting my entire life, which had been an incredibly long time. A fight that was, in truth, all I lived for. It had swung backwards and forwards across millennia, across countries and continents, both of us existing solely to seek out and battle the other. We had both won and we had both lost in equal measure; small victories, small losses. And now? Now he was refusing to fight. I wondered if that made me the winner. I knew almost before the thought had formulated that I wasn't. I couldn't be. The fight was ended, but that meant so much more. It meant something so much worse. We *had* to fight. Those were the rules. Rules we didn't ever make, but rules we were bound to as much as we were to each other. I sighed, flicked my cigarette out of the window, watched it sail to land in the red dust, and began pulling on my clothes. I was going to go and find him.

I did a U-turn in the Motel's dusty parking area and pulled across the road to the gas station. The more I concentrated on it, the more I knew I would have a long way to go. I already knew that in the time I had been recovering from my body-hopping and living deep in my thoughts, watching the sun rise on this new existence, the Kid had already passed me, was heading away from me. North. He was heading into the cold. Neither of us had to sleep or eat often, and he was stronger than me now. I felt him pulling further away, increasing the gap even as I stood there. I sighed, feeling queasy. I needed gas.

I had the uncanny ability to always find what I needed, be it food, shelter, or money – despite often taking jobs, I'd never *needed* to work; there was always a bill of notes in my pocket when I had to buy something – but I couldn't magic gas into a truck tank. I could, however, guarantee I'd find a gas station with a full pump when I needed to fill up. I slid out of the truck with an arthritic groan as a sharp pain shot down my thigh, filled the tank from the single pump, then pushed my way through the door of the store; a bell rang somewhere behind the counter. The radio on the counter was trying vainly to pick up an oldies station but kept slipping into crackle and high-pitched wailing.

The old boy sitting there looked up as I entered, did a quick once over on me, but returned my brief smile as I took myself a basket and headed up one of the two cluttered aisles. There was fishing equipment next to ladies' lace-top hold ups, a swivelling rack of dog-eared paperback books next to the glass jars of instant coffee and boxes of Tampax. I found a shelf stuffed with a selection of family sized Doritos and put two into my basket. I added three cans of Coke, a fistful of Hershey Bars, a small travelling wash kit complete with tiny Mechano-style toothbrush and a bar of hard, greenish soap. And then, because I never did do well with the cold, I added a pair of fisherman's socks, thermal gloves and a large cable-knitted sweater that had obviously been made for some kind of mythical giant with chimp-arms. It would fit me; I didn't care. I headed back to the counter and sat my basket beside the register. The old boy began taking each item, looking at it, tapping a figure into the cash register and putting into a paper bag.

"Do you have a rest room?" I asked.

The man paused, as if unsure of the answer, then – "Sure do. Back there." he pointed.

I nodded. The man tallied up my shopping, I gave him the money.

"Could I leave this here, while I go freshen up?" I asked.

"Sure, son, sure. You been on the road long?"

I had started to rummage in the grocery bag for my soap and dwarf wash kit, but his words stopped me. *Son?*

"A few days," I replied absently, because an answer was expected of me.

"Looks like you ain't slept for a month, boy. I ain't sure if you're safe to drive. Would you take a cup of coffee?"

Boy? My hand tightened on the wash kit and, without my usual caution, I flung myself into the old fella's thoughts, desperate to know what he thought he saw. He thought I was running from something. He didn't care much, I didn't look like I'd killed anyone. Almost only customers this guy ever got were on their way to or from somewhere else. The few townsfolk had their supermarket with thirty different types of toilet tissue. But he liked my face. Honest. Tired. Too tired for someone so young. My teeth were clenched.

"I said, want a coffee?" he reiterated, cocking his head at me. Now he was thinking I might be a little backwards or slow-witted.

"Yeah... yeah." I turned and headed for the rest room. "Um, thanks," I added.

I almost ran through the store, knocked a stack of boxes with my shoulder, flung myself into the bathroom and shut the door. The cracked mirror was hanging over the sink directly opposite me. I stared at myself, leaning against the door. The queasiness I'd felt since waking up in the motel overtook me and I wretched suddenly, unexpectedly, spat bile into the sink. Wasn't sure whether to laugh or cry. Looking back at me was a face I hadn't seen for months – a sun-browned, wind-blasted face, deep auburn hair curling over my forehead and ears. The green of my eyes stood out against the tan of my skin. I was lean, muscled. Beautiful. No more than twenty-five. The only lingering evidence of the body-hopping and the worry were the deep dark circles under my eyes. I really did look like I hadn't slept in a month but, other than that... What the hell?! By now, I should've looked as old as that good ol' boy waddling into his back room to fetch me my coffee. I let this thought dangle over the gaping precipice that had opened inside me, bracing my hands on the edge of the sink and staring at my face.

"You've done it now, Kid," I muttered. "You've gone and blown it wide open."

Was I talking to myself? Perhaps. But mostly, I was directing it through the white to the solitary mind at the end of that connection that bound us together. *You've done it now, Kid.*

Yeah? Well, the party's started. His voice was distant. But still there; still connected.

My head dropped forward, eyes closed. It unnerved me that I was relieved he had answered. He had sounded petulant, defiant. Alone.

"Shit." I said it aloud.

And then I turned the faucet on and unwrapped the soap from its plastic wrapping. Scrubbed my face with my palms until I stung. I couldn't meet my eyes in the mirror; it made me feel like vomiting.

The old man passed me a chipped mug of gloriously hot, strong coffee, and I had to cup it in both my shaking hands to keep it from slipping to the floor. I sipped it obediently and knew, without pushing at his thoughts, that the man wanted more from me than a mumbled thanks. So I met his gaze and allowed him to ask the questions that hovered on his lips like a stutter.

"Where abouts're you heading?"

I swallowed, then said, "North."

The man laughed, one gunshot burst. "North's kinda big, son."

I suppose the shock was beginning to wear off, or maybe it was the caffeine lacing into my blood, but I conceded a laugh too, and nodded.

The guy looked pointedly at the gloves, sweater and socks in the top of my grocery bag. "You goin' a heck of a way if you're expecting to need *them*."

I wondered how on earth I could begin to explain, and in the silence that grew, I found myself honing in on the white-noise whine of the radio. As I stared at the little transistor, the static cleared into a female voice.

"*...when the tornado hit. Reports are coming in of at least one hundred and fifty dead, and the total is expected to rise steadily...*"

I shuddered and the radio crackled again. I had been dreading this, ever since the Kid had muttered 'to hell with it' and abandoned the fight.

"I'm looking for someone." I held the mug into my chest for the comforting warmth. "He's gone North. Canada. Maybe further. And I gotta find him."

"He owe you money?" The old man turned his head to one side like some strange bird-creature. I shook my head.

"No. He just... bailed... on this damn job we have, see? And I have to get him to go back to work."

"Don't seem too keen on the idea yourself."

"I guess not," I admitted after a pause. "But we're the only ones can do it, and if we don't..."

"...say that whilst it is not unusual for tornados to manifest in North Carolina, it is certainly highly unusual for a tornado of this scale to touch down and wreak so much devastation. Meteorologists in Silver Spring, Maryland are endeavouring to..."

What would happen if you didn't fight? Oh Cate, it's happening already. It's begun.

"Everything unravels," I finished somewhat lamely, scraping my hair back from my face and trying desperately to block the news broadcast that kept filtering in through the radio; realising, as I had whilst staring at myself in the mirror in the tiny bathroom, that I would feel it somewhere in my belly anyway even if I blocked my ears.

The old man raised his eyebrows, then pursed his lips and sucked on his teeth. I could feel the shape of his thoughts shifting to drugs, mobsters... I waved my hand, absently. "Forget about it."

I began gathering my groceries, patting my pockets for my keys.

"I ain't gonna pretend I know what it is that's troubling you." He pushed himself to his feet with that old-person groan and accompanying knee-pop. "But it'll come right in the end. You'll see."

I inclined my head and allowed a little placatory smile to hover on my lips.

"You don't believe me. You kids these days with your Apple-this and Googly-that." He waggled a finger and I knew he was teasing me. "But there's something to be said for going 'round the block as often as I have. Things come back around, no mistake."

I stared out of the window at a dog barking at a UPS truck. "That they do," I agreed. He really had no idea. Except, *except...*

"But if you're goin' any further than Saskatchewan," the old guy shuffled into the back room, speaking over his shoulder to me and interrupting my brooding, "you can't go wandering around in nothin' but that God-forsaken sweater."

He returned and presented me with something that looked like a synthetic electric-blue cloud. I took it and it unfurled into a thick padded ski coat with a fleece-lined hood, the sort you find in outward bound stores. He charged me ten dollars for it, and that was only because I insisted. When he held out his hand to take the money, it was missing the thumb and the tip of the index finger – *landmine, Gulf War* swam up in his mind – and I wondered when I had last looked at a person; really looked and seen the human being rather than a vehicle for my body-hopping or as a transient object. I wondered what else besides blown-off thumbs I had missed.

"Thanks," I said. I meant it.

I drove along the main street with a full tank and an unnerving amount of youthful energy, mixed with that deep-belly tightening that had started beside a smashed-up car on the side of a highway, taken hold when I'd seen my face in the gas station mirror and only intensified when I'd heard the first news broadcast about that unprecedented tornado. I bumped across the train tracks and wound down my window as I drew up alongside the Border Control Check Point. The passport and Green Card I presented to the official were mine, but the Social Security Number, birth date, even the name, were invented. Not by me. They were just in my pocket when I put my hand there to find them. While she inspected them, I looked back at Portal in the rear-view mirror. I could see the gas station with the old guy. The guard handed me back my papers and waved me through. No going back now then.

A few kilometres down the road, I pulled over, and concentrated.

"Where are you going?" I muttered to the wind blasted hills. *Where are you going?*

There was a strange snapping sensation in my mind, almost the reverse of getting a migraine – sudden clarity – and then... water, snow, cold wind, vast expanses of ice. I frowned, then realised I was catching a glimpse of where he was headed. Whether it was a conscious acknowledgement, or a random surge on our mental link, he was letting me know his destination. The knowledge blossomed in my own head. Alaska. Fuckin' terrific. I popped a can of Coke, took a gulp and pushed it between my thighs. I took a road heading North West.

I'm coming, I told him. I didn't know myself if it was a promise or a threat.

IV

It took me nearly three days of solid driving to find him. I only stopped to fill up with gas and to check the news and weather. I had felt the uneasiness in my stomach growing as I'd pushed through Canada; felt the sense of being out of kilter as I clipped the edge of the Yukon; the frayed edges of the world unravelling grated my brain as I turned up into the mountains at Conrad, where the cold had really started to bite into me and I was forced to pull on the deformed sweater. I had found my answers broadcast in bulletins, headlines, breaking news, Twitter, Facebook – Smoke seen billowing ominously from Yellowstone, earthquakes strong enough to topple houses in Margate, England. I read about flash floods, freak squalls, a hurricane that ripped through New Jersey. Snow in New Delhi. Sinkholes, fault lines, freak weather, wildfires. All these and the rest I had felt inside myself. I'd been waiting for it to happen. Seeing it confirmed made me press on along the roads with a grim determination. At Fraser, just before I dipped back into the States at the Alaskan border, I pulled my denim jacket on over the sweater. I looked like the Pillsbury Dough

Boy, could barely move my arms at the elbows, and still the cold ate into me. I sat in the truck on the ferry from Skagway with the engine running, just for the radiator, and kept looking at my reflection in the wing-mirrors to see if I had changed. I hadn't. I had never been young and cold at the same time before. I had never, I realised, as I drove off the ferry into Haines, really known cold before. Not like this. I had never been around long enough to experience it. And here I was, pushing myself further into this strange land of ice, wind and cold, so out of place, feeling uncomfortable, confused and irritable. I blocked out the bullet grey sky and the snow that had started to fall and the bitter wind that rocked the truck and the queasiness in my stomach; grit my teeth against the world heaving up and dropping down and spinning wildly, and focussed on the drag of the Kid's presence. My own mind was a Geiger counter that clicked like crazy when I was heading in the right direction. I hung a left in the truck, drove for a half-mile along the edge of a vast expanse of flat silver water. It wasn't the ocean; I could see the far shore, misty and black. It was the Chilkat inlet, wide, deep and cold enough to rip the breath from my body in less than a minute. Birds wheeled high above. I thought they might have been eagles.

It wasn't until I had passed several buildings that I realised I was driving through a town, though 'town' was a loose description of this place. A sign in the window of the bar told me I was in Mud Bay, and that it had a population of 137, and thanked me for visiting. There was a small bar and restaurant, a fishing store with a display of rods outside the door. People milled around. Fishermen on the quay beside fishing boats, people hauling baskets and crates to a few trucks parked close by. Children running about, teens half-heartedly bouncing a basketball around a square of concrete. I passed a building that might have been a postal office, a bank or a sheriff's office, or possibly all three, and a small convenience store. There was a girl sitting on the step of the store; she wore a red parka with the hood up. She was poking a stick very purposefully into the dirt at the side of the step but looked up as I passed. Her face was round, dark-skinned and capped with thick black bangs. Liquid black Alaska-Native eyes followed me. The girl stared, I guess, because she didn't recognise the truck or the driver. Strangers would be odd here and I wondered, as our eyes met, whether she had seen another stranger pass through here recently. But within seconds, I had coasted past her and my mind returned to the buzz pulling me on. I left the town, drove on with the flat mirror-sheen of water on my right and tall sweet-smelling cedar trees on my left, and suddenly, I knew I was there. I had found him. I had nothing but the electric tingle in my brain to go on, but it was enough. I slowed, stopped and, after a pause, turned the ignition off and sat with the keys in my hand. The engine went through its ritual of clicks and clanks as I slid the thick blue ski coat over my denim jacket, hitched the hood up over my head, rammed my hands into the gloves and dared myself to get out. With a grunt, I flung myself out of the seat and slammed the door behind me. Jesus, it was cold. The wind found its way in under every edge. Neck, cuffs, waist; it flogged at me. I wondered, as I shivered, whether my regained youth and strength meant I had regained other abilities. Only one way to find out. I gathered my strength, winced, felt a popping along my skin like thousands of tiny blossoms bursting into bloom. Felt warmth on my face. The clouds broke and a watery sun shone through. The icy winds fell away and out in the inlet, fishermen on a schooner stopped on deck, turning to look up at the sudden, unexpected change in temperature. It appeared I had recovered all my powers. It felt strange. Cheating. I struggled between my conscience and fear of hypothermia for a moment, but in the end pulled my influence away, let the sky cloud over and the temperature plummet again. I began to walk away from the truck.

I dug my gloved hands into my pockets, crunched across the gravel at the side of the road, and finally got my first glimpse of the place the Kid had been staying. A corner of roof and white weather-boarding, a single upstairs window winking at me through the dense trees like a stripper revealing the first bare shoulder. There was an old beaten up brown '72 Dodge Challenger R/T parked beneath the trees complete with snow chains; the Kid must have driven it here. The wind fell away into stillness and the temperature dropped as I drew closer to the building. When the trees pulled back entirely and the house stood complete, naked, my breath puffed and I was glad for the ski coat. It was a colonial-style building, porch supported on pillars. It was riddled with wood-rot and damp and leant slightly sideways. But it would have been impressive in its day. It made me think of tired old women who shuffled along city streets clutching to their independence – ashamed but defiant, the great beauties of a forgotten time. And on the top step up to the porch, framed by that glorious building, sat the Kid. He looked to be the same age as I was now. For the first time in all my memory, we were equal. I had never seen him at the peak of his strength before and I was dazzled by him. He wore no coat, no gloves or scarf, just a black T-shirt and pale blue jeans, dark brown boots. His silver hair glinted against the pale of his skin and the dark of his shirt. He had one leg hooked up on the step beneath him, the other hanging down loosely. It registered that he looked as I must have done, days back, sitting on the hood of my truck, basking in the sun. The Kid was basking in the cold. It seemed for a moment that there was a sort of shimmering aura around him of pure almost crystalline air that, should you breathe it in, might freeze your windpipe.

V

Though he didn't acknowledge me – he was picking at the flaking paint of the step between his legs, his face lowered – I knew he was out here waiting for me. He would have known, felt me approaching. There was a cell phone and a stack of newspapers beside him as if he'd read them and discarded them with disgust. I knew he had been drawn to the news as I had, by the rolling feeling inside, to find out what his going A.W.O.L had cost the world. I stepped towards him and pushed the hood back from my head and the rush of cold air around my ears was coupled with... something. Relief? Irritation? Sadness? I wasn't sure. All or none of these things. As my booted feet crunched in the dead twigs and leaves, he took his hand away from his mouth where it had rested, and gestured vaguely without looking up. "Figured you'd turn up eventually."

I found myself unable to think of a single thing to say to that and so I remained silent.

"Why?" he asked. His voice was small, full of things that registered a deep thrum chord in me.

I clumped towards him and hunched my shoulders as the temperature dropped further, until I stood at the foot of the steps. I turned to look back the way I had come; I could see a slice of the grey uncompromising water between the trees.

"I... I don't think I had a choice," I said.

He laughed, a snorted derisive laugh that shook his silver hair back from his face. Still, he didn't look at me. "And there I was thinking it might be a social call. Have a few beers, shoot some pool, laugh about the old days."

I rooted inside my many pockets until I found my cigarettes and lighter. I lit two, difficult with the gloves on, and passed him one. He looked down at it, a little surprised, then plucked it from my fingers and inhaled deeply on it. Then he rested his elbow on his raised knee and finally squinted up at me, an appraising expression on his face. He exhaled smoke down his nose.

"So that's it," he said. "I was wondering what you'd look like."

I held out my arms, inside my layers of clothes, bulked out and stiff with cold. "It's my summer look."

He smiled. It was a little sardonic, but more genuine than the one he usually wore when he saw me.

"You look ridiculous," he dead-panned, but his eyes defied his words. He was as impressed by me as I was by him. I wondered if he saw a shimmering heat haze around me, smelt baked earth. I laughed despite myself as we both smoked in silence for a moment.

"It's started," I said, eventually, kicking at the earth by my toes, my voice quieter now. "It's unravelling."

He was looking past me, back out towards the water, flicked his ash over the side of the steps into the dirt. "Is that what you came here to tell me?"

There was a bite to his voice.

"You already know it. You've felt it too. Everything shifting. You've seen it, read about it, listened to the news. I came because I didn't have anywhere else to go."

"That is bullshit," he snapped, thumping his hand on the wooden deck. "I come out here to get a bit of peace and quiet and instead get a visit from the Jolly Green Giant. Haven't you got anything better to do? Go... play with all the little woodland folk. Farm things. Find yourself a woman."

I felt the chill of his stare fall on me. The wind howled across from the inlet, moaning eerily in the trees, holding the promise of ice and snow. It lifted my hair and numbed my ears. Instinctively, I pushed back with my own renewed strength, pulling heat from my blood and spreading it outwards. The sky opened up like a promise, and the water in the bay skittered and danced with a hundred starbursts of light. There was a smell of ozone as our influences collided. He glanced up at the brilliant bowl of blue sky and flinched, as I had stepping out of the truck into the immense cold he had breathed onto everything.

"I had a woman," I said. "She died."

Under the glare of the sun and the weight of my words, he sagged, dropped his head forward. The wind he had been buffeting me with died.

"To hell with this," he muttered.

I felt my anger drain out of me, too. The sun faded. I climbed the steps and sat beside him. "You said that before. Won't make me go away."

I felt him chuckle. "Never getting shot of you am I?"

I sat there, contemplating the truth of his words.

Then he shifted. "Remember Ypres?"

I stared at the inlet beyond the trees, grey again now that I had let the sun pull back behind its heavy clouds. Unbidden, my nose filled with the scent of decay and damp and rotten flesh. I could almost feel the mud slicked across my face as shells rained down into the vast shipwreck of war. I nodded.

"It was easier there. Easiest it's ever been for me," he said. "With everyone dying all around us, it was easier to let you stick that bayonet in me. Easier to just let it happen. Easier to just march up to you, following September, and throw gas in your face."

"It was easier when you didn't feel like you were leaving anything behind," I pondered.

"Never kicked up much of a fight when there was a war on," he added. "Just sort of turned up, did it, went on for the next few months and then sat and waited for you to turn up again."

"And now there is war everywhere." I said, "and I never go to Afghanistan or Palestine or Yemen or Syria to wait for you."

"No, we kinda stick to America now," he agreed.

"Guess maybe it's because here, no one really sees any of the dying, not even the death on their own doorsteps. Just blindly looking through it all, pretending it's fine while they all drown." I chuckled at my own cynicism. "Like lobsters in a cooking pot. It's easier to stick it out here in a country that's stopped caring. Like Ypres, but without the mud or trenches or explosions or uniforms everywhere you look. Just... numbness."

He studied the cigarette I had given him, half-smoked now. "You sound like I think."

"S'pose that's unavoidable when you live as long as we have, with only each other for company," I quipped. "Did you really think it had never occurred to me to just let this thing slide, to see what happened?"

"Yeah. I guess I did. I always thought you were the sensible one. The 'good' one." he made little air quotes and I pulled a face.

"Fuck off!"

We laughed, the surprise, the easiness of our talk bubbling up through us both. It felt good to laugh. It felt easier than I'd expected it to be, sitting here with him, just the two of us.

"Do you remember England?" he asked me now.

"Sure. Spent a lot of time there."

"Yeah, but do you really remember what it felt like? What it *smelt* like? Sometimes I try and remember the first winds of autumn, still kinda warm. I liked that, you know? My life is spent in the cold, and to get that taste of warm dust in the air, it was nice. But now, I'm not sure I can really remember it."

I tried to conjure crisp English spring rain, and the haze of a summer evening, the fields smelling of grass and earth, and the long quiet sky split by a church bell tolling or the starlings coming in to roost. I thought maybe I could... but... all I could see was that field circled with burning torches,

Cate in her dress, the one that might have been green or red. The last time I had seen her. I had been as old as I ever get - people guessed at sixty, sixty-five - but Cate had been so much older; her hair a wispy white mane that was the closest I had ever been to snow back then. She'd been a strong lass, a farm girl, rounded yet solid and sturdy, but the years and the sickness eating her lungs had stripped the vitality from her, made her start to seem small. I had gripped my sword and tried to hold it higher than my guilt; I would have to leave her again, leave her alone with only her frail arthritic bones and that deep cough that ripped through her. The Kid was watching me.

"You came over here when she died," he said, and I wondered if my feelings showed so easily in my face. Or was he just picking up ripples of it through that strange link we shared?

I nodded. "Couldn't stay there. She was in every blade of grass and every tree."

I'd taken a ship over the ocean, letting the storms and waves and wind batter the pain from me. It hadn't worked, not really. Europe. The Mediterranean. India. Then I washed up on the shores of the new world back when it was still new to white men.

"She fought, you know," he said, quietly. "Right through that winter. She held on, stubborn as an ox she was, despite the cancer. She... just *refused* to let go. She wanted to see you again, see you with May blossom in your hair, she said."

"How...?" I stared at him, feeling that old sensation of walking across ice, of the tremendous riptide I felt whenever I thought of her.

He looked down at his thin, elegantly long hands, studying the light on his mirror-smooth nails. "I went to her, that last winter. When you were gone. I went to her home. I don't know... I think I thought that if you couldn't be there with her at the end... maybe she shouldn't be alone..."

"You were with her when she died?" My voice creaked, hollow under the strain of it.

He took a drag on the cigarette, studied the trees and nodded once. "She knew me as soon as she saw me. Said she'd seen me every year, when I had come to fight you, and you know, in the forest, in the shadows. She was peaceful, at the end. Not much pain. I made it snow for her. Helped her to sit up so she could see it. She was so light. Like a little quivering bird..." he trailed off.

"I didn't know," I said.

"I didn't tell you." He smiled wryly.

I found myself wanting to thank him, both for the surprising gentleness he had shown Cate and for not telling me back then when I was still open and raw. All I could manage was a strange little grunt.

The Kid chewed on his bottom lip, then puffed his cheeks and exhaled. A patch of leaves on the nearest tree turned white with frost. I shivered. The frost melted.

"She was beautiful," he said, almost to himself. "I was so jealous. Every spring you had her to go to, almost like you had a home. You were loved. I wish..." but he shook his head, cutting off whatever he might have said then.

"*I* was jealous of *you*," I countered. "That you could be near her in the cold and dark months. You could've gone to her; she would have fed you and been company for you..."

"No." He shook his head definitely. "I never could, as much as that might've been... nice. She was your wife. That was your life. She was always the May Queen."

"Is that why you were so angry?" I said. "When I body-hopped into that girl at the fair, back in North Dakota?"

118

His clear eyes darkened and he looked away.

"I just... someone to be there every year, waiting for me. Someone who knew and understood what I was and waited anyway."

I hung my head. I couldn't deny him his longing, but I needed him to see how it had been for me. "But you have to watch them grow old, and know they'll never be young again in six months, like we are. You have to watch the person you've come to depend on to keep you rooted to the world get old and die. You have to see how transient the world is."

"Does it make you care more about what we have to do?" he asked me. "Does it give you a reason to die every six months?"

"It makes you hate that you care." I shook my head. "Which is maybe worse than not caring at all."

"I wouldn't know. Never had anything to hate caring about."

And that, right there, was the reason he had run away from our fight. He could see no sense in fighting me when he didn't care what we were fighting for. And if I were honest with myself, I couldn't see much sense in it either. The world had lost all its colour. Losing Cate, yes, but everything else had soured too. I fought the Kid every six months, when I was young and then when I was old, over and over, let him kill me, let myself return and go find him because there was nothing else I could do. The only person I could depend on now was sitting right beside me. It was the reason I had come out here to find him. I didn't want to fight him year in year out. I *wanted* to get drunk with him, shoot pool. Laugh. Forget. Forget what we were, forget what we had to do and why we had to do it. I wanted to say to him, *hey, yeah, to hell with it. Let's hang up our guns and kick back with a beer and a packet of smokes and...* but the Earth wouldn't let me forget. It was protesting to us already. It knew we weren't doing our job and was sending us these alerts in the shape of freak weather and natural disasters and chaos and deaths. I felt it vibrating through me, even now sitting on the steps to an abandoned house on the outskirts of Mud Bay, and it would only get worse. That was what 'unravelling' meant; what happened when the two of us didn't fight.

"I need a drink," the Kid said finally, and pinched what was left of his cigarette out between two fingers. It hissed. He rose from the steps in one graceful twist of his body and dropped the extinguished cigarette-end into the pocket of his jeans. He glanced down at me. "And so do you." he held out a hand and hauled me up.

VI

The inside of the house was filled with an odd light, mottled with strange shadows, dust and memories. Sounds were distorted. Bare hardwood floor that somehow swallowed the sound of my heavy bootsteps. Green and gold flock wallpaper, the sort that was de-rigueur around 1972, was curling and peeling like fern fronds on the walls. Aside from a single armchair, which was another horrific 70s relic of faded ripped orange and mustard velvet, the room was a lot like being deep in the dark forests. A pile of blankets in the far corner. An open can of peaches in syrup sat beside the chair on the bare hardwood floor. Its lid was all jagged-edged and sticking up at an odd angle where it'd been hacked open with a pocketknife, the way we'd done it in the trenches. On the arm of the chair, a dog-eared paperback copy of 'One Flew Over The Cuckoo's Nest' and a stub of candle. He had made himself as much at home as we ever were.

"It's deserted," the Kid called from another room. "Falling down. Guess I'm squatting."

Things had a way of turning up when we needed them. Like blankets, or cans of food. Empty houses that smelt of mulch and secrets. Or a book to read at night when you got sad and lonely. I stood in the centre of the large front room, watching dust motes spiralling in front of the window, remembered my earliest memories of pine and oak trees, deep quiet and old magic, of shadows that took shape and stories that seeped into the rock and took form. I turned in a small circle, my mind turning over the lines of the old children's rhyme like a mantra – one flew east, and one flew west and one flew over the cuckoo's nest. One flew east, and one flew west and... who flew over the cuckoo's nest? I spread my arms out as if I could grab hold of the time that had seeped into the peeling wallpaper and creaking floors.

"It's great," I answered.

He reappeared in the doorway, holding a bottle of Glenlivet Scotch in one hand and two glasses in the other, set the glasses on the mantelpiece amid the pillar candles, the curls and hanging blobs of wax, and unscrewed the top of the bottle. I could smell it from where I stood, malty and sweet.

"I found that back in Canada. You can't get it out here for love or money," he told me, as he poured three fingers worth into each glass. I made an indignant noise and he poured out a good slosh more.

"How long you been here?" I asked, as I pulled a glove from my hand with my teeth and took the glass he passed me.

He held his own glass up into what little light there was, peering at the swirling contents. "Got here just about when you were leaving Saskatchewan." Then he glanced at me. "I felt you coming up behind me. Made it barely a day before you. Challenger wasn't up to the mountains much."

"I'll bet."

"How'd you like all that snow?"

"Hated it."

It was small talk, idle bullshit to save us from thinking about everything else. The silence that rose around us filled the house so that it creaked.

He raised his glass in a toast, then, and looked tired, sad. "To us. To this whole fucking thing."

It wasn't a hopeful-sounding toast but I doubted I would've come up with much better, so I took a gulp of the burning liquid. I could feel the Kid's power pushing against my own like a magnetic field and I flexed my fingers as if warding off cramp. The air between us shimmered as our influences pushed at each other and crackled. He looked as if he might say something, but he didn't. Instead his breath stammered out in a puff of cold air that made me shiver. His eyes, I realised, were the colour of the Chilkat inlet; just as deep, unfathomable and deceivingly tranquil. Neither of us could think of anything fitting to say, anything that wasn't evasive, undermining or just plain dumb. Then he smiled a resigned little smile.

"Wanna see something neat?" he said, eventually, opting for the evasive-and-dumb tactic.

I felt something a lot like relief. Without waiting for my answer, he threw the last of his whiskey into his mouth, slammed the glass down on the mantlepiece, then stalked over to the window and braced his hands against the glass. Instantly, curls, spiderwebs and leaves of frost leapt out from his spread fingers and danced up the glass. I watched them, mesmerised. People called us many names, but he'd always been good at being Jack Frost. Then he lifted his right palm until only the fingernail of his index finger remained in contact with the glass and began to trace a more precise shape. The edge of his tongue poked out between his lips as he drew. I moved closer as he put the finishing flourishes to his ice sketch – it was a girl, *the* girl, I realised, from the fair ground in North Dakota. Alison Maddison, solemn and graceful, glancing back over her shoulder, long hair whipped up by an invisible wind. And though there was no colour except the lines of ice, the girl seemed flooded by moonlight. The girl made of starlight. He let his hand fall and stepped back beside me, turning his head to contemplate his work. I was speechless. She was perfect; fragile.

It made me ache inside. I didn't want to breathe, afraid she might melt. But she hung there on the glass, glittering.

The Kid turned to me. "Your turn."

The refusal that wiggled its way up my throat never made it out of my mouth. Instead, I cast about for some inspiration, peering into all the shadowed corners. My eyes fixed on a small hole down on the skirting board, where the slowly sinking wall had begun to pull away from the floor. I smiled and dropped to one knee, reached my hand out towards it and brushed the tiny opening with the fingertips of my one bare hand. I let myself expand and search down for earth and water beneath the building. Then I began to coach and urge, felt my jaw clench briefly with the effort. *There.* A sigh whispered through my body and I sat back on my heel. The Kid was leaning over my shoulder, his hands on his knees, and together, we watched as a tiny green shoot wound its way out of the hole and began to snake and unfurl tiny new leaves. Finally, three buds swelled then burst open into small blue flowers with yellow centres. Forget-Me-Nots. They'd grown wherever I'd lived, all summer long, for as long as I could remember. I was smiling, an artist proud of his creation.

The Kid nodded with raised eyebrows. "Impressive." He leant further forward, to inspect the details on the leaves, to brush his finger along the fuzzy stem. "OK," he nodded, "OK. So how's this then?"

He held out his hand, palm flat and down-facing, over the flowers. Then he closed his eyes and I felt a shiver ripple through me. Miniature snow had begun to fall slowly, majestically, from his outstretched hand, settling on the Forget-Me-Nots like icing sugar sifted onto a cake. I laughed a genuine childish giggle, pulled off my other glove and poked my finger into the snow, feeling the cold on my skin. Then I pushed myself to my feet and he straightened up. The snow stopped falling over our little flower as we contemplated the beauty of it, staggered at the sheer unnatural otherworldly quality it held as it sat there against the wall, glittering and surrounded by a small neat blanket of white crystals. He turned to me with a pointed, challenging raised eyebrow, the foppish Lord-ling all over again. I moved to sit on the crumbling windowsill. My gaze fell on the giant cedars creaking around the house. That would do, I thought. It was coming easier to me now, the power, and I tapped into it faster, sent my influence out to the tree. The Kid moved over beside me and we watched the tree shudder, sway, then explode outwards and downwards simultaneously. When the torrent of leaves had stopped falling, I could admire my work – the tree that *had* been a cedar was now squat, branches dragged down low with hundreds of round, swollen apples.

The Kid's surprised laughter ricocheted around the room. "No way...." He shook his head in disbelieving wonder and ran for the door.

I stayed on the windowsill, watched him leap down the steps in one jump and rush to the tree, reaching up into the boughs. He plucked a fruit, bit into it, laughed, danced a strange wild little jig, stamping his feet. I realised I was grinning inanely, watching him, and when he saw me, he stopped, pursing his lips and shrugging off his embarrassment. He tossed the half-eaten apple into the air, caught it, then swung round in a circle, pointing to the new apple tree as if he were a cowboy shooting from the hip. The branches bowed even lower with the weight of the icicles he had just hung there alongside the fruit. I was up and running to join him a second later, snapping one sharp point of ice off a branch as he had with the apple, couldn't help giggling as it slid through my fingers, caught it and touched it to my tongue. It had a pure clean taste as it melted against my lips and dribbled down into my scarf. We stood there, he with his apple and I with the icicle, like two boys in the proverbial candy store, laughing at each other and at ourselves. I called on the heat of my blood again, sent it out through my hand so that the icicle dissolved in a rush, and directed it out. Just out. Everywhere. It pulled at me, the atmosphere drinking in the warmth in long draughts until the sun was blazing low in the sky, and

124

the wind was hot, dry and sand-blasted. I ripped the coat, jacket, the ridiculous sweater off. Tossed them aside, peeled off the scarf, and threw my head back. The apple slid out of the Kid's hand as he shrank from the sudden heat, turning his head and shielding his eyes. He stepped instinctively into the shade of the apple tree, and then, glancing at me, eyes wide with wonder, he held out his thin, pale hand into the brightness, watched the play of colours shifting across his skin. Then he plunged out into the sun, his hair brilliant white in the glare, a halo around his shoulders that threw ripples against the trees like light reflecting off water. He spun on his heel and raised a hand, bringing the snow. It came from nowhere; the sky was still hot and blue. The snow was thick and fluffy, Christmas card snow that danced and whirled and spun in gusts. I threw my head back into it, let it settle on my eyelashes, lifted my arms and spun slowly round in it. The heat from the baking sun and the cold kiss of the snow was intoxicating. We stood there, drunk now on the things we had never experienced before, maddened by the wrongness of it all and the rush that using our powers brought. My blood sang, crackled with burning grass and the cool green smell of sun-dappled oak leaves. I felt my skin scorching with the blaze inside me, the heat and fire of the summer. I looked at the Kid and his eyes were white with the winds and ice of winter. We were Elementals then, Ancients, and we felt it filling us, overflowing, spilling outwards. There was a rushing sensation, a sudden void. Then there was screeching, wailing, echoing sound – I thought it was inside my head until the earth jolted beneath my feet with a thundering boom. It sent us both stumbling. I ended up on my knees, clawing my fingers into the dirt, my breathing ragged, my body boiling with the power I had suddenly pulled back inside myself... because something was terribly wrong. I looked sideways at Winter; he was sprawled against the apple tree that had no right to exist, arm thrown over his face.

"Hurt?" I managed to ask.

125

He uncovered his eyes, stared at me. His gaze was still frozen, pupils and irises still blank with the snowstorm that raged inside him. He shook his head and when he carried on staring at me, I knew my eyes were ablaze with fire and heat.

"What did we do?" he asked at last.

There was no denial, no passing of blame. *We* did it, whatever it was, and now we had to find out what. We got to our feet and turned in the direction that the twisting screeching wail had come from. Out over the inlet. And then we were moving forwards, concerned jog turning to full sprint as the effects of our games became apparent. We emerged from the trees onto the side of the road and stared. The inlet had frozen in a gnarl of angry water and huge flames leapt up from it in the centre. The fishing schooner was held aloft out there, stuck in the twisted ice, half ablaze, but the men had abandoned it, had already made it to the shore. The sudden heat that had thrust itself up into the cold air crackled and sparked, charging the atmosphere so that it shimmered iridescent. The sky rolled and thrashed, iron-grey and heavy. A cumulous cloud towered above us, nipping in at the waist then billowing out again into a flat anvil shape miles above us. Then the wind started up with an eerie howl that intensified as it roared towards us, bringing with it a wall of snow, until it engulfed us, filling my eyes and lungs with sharp particles. The blizzard stretched itself out across the bay, smothering the town in seconds, making it a vague black shape in the grey. I had heard stories of Thundersnow, but never seen it until now. I had a moment to rake in a deep painful breath before the first crack of thunder reverberated over our heads, so loud and so close that I felt it in my teeth. The blue-green lightning followed immediately in a blinding flash as it lashed out across the bay. It struck somewhere in the town, with a shuddering bam. We could see the flames from where we stood. It was followed almost at once by several more crackling forks. I think I must have said something, sworn some curse, but the grey swirling sky swallowed it, and I don't remember what I could have said. We just stood there, on the edge of the inlet, watching with an awful dumb fascination. Stood and watched as the world which we were supposed to hold together began to fall apart. Nature unravelled exponentially now, and we had done this, let it happen. Fire and ice, heat and cold, whipped through the inlet, tore through the town, scattering itself through people and buildings, uncaring. It was wild. Because we had let it become so. Without us to keep the balance, to tie the knot between extremities, the ends flailed around like crazy power cables.

Did I care?

Did I care.

I looked at Winter, saw the shock, the pure horror on his face. His gaze met mine. We were running towards the town when I realised the decision had been made.

VII

We moved faster than any human, faster almost than the wind, but not quite. Our feet barely touched the earth, and with each step, the guilt pounded up through me, magnified by the power I had no right to possess now. We flew into Mud Bay, blind from snow, deafened by the thunder and wind, dizzy on power. Around us, adults and children ran in and out of the dense blizzard, faces illuminated alternately by the flashes of lightning and the flames that leapt from where it struck. Some were shouting, some silent. The convenience store was ruined. Houses lay with their spines broken. The quay had been destroyed. Boats were on fire and mountainous drifts of snow were piling up against anything that didn't move. I floundered as another clap of thunder roared overhead. There was too much – lightening flickered and hit a tree to my right. Where first? What should I do? Winter grabbed my arm and the sharp freeze of his hand on my bare skin made me wince and focus.

"It'll take everything we have. We work together." He pulled me forwards, and I moved, given purpose.

Together, we began to try and rectify what we had done. It was a tiny place, hardly deserving the title 'town', but the supernatural thundersnow hammered it in revenge. I could feel the world rising up and fighting against us but Winter and I went on, mindlessly, and it took every inch of what we were to hold it back enough to do any good. I poured heat into frozen snow drifts until they melted, while he shifted the snow with his hands, lifting great piles of it and sending it disintegrating into nothingness. I pulled the flames of the burning buildings into myself while he sent icy wind blasting through them, clearing the smoke until they were left charred and dead. Winter held back the wind and snow as much as he could, and I found myself conducting the lightning through my outstretched arm and out of my feet rather than let it hit more buildings or people. We didn't stop, didn't think, didn't tire. I ploughed my weight against girders and lumps of stone. Winter lifted bodies from the wreckage, sometimes two or three at a time, hauling them as if they were no more than sacks of grain. It was our penance. Occasionally, men worked with us to shift debris, or to guide families out of their houses while Winter or I held up the roof. They never said a thing to either of us, but I caught fleeting glimpses of their thoughts, tangled with fear and the same mindless drive that was pushing me on. They saw two men. One huge and broad, the other tall and thin. Strong men. Strangers. But we were helping and if they saw that neither of us wore a coat, noticed the strange glow to our eyes or the peculiar shimmer to the air around us, they let their minds rearrange it into some sensible explanation of shock and adrenaline.

I was herding a family towards the centre of the main street where it was safest when I heard Winter shout to me. I swivelled on my feet and sought him out in the blizzard; ran to him. He was siphoning snow frantically, sending it spinning off back into the air with his hands. I could see the tailgate and part of the roof of a pick-up truck had been flung onto its side by the howling wind and was held down by the weight of the ice that had fallen around it so quickly.

"There's a kid under there." He gestured with one hand to the far side of the truck.

I didn't ask him how he knew. Once he'd said it, I could feel it too – the tiny, slow beating of a heart that was about to give up. I put one foot on a wheel that Winter had just unearthed and vaulted over the roof, landing on the tarmac on the far side. I laid my hands into the snow there until it began to thaw and trickle. Finally, I found a tiny hand poking out from the wheel arch.

"Here!" I called, and then I crouched, curled my hands under the body work, and straightened my knees, lifting the truck and tossing it right way up. Winter was there, dragging the small red parka-swathed kid out by her shoulders. It was the girl I'd seen on my way through here earlier. Winter lifted her limp body, her coat soaked and dragging on her, cradled her head and knees, and presented her to me.

"I can't stop the cold," he said.

I nodded, rubbed my palms together and placed them on her face. As I sent heat through her body, felt her heart thump-thump, watched her coat begin to steam into the cold air, saw her take a gulp of air, she squirmed in Winter's arms. Then she looked up at him with her large black eyes. Really looked at him and really saw what he was. Her mouth opened in a tiny O of surprise, and he nearly dropped her, startled. Some humans have just known what we were. Cate. The witch in New Orleans. This girl. She twisted to gaze up at me and instinct told me to draw away when she reached her hand out to my bare forearm. But I held still and she felt the heat radiating out from me.

"You can fix this," she whispered.

I met Winter's eyes over her head.

Then I looked down at the girl. "Yes."

We stood there, Winter and I, just looking at each other. Eventually, he nodded. And the wind stopped. The last roll of thunder echoed away into silence. The snow in the air drifted lazily to the ground. The townspeople out in the street stared about them, finally able to see the damage the storm had wreaked. I closed my eyes, could already feel it inside me, the world settling back down again, the power receding slowly inside me, the fire in my blood cooling to a throb. It was not my turn to be strong now. It wasn't summer. When I opened my eyes again, I felt Winter's gaze on me. I wondered if I had already started to age, but I turned to the crowd of people. "Do you see your family?"

The girl twisted and searched the crowds, then pointed. Dumbly, Winter carried her over to them, presented her to a man with white hair tied back in a braid and a gnarled walnut face. There was laughing, tears, thanks. But Winter looked down at the girl who knew what he was, and I saw his sharp features, all those angles and planes and cheekbones, soften just for a moment into a gentle smile. He turned and walked back to me, stopping short by a few feet, studying me with his cool snowstorm stare.

It didn't feel like there were words enough, but I swallowed, looked up into the grey sky and said "It has to be done properly." It felt like I was dredging the words from the bottom of a deep well. "Like in the early days. Just to be sure..."

"Yeah. Whatever you say, old man," he said.

I looked at the townspeople, the adults, the children. Beautiful transient things that made the world what it was; made what we were have purpose. They didn't see us now. But the girl in the red parka, she saw us. She waved. I waved back. And then I found myself focussing on the tiny point of light in my mind, felt it growing. I plummeted into it. A moment later, Winter followed.

When we stumbled out of the white, I was shivering. My body ached from the assault I had put it through. I could barely stand, and Winter supported me with my right arm flung over his shoulders. We were outside the old house where he had been staying.

"This was the only place I could think of," he said quietly and laid me on the ground under our apple tree, so that I could see the sky through the branches. The sky was gunmetal grey. The branches were bare now. No fruit. No leaves. I coughed, winced, looked down at my hands, papery and blotched with age spots. I was so old. Older than I've ever been. My jeans flapped around my legs, too loose now, and the cold bit into me like a rabid dog.

"It's a great place," I said.

He nodded, looking solemn. Then he slid his arm around me, lifted me against his chest. I was so light, like a little quivering bird. And then he leant down over me, his silver hair touching my cheek. His lips were frozen and his kiss sent ice into my lungs. I hardly felt the blade of his pocketknife as it slid between my ribs. The blood was hot and stained the snow that still lay beneath me.

"See you in the spring..." the words buzzed from my lips, and I was gone.

VIII

There is a moment of stillness – then with a lurch, I feel my heart hammering in my chest. I'm not dead. I can still feel the blood clinging to my skin, dried and tight; can taste the wind and snow on my lips... But when my eyes open, the sky is clear and blue. How long have I been laying here? There is a blind panic as I try to establish how I came to be sprawled beneath an apple tree, covered in blood...

And then I remember and I flex my fingers, watching the marble sky doming above me. I can feel the first buds of power in me and it warms me. Gingerly, I sit up. I can see the house, the same house with its weather boarding and porch and steps and tall cedar trees, but it's not leaning to one side anymore. It stands tall and proud, in the first flush of womanhood. Someone has started to paint it, too. The apple tree I made is covered in blossom and as I move awkwardly to stand on new feet, it rains into my hair. I'm small, compact and, at a guess, about eight years old. There is a wrinkled, old man sitting on the steps. He's lean, whip thin, a shock of silver hair and beard. He's watching me, one elbow resting on a knee, his hand cupping his chin.

"How was your Christmas?" I ask.

His laugh rumbles out around me and he rises to his feet. "Piss off."

I look down at myself, my jeans, striped grass-stained T-Shirt all smeared with dry blood.

"Did it work?" I ask at last. "It's not unravelling anymore?"

The old man nods. "It worked. You need to get cleaned up, and then we'll eat. You must be starving."

My stomach growls loudly in response. I've got a lot of growing to do. "Got any pancakes?" I'm brushing dirt from the seat of my pants, give him a rueful grin. "And please tell me you kept that awful armchair."

He studies me for a beat, a long cool stare, then cackles, turns to the house. "Hey, Annie! He's here!"

There is the sound of running feet and the door is thrown open. The girl we pulled from the snow, the one who'd really seen us, stands there, her long black hair is loose and moves in the breeze around her dark face.

132

She's probably a couple of years older than I am now, and she's gripping a box of cookies in one hand. She grins and I grin back at her.

"Grandpa sent these over for you," she tells me, thrusting the box out towards me. I remember the walnut faced man that had taken Annie from Winter when we pulled her out from under the truck. Things have a way of turning up when we need them. When you're sad and lonely.

"Awesome!" I say and bound up the steps towards her to take one in a pudgy fist.

She looks at me with her liquid eyes, unsure for a moment. Then she puts a hand on my arm and feels the warmth radiating from me. "Just checking." she smiles.

It's been so long since I had a home to come back to, someone waiting for me. I think of Cate, and I feel a little bit seasick for a moment, but I feel Winter's chilly hand on my shoulder as he steers me into the house, and the sickness passes.

It passes as the seasons must pass.

* * *

Fee Fi Fo Fum

You want me to tell you about my brother?

Can I play with the Lego instead? Legoes are the best.

OK.

If I tell you one thing, can I have a biscuit?

My brother is the biggest and the best and he's better than all the other brothers, and probably all the mums and dads.

My brother is the smartest and the cleverest-est. Maybe he's the smartest person who ever lived. I bet he's smarter than you.

My brother learnt to be really, really quiet so no one would ever see him or hear him. Ninja. Ghost boy. Wizard. He tells the best ever stories about magic and knights and heroes and kings and lands where everyone is happy every day and never sad or hungry. I think when I'm big I'm going to be a hero too. Just like my brother Jack.

One time he sneaked right down the stairs while the telly was on and he took the treasure from the Giant's pot without being seen and then he sneaked back up the stairs, and no one heard him at all 'cause he was the quietest, and then he went out the window on the magic beanstalk.

I was afraid my brother wasn't coming back and I was scared that the Giant would look away from the telly and see the treasure was gone and come stomping up the steps and bang on the door and, if my brother wasn't there, it wouldn't be our castle anymore, it'd be just a bedroom, and I wouldn't be invisible and I'd be just a boy again. And I was scared the Giant would see me this time and get angry and hurt me like the times before. Like that time when my brother came home late after three days and saved me by making me invisible, so the Giant stopped seeing me and only saw him.

But my brother came back, because he's the best brother.

He was gone for ages and ages but he came back with McDonalds which is the best food ever, even better than the magic beans he found us that time when he swapped some of his favourite Pokémon cards for them at school. McDonalds is even better than the magic golden egg he found after Easter that we ate all in one go and got tummy aches but he still let me have the biggest bits.

But I had to eat the McDonalds in the wardrobe, which is also the secret cave, so the Giant wouldn't smell it and come to eat me.

My brother let me have all of his fries, and extra ketchup too.

One time it was dark and I was sad and my arm was hurt. I don't remember why. Maybe the Giant. Maybe... I don't know. I don't want to. But my brother found a radio in the skip outside the flats and he got some batteries from somewhere and we listened to the radio. All the music came by itself, and we were in the bedroom which is the castle and even though I was sad and my arm was all funny, we danced and my brother made it so the radio was magic and singing us songs. He said it was magic and the songs would make me feel better so they did. And we'd listen to the radio in the night-time instead of sleeping and we'd hide in the secret cave so the Giant wouldn't hear, but it was the best. My brother is the best.

Then this one time my brother made me hide in the secret cave under all the jumpers and the dressing gown that is sometimes the magic cape. I had to hide and be invisible and super quiet when the Giant and his Giant friends came to find us. They were singing the football songs and smelt like beer and they was saying they was going to have fun and my brother wasn't even a man so they would make him a little bitch and I hid and the Princess was screaming really loudly and my brother was shouting and there was all the banging and I thought maybe my secret cave wasn't really secret anymore but they never found me because my brother turned into a dragon and breathed fire on the noisy Giant friends so they all ran away scared, because my brother is the best. But the Giant was angry after that, 'cause my brother hurt his friends, even though they'd hurt him first, and there was burnt bits on the carpet and that's when the Giant made the big round red circle mark from the cigarette on my brother's arm, which maybe is magic like the Power Rangers or something.

I didn't see but I heard.

And then the Giant got bored or hungry or wanted the telly on or to go to the pub so he went away and my brother climbed into the secret cave with me and the Giant had given him the big cigarette mark which wasn't a scar yet but just all red and hot and then it went all blown up like a balloon and yellow and infected, and I had to get the Savlon from the bathroom which is also the ocean where the mermaids live. I had to find the Savlon in the big cupboard even though I'm not meant to ever *ever* go in the big cupboard 'cause of the medicines and it's dangerous. But the mermaids helped me be brave and we sang the brave songs and it was fun 'cause the ocean in the bathroom makes my voice sound big. And I found the Savlon and took it to my brother and he said it was a quest, a hero's quest and that I'd saved him. I was the best brother that day.

But then because of the maybe magic cigarette circle mark and them making him a little bitch, the Giant stole my brother's voice and he was sad so we hid there for years and years. Maybe a whole week. I don't remember. The Princess got us sandwiches then, but we didn't even have to go to school which was awesome.

You want to know about last week? What was last week?

I don't know.

I don't remember.

It was very loud.

I don't want to tell it.

I want to play with the Lego. Legoes are the best. You can make anything you want from the bits you've got.

OK.

Yes.

It was Sunday which is the worst day because that's football and pub day.

The Giant came home all loud and stomping. I thought we would hide in the secret cave again, but my brother got big. He suddenly got so big like he wasn't a boy no more and he said the bad words and he got his sword and he went down into the dungeon because the Princess was crying and then my brother rescued the Princess and she turned back into our mam. It was our mam with her hair all cut off and a black bruise on her eye and it was all swelled shut and puffy, so I hadn't recognised her before. But it was Mam. Then she and my brother, they got big. All big and strong and they got bigger than the Giant. Bigger than the world. Bigger than the whole house even and they roared and had a battle and made the Giant go away.

Mam who is the Princess says he won't come back no more. I know the Giant won't be back no more because my brother is the best brother and I saw him. My brother is called Jack and he is Jack the Giant Killer.

Can I play with the Lego now?

Where's my brother? Can I see him? He's been gone for ages now.

Is that a really real policeman's hat? Can I wear it?

* * *

137

Hoof And Horn

The hospital is a labyrinth of squeaky floors, flickering lights and uncomfortable chairs that sprout into corridors in little groups of twos or threes like strange fungus. In this respect it is much like every hospital ever. Adelaide Ward smells of hand sanitiser, gloopy hospital food and unmistakeably, faintly, of wee. It is also unbearably hot in here. Again, in this respect, it is exactly like every other hospital I have ever spent any time in. They tell me the Air Con is on, but I don't believe them. I can feel the wetness in my armpits, at the nape of my neck. This corner of Adelaide Ward houses four beds. Only two are currently occupied; one by Darren who is nineteen and has a brain tumour. He is asleep every time I come here, but sometimes calls out fitfully for his mum and someone called Charlie. Today his mum was pacing the long hallway outside the ward. I saw her when I arrived. She had that bleak, faraway look in her eyes that I know from the inside. She walked angrily back and forth, a tissue gripped in her hand, pressed to her mouth. It was soggy and limp and, when she saw me approaching the ward, she pulled it away to smile thinly.

"Not great, today," she'd told me, and I'd squeezed her arm.

The other bed in this end of Adelaide Ward is occupied by my grandfather. He is awake, sour and bitter and gumming an orange slice. He says the chemo makes his gums hurt, so his teeth are floating in a plastic cup on his table.

I'm sitting on a high-backed vinyl foam-padded chair at the side of my grandfather's bed. I'm too hot and the air is stale. There's a fan on a tall pole slowly rotating, moving already-hot air over us every once in a while. The T.V is on and we are watching the news. It's a segment about the heatwave across Europe right now. Paris, the presenter tells us, is marking today as the hottest recorded temperature *ever*, and that architects working on the restoration of Notre Dame Cathedral are concerned that the heat will cause exposed beams to dry, shrink and collapse, or possibly to catch fire once again.

"Bloody Frenchies..." my grandfather mutters, rolling the orange slice around into his good cheek. He's eighty-seven and he has terminal liver cancer. It's in his spleen and his blood too, they say. He had a stroke three weeks ago just before a chemo session and the very abrupt but kind specialist told me it was probably linked to his cancer, that we were talking months if he was lucky, and they were already talking with the hospice down the road to take him in if he got to a stage where he could move out of Adelaide Ward. It was silently implied that this might not happen, given his age and what-have-you. They've had to stop his chemo after the stroke because the cocktail of drugs would kill him quicker than the ailments.

My grandma died in this hospital twelve years ago; she'd had a fall and then, I suppose, her body just decided it was time, and she hadn't come home. My mum, too, last year. With her, it had been throat cancer. So here I sit, clammy and uncomfortable, in a hospital I've spent far more than my fair share of time in, in a cancer ward full of dying people, with my grandad who is also dying and doesn't like me very much. Grandad doesn't like anyone very much. I suppose he must have liked Grandma once, years ago. Now, he is shrivelled and too skinny, like Gollum. He's paralysed on one side, so his left arm is curled and folded into his lap, his left hand bent and claw-like. His face is sagging on that side too. He's only, within the last week, regained his ability to swallow properly so now he is allowed to eat soft solids under supervision. He swears about that too, says they give him 'effin' baby food'. I thought he might appreciate the orange, and since he's not commented on it, I guess that's a win. He's toothless, mauling the orange slice to death with the gums on the good side of his face, dribbling orange pith down his chin, angrily swearing at the T.V because the presenter dares to say France is having a worse time of this heatwave than us. Miserable old fuck, but he's the only family I've got left now. Stef says I don't have to sit here and watch a bitter old man die. But. I look at Darren, bunching his sheets into his fists in his sleep. I look at the empty beds that weren't empty last week. I see the people that get admitted here and get no visitors, no one to watch the T.V with or bring them oranges. No one should die alone, I think, and I've become quite adept at the half-life of visiting hours and canteen food, and the strange silence in the world that comes after death.

The news segment is now doing a fill-in piece on the fire that destroyed the spire and roof of Notre Dame earlier in the year.

"Bloody terr'ists..." Grandad mutters.

I sigh. "Actually, Grandad, the fire wasn't terrorists. They don't even think it was arson. It was most likely 'cause of the renovations they were doing at the time. Like when Windsor Castle caught fire."

Grandad swivels his eyes to look at me as if I've just magically appeared in the chair. Sometimes, I wonder if he forgets I'm even here, every afternoon from 2.30 'til 4 p.m.

"Haven't you got work?" he slurs. The orange slice plops out of his mouth into his lap, wetly. He uses his good hand to push it back in, not taking his eyes from me.

I sigh. He knows very well that I quit my job after Mum died.

"Poems isn't a job," he tells me, "*actually.*" He smirks and manages an eyebrow raise, and he's peering into my soul with his watery eyes. Since the stroke, he only speaks in short cannon-fire sentences. It's taken me a while to learn to decipher what he's saying through the slur.

"I know, Grandad." I place my hands on the arms of the chair and look only at the T.V despite his challenge.

My spoken-word poetry and art have been making me pocket money over the last eight months. I bought a house outright with my inheritance,

140

once I'd cleared and sold Mum's place and got all the probate sorted. Hours and hours of paperwork and sorting through files, speaking to lawyers, signing things and making copy after copy of the death certificate to send off or email to a million people, when all I'd wanted to do was sleep. But the house I'd finally bought, *my* house, was a 1930s semi on the outskirts of the city. It had previously been owned by one person that had used it as two flats, with the owner living downstairs and renting the upstairs out. One external front door but two lockable inner doors, one leading up the stairs. The Estate Agents had been struggling to sell a single house with two kitchens and two tiny bathrooms. The woman who'd showed me round said I could make the upstairs kitchen into another bedroom, or a family sized bathroom, take out the two inner doors. *Unify the property,* she'd said. But I took it just as it was and kept it that way. I live downstairs and lease upstairs to my mate. I charge Stef way lower than market value, but I live off her rent. I do poetry gigs at bars and cafés that cater for the crowd that wants something between awkward singer-songwriters and swanky jazz bands. I stand up and recite sad poems and sometimes, I accidentally cry in front of strangers, and they pay me for it. My self-published book does OK at the gigs; people feel like they ought to buy one, after I stand up there and bare my soul at them about grief and trauma. Stef says it's like paying the ferryman their silver coins, although I'm not sure what my poems ferry them to.

All in all, I'm lucky. White-girl Grammar-School privileged. My mum worked hard and saved and had money tucked away in all sorts of weird stocks and bonds. I've got no siblings. No children of my own. I'm set. Except... losing my mum, my best friend, my fixer of things, my mender of broken hearts, my comrade and confidant, before I was thirty, has done something to me.

Have you ever heard of the Rose of Jericho? It's a type of resurrection plant; a fern-like tumbleweed-y thing that lives in the desert and can survive

141

without any water. During drought it dries up and curls up into a tiny ball like a hedgehog, looking like a brown brittle ball of dead twigs. It's not dead, but it only uncurls, reborn and green, if it gets exposed to moisture. That's me. I'm dried out and rolled up tight. I do the poetry and it's a release. I hang out with friends, drink wine, laugh. Sometimes I sleep with Tan. I have a large black and white cat called Tomlyn that I spoil. I write and I paint and I make things out of clay and I sell my little bits and bobs online. I do craft fairs. But I'm curled in on myself. Dormant. Not dead, but not exactly alive. There is drought. I *am* drought.

"Did you know that Notre Dame was built on the site of an older church?" I say. Grandad is studying me, masticating his orange and dribbling. "Before she was Our Lady of Paris, that bit of land in the middle of the Seine was a church to Saint Stephen, but under that, there was remains of a Romano-Gallic temple to Jupiter. Before *that*, some reckon, it was a sacred site to the goddess Isis."

"Isis like terr'ists?" Grandad's eye brighten. He loves a good rant about the 'terr'ists'.

"No, Isis like the Egyptian goddess," I say and he slumps back, turns his head back to the T.V, disappointed.

The T.V is showing footage of the fire, the crowds in the square singing hymns as the flames roared. "And then she burnt..." I finish.

Grandad mutters, "But still she stands."

I'm taken aback by this rare moment of poetry escaping his drooping, drooling mouth. But it's not long-lived, as he farts then says "Wasted that degree of yours."

There's no question there. Just a statement of reality to him. I have wasted. I am wasted. I waste. I suppose, beneath the surliness, he is trying to tell me he thinks I am smart. It's the nicest thing he's said to me in years.

I peel him another segment of orange and slide it onto the hinged table over his legs, mop at his chin with the paper napkin that the nurse left me. He grunts and rolls his head away from me, then says "Find that nurse, I need to piss."

I do as I'm bid, pass Darren's bed and Darren's mum who's curled up in her chair reading her magazine, still gripping her soggy tissue. We swap tight 'relative of dying person' smiles and I go in search of a nurse or HCA.

When the two care assistants pull the curtain back from around Grandad's bed, he's already sleeping. The stroke, the chemo, it all makes him so tired. Asleep and unclenched, he looks as frail as dandelion seeds. I kiss him on the top of his head, hair patchy and skin waxy, then wrap the remaining un-gummed orange segments in a sandwich bag and gather my things.

I navigate my way back to the main entrance (straight along the corridor from the ward, third left to the stairs, down three floors, right, left, straight). Mum had been on Kingfisher Ward. The ward sister there is called Colleen and she's the one that called me in the middle of the night to say Mum had gone. I'd been there for forty-eight hours without sleep, reading to her, holding her hand, watching her slip away on her morphine train. Eventually, Colleen sent me home, told me I'd be no good to anyone by making myself poorly too. Stef had collected me, bought us Chinese that we ate in silence. I'd showered and slept for maybe about an hour when the phone rang. Of course, Mum had waited for me to leave her in peace. Of course, she hadn't wanted me to be there at the actual moment she'd paid her own ferryman. Colleen was the one who had straightened Mum up, made her look serene and smooth before I came to see her. Colleen had met me at the ward door and hugged me and given me Mum's jewellery before I'd forced my legs to carry me into that little side room where she... I blink and grit my teeth. No.

143

I hate hospitals. I loathe them. The air in here is heavy and sticks to me like mucous. I can almost feel it trying to suck me back in. The energy in the walls is so fractious. I always feel like I can't breathe here, am always desperate to get out. As I approach the huge glass atrium with the electronic doors that hiss open and shut repeatedly, I almost want to break into a run. I can feel the intense heat radiating in from outside. The heat out there has got to be better than the smell and the memories in here, so I don't even stop. I just plough right out into the baking, humid English sunshine and dash to my car.

The steering wheel is almost too hot to touch. Though my little car has A/C, I wind all the windows down and let the hot air blast me, lifting my hair at the roots. I'm heading home, but all that awaits me there is a dozen unfinished poems, the novel that's sucking my soul out through my eye sockets, a heap of ceramic pots to list on my online shop and an un-mowed garden. Stef is at work until five. I consider stopping at Asda for wine and one of those boxed up curry meals for two. I again get that caged in, hollow feeling. Like, the Universe knows underneath all this, I am brittle and dry and... not dead but... waiting. I consider calling Tan, see if a little afternoon delight wouldn't go amiss, wouldn't maybe kindle some kind of spark of life in me. But Tan works in Woking and it's a Thursday and the traffic will probably be bad since it's school-chuck-out time. And I am so sick of myself right then that I thump the steering wheel and open my mouth and yell and honk the car horn repeatedly on an empty stretch of B-road.

This road back from the hospital is winding and lined by old, moss-covered and crumbling drystone wall. The woods grow up on either side here. Some of the trees meet overhead. Mum used to call these mottled patches over the road where the sky is blocked out with a leafy canopy 'tree-places' and, out of habit or refusal to let childhood memories and tradition die, I call out, "Tree-place!" to the empty car and road.

144

And then there's that choking vice-grip around my throat again and I can't see straight. And it's so, so hot. I can't breathe. So I pull into the driveway of the nature reserve a little too sharply, drive down to the parking area and find a shady spot, turn off the engine, grab my bag and get out before I really know what I'm doing.

It is still hot, but not as hot as out there. It's dry here. Not humid. There's a cool breeze. There are butterflies. Birds calls out, their mates or children or enemies or second cousins once removed call back an echoing reply. I have not bought hiking shoes, only my chunky open-toed sandals. I am not wearing hiking clothes, but rather the too-long tent-like dress over leggings and sports bra. But I walk. I don't even consciously choose which of the trails I am taking but I walk slowly along a mostly shaded flint path that has cracked in the heat. The sun breaks through the tall trees in defiant bursts to remind me it's still there, but as I walk further into the forest, even the sound of the traffic on the motorway fades. I am alone and the forest takes me in, like the ample bosom of a doting aunt.

It's not like I haven't grieved. I cried for hours, days. Sometimes I think the last year has been nothing but tears and weird sleeping patterns and that horrific choked up feeling like something has got my throat in a choke hold. I'm not bottling my emotions up, honestly. I talk about Mum a lot. I cry at everything. Dog food adverts. Songs in T.V shows. I cry when I see daffodils and when I see Happy Birthday Mum cards in Tesco. Sometimes, I just cry when I run out of coffee. Believe me, I have grieved. I am grieving. But I'm hollow.

I do all the good stuff, too. I surround myself with life and light and good people who have carried me and all my unravelled edges across this ravine. I read all the stuff about bereavement. All the books and blogs say this grief now will just shift into something less raw, but never not be here. I get that. I've got sun-catchers in all the windows. I meditate, I do yoga, I take long powerwalks and I journal. I create. Christ, there's nothing like bereavement to shove a creative firecracker up your chuff. How many poems have fallen out of me in the wake of losing her? But. How can I explain it? Everything is so close to the surface, all the emotions right here on top all the time, but beneath that, I'm just sort of... nothingy.

I follow the path and it is relatively flat and cool and I'm not even really looking at the trees, I'm so lost in my head. Usually when I've been here before, it's been full of dog walkers or BMX-ers or kids toddling around while their parents try to stop them eating whatever they pick up or killing themselves by pitching headfirst in the brambles and stinging nettles. Today, it's been deserted, and I haven't seen or heard another human in, I check the time on my phone, nearly an hour. How can that be? One minute I was on the verge of some hysterical melt down panic attack in the car and the next, I am swallowed by this place, this cathedral of tall trees and sunlight and quiet. The forest has stretched out sounds and space and time. It could be now or last year or thousands of years ago or a million years from now and this place, I bet, would be just the same. And, like cathedrals, and even hospitals I guess, this place has a weird pulsing stillness.

Something darts through the undergrowth. A squirrel, perhaps. Leaves and twigs drop occasionally from the canopy. I can see pollen drifting like pixies in the shafts of sunlight. And the birds, lively, incessant, flit above me. It's very alive, in a quiet, secret sort of way. But I'm still sweating, and my eyes are drawn to the shaded centre of the woods. Something in me craves that cool, sheltered place – true solitude, away from the path even. I step off of the flint track into the mulchy undergrowth, hitch my dress up so I don't trip, and walk into the heart of the forest.

Gradually, it changes. The forest, the air, the light, the feel of it. It grows darker. Less 'cathedral to nature and peace' and more like something out of Hansel and Gretel. There are more fallen limbs to climb over or round. The trees here are older and closer and their barks sport gnarled faces.

146

Even the birds sound different here. I can't see the sky now. I've got bramble scratches on my shins and bare arms, and I have no idea why I thought this would be a good idea. I'm not hot anymore, I suppose. It even smells different here. Back on the sun-dappled path it smelt dry and baked. Here, it smells damp. Like the underside of a flipped log or paving slab, when all the wiggling bugs and worms freak out and try to hide. That soft, peat-y, mossy smell of deep-down decay, but also the smell of green. I can't describe it better than that, but do you know what I mean? Green, like grass cuttings and growing things and dirt. The ground here is uneven, all the tangled twisty roots making dips and hollows full of murky pools and slippery leaves that could easily catch a foot and break an ankle.

There are occasional snaps and cracks in the undergrowth, and after a while, I become certain I'm being watched. I stop in a small clearing, dazzled by the suddenly-very-bright and hot sunshine, shielding my eyes, and look about, peering into the knee-high oak saplings all around, squinting into the darkness of the trees beyond. There is movement. Could it be a badger? Rabbit? Axe murderer? I think I see something move from the corner of my eye – not down low, but up at eye level. Axe murderer it is, then. I'm envisaging news headlines – *local young woman is moron and takes a walk through Murderer Wood*. I do that thing where I'm trying not to look nervous but I know my shoulders are slowly making their way up towards my ears. A female deer explodes out of the thicket with a crash, leaps across the clearing I'm standing in and disappears into the forest behind me. I exhale, tell the already-gone doe to fuck off, hitch my bag onto my shoulder, laugh, and only then wonder what startled the doe.

Still, I feel eyes on me. There could be a whole herd of deer staring at me from that dense thicket. All sorts of animals. A thousand eyes and ears trained on me. Maybe that axe murderer is just biding his time. Could be a her, I suppose. I'm glancing all around me, knowing I'm being ridiculous to get spooked in the middle of the woods but unable to shake this strange watched, uneasy feeling that has settled on me. I see, or almost see, something move again. Movement from the corner of my eyes. I can't tell if I'm imagining things, or not.

I'm tired. I'm exhausted. Soul-weary. This is why. I'm pushing my body too hard, after everything, with Mum, now Grandad, in this stupid heatwave. Why is it so fucking hot, anyways? Global warming can do one if it's going to give me the heebie-jeebies around some stupid trees. That's why I'm feeling unnerved. I'm hot and tired. There's nothing there. I know that. My logical brain is repeating all this but that doesn't stop me feeling a creeping sense of... something. Bated breath. Even the odd, sad-sounding birds have fallen silent.

I feel my skin raise into goose bumps, feel all the hairs on my arms stand on end. I've only ever felt like this once before, when I ventured into the attic space of Tan's dad's friend's Victorian B&B to help them look for a leak, and a chair moved on its own and I knew there was something up there. I booked it down the stairs as fast as I could and I knew that it was haunted.

From somewhere, nowhere, everywhere at once, I can suddenly hear the sound of horses racing towards me. Startled, I spin around in my little clearing, unable to see anything. The sound is close and all around me now. Not trotting, not gently ambling, but galloping. Hooves pounding the earth, bracken breaking, snorts and neighs. Dogs barking, too. I can't see anything. No dust thrown up into the air, no horses, no riders, no dogs. Nothing. But I hear it. I feel it, reverberating up through the ground, through my legs and within my chest, like the deep bass at a music festival. I can smell it, rank wet fur and the iron smell of blood. The heavy scent of stale sweat and urine. The panting of horses and dogs, their spittle, the hot air of their breath. There's the clanking sound of metal on metal. I feel like, if I stretched out an arm, it would be shorn off at the elbow by some sweeping, invisible blade. I am being corralled by some unseen group of riders. A horn blares, mournful, filling the clearing, and I can barely breathe. My brain can't make sense of what I'm hearing and not seeing. I'm sinking down to my knees, pressing my palms against my ears, it's so loud! Too loud! My mouth is hanging open in a silent scream. I screw my eyes shut.

And then it stops. The crazy churning charge of circling horses and dogs and riders doesn't gallop away into the trees. It doesn't fade away into silence. It just stops very abruptly. I'm crouched painfully amid broken twigs and leaves and soggy earth, feet and dress and leggings and shins all muddy. My heart is racing, but it is now the only sound I can hear. I carefully look around me, at the empty, still clearing in the middle of the twisted forest. I hear birds again. I think, vaguely, that I should perhaps wonder if I'm having some kind of psychotic break, but I know I'm not.

Very slowly, awkwardly, I stand up, pull my little canvas bag back onto my shoulder, push my hair out of my face, decide to file this in the 'weird shit that has happened to me' bank ready for future pub or late-night BBQ sessions, and walk out of the clearing the way the doe ran earlier. The trees close back in overhead.

I wonder why I'm so calm, why I'm not running the hell back to my car and calling Tan or Stef in a panic. I'm muddy, with green smears all over me, just casually strolling back into the forest. I think, as I walk, it must be because, by this point, after everything, I have lost the ability to sustain fear for very long. Every single day since my mum fell ill, since her diagnosis, through every meeting and appointment, through the hair failing out and the night-time vomiting while I stroked her back, through them telling us the treatment wasn't working, right up until the day she died, I was afraid. I don't think anything else will ever be as terrifying. It's all part of that strange void I feel at the centre of myself. So I carefully pick my way through thicket and undergrowth, crouch beneath a fallen tree that lays diagonally across the path I've decided I'm taking, and find myself straightening up in front of a man with antlers growing out of his head.

He sits, bare-chested and cross legged, beneath a huge, knobbly, old oak tree. Now I know my brain isn't catching up with reality, because I spontaneously say, "Oh!" and nothing else.

The cross-legged, antlered man says, "All right?"

He sounds a bit cockney, so it comes out more like '*Or-wight?*'. Then he grins, and holds out a tinfoil container like you get from the takeaway, and asks, "D'you want an onion bhaji?"

Now, I can't say I've much experience of spending time around mystical forest people with antlers, but this is really not on the list of things I expect them to say. He seems to clock the look on my face, makes an 'ah' expression, lowers the tinfoil takeaway tray to the floor, straightens his back and says, in a deeply booming voice,

"Welcome, traveller. I am Cernunnos, Lord of the Forest. Sit, and we may speak a while."

I'm not scared. I'm not confused. I know I'm not dreaming or drunk or 'having an episode' or anything. This middle-aged bloke with the full on, velvety-looking antlers sprouting out of his mop of brown hair, with his bare barrel chest all covered in reddish brown hair and the dirt-coloured trousers, with the bronze torcs around both his biceps and the tawny, honey coloured eyes, this bloke who looks a bit like Tan's uncle Dave, is absolutely, one-hundred percent Cernunnos, Lord of the Forest, and I am utterly calm.

I slouch onto my hip. "*Traveller?*" I say, incredulously.

"It's gender neutral, innit." He shrugs. "Big thing, these days. Have a bhaji. They're fuckin' blindin'."

Cernunnos is grinning. There's a twinkle in his eye. He's big, has a gut that's solid rather than flabby, but there's something quick and alert about him, a darkness to the edge of him. I can't help but think that he reminds me of those blokes down the pub with their faded tattoos and sovereign rings. The sort of blokes who know someone who can get you whatever you need for cheap, no questions asked. Big teddy bears who will call you *darlin'* and not mean anything weird by it, but just as soon as break someone's leg on the quiet as grin at you. His big smile lessens a little as he appraises me standing before him, and he leans back against the trunk of the huge tree, crossing those massive arms of his. The torcs dig into his forearms. His antlers scrape against the tree bark.

"Look, I didn't get all dressed up for nuffin'," he says. "I've got other things I could be doing. The Chase is on, you know. Sit your arse down and let's have a chat."

So I do. I promptly drop down to my bum, tuck my now-muddy tent dress around my knees and stare at him.

"It has been a *really* weird day..." I mumble. Day? More like year.

"Tell me about yer mum," he says, out of nowhere.

"Excuse me?" I frown at him. He just grins again and waits.

I puff my cheeks out. You don't avoid questions asked to you by a real-life Lord of the Forest with antlers, do you? Saying 'I'd rather not, if it's all the same' somehow doesn't feel like it's going to wash.

"Uhhh..." I look at my toes, grubby now, nail polish chipping off. I wiggle them. "Her name was Jan."

"Good name, that is." He nods approvingly.

"She was, um, just turned fifty-three when she died. She..." I steal a look at Cernunnos, and though his expression is open and kind, I somehow know that this isn't quite right. He seems to be expecting more than stats

151

and facts. He stretches out a bare foot and nudges the tinfoil tray towards me.

"It'll help, honestly. I dunno how Sanjay up the Delhi Belly on the high street does it, but these things are little mouthfuls of magic."

I obligingly pluck a fist-sized oily, crispy globe out of the tray, pick off a bit of golden fried onion and eat it thoughtfully. The cumin and turmeric blossom on my tongue. It's buttery, warm, comforting. I take a bite, contemplate its taste, lick my lips.

"She was big and brash and loud and wonderful." I smile, pulling apart the delicate bhaji, watching the yellow oil ooze over my fingertips. "She was... radiant. She was my home, my north star, and..." I stop. No.

"Yes." Cernnunos says gently.

I shake my head.

"We ain't going anywhere till you do."

If he knows what I'm clamping my teeth down on, then why does he need me to say it?

"I wouldn't be here if you didn't need me to be, would I? If you didn't need to say it." He's casually cleaning dirt out from under his thumb nail with a small twig, raises his eyebrows at me.

It's as if his gentle tawny eyes, his insistent kindness, undoes something. I don't often let people just be kind to me. It hurts too much, and I am too bruised to receive nice things that might be snatched away without warning.

I unclench my jaw, "It's... it's not fair..."

I'm crying now. Again. It hurts. Again. It's all there, again. The fear and the exhaustion. Watching her waste away. Seeing her lovely face contorting in pain that she refused to complain about. The way she would call out when she lost consciousness, like Darren in the bed beside Grandad's

152

does, incoherently. And it's that phone call all over again. And it's seeing her laid in the bed afterwards while I'm clutching her rings and gold chain, and she looks beautiful and all the pain has melted from her face but she is utterly gone from that body. And now it's the funeral again and I am reading my eulogy and I'm not crying at all and everyone is surprised but they don't know I'm not even really there. And now I'm sitting in the middle of the empty dining room on the bare floorboards of the house I grew up in again, and it's empty and I am empty. I am empty.

Cernunnos opens his arms and I scooch over and, yes, I climb into his big lap like a forlorn kitten mewling for its mother. It's an ugly cry, with the snot and the hiccups and the scrunched-up face. I'm still cradling the bhaji in my open palm and it's leaked oil everywhere. Cernunnos holds me against his big chest and strokes my hair, makes soothing low noises. I am so small and I am too big and awkward and nothing fits right anymore.

Cernunnos holds me until my sobs settle and I'm sniffing back snot. Then he waits without saying a word while I sit in his lap and finish off the bhaji – it really is the best bhaji I've ever had. I wipe my oily hands on the mossy grass. Then he urges me to stand up, unfolding himself in the process. He is almost impossibly tall – well over six feet and that's without the antlers. He puts his hands on my shoulders and I look up at him. He smiles. It's a small, simple, kind smile that isn't all full of the bullshit most people's smiles are full of. I wonder why this isn't weird. It should be all the levels of weird. But it's not.

"Better?" he asks. I sniff and nod. "Lets go find you somewhere to wash your face." He turns and stalks away into the trees.

I grab my bag and follow after him, and he takes me to a little stream. I crouch down and let the cool water run through my fingers, wash away the remnants of the bhaji, scoop some up and splash it on my face and the back of my neck. When I look up, my skin feeling tight and squeaky, Cernunnos has settled cross-legged beneath another tree. A squirrel, a couple of rabbits, and a lot of birds are hanging out around him. He's petting the squirrel.

"Do you..." I hesitate, and he looks at me, "do you live here?"

He mulls it over for a moment, scratching his belly, then says, "When I need to. I like it here. Not a bad gaff, is it?" He gestures to the vaulted trees. The squirrel runs back up into the tree. The rabbits are doing their thing in the grass. A bird of some kind flutters down to sit on his knee.

"What are you?" I ask. He fixes me with a hard look and I almost feel embarrassed. "Are... you..." I remember the stone pillar dedicated to Jupiter found beneath Notre Dame Cathedral, on the island in the middle of the river, with its many carvings of gods. I know Cernunnos was on that pillar.

He laughs at my awkwardness and the bird takes flight, then he scratches at his hair, places a hand on an antler thoughtfully, as if checking it was still there. "I'm a story. That's all. A story told so many times by so many people that I just sort of... happened. Seeped into the roots of the wild places. I'm a ghost. A thought. A symbol. There's always been stories about the green places, the wild places, the lost places, the journey places, and things that live in them."

I nod, not sure I entirely understand. "What now?" I ask.

"Now?" He grins. "Now you need to let go my girl, and get back on with your life."

"Let go? Let *what* go? D'you mean my *mum*?! Because I am not letting her..." I feel indignance thrumming in my voice. The other birds sitting in his antlers and pecking at the dirt and grass around him fly off, startled. Even the rabbits look at me, annoyed.

"Not that." He smiles. "That story's a part of you like I'm a part of the trees. You can't shed that even if you wanted to. No. I mean you need to unfurl. Let in some of the Sun, the water. It's time to stop holding on so tightly and wringing the life out of yourself. Go into that space inside. Don't keep it locked up. Breathe into it. Flow into it."

I remember the Rose of Jericho. I am parched and I am waiting. "How?" I ask.

In response, Cernunnos grabs up a meaty fistful of leaves from the forest floor, rises to his feet and holds his fist out over the stream. He looks at me to make sure I'm watching. Then he releases the leaves, lets them fall into the water. We watch the leaves drift away.

"Am I the leaves, or the water?" I ask.

He cuffs me gently on the top of my head. "Both, you idiot."

I rub my head. "Alright, *Yoda...*"

He laughs. It's a harvest laugh, deep and full.

"Before I bumped into you, earlier, I heard..." I sit back on my haunches, struggling to describe the sound of phantom horses I'd experienced earlier.

"The Wild Hunt," he tells me and once again my bare arms break out in goosebumps. "It's part of my story, too. Or maybe even an older story. Maybe it's all just the same story."

I look up at him, and he's sort of fuzzy around the edges. Soft and unfocussed. He doesn't quite look like him anymore. He is still tall, still antlered, but now he is wearing furs and pelts and he holds a sword.

"The story has many versions, and there are many names," he says and his voice is different, a voice seeped into soil and root and leaf and blood.

His form is shifting, melting, changing. He's Cernunnos and then he's Herne the Hunter of the Wild Hunt. Then he's Pan with his faun's legs and short curled horns. Then the horns are gone, and his hair is long and flowing and he is Oberon. Then he's cloaked and shadowed, his face unseen beneath his hood of green and he wields quarterstaff and long bow with a quiver of arrows on his back. Then he is an old man, haggard, one eye missing and he holds a spear and there are ravens on each shoulder. Then he is a stag, and then he is a man-like shape made of leaves, and then he is the wind through branches and the sound of wolves. Then he is the darkness. And then, he is gone.

When I get home, finally, it's dusk. I can see the lights are on upstairs. I have a missed call and three messages from Stef, and a couple of messages from Tan. I send a quick 'all is well' message to them both. Then, after a moment's contemplation, follow it with a message suggesting we all try out the Indian on the high street next week. I'm covered in mud and moss. There are twigs, pollen and spiderwebs in my hair. There are green stains pressed into the whorls and lines on my palms.

I drop my bag in the hallway and leaves, acorns, feathers, pinecones, the strange split cases of seeds, stones, all the forest gifts that I collected, spill out. I kick off my sandals, and walk barefoot through the kitchen, throw open the back door and pick my way carefully into my un-mowed, overgrown garden, all lopsided daisies and clover and knee-high grass. Somewhere out here, Tomlyn the cat is stalking his prey; I can hear him making little chirruping noises and pinging around.

The sun has set and the sky is a wildfire. It is still so hot, but I can breathe now. I lay down on the cracked dry earth and close my eyes. I think about Notre Dame and the fire and wonder if any of her beams shrank and collapsed today. I think about the bones upon which she is built, the past holding her up, the stories seeped into the ground beneath her. Still, she stands. After everything.

I can feel the sweat beading in my hairline, trickling behind my ears, dripping into the gasping earth. My tears follow, hot and slow. I can almost hear the dry ground hissing. I breathe deeply.

I feel the clenched fist at the centre of myself begin to unfurl, and, despite all signs and suggestions to the contrary, know that somewhere inside, there is green. I'm as light and frail as dandelion seeds but...

Something is stirring in me.

Something is growing.

I am a leaf in the stream.

I am a holy island in the middle of a river.

* * *

And I Shall Go Into A Hare

"I shall go into a hare,
With sorrow and sych and meickle care..."
(From the recorded confession of Isobel Gowdie, 1662)

I first saw her through the living room window. She was struggling in through the front door with her groceries, peering over a big bag of Monster Munch balanced precariously on the top of her shopping as she struggled to get her keys into the front door. I could see she'd gone for pickled onion flavour. When I'd been working in New Zealand, I'd ask anyone that came to visit from the UK to bring me pickled onion Monster Munch and McVities chocolate Digestive Biscuits. It's funny the things you miss when you're away from home. Here, in this short-term rented flat on the ground floor of a townhouse with bricks gone black with soot, on a hill that hugged the edge of the Yorkshire Dales, what I missed most was my own bed. I'd been sent here for work, too. Like New Zealand. Easier to get back to see family on the weekend, but with significantly fewer trips to the beach.

I was, at the time I first saw the girl, working for a software company that sold accounting packages to businesses. I'd been sent to be an on-site rep slash glorified salesman, solving their problems by offering them additional packages at a cost. The girl lived in the upstairs flat. I knew of her existence by the post I moved from the doormat and set on the console table for her in the hall, by the Amazon parcel she'd obviously taken in and left propped against my door for me, by the sounds of her moving around up there and the occasional wafts of delicious-smelling food (I, working all the conceivable hours under the sun, was living off microwave meals for one and the occasional kebab, even though work were covering all my expenses). I knew her name was Isobel, based on her post. I had always imagined Isobels to be slight and blonde, probably based on encounters with a few women of that description and name, a few characters in T.V shows or books. But Isobel-from-upstairs, as she struggled with her Monster Munch and the stiff front door that swelled in the rain so that you had to kick it open, was a tall mass of wind-tossed dark tresses and pink round cheeks blasted from the walk up the hill from town. She wore a huge green woollen peacoat and a chunky scarf that covered most of her face, but still, it was nice to finally have a sort-of-face to put to her name and her footsteps overhead.

The next time I saw her, I was the one kicking the front door open and trying to get myself inside the hallway without closing my umbrella, trying to avoid getting myself or my laptop bag wet. I'd failed abysmally and had been forced to snap the umbrella shut before getting through the doorway. She'd been leaning out of her upstairs window pruning the window box – leafy things that I would later realise were herbs. She'd grinned and waved shortly in a way that suggested we were on the same team against the poxy British weather. That day, her mane of long black-ish hair had dangled over the basil and dripped at me.

She told me, when we reached the stage of swapping hellos in the hall, to call her Izzy. So I did. When I was leaving for work one morning at the same time as her, both of us wrapped against the wind, rain and cold, and she asked how I was doing, I told her I'd woken with a banging headache that coffee hadn't shifted, and she genuinely looked concerned. I came home that evening, peering through the fog of migraine, to find a tiny glass jar, like the ones you get jam in at B'n'B's, sat on my fraying doormat. It had a little hand-written luggage label on it that declared this was a peppermint and butterbur balm to soothe headaches and migraines, and that I should rub small amounts into each temple. It was incredibly sweet of her to have left what I could only assume was a homemade remedy (I remembered the herb window box), and after chewing Anadin and Ibuprofen all day to no effect, I was willing to try anything. As I pushed into my own soulless little flat, void of any kind of personality whatsoever,

159

I unscrewed the jar. It smelt odd. Not awful. Very peppermint-y, but also a coconut base to the balm, and under that, there was a faint dank, rotting almond scent. I guessed that must be the butterbur. But, with the ache in my eyes and the back of my head pressing in, I steeled myself and used it as directed. The headache was gone halfway through my first episode of C.S.I.

So, the next time I was grabbing myself some microwave meals and bread, and I saw that the supermarket was selling little pots of garden herbs for the kitchen – basil, coriander, curly parsley and what-have-you, I grabbed a little pot of rosemary for a quid and took it up the stairs to leave outside her door. I could smell the incense, that cheap but good stuff all the jangly hippy shops and stalls outside train stations sell. There was a dried bunch of odd-looking flowers and something that might have been a Christmas tree bauble hanging on a piece of string stuck to the door with Sellotape. It made me smile. *She* made me smile, with her herbs, her incense and her doorway charms. I was standing there admiring the pearlescent oil-slick sheen of the bauble when Izzy opened the door and looked at me, cautiously. I hadn't knocked. Maybe she'd heard me coming up the stairs.

"Are you lost?" she raised an eyebrow. She was wearing a hugely over-sized black jumper that slid off her shoulder, a collection of silver pendants and stones around her neck, a pair of ribbed grey leggings and thick rainbow-striped knee-high socks. I also noticed parts of her mane of hair were woven into braids. She was eating a Pot Noodle and there were little tomato-y stains in the corners of her full mouth.

I held out the pot of supermarket rosemary. "Thanks for the balm."

She looked from me to the plant in my hands, and her round face broke into a huge smile. She placed her Pot Noodle on some unseen surface on her side of the door and took the plant from me like it was a favourite kitten I had rescued from a tree. She stroked the silvery fronds and the smoky smell of it filled the landing for a breath.

Then she fixed me with her unflinching eyes, blinked once, and said "Don't take the offer. Wait. They'll double it if you hold off."

I frowned, but she was smiling at her little cheap pot of droopy rosemary that desperately needed a water and closing the door on me.

Three days later, one of my clients, a small-ish company that sold wooden children's toys and had their head office in Harrowgate, offered me a permanent job with them, working remotely from my home – my actual real home – on a consultant salary almost £5k a year more than I was making with the software company. Izzy's words came back to me, and with clenched jaw, I turned them down, feeling every inch of my insides squirming with lost opportunity. A week later, they offered me a wage £10k more than my current one.

I took their offer then, obviously, but would need to work three months' notice at the software place, since I'd been with them around a decade. But what were three more months if I had this dream job sitting there waiting? I wanted to thank Izzy, but I didn't know how. What does one buy a friendly neighbour witch that just helped you land the career move of the century? Nice bottle of wine, maybe? But what if she didn't drink...? All the esoteric ideas my uninitiated brain could come up with seemed ridiculous, or things that she probably already had covered. Tarot decks and crystals seemed a bit... I don't know, like someone presuming to know how much milk you like on your cereal. I could get her some nice incense, but that didn't seem to match up to what she'd done for me.

The following morning, I woke before it was properly light. I wondered if the job offer was too good to be true, whether it'd all fall through, whether I really would get to work from home and really get to spend more than two days a month in the house I'd bought the year before in Shropshire.

The house that, though I'd unpacked everything, still felt unfinished and half empty. The house that seemed to be some great, bland metaphor for me and where I found myself at thirty-five. I looked around my temporary home, in a temporary flat devoid of anything personal, and felt decidedly temporary in my skin. I thought of Izzy with her multicoloured socks and comfy sweaters, how even her front door screamed out colour and something... something decidedly *her*. The way she hadn't waited for any kind of permission or non-verbal indicator from me before she shut the door, although she was clearly pleased with the silly pot plant I'd given her. She had boundaries like no one I'd evet met; she projected them through the floorboards, and I'd only spoken to the girl, woman, a handful of times. Maybe that's all being a witch really is. Just – knowing yourself so deeply, so entirely, being so OK with that, that you stop looking for any kind of context or permission in others. Maybe all the weird woo-woo knowing stuff before she could was just what happens when you go so far into yourself that there's no interference, noise or chatter getting in the way. I think I'd been swimming in a sea of radio static for years, pinballing from what one person wanted of me to another.

I knew I'd get no more sleep, and since it was a Saturday, I decided to take a walk onto the Dales to blow the cobwebs out. Maybe somewhere along the way I'd come up with a nice present idea for Izzy. October was blustering into November, but that morning was bright and clear, with a low mist still clinging to the grass. My favourite kind of weather. You could walk for miles, climb hills and scramble boulders without breaking a sweat on a day like this. So, I walked and I thought, about Izzy and about witches. My Gran had read tea leaves. She'd also read Tarot until it stopped being a silly after-gin party game and the stuff she was reading in the cards started to happen. Then she'd wrapped up her cards and put them in the drawer with her medical stockings. They would've made a good gift for Izzy. The old Tarot deck, not the stockings. I didn't want her to think I was some creepy neighbour trying to buy her affection or her, whatever it was, skills.

Services. Any phrase I applied seemed to be a polite insinuation that she was a prostitute. I wanted to do her a good turn in return for her good turn to me. It seemed only right to thank a witch with something useful. I just wished I knew what she might find useful.

In New Zealand, there were spiritual Maori healers. I'd gone to Rotorua, where the land breathed into the air, where sulphuric steam jettisoned up out of street drains and yellowed lakes, and some of my work colleagues had wanted to go see this healer. He was a local tribal elder who, they said, could help cure my bad back that occasionally, for no reason that I could discern, would seize up and render me practically immobile. I'd gone, but felt awkward, embarrassed at being a tourist for something so deeply indigenous, something that my own forefathers had tried to quash and make illegal. The guy, swirled in these intricate patterned tattoos, had placed his hands on me, not even asked what the problem was, looked deep into my eyes with that same unflinching knowing that Izzy had, and told me my problem was that I was overworked and disconnected. He told me to walk in nature, often and with an open heart, and to let it fill me. I hadn't been sure exactly how to do that, but I'd taken it at face value and walked into the big quiet open spaces whenever I could. I didn't get back aches like that anymore. The migraines were a new development, but I suspected if I were to go back to that same tribal Maori, he'd tell me nothing much had changed on the overworked front and that, despite my long hikes when I could squeeze them in, I was still hopelessly disconnected. I was hoping this offer from the toy company would allow a little more freedom, a little more connection. Doesn't that sound perverse? That a job working from home rather than in offices all over the world should let me be more connected. But... but it would. I felt that with a strange certainty.

As I walked, my feet pulling me high into the land of rippling grass and the shadows of clouds scudding, deep in thought, a hare darted out of the bracken onto my path, ran a few paces ahead, then stopped, rose on its haunches and looked at me. It was sleek, its back legs long and powerful, the tips of its ears black as though dipped in ink. It sniffed the air, its nose twitching as it stared at me with huge great orbs for eyes. I tried to stay as still as I could, one foot still hovering above the floor midstep. It bobbed its head at me, almost like a greeting, flicked its ear and took off over the moorland, its dark tail flashing little flares of its white underside as it disappeared into the mist.

I'd never seen a hare up close like that before. Rabbits, yes, but even those only as pets. A friend of my parents used to have a huge pet rabbit that was terrifying and used to hiss and bark like a dog at the postman. I was thrilled by this encounter, like nature had sat and stared right back into me. I did feel connected, filled with a calm electricity. The rest of my walk was a bouncing of my heels, though I still hadn't thought of anything I could gift to Izzy.

I didn't see her for a while after that, though. I knew she was around, heard her coming home late at night, heard music or the laughter and clattering of crockery, or the marijuana-like smell of burning sage, but we just kept missing each other. I did find I was listening for her, though, like her routines punctuated my days, like her vibrant existence somehow shone colour into my own dreary little existence, sunlight through coloured glass onto my nine-to-five working-away-from-home life. I was really quite concerned that this wasn't healthy. I didn't want to get weird, was worried I'd start turning into some kind of crazy stalker, so it made me especially wary of seeing her. If I was about to leave for work and heard her on the stairs, I'd wait until I heard the front door slam before heading out. If I was coming back and she was climbing out of a taxi, all long legs and draped flowing kimonos, I'd hurry inside with a quick wave. I think she knew. I think she found it funny; she always gave me this knowing little smile. She liked me, I was sure, but my nervousness at not overstepping her very carefully set out boundaries entertained her.

Then, one Friday evening after work, I was invited out by one of the clients I'd been on site with, unravelling the mess they'd gotten their accounting reports into. Drinking piss-warm gassy lager in an over-crowded pub, pretending to be their mate, was the last thing I wanted. I'd rather be tucked up in the bed that wasn't mine with a packet of Jaffa cakes watching endless soothing American crime shows. I know, I know, all that blood and murder and suspense is hardly soothing, but there is something comforting to me in their formulaic predictability; everything wrapped up neatly in an hour before moving onto the next crisis. That the episodes of the same series rarely ran in chronological sequence added to the bubble of escapism. But I owed the software firm. They had accepted my resignation letter after a conference call, seeing as I was away on site. They offered me more money, an executive office, a car... I didn't want any of that, but I did need a decent reference, and I didn't like to burn any bridges. It also wasn't this particular client's fault that our software had eaten their accounts. And the guys that had invited me out seemed OK, in that corporate extrovert way. And I hadn't been out socially in bloody ages. So I went. And it was all right. We got pizza. I had too many pints. And then, as I was propping up the bar after a Jägerbomb that was definitely a bad idea, I saw her. Izzy.

Dressed up for a night out. Jeans, black lace top, biker boots, wild tresses full and glossy and black. Silver dripping from throat and ears, eyes made dark and sparkling, full mouth turned up at the corners which had once, on her landing, been stained with Pot Noodle, but which now cradled that deeply knowing and slightly cynical smile. She was with friends, I guessed. She raised her glass at me in a small salute. One of the lads I was with clocked her and asked if I knew her. I said she lived upstairs from me. He said something about it being all right for some, asked if I'd

165

asked to borrow any sugar yet. The others saw her, and there was a lot of nudging and *phwoars* and, "not bad for a chubby lass, eh?", and someone else laughingly suggested I drop something in her drink so I could take her home. Which pissed me off. It would have been so easy to swallow it down, ignore the banter that skirted the edge of this kind of bullshit. It would've been so easy to laugh along and finish my drink and go home. But three pints and a shot had made me bold. I'd handed in my notice anyway, so I told the lads to fuck off, that they were the reason women went to the loo in pairs, and that it didn't matter that it was 'only a laugh, like'. I gulped down the last of the god-awful lager, grabbed my coat and headed for the door.

It was raining but I was drunk and angry, so I pulled my collar up and stomped back to my not-home. Sometimes you need to pound out indignance through your feet. Sometimes only the heavy slap-slap of heel and toe on pavement will suffice. I stamped my way home, slammed into the not-my flat and threw my now-drenched jacket and bag into a pile in the corner. Sod the laptop. Sod work. Sod this crummy little flat where the white caulk along the back of the sink was peeling off in stringy, grubby handfuls. Sod this crummy village trying to masquerade as a town, where you were expected to go out on the lash with a bunch of troglodytes and join in with that sort of bollocks. I grabbed the open box of Jaffa cakes and went to bed to find some C.S.I or N.C.I.S or some other abbreviation to oblivion.

I woke with the T.V still on, the mostly empty packet of Jaffa cakes on my chest gone gooey, and my neck at a weird angle. I blinked, blearily, fumbled for the remote to turn everything off, vaguely aware that a sound had stirred me awake. Maybe it was the rain, or a car outside. Maybe it was something on the T.V. My mouth felt furry and my face felt distant, like it might belong to someone else, but I sat up and drank from the glass of water on the bedside table. Then I heard it again. What I can only assume was the sound that had woken me. A scratching, scrabbling sound coming from the front door. I know it's not really possible, but in my memory, I recall having this ball of dread in my stomach as I slid out of bed, pulled on some pyjama bottoms, and picked my way through the darkened flat feeling this pit of fear and of steeling myself. It's just not possible that I could know what I would find, but in my mind now, that's how I remember it.

I opened the front door of my flat into the dark hall. The console table was still askew where I'd knocked into it coming in earlier. I looked up the stairs, but they too were quiet and empty. The scratching sound came again, from outside, on the main front door. I clenched my jaw and twisted the latch, feeling the heavy old door press in on me with the wind and rain still howling beyond. There, on the doorstep, bedraggled, staring up at me with those huge globe eyes that reflected the streetlight, front paw raised where it had been scratching at the door, was the hare. As soon as I had opened the door and looked at it, it collapsed.

It was trying to hold its head up to look at me but could barely seem to manage that. It seemed to be panting as if it had leapt and sprinted for miles in the dark, cold, wet night. I stared down at it and it shifted slightly, pelt slick and shining in the rain, and showed me its back leg. It had a nasty, deep, oozing gash on it; blood had stained its grey-brown fur down to the long foot and was all smeared on its belly. It lay there on the doorstep, panting and bleeding, so I bent down, with my head hurting, and scooped it up. It was heavier than I'd anticipated, but I cradled it against my chest and brought it into the hallway, closing the door with a hip. Then, into my flat. The hare made a sound a little like a mewl and flinched.

"I'm sorry, OK?" I muttered and set the animal down on the breakfast bar where it stayed, unmoving, panting and watching me. I wasn't a vet, had no idea what I should or shouldn't do, but I felt that I needed to clean the wound, and dress it, possibly take it to the vet in the morning, if it made it through to morning. I put the kettle on, knowing boiled water was sterilised, then rooted around in the cupboard under the sink with all the junk in it, pulled out a first aid kit. When I stood straight, as the kettle filled the air with steam, I saw that the hare was attempting to lick at the wound.

"I'm not sure you should," I ventured, remembering a cat we'd had when I was young that had ripped out its back claw and then made the whole foot green and stinking and infected by licking at it. I nudged at the hare's head and it snarled at me, lashing out with its powerful other hind leg. It startled me and I dropped the first aid kit so it cracked open and threw its contents across the floor. Sighing, I picked up the gauze and tiny pipette bottle of iodine and held them out to the hare. It sniffed, whiskers twitching, and lay its head down on the worktop, laying still. I took that to be permission. I poured a mug-full of warm boiled water into my coffee cup that sat clean on the draining board, poured in a teaspoon of table salt, stirred it and dipped a piece of folded kitchen paper towel into it.

"Hold still," I whispered, and laid my hand on the hare. I could feel it trembling, its heart beating so furiously beneath my palm. Its eyes had closed. With the other hand, I cleaned the blood from the fur, inspected the wound. It was deep but it oozed a clear-ish liquid, not the brackish thick greenish yellow puss I remembered from the poor infected cat. I dripped on some iodine, felt the hare convulse in pain, then placed the clean gauze over the gash, followed by a clean bandage from the first aid kit. It was far too long so I cut it with the kitchen scissors, secured it with a knot around the hare's hind leg, and stepped back. The hare opened its brown eyes, flicked its black-tipped ears at me, lifted its head as if to try and get up.

"You shouldn't. Rest, heal. For Christ's sake, don't lick or scratch at it, we'll get it sorted properly in the morning. Don't die," I told it. I grabbed a discarded sweater of mine from the back of the sofa, made a little pile of it on the pillows and then, gingerly scooped up the hare and placed it on the little nest I'd made. It glared at me indignantly but didn't try to kick me again. Shaking with spent adrenaline and the gnawing concern that this lump of half-eaten wild thing would stop breathing at some point in the night, I slid to the floor, still in only my pyjama bottoms, grabbed a blanket throw from the sofa for myself and clicked on the big T.V. There was always a crime show on, somewhere. We found an episode of Law and Order Special Victims Unit and watched it together, the hare and I. Then we watched some really old Inspector Morse. Then I dozed off again.

When I woke for the second time, it was daylight. The rain seemed to have stopped, but I could tell by the way the light fell across the floor, the thinness of it, that it was still early. I blinked, twisted and looked at the sofa behind me. It was empty, save for a little bloodied stain on the sweater-nest. I scoured the flat, but it was empty too. Then I did the only other conceivable thing I could think of and ran up the stairs to hammer on the door up there. She opened it. She was wearing a large baggy white T-shirt that came to her knees, and her legs were bare. She was pale, the dark circles beneath her eyes were like bruises, like thumb smudges of soot. Her hair was matted. She held the door close against her hip. I stared at her. I didn't know what to say as she scrutinised me silently. Then she licked her cracked lips and said,

"Thank you. For last night. I owe you a debt."

"No." I shook my head. "Consider it me repaying you for the job."

We spoke in half sentences, dancing around the truth, never quite saying it, but not needing to. She looked down at her leg and I could see it was bruised terribly, swollen, and that she'd clearly re-dressed it with new bandages.

"What happened?" I asked.

She snapped her eyes back to my face and I was reminded of the fierce, pained look in her eyes the night before. But her face softened slightly.

169

"Men." She sneered. "Men that wanted to take what wasn't offered. They chased me."

I didn't know whether she meant that men had chased her, in her black lace and silver jewellery, or if men had chased her as a hare. Then I realised it didn't really matter.

"I'm sorry," I mumbled.

She placed a cool hand on my arm. "Never apologise for what's not yours to pick up. If you hadn't helped me..." She left that sentence hanging like the mist on the moors. She smiled thinly, nodded, pressed a single cool kiss onto my cheek, fixed me with her solid brown eyes and her inky hair, and she closed the door.

I walked on the moors that afternoon, then came back and bought myself the fixings for a vegetable stew, complete with thick golden crusted bread that I needed to saw into doorstep slices, and golden butter – the real stuff. I opened all the windows, let the wind and the light and the smell of the grass fall in from the hills. I cooked and I ate, content, and wondered if she could smell my cooking, upstairs. Wondered if she could see the light reflecting on all her surfaces. I left a bowl of it out for her on her landing.

When I left for work on Monday morning, there was a bundle of rosemary sprigs, bound in purple ribbon, hanging on the outside of my door.

She moved out a few weeks after that. She let me make her a meal before she left. We even sat in the same room to share this one. We barely spoke. We didn't need to. She still limped when she walked. She left me her window box. I promised to keep the herbs alive. She told me she knew I would.

I worked the rest of my notice, polite but distant when dealing with those men I'd gone drinking with. I'll never know if it was them that chased her. I moved back home, at the end of my contract, and I made sure to make it *my* home. I filled it with personality and colour. I wanted people to know exactly who I was when they knocked at the door. I grew basil and mint. I painted the walls and hung art.

Sometimes when I walk in the big wide-open places, I see hares. Sometimes I see a hare with a limp. I wonder, sometimes, if she comes to check up on me. I leave the window open in the lounge, just in case.

* * *

Once Upon A Meeting...

Dreams are in-between places. The ones we sort-of remember are, anyway.

The ones we have in the dead of the night that have us writhing around with our eyes twitching beneath closed lids and possibly shouting things like *'Save the brie! The satsumas are rabid!'* are very definitely on the far side of the line. Conversely, those moments when you're lying in bed all snug and cosy and you've just remembered with chilling detail last night's cocktail party where you unceremoniously projectile-vomited all over the bar; that's very firmly on this side of the line. Ah, but the moment where the remembering comes rushing into the void – the exact moment between not remembering and cringing – that is an in-between place. It's a split-second, less than a hair's width moment of transition. And the dreams that you half remember, the vague shape or feeling that you can't quite grasp but which flavour your whole day – they are an in-between place too. Neither one thing nor another. A threshold.

The Meeting, this time, was being held in the In-Between, at the Edge of Dreams, between sleep and awake.

It could have been held in that Unforgetting place, or the Moment The Phone Call You've Been Waiting For Comes But Before You Know What The Answer Is place. It could have been in the Shoreline. It might have been in the Garden Wall place, or in the Dusk, or in the Infinite Reflection Of Two Mirrors Facing One Another place. It could even have been in the threshold between life and death. But since Queen Mab was chairing the meeting this time, she'd chosen the Edge of Dreams, which also, funnily enough, looked remarkably like an enchanted forest.

This forest of the In-Between was bathed in twilight. The trees here were giant; so tall and wide that they disappeared into the darkness above. They were perfect executions of enchanted forest trees, full of faces, gnarled of limb, twisted of trunk. Grass and reeds sprouted several feet high. The ground was carpeted in huge curling leaves and pine needles as long as lances, scattered with acorns the size of bowling balls. Pinecones that were altogether surprised and frankly embarrassed by their size tried to bury themselves into the gaps between roots. Towering toadstools in glistening reds and yellows, with just the right number of white spots, sprouted in clusters. Giant fans of fungus sprouted from tree trunks and fallen logs.

Haunting lights moved in the gloaming; pale iridescent things that buzzed and flitted in pinks and silvers and electric blues, the sort of lights that could lead a wayward traveller from their path. There was music that sounded vaguely like the wind blowing across glass bottle tops, and dewdrops glistened immaculately on everything that wasn't already covered in moss or lichen. In some places, dewdrops clung *on top* of the moss and lichen, you know, to really drive it all home. The air was alive with chirps and croaks and whistles. Everything sparkled and chimed. Someone had really gone to town with the glitter. It was all designed to ensure you knew you could quite possibly stumble upon a mildly terrifying hat maker having a tea party, or possibly a headless horseman, just around the bend. *Of course* the path shifted and shimmered and dissolved. *Of course* the trees got up and wandered off. *Of course* eyes followed you, owls hooted and other unseen but huge-sounding things crashed about and occasionally muttered, "bugger..."

And in this dream of an enchanted forest, there was a boy. He was at that awkward in-between stage, himself – not quite child and not quite man, made of awkward angles; all Adam's apple, elbows and sniffy red-tipped nose. He was also, strictly speaking, not a boy. Not a human one, leastways. His name was Perran, and he was lost.

He was also, if you listened very hard, reciting a speech under his breath as he walked. "Members of the Council... esteemed members of the

Council... thank you for your time... no, it is an honour to... uh... stand before you today and... uh...” He glanced down at a crumpled piece of paper in his hand that had been folded and unfolded far more than was strictly good for a piece of paper. It was covered in spidery, splotchy scrawled writing as if whomever had written this had done so in the dark, bent over the light of a candle with their tongue poking out in concentration. Which in fact, was exactly what had happened.

“...draw your attention to the plight of, uh...”

Something screeched in the darkness, the sudden but definite sound of an ending.

Perran paused, beside the huge hanging bell of a giant bindweed flower, and looked around anxiously. Nervousness oozed out of him. The helmet he wore was made of tin, with a large circular protrusion on the front which contained a burning candle. Though the candle was impressively dribbly, the sort of dribbly that takes years of concentrated dribbling by expert candle dribblers, the wax never seemed to drip off of the little plate it stood on and the candle never seemed to burn out. The helmet, however, was at least two sizes too big for his head and kept slipping over his eyes. Perran shoved it back absently as he tried to lean his pickaxe against his thigh and flatten out the creases in the paper against his chest. The pickaxe took a sideways slide and fell onto his boot with a clang. Perran looked at it and tutted audibly, then held the soft, yellowing page up into the torchlight of his helmet, squinting at it. He turned it over, looked at the much neater printed side, with straight lines, fancy headings, time slots and *bullet points*. Then he squinted at the path he stood on, turned and squinted back the way he came. He sighed, and shoved the paper back into his pocket.

“Jago?” he called cautiously. The forest swallowed his voice; made it muffled and too close.

“Jago?!” he tried again. Nothing but the hooting of owls replied.

He'd been supposed to stick with Old Jago. That's what The Foreman had told him – "Stick with Old Jago, he knows the way. He'll get you there in one piece. And remember, Perran, we're counting on you."

Which, of course, doomed them to failure from the start.

They'd started off well, though. Jago with his knees that barely seemed able to support his wiry old body and his knobbly walking stick that he liked to bash Perran on the head with, and his big old white beard and spotted neckerchief, had wheezed and shuffled and muttered to himself, but they'd made it up out of the mines onto the clifftop. They'd made it all the way to the cove where the lighthouse blinked and the waves turned white against the rocks without getting seen once by a human. Jago had even brought them pasties, squashed up and mangled though they were, in his little haversack, and they'd sat and eaten and brushed golden pastry crumbs, lumps of fallen meat and potato from themselves as they waited for the tourists and the beach goers to pack up and head home. Then Old Jago had heaved himself to his feet and untangled his boot-points with his walking stick – he still wore the curled pointed felt boots that went out of style four hundred years ago, refused to acknowledge that maybe the tin helmets and steel-toe-capped boots might be a smart investment, said they were "bloody flimflam, like that electrickery. Didn't need none of that back when I were a lad, mark my words..." – and stood facing the setting sun.

He showed Perran how to wait for the exact moment the sun touched the horizon, how to squint into the light, how to turn and step sideways into the In-Between and into the mists of time, how to walk out into the Edge of Dreams. All that had gone relatively smoothly, considering it was Perran's first time. He hadn't even felt airsick. But as soon as they had emerged into the enchanted forest, Old Jago had taken one look around him, as a pink glowing light zinged past their heads, grinned a gappy, yellowing grin at Perran, whapped him on the back of the head with his walking stick and cackled, "Last one there's a stinkweed," and hurtled off in a limping run into the trees.

Bloody old bastard. Perran sighed again. He wasn't sure he'd be able to face The Foreman again if he was late to his very first meeting, especially when he had this whole speech he was meant to deliver, that he'd been practising for ages whilst desperately trying not to think too hard about the hundreds, thousands, of eyes that would be staring at him as he delivered it. And his voice still didn't always behave itself and liked to hitchhike up an octave when he was nervous... his mouth filled with saliva. Didn't matter though, did it? 'Cause he was lost in a bloody cabbage patch and likely to get eaten by something much bigger and less awkward than he was.

Right on cue, something crashed and thudded in the undergrowth out there beyond the path's edge, followed by a muffled, "Ouch."

Perran grabbed up his pickaxe, held it out at arm's length. "I've got a... a stick with a pointy bit on it, and I'm not afraid to use it!" he told the darkness.

The branches closest to him shuddered, shivered and turned to face him. "That's awesome, mate! Good on ya! No point in having pointy bits that you're scared of is it?"

It was a walking tree. No, it was a Spriggan. He stepped out of the forest onto the path and moved the bindweed flower carefully, holding the petals between long spindly fingers, to look down at Perran. His arms and legs were corded and twisted like vines, his face was sort of triangular and sprouted leaves. There was a bird's nest wedged behind his ear though it didn't seem to currently be occupied.

"Uh..." said Perran.

"I'm covered in pointy bits, me." The Spriggan chuckled. "Wouldn't get far if I was afraid of 'em."

"...right?" said Perran.

The undergrowth rustled again and a Boggart stepped out onto the path, rubbing its head. "Should put signs up, they should, stop people walking into trees like that..."

The Boggart was grey and lumpy-looking, with all the physical characteristics of a sneeze on top of a half-melted ice cream, topped with a fantastic thick crop of dark hair styled in a bowl cut.

"It's a forest... it's sort of filled with trees, mate." The Spriggan raised an eyebrow. "Kind of its modus operandi, if you like."

"Yeah, well, it hurts, don't it, to headbutt one." The Boggart was still rubbing its head. "I ain't done nuffin' to modus its operahandee."

The Spriggan blinked, reconsidering the advice he'd been about to offer that perhaps his travelling companion *not* headbutt the trees, realising it would very likely be a little like talking to mud. Instead, he placed his hands on his hips, tilted his head at Perran. "You going to the meeting?"

"Yes! Only..." Perran lowered his pickaxe, shoved his helmet back on his head. "I got lost..."

"Ah..." The Spriggan nodded. "Yeah, well, this place is all a bit disorientating, isn't it? Easy to get lost if you've not been here before. First time?"

All the air seemed to get sucked out of Perran as he sniffed, rubbed the end of his nose. "Is it that obvious?"

"Nah, mate, nah, it's all good, everyone has a first meeting, don't they? Eh? Nothing to be ashamed of. It's exciting! A creatures' first meeting? Rite of passage, you might say. You can come with us if you like?" The Spriggan's face split into a smile, which was a little horrific, what with the splintering of wood, but Perran appreciated his friendliness.

"Thanks, I– that's really nice of you. I was with someone, Jago, but he buggered off. Said I was a stinkweed..." Perran sniffed again, hitched his pickaxe up onto his shoulder.

"You don't look like a stinkweed to me." The Spriggan brushed a fallen twig from Perran's shoulder. "Does he, Gaz? This 'ere Knocker don't look like a stinkweed?"

The Boggart leant in towards Perran, gave him a good sniff. Something gurgled under the surface of its skin; a large watery bubble rose on its cheek and burst with a small plop. "Nah, not stinky at all."

"That's settled then." The Spriggan clapped his hands with a shower of twigs and leaves. "You're coming with us. I'm Trungle, this bubbling cesspit of ineptitude is Thick Gary."

Thick Gary the Boggart leant in conspiratorially. "They call me that 'cause I'm not very smart."

"O-oh." Perran nodded encouragingly, as if it hadn't occurred to him already that this thing was a few rocks short of a barrowful. "I'm Perran."

"And *I'm* about to lose my god-damn mind if you lot don't get a sodding move on!" a female voice yelled from the gloom. "We are running late!"

There was a whooshing sound from above. A small, lithe Piskie swung on a rope down through the branches and tall grass, somersaulted off a toadstool and came to land in an impressive crouch beside them. The Piskie was dressed in various layers of ripped and deliberately laddered green and brown garments, had a nose ring and a purple mohawk. Her left arm stopped just below her elbow, with the cuff of her sleeve on that side rolled back. There was a collection of fluorescent elastic bands around her stump and she wore big, clumping, scuffed up red boots with thick soles, yellow stitching and little tags poking out the back of them that read 'FairyWare'.

"That's Roz." Trungle grinned.

Roz tugged on the end of the rope she had swung from and it slithered neatly into a pool at her feet. There was a grappling hook attached to the other end. She scooped it up, using her left arm to loop the rope over, twisted one end around the coil with her right hand, and slung it over her head so it sat across her body like a sash. She wore a selection of sharp things in her belt made from what looked like slithers of glass and flint.

Perran felt everything in him, including his jaw, go slack and bendy like he was made of melted cheese.

"Roz, this is Perran. He's coming with us." Trungle clapped the young Knocker on the back so that he stumbled.

Perran righted himself, shoved his helmet out of his eyes, faced Roz. "That was, I mean, you're very, uh, hi. Uh. Wow."

Roz raised an eyebrow at him, looked at Trungle, and said, "Really?" in a withering voice. She looked back at Perran, tutted, and strode away along the path,

"She tuts a lot," Thick Gary whispered. He wasn't very good at whispering.

"Come on, morons, it's this way." Roz's voice echoed back to them. "You want to explain to Mab why we're strolling in late?"

* * *

Throughout all of time, across all of the Multiverse, stories have existed, floating around in the ether waiting to be needed, waiting to be told, but always, they are there. The oldest story is "NOW", often hurriedly followed by a stumbling, "Wait, no, hold on a second! Shit..."

Some stories are lucky enough to survive the passage of the millennia; manage to adapt, shift and shape themselves to suit the modern needs, colours and movie screens. Others serve their purpose and become lost, unneeded, drifting endlessly in the void of the mists of time. The world no longer needs the stories of Darkness and Fire, but they linger, on the periphery, just in case, lending their ancient necessity to other tales. Then there are the myths, the legends, the folktales. Important enough to have survived, but old enough to have slipped through the cracks, to not be swept up in the endless cycles of stories repeating themselves as History. These are an altogether different breed of story. They breathe. They have taken form in minds, taken root in the countless tellings, each voice that speaks them giving shape and solidity. These tales, the mythic, the legendary, the folk-law, they are very much real. The characters are memories, ghosts, thoughtforms, and they exist in the In-Between, waiting to be needed. And with all collections of anything that have their own identities, needs and wants outside of their prescribed roles, sometimes, they get restless. Sometimes, they get ideas into their heads that aren't necessarily good for the wider community. Sometimes, stories go rogue (ever heard of Hat Man? Don't look him up...). Sometimes the same stories grow new offshoots and there are multiple variations on a theme existing in the In-Between. Sometimes they don't all get along.

And so, just like with any other group of individuals ostensibly all part of the same team and spread far and wide over the Multiverse, it becomes important to have some structure, to have fixed points at which to collect, recalibrate, get organised so no one gets funny ideas or indeed gets left behind (poor old Sfpubsdlj – lost now forever floating somewhere in the Forgotten). Also it's nice to get everyone together once in a while, isn't it? Nice to have something on the calendar besides weddings and funerals. So, there is the Council, and across all the planets and across all the planes of existence where stories are born and told and exist, there are the Committee Meetings. Within the British Isles, by all accounts a tiny collection of floating rocks on a slightly larger rock floating around the star called Sun, the Meeting is held once every fifty years (within the human understanding of time). It's a bit of a to-do, really. There's an agenda and everything.

* * *

As we zoom back in from the Multiverse to the floating rock of the Earth, to a funny little collection of islands with ideas of grandeur, to the Edge of the Dreaming just beneath the surface of the human world, in the middle of the enchanted forest, we find a clearing. It was nothing particularly special, just a big gap in the trees, where the grass was short and soft and the hulking spotted toadstools kept to the side-lines. There were coloured lights and lanterns strung up in all the trees here. Chandeliers of wisteria and ferns hung from the canopy, strung with hundreds of twinkling golden lights, and the air smelled sweet and heavy. It was a pretty big clearing, but then, quite a few people were expected. Above the winding path that entered the space, a faded blue cotton banner was strung between two trees. The banner was patched and much repaired, and it said, in slightly grubby white lettering:

Welcome! To The Officially Recognised Members of the British Isles Legends, Myths and Folklores Association (B.I.L.M.F.A)

Semicentennial General Meeting

(It was a very long banner, and it was a bit saggy in the middle.)

At the opposite end of the clearing there was a row of huge fan mushrooms, dark and rippled. On the top of the flat fungi, seven glasses of water, seven lined notepads and seven blue plastic biros with the letters B.I.L.M.F.A on them were set out neatly. Each place also had a single sheet of paper with the word AGENDA written across the top in beautiful green calligraphy (these were the same, albeit far less crumpled, as our friend Perran had written his notes all over the back of). Behind the fungi, there were six padded office chairs on wheels, all of them currently empty. A lectern made from a single thick rhubarb stalk and flat, smallish angled

181

leaf, had been set up in front of the fungus desks. It had a tiny microphone. And, because there are just some conventions that should never be messed with, enchanted forest in a dream or not, three wobbly trestle tables covered in white paper tablecloths had been set out along the far side of the clearing, with an ancient and dangerous-looking hot water urn cheerfully popping and steaming behind a sea of too-small white ceramic mugs.

In the shadows at the side of the clearing, unnoticed or perhaps ignored, two suited figures stood in matching striped ties and slicked-back greying hair. They were identical, except that one of them wore a thin, rimless pair of glasses. They were watching the clearing slowly begin to fill.

"Remind me," one figure asked, "are these the ones with the angry blue lady with all the arms?"

"No, no," the other, with the glasses, responded. "Same planet but that's somewhere east of here I believe."

Both figures carried huge leather-bound and metal-clasped books under their arms. These books contained all the stories ever told, ever, anywhere. These figures were the Storykeepers and they were here as representatives of the Council.

"They all ruddy well start to look the same after a while, don't they? These little countries with their folksy little tales," the first figure snorted.

"This best be over and done with by four. I've got golf with a supreme being at six." The bespectacled figured raised its eyebrows at the collection of odd-shaped creatures wandering into the clearing slowly.

The first sniffed. "I hear they've got a woman chairing this time round..."

"Mmm. The Wizard is here too."

"Oh, is he? *Good,* good..."

"Yes, but remember what a ruckus he caused with the whole equal opportunities thing? Round tables and what have you."

"True. Messed up the story good and proper that did. Took years to get that one square in the psyches of the people. Good job we put a stop to that sort of thinking at these things, or else we'd be here for the next fifty years *listening* to everyone..."

"Do you reckon they've got cake? Last time I had to come to one of these here, they had this delightful little thing called Battenburg."

"Didn't he get blown up on a boat?"

"It's a cake. With almond paste. I don't know about any boats."

* * *

"So, uh, that's a pretty cool set of knives you've got there." Perran was desperately trying not to fall over his own feet whilst exuding an air of nonchalant sexual prowess. "Not like the ol' Fortune Maker, though." He patted his pickaxe. "Nope, you need something a bit heftier down there in the mines. What with the heat and the heavy lifting, and the danger of cave-ins. Sometimes we get Trolls down there. I'm lucky to be alive, really." He puffed his chest and raised his eyebrow in what he thought was a deeply provocative yet heroic manner.

"Do you have indigestion?" Roz stepped over a tree root. "You look like a burp died trying to escape out of your nose or something."

"Oh... I, no, I, er..."

"You really shouldn't walk with your shoulders pushed back like that, if you've got indigestion," she continued, pushing a trailing vine out of their way. "Better posture might help."

"Right." Perran stumbled over something, got tangled in the vine that Roz had let go of, shoved his helmet out of his eyes. "Good."

Behind them, Trungle and Thick Gary were deep in discussion regarding Gillingham F.C's chances of being relegated down a division this season.

Roz glanced at Perran as they walked. "The pickaxe is cool, though."

Perran sighed. "I'm only a barrow boy, really. I don't do much of the digging or the explosives or anything, just bring the rubble up to the surface. The pickaxe just sort of goes with the territory."

Roz shrugged. "There's a part for everyone, and everyone has a part. We make do. We adapt."

Perran found himself looking at her missing hand. She saw him looking and waved her stump with its collection of colourful armbands at him sarcastically.

"Sorry." Perran blushed, looked away.

"It's not contagious." She laughed. "I just figured out my own way of doing things, is all."

"What's your part, then?"

"Me? I'm a Finder. Help people find the things they lost. Car keys, important letters from the bank, cats – though cats are arseholes that don't like being made to be found until they're ready. Ever tried herding cats with only one hand? Sometimes though, I get to help people find cool stuff, like courage. Sometimes I get to find weird boys lost in the forest on my way to the Meeting."

Perran frowned. "I'm not weird!"

"You gave your *pickaxe* a name..."

He opened his mouth to argue back, ready to set out a list of reasons why naming a tool was just what you did, if you wanted it to be good at its

184

job and that this in no way made him weird, when he realised they were walking beneath a shabby looking banner and into a clearing in the trees.

There was already quite a crowd. At least fifty, congregating into smaller groups. More were streaming in behind them. Greetings were called out, arms raised in welcome. There was laughing, shouting. All manner of creatures and characters were there. Giants strode across the clearing, making the earth tremble. A huge green Dragon leapt up into a nearby tree to lay along a low branch while continuing its conversation with a Gnome who was eating a fondant fancy, "Well I don't think one can say it's post-colonial but I *do* enjoy a good Morris dance–"

Fairies of all shapes, sizes and ranks, Goblins, Ogres, Imps, Pookas, Lubbers and Hinkeypunks, all milled around. Hags with warts, Witches with pointy hats and women with knowing looks in their eyes. Men with swords, and men with bows. Things made of light, things made of leaves, things with horns and others that flew.

At the far end, Perran could see the Committee members taking their seats. There was Merlin with his pointy hat and long beard. There was Mab looking every velvet-clad inch the Queen of Dark Desires. And Perran could see the lectern. And he remembered that he'd have to stand up there and speak, and his breath got stuck somewhere in his windpipe. All his nervousness came flooding back and made it impossible to move. His legs were sacks of water.

"What's the matter with you?!" Roz dragged at him. "Come on, you're in the way!" She pulled him out of the path of a procession of fairies and goblins bearing trays of food as they rushed through the clearing.

Oberon was directing them. "On the left... the left... *left* by the fucking teacups you imbeciles! Do I have to do everything myself?"

The very tall, very blonde and very handsome man with the silver circlet around his head flipped his enviable long tresses over his shoulder, huffed, and marched in his thigh-high grey velvet boots over to the buffet tables. "And now there's butter on the tablecloth... I don't have time to be... oh for the love of Circe, why would you put the tarte tatins beside the cheese and onion sandwiches? Where's the consistency and flow here? We want it to look *nice,* people!"

Without being able to take his eyes from the lectern, Perran reached into his pocket and passed Roz his notes.

"You're on the agenda?" Roz looked incredulously from the paper in her hand to Perran. "You?!"

Her tone shook him out of his stupor. "Yes, me, and I'll have you know... I'm a little nervous about public speaking..."

"Ah, I wouldn't worry about that, kiddo." Trungle scratched at his birds' nest.

"You're not the one who's got to stand up there and..."

Trungle was shaking his head. "Honestly, mate, it's not that sort of a do."

Roz looped her arm through his and guided Perran into the clearing.

"But... but... I have a timeslot..."

"At these things, think of it more like a polite acknowledgement of your existence." Trungle was peering around. "You stick with us, you'll be alright."

"But the Foreman said he was counting on me!" Perran dug his heels in, refused to be dragged further. Trungle, Roz and Thick Gary all turned to stare at him.

"On *you*?!"

"Yes, *me*, thank you very much. And I'll have you know that I... that I... Oh my Gods and Goddesses, is that Robin Hood?!"

Perran had spotted a group of guffawing men raucously cheering and slapping one another on the back, all dressed in green. They were all there – Much the Miller's Son, Alan A'Dale, Will Scarlett, and, towering at least a head and shoulders above the rest of them, with a quarterstaff braced across his shoulders, there was Little John with his swathe of dark curls, deep booming laugh and six-o'clock shadow. In the middle of the group, sitting upon a tree stump, was a young bearded man with a long bow propped in the dirt beside him and quiver full of arrows upon his back. He wore a Lincoln-green tunic and a mossy woollen cloak with a hood. He was smiling, nodding and raising his hand at a small crowd of admirers. He stood up to take a selfie with a couple of Banshees.

"Wow!" Perran gawped. "He's... he's actually quite short."

"Yeah, but he makes the others all stand in ditches so he looks bigger." Roz rolled her eyes. "And rumour has it that the long bow is definitely compensating, if you know what I mean."

"Still, he's like the Dude though, right? He's got it made. Lucky son of a myth. You reckon I could get his autograph?"

"Not a myth." Roz sighed. "He's a legend."

"Same thing." Perran shrugged.

"Nah not really mate." Trungle had plucked a pork pie from a passing silver platter and took a bite. "Myths are creation stories, like your basic gods and goddesses, and Vincent and Goram over there– alright lads?" Trungle waved at a couple of Giants drinking cider. "Legends are things that maybe might've once had a root in reality. Like your Robin Hood, your Rob Roy, your..."

A fanfare erupted in the clearing that made Perran drop his pickaxe. Four heralds strode into the clearing, dressed in red and gold tunics. Their trumpets were long and spindly, and their hairdos were the sort that told

187

you they probably had a hard time with the other kids at school. Perran's jaw dropped as a group of men on horseback slowly trotted into the clearing. The crowd cheered. The men were all in armour, with chainmail and white tunics sporting a red dragon. And there, at the front, with a hefty gold crown nestled in perfectly shining golden hair atop a dazzling smile, was Arthur. Once and Future King. He waved, he posed, he even pointed and made little finger-guns at people which, honestly, killed it all for Perran a bit and the boy lost interest. He saw Roz indicate, with a waggle of her eyebrows and a tilt of her head, back at Robin and his men. Perran turned and saw the Merry Men had all gathered into a knot of testosterone in the centre of the clearing. Robin stood on his tree stump with his arms crossed, sneering at the knights. Arthur's white horse came to a halt in front of him and the golden-haired man slid, with a clank of armour, to the ground. The rest of the knights followed suit and the horses were led away by a group of imps. Arthur was making a show of removing his gloves and gauntlets. Robin stood, arms crossed, chin raised.

"Really very lovely to see you again, old chap." Arthur grinned. "And still in those splendid tights, I see."

Little John growled and gripped his quarterstaff so that it squeaked between his hands.

"They're leggings," Robin muttered. "Thermal. Keeps out the cold when we're sleeping outdoors, in the forests. Not that any of you lot would know what it's like to have to rough it."

Arthur laughed. "Now, now, let's not be off on the wrong boot here, eh lads? We have, you may recall, had our fair share of quests."

"Yeah, and what did you do with all that loot, eh? Keep it for yourselves? Like you bloody need it."

"And I suppose a rabble of petty criminals like yourselves need all the purses you've lifted over the years?"

188

"We do it for the poor!" Alan A'Dale growled.

"We do it for... for..." Arthur stalled.

"For the *glory*!" Lancelot offered.

"Yes. That."

"Oh, how bloody *glorious*." Robin shook his head incredulously. "You wouldn't last a bloody minute in our neck of the woods. Lot of damp pansies, the lot of you."

"Wait, wait, I think we've heard this one before, boys! Why don't you go sit with the other Green Man depictions." Bors pushed his way to the front, poked Robin in the chest. "Little forest man."

Little John squared up to him, poked him back in his metal armour-plated chest. "Yeah? Say that again, tin man."

Arthur sighed. "Look, it's simply not our fault that the people prefer our story to yours." He shrugged, looking to the crowd. "Titania, baby! Loving the hair!" He winked at the blonde Fairy, who was engrossed in a hand of poker and held up a middle finger to him.

Robin snorted and spat a great glob of snot on to the ground by the King's foot, stepped down from his tree stump to sneer up at Arthur. "Is that so? Think maybe you ought to ask again, pal."

Arthur was looking at the glistening puddle of snot, repulsed. "He *spat* at me! A King!"

From the other side of the clearing, a strong Irish voice rang out. "You're not the only royalty here, Goldilocks."

The Celtic contingent had risen to their feet. Lugh O'The Long Arm, huge, red haired and covered in swirling blue woad, cricked his neck on his shoulders.

O'Neill the One Handed waved sardonically. "Yoo-hoo, Remember us?"

The silence that had descended on the clearing then was meaty, like you could chew it. All eyes were flitting between the three groups, waiting to see who would throw the first punch. Perran felt his heart beating in the palms of his hands.

Beside him, Thick Gary said, "This is always my favourite bit! One year Lancelot headbutted Much."

But then a dog barked, and it wasn't the yappy little scrappy sound of a friendly, if potentially annoying, lap dog. No, this was the deep throaty bark of a dog that could herd nightmares, a dog that could hunt fear. It was the bark of a hound. This was followed by the striking of a drum that reverberated through the trees and a single mournful blast of a horn. Yet *another* band of men were strolling into the clearing, but these were grim men, scarred men. Men in furs, men wearing skulls of things they had slain for helmets (this effect was rather spoilt by one fat man with braids in his beard wearing the skull of a frog balanced daintily on top of his wild mane of hair). These men reeked of sweat and urine. They carried lances, pikes, maces, short swords. They were grizzled. The crowd parted, as much from the overwhelming smell as out of respect. Their leader, whose stag horns did not belong to a dead animal but rather sprouted from his head itself, was picking some kind of petrified slug out of his beard. Petrified as in old and turned into a mummified husk, but also, probably, terrified.

"Who is *that?*" Perran whispered to Roz.

"Herne. They're the Sluagh. The Wild Hunt. Original lads on tour."

Herne ambled towards Robin and Arthur, picking leaves and slimy things from his beard. Both men were looking about – at the sky, at their feet, and their hands, at anywhere other than this beast of a man.

190

"Lads?" Herne rumbled.

"Af... afternoon, Her-Herne," Robin stammered. "Your, your Lordship," he added as an afterthought.

"Jolly good to um, see, yes, see you again old sport..." Arthur held out a hand. Herne looked at it and placed the pickings from his beard in it, then brushed past. Arthur was staring into his hand as if he might pass out. The rest of the Wild Hunt followed, all wide shoulders and jutting elbows.

"Sit down, and shut up," Herne called back over his shoulder.

Robin and Arthur dropped to the floor, cross legged. To a soul, every Knight and jolly Merry Man did the same. Except Little John, who was trying to look small (difficult at nearly seven feet tall) and step sideways into the crowd. Two of the wild men of the Hunt glared at him, and he pointed, sheepishly, to the desks at the front of the clearing, where Mab and Merlin sat watching all this unfold with barely contained boredom, "I'm on the Committee," and he scuttled away to take his seat.

Lugh sniggered. Herne fist-bumped him, then, upon spotting a fat and ruddy-cheeked Friar in a shabby-looking habit, roared, "There you are, you fat turd, Tuck, is there some bloody beer in this place? I thought this was a gathering?!"

The crowd cheered, the crowd breathed (although, not too deeply, because the Wild Hunt really did *hum*), and the buzz of conversations and eating resumed.

Perran was almost giddy. "That was *awesome!*"

Roz smirked, tossed him a chicken leg.

"Sod Robin Hood, I want to be Herne when I grow up!" Perran took a huge bite of the chicken leg and said, around a mouthful, "So, what is he then? Myth? Legend?"

"Myth," Roz said.

"Legend," Trungle said, simultaneously. They looked at one another and shrugged.

"And what about us?" Perran pushed his tin helmet back out of his eyes.

"Folktales and Fairy Tales, ain't we?" Thick Gary had somehow acquired an entire plate of vol-au-vents and was daintily dropping them one by one into his mouth. "Though undoubtedly falling within the umbrella of the mythical pantheon, since we characterise ideas and symbols rather than historical occurrences, by which the humans can pass on knowledge... ooooooh, *scones*..." He wandered away from Perran's mildly disturbed expression.

"He's only smart when he's not thinking about it," Trungle explained with a shrug. "It's a skill."

* * *

Merlin was peering over the rim of his spectacles. He'd been rather concerned he might have to get up and intervene with the whole Robin versus Arthur debacle, which could have proved tricky given his narrative affiliations, but then Herne had arrived and there was nothing like a six-foot, barrel-chested, stinking brick out-house with antlers growing out of his head to dissipate some legend-based rivalry.

"Thank Tír na nÓg for that." Mab sighed, beside him. "Thought we might have to get the Dragon involved."

Merlin went back to squinting at his phone. For some reason known only to people over a certain age, he could only work a smart phone by holding it at arm's length and squinting. He liked Twitter for the social commentary, Facebook for the dank memes and Instagram for keeping tabs on the kids. Beside him, Mab flicked through a stack of papers in a

192

manila folder, tapping a long, painted fingernail on the desk. Since it was made of a huge great fungus, this made a strange sort of hollow drumming sound. Mab had finally managed to convince the Council to let her chair, and since this was her patch of the In-Between, she'd worked hard to make everything just so. Her choice of outfit mirrored this attention to detail. Just enough of a plunging neckline to remind everyone she was the Queen of Air and Darkness, Queen of Dreams, Queen of Dark Desires, just sleek and dark enough with just the right amount of shoulder pad to remind people she took no nonsense. She was a formidable woman, fiercely beautiful. Long black hair, of the sort that poets described as beguiling, hung past her waist. Her wings, like those of a large Red Admiral, fluttered impatiently. Her look said part school headmistress, part dominatrix, like she'd have no qualms telling you off but knew you'd probably quite enjoy it. She was sipping from a large steaming mug that had the words: 'COFFEE! Because Crack will get you fired!' printed on it. Merlin nudged her, held up his phone, and Mab smiled her most dazzling Queen of the Night smile. Merlin made a rock-on bull's horn sign with his other hand, and he snapped the selfie.

"...hashtag... fierce at work..." he mumbled, tapping each letter with his index finger.

Beside Mab floated a pale blue Will O' The Wisp, bobbing superciliously up and down. He was clicking the top of his biro as he sneered at the gathering crowds. "We really ought to get going soon," he spoke with a suitably snivelling voice, "if we're to stick to the agenda."

Mab rolled her eyes. "We can't very well start before the rest of the Committee get here, can we?"

Little John sidled into his seat, avoiding their faces. "Sorry 'bout that, you know how it gets..."

"Yes," Merlin raised an eyebrow, "after several centuries, we know exactly how it gets."

Mab tapped one of the sheets in front of her. "John, it says here we're four hundred florins short on the subs."

"Ah, well, yes, ma'am, you see," he scratched his head awkwardly, "Jack won't pay his subs."

"You *are* Treasurer, are you not?" the Wisp snipped.

Little John sighed. "I am..."

"And therefore, I mean, correct me if I'm wrong, ahaa haa, but therefore isn't it your job within the Committee to ensure all subs are paid on time?" The Wisp had a funny little habit of laughing condescendingly mid-sentence that made you want to shove his pen up his nose.

John clenched his teeth. A vein throbbed somewhere in his temple. "Yes, Frank, it is my job."

"Then, ahaa haa, as Steering Committee member, whose job it is to ensure we all stay on track and that everything runs smoothly here in BILMFA, I have to ask, ahaa haa, why..."

"'Cause I don't know which bloody Jack it is, alright?" Little John thumped a meaty fist onto the desk. "There's a lot of the little buggers. Jack Spratt, Jack the Giant Killer, Jack Frost, Jack O' Lantern, Jack in the Greens popping up like god-damn daisies left right and centre. All I know is there's a Jack on the books who hasn't paid since 1519, and all of 'em refuse to tell me who it is. I reckon it's Puck, the little shit."

"Isn't he a Robin?" Merlin was trying to get a crowd shot of the clearing to Tweet.

"Oh, he's whatever the hell he wants to be, is our darling Goodfellow. Wouldn't be surprised if he did it just to drive me insane..."

"See, this..." Frank the Wisp bobbed towards Mab and muttered in her ear, "is why I have to voice my concerns about letting a thief hold the position of Treasurer."

Little John's lip started to inadvertently curl; he couldn't stand this officious little prick and never had.

Mab, however, simply swatted the Wisp away, not even glancing up from her paperwork. "You think that Merry bunch of reprobates would have survived as long as they have if Iwan here wasn't good with the pennies?"

Little John blinked a few times, felt a worrying blush start to creep up from his collar. "No one's called me Iwan in centuries..."

Mab glanced at him and winked. "I'll speak with Puck."

John leant back in his seat, crossed his ham-hock hands over his belly and grinned, smugly, at the Wisp. A Giant in a kilt was making his way towards them with a cup of tea in one hand and a laptop in the other. The Wisp wilted and John's grin broadened, as he raised a hand. "Finn!! How's it going?"

Finn McCool very carefully placed his laptop on the table and opened it. Then he sat cross legged beside John very slowly and gently, holding the cup of tea gingerly. In his giant hands, it was essentially an espresso shot. He raised it to his moustached mouth with both hands and slurped it empty with his little fingers sticking out.

He smacked his lips. "Oooo aye, canae beat a decent brew..."

Frank the Wisp flittered back towards Mab. "I have to say, ahaa haa, I have similar concerns that our Secretary is..."

"Is a Giant? Whit's wrang with Giants, eh? Ye puff of hot air?" Finn leaned forward to glower at the Wisp. His accent was fantastic – geographically, it danced all the way from Limerick to Glasgow.

"Is... too large to type the minutes without bashing every key on the keyboard," Frank finished.

In response, Finn plucked two chopsticks from his sporran, thrust them out so the Wisp saw them, then used them to very deliberately type on his laptop. He then turned the screen towards the others:

THE STEERING COMMITTEE MEMBER IS A GREAT FUCKIN BAMPOT

John guffawed, slapped Finn on the arm.

"Awa' ye flittery choad, and chew mah banger, so you can!" Finn McCool declared loudly (which, in case you're wondering, roughly translates as 'get away with you, you large pile of excrement, and you can chew my sausage'. It has a certain ring to it that only a mythical Scots/Irish Giant can offer).

"Personally," Little John grinned, "*ahaaa haaaaa*, I can't think of anyone better suited for the role of Secretary."

"Duly noted." Mab was marking something in her notes in yellow highlighter.

"Can we *please* get started?" Frank the Wisp whined. "We are now technically twenty minutes late in starting."

"Ah, well, yes," Merlin placed his phone down on the desk, scratched the end of his nose, "We can't technically get started until the other two arrive." He gestured at the two remaining empty chairs at the end of the line. "And Christ knows when they'll decide to pull their fingers out. Bloody senior management. Always operating on their own timescales."

* * *

Perran looked around him at the only vaguely controlled chaos. There were Witches swapping crystals and reading each other's Tarot cards. A bunch of medieval-looking Welsh people standing with Lugh were trying to teach a group of Brownies a song, apparently, about saucepans. Some of the Merry Men and some of the Knights had begun a game of cards. A bunch of various Green Man depictions including Puck, a walking pile of leaves, a Jack in the Green and a young freckled boy with a feather in his hat and rather detached shadow, were passing a plate of biscuits around while the Green Knight poured tea for the Morrigan. Some Leprechauns were swapping gold pieces for jewels with a couple of Wyverns. Perran puffed out his cheeks. This was not really what he'd been expecting, but it *was* exciting. He was trying to pick his way back from the buffet table with a paper plate piled high with sandwiches and little bread-crumbed nibbly things. He still diligently carried his pickaxe in the other hand.

Roz, Trungle and Thick Gary had found a spot to sit on the soft forest floor with a group of other Unseelies. As Perran approached, Roz patted the ground beside her and Perran felt a surge of something warm, bubbly and not entirely unpleasant in his stomach. He fumbled with his pickaxe and narrowly missed dropping it on her head. But she didn't seem to mind. She helped herself to a cheese sandwich from his plate. Trungle was happily tucking into an onion bhaji that Herne had bought and set out on the buffet table next to the little pots of sliced grapes and peeled orange slices, much to Oberon's annoyance. As Perran settled himself, he saw Old Jago hobbling towards him out of the crowd carrying an entire quiche.

"Made it, then, did you?" the old Knocker said. "Good lad, good lad."

Perran scowled at him. "I could have gotten lost, or been eaten by something!"

"Like a really big hamster..." Thick Gary pondered.

"Like a really big hamster!" Perran ran with it, refusing to let his anger be quelled.

"But you wasn't though, was you?" Jago waggled his extensive eyebrows. "And you made some friends, and that's nice." He looked at Roz and then winked hugely. Roz rolled her eyes but said nothing. Jago sniffed. "Now, since you're here, I'm off for a snack, and a nap. See you tonight."

Perran shoved his helmet back up on his head and balled his hands into fists. "You can't! The Foreman sent us here to talk about the Miners' rights! He's counting on us! We're on the *agenda*!"

Jago sucked on his few remaining teeth, leant his wizened arm over the top of his walking stick so that the pan of quiche he held threatened to tumble wetly into Perran's lap, leant down and said, "You don't really think anything's actually going to happen here, today, do you? You don't *actually* think any of them Committee peoples is going to be listening to anything a pair of scrawny Knockers like us have got to say, do you? You mark my words, laddie, there's going to be a lot of ballyhoo and people what like the sounds of their own voices, a bloody good buffy lunch, then down the pub for a beer or twelve."

Perran was angry. The sort of angry that can make an earnest, if somewhat awkward, young folktale character say stupid things. In this instance, it made Perran climb to his feet indignantly and declare, slamming his fist into his palm, "Well, I shall see about that, shan't I? I'll show you!"

Somewhere in the ether, the, "I'll show you" stories zinged and pinged and crackled, and laughed, because they knew exactly what happened when anyone indignantly declared, "I'll show you!". This was up there with knowing exactly what happens when someone shouts, "Oi, watch this!" (and sometimes, "hold my beer").

Roz put her head in her hand. Trungle shook his head, showering leaves.

* * *

198

Approximately forty minutes after the agenda stated that the meeting would start, the two Storykeepers appeared at the side of the clearing and silently made their way to the two remaining empty chairs at the desks. The only one who seemed remotely bothered that they had arrived, or that they were late, was Frank the Wisp, who was wringing his hands and twitching from left to right. The Storykeepers sat, in their identical suits with their identical pale faces, and folded their hands identically over their huge tomes. They did not make eye contact with anyone. Anyone who has ever sat and waited for a grey, pale, man in a suit to arrive at a meeting for forty minutes will not be surprised to learn that neither of them apologised for being late.

"Well, lovely, since we're all here, we can..." Frank began.

"Let's get this over with, shall we?" The bespectacled Storykeeper sighed, looking at his watch.

Mab drummed her fingernails on the desk and her nostrils flared. But she took a deep breath, pressed her palms onto the desk and pushed herself to her feet. She raised one elegant hand into the air and there was a flash of lightning followed by a loud clap of thunder. It was a little trick she'd learnt from Thor. The crowd in the clearing fell silent and all eyes turned towards her. She smiled her glossy red lips.

"Good afternoon, welcome, I'd like to thank you all for coming." Her voice was amplified – it seemed like magic to everyone except the Committee, who could see the microphone pack clipped to the back of her dress – "I know some of you have come a long way. I'd also like to thank our Council members for joining us today..." She threw a hand towards the Storykeepers, who did not move or acknowledge her remark, "...who are *thrilled* to be here... Now, we've got a lot to get through, so let's make a start." She took her seat again.

The Wisp floated up from his seat, drifted forward over the desk holding a ream of paper that he let unravel. It hit the ground. Behind him, Finn McCool flexed his fingers and picked up his chopsticks, poised with them over his laptop keyboard.

"First off," the Wisp began, "I shall acknowledge the apologies. Ahhaa haaaa... Peaseblossom the Imp, the Beast of Bodmin, the Elemental known as Summer and the Elemental known as Winter who are currently renovating a house in Alaska but send their regards, Gatlin the Hob, Bridgid, Bran the Blessed, the Ogre of Liverpool Street..." His voice was nasal, whining, boring beyond all belief. His voice was not amplified as Mab's had been and though he tried to project, those at the back could barely hear him and so they started to chat quietly amongst themselves.

"...the lady Marion, Bob the Troll Fol De Roll, the Finnmen of Orkney, the..."

The chatter rippled through the crowd, growing in momentum like a wave hitting shallow ground. Soon enough, Perran couldn't really hear anything that was being said. He thought he made out the names, "Loch Ness Monster" and, "Blue Men of the Minch" but it was really hard to hear. No one else seemed to care that no one could hear and that no one was listening. Not even the Committee. Perran looked at Roz. She made a 'told you' face and went back to attempting to peel a hard-boiled egg. She had attached one of her flint knives to her arm stump using the fluorescent elastic bands and was using the sharp end of the knife to keep the egg still while she peeled away the shell with her right hand.

* * *

Mab leant over to Merlin. "Not a single representative from the water stories. Not even the Kelpies could be bothered."

"See a lot of water here in your enchanted forest, do you?" Merlin quipped back, as Mab's face fell into an expression of chagrin.

"...fuck..." she whispered.

Merlin gave her a sarcastic thumbs up. "Inclusive design for the win. Always next time, eh?"

Mab scribbled on her legal pad furiously and underlined 'send fruit baskets as apology'.

Finally, Frank got to the end of the apologies, rolled up his list and floated back to his seat.

Merlin stood up. "Now, first order of business," he started, then paused, as the crowd continued to chatter. He snapped his fingers and spoke again, "First order of business!" His voice, this time, echoed around the clearing

"That's more like it!" Perran said enthusiastically.

"...Is the international delegation for the summit," Merlin boomed. "May I remind you all to check your inboxes and respond, if you require tickets, to Freya's email invite. We need to get numbers to Ganesh by Thursday, OK? That's *Thursday.*" He lifted up his phone to read from the email, squinting at it. "Some of the listed keynote speakers are 'Misunderstood Villains in Myth and Folklore' with Baba Yaga and our very own Mordred, 'LGBTQ+ Representation' with Tu Er Shen, Gardening Workshops with Cronos, Q'uq'umatz and Oko, and 'Dragons – We Don't All Look The Same' with Fafnir and Ryu. And, of course, there's the midnight mixer with Orpheus on the decks. I am also to remind you that if anyone requires the vegan or gluten-free menu options, to make sure you include that on your invitation response. Next–" Merlin paused to take a sip of water, "I understand we've an update on the situation at the border from our Defence Committee representatives..." He looked over the edge of his phone as a Redcap and a Goblin with an AK47 slung over his shoulder came to stand at the lectern. The Redcap removed his burgundy beret and tucked it under his frog-like arm, then saluted. Merlin vaguely waved a hand back in his general direction.

"Sah!" the Redcap shouted. "Pleased to report, sah, that the situation at the border is that the men are angry and soaking in the blood of their enemies, sah!"

Merlin nodded slowly, glanced at Mab, who shrugged.

"Right, er, jolly... jolly good, eh? The blood of their enemies, eh?"

"Yessah, absolutely, sah. Lots of enemies."

"And um, how, how is all this blood soaking affecting the, er, Beanstalk Day Agreement?"

The Redcap turned to his Goblin aide, who whispered something in his ear, then said "Oh, couldn't be better, sah. Golden eggs all round. The lads are keeping the bloody hand of the English out, sah!"

Merlin frowned. Mab looked panicked and flicked through the papers in her file.

"Um, just to be, you know, absolutely and a hundred percent clear on this, General," Mab smiled widely and encouragingly, "What side of the border are you defending?"

The Redcap leant back towards his aide, who whispered something again. "Both, Ma'am!" the Redcap saluted. "Blood baths all round, Ma'am!"

Mab massaged her temples. "Let me try to understand..."

But Merlin, wincing, interrupted with, "Very good, chaps, very good. Keep up the sterling efforts. Send the Council's very best to the lads at the front, one big push and home for Solstice, eh?" The wizard saluted.

The Redcap General looked as if he might cry with pride, returned the salute with a flourish. The Goblin aide lifted his chin high and also saluted.

"Sah, tis our honour and our duty!"

"Yes, well, thank you General... er, dismissed."

The Defence Committee stepped back from the lectern and marched away. Merlin threw a hand up in apology to Mab. "I'm so incredibly sorry, my dear, but if you question them too hard on it all, they go a bit loopy. They've been known to rip their uniforms off and start screaming before."

Mab indicated with a complicit nod of her head and a raise of her fingers that she understood. She was, she realised, starting to get a headache. "Fine, fine. Next?"

Frank checked the agenda. "Nomination Committee."

A Hobgoblin, a Pixie and a Brownie wearing a sash covered in fabric badges came to the lectern. They huddled close to one another, but it was the Hobgoblin who spoke. "Good afternoon, my name is Pip and this is Niff and that's Sooz. We are the BILMFA Nominating Committee and we've been working hard to process all of the applications and suggestions for membership. I think you'll find that..."

"Yes, yes," Frank the Wisp waved a hand, "get on with it, will you, we're trying to keep this ship sailing."

Pip the Hobgoblin rolled her eyes, pulled out a stack of application forms from her pocket. "OK. So, the nominations for induction into BILMFA, for your consideration are as follows... James Bond-"

"No, absolutely not, ahaa haaaa," Frank wheezed a shrivelling little chuckle, "he's a fictional character!"

"We're all fictional, ye muckleheided nitwit," Finn McCool grumbled, pausing his typing.

"Well, he's neither legendary, mythical, nor folkloric, is he?" Frank crossed his skinny arms over his glowing chest.

"Well, technically..." Mab was tapping her pen against her teeth, "Bond is a culmination character of several real agents known to and including Ian Flemming, so...?"

"That'd make him eligible for the Legends category. Modern Robin Hood, isn't he?" Little John nodded. "And you *did* let the Peter Pan lad join last time on the basis of him being a Green Man forest spirit theme?"

Frank scowled.

"Motion to consider application." Mab nodded, as Finn Typed.

"The other nominations," Pip read from her notecard, "are William Wallace, Guy Fawkes, the Highgate Vampire and, uh, David Bowie."

Frank scoffed, tossed his head in exasperation. "That scrawny lad with the weird eyes and spaceman schtick? He's not been dead long enough yet. Tell him to try again in fifty years. And we don't *have* Vampires in BILMFA, they're not a British Isles native story."

"Well, it does raise some interesting questions about where we draw the line," Merlin mused, twirling his beard around his finger. "You go back far enough and we're all Nordic, Scandinavian, Central-European, Greek, Egyptian. We don't want to be xenophobic, do we?" He looked pointedly at Frank.

"Good point, but don't want to be appropriating other culture's myths and legends," Mab said. "Mithras knows we've got enough imperialism to go around here already."

"I say, if there's members of those groups here on the Isles wishing to join, let it be a motion that we will allow it," Merlin suggested.

Mab conceded, "OK. Agreed."

"What about the other two?" Pip asked. "Wallace and Fawkes?"

"To be quite honest with you, I thought we'd already invited them." Merlin looked sheepish. "Poor form on our part. Process their applications immediately. Won't look good if Wallace sees Robin Hood, Ivanhoe and Rob Roy are already in. Is that everything, Pip?"

Pip nodded. "Yes sir, all the ones worth mentioning. We did get an application from a Jack B Nimble, but after a bit of digging, we think it's just Puck being a dickhead."

Little John thumped the desk. "I knew it, the little shit!"

"Right you are, thanks ever so." Merlin nodded as Pip, the Pixie and Brownie shuffled away from the stand in unison.

"Do you think the other two actually speak or are they just attached to each side for moral support?" Mab wondered aloud. "I'm not sure I even know which one is which... right. What's next?"

"Treasury update," Frank the Wisp said.

"Skip it." Little John waved his hand. "We've already done my bit earlier."

"But, but, it's– you *can't* skip! You're on the agen..." Frank flapped.

"No one gives a flying hoot about the sodding agenda!" Little John sighed, leaning back in his chair and putting his feet up on the desk. "I'll drop it all in an email to Finn and he can include it in the minutes, alright?"

Frank's iridescent blue colour flushed purple. "This is highly irregular and against Council protocol!"

"Ah, get tae fuck," Finn McCool growled at him, lifting his huge shaggy head from his laptop, chopsticks poised, "Ye wee arsepiece."

Frank spluttered. Mab hid her snigger behind her coffee mug. Little John braced his arms behind his head and closed his eyes in satisfaction.

"Oh, before I forget, it's not on the agenda, but," Merlin checked an email on his smartphone, "I believe the Social Committee would like to give us an update."

"It's not... on the agenda..." Frank shrank to a small flickering pale blue light. Merlin pretended not to hear.

A large vomit-coloured Troll in a slightly-too-small pinstriped shirt was clambering through the crowd, shuffling a sheaf of papers. He dropped some, stopped to picked them up. "Thanks, sorry, sorry, haha, oops, sorry about that..." By the time he'd made it to the lectern, he was sweating profusely and grinning too widely. He insisted on turning the lectern around so that he could see the crowd, and he gave a friendly little wave. "Hello! That's better, isn't it? Now we can all see each other and be friends. My name's Dennis, Dennis Snotlouger? You might remember me from the France versus UK volleyball tournament last year? Or the Christmas karaoke pass the parcel? That went down a treat?" His uncertainty and nervousness and absolute resolve to make lots of friends via organised fun, despite all evidence to the contrary that this worked, made Dennis' voice go up at the end of every sentence, like he was asking permission to exist. "Anyways, I just wanted to take a moment to run through some of the upcoming events and mixers on the social calendar? First of all though, can we just take a moment to show our appreciation to Oberon for an absolutely phenomenal buffet he's laid on for us all today? Yeah? Let's give 'im a nice thank you round of applause?"

To give them their due, though most of the people in the audience made it a point to avoid Dennis, they knew he was harmless really, and they did, on this occasion, give a hearty round of applause. Oberon did lay on a nice spread, after all.

"Great work, really," Dennis continued. "OK, so, as you'll all know, we've got the Forestry Games coming up. If you'd like to register a team, speak with the Woodwose? A reminder that aquarobics is on Wednesday evenings, and anyone can sign up at all, just email your local Merfolk rep. Oh, and this one I am *beyond* excited about? In September, we've got the Fisher King's Bake Off! Your chance to win the grail. Best get your buttery biscuit bases and your soggy bottoms sorted!" He laughed at his own joke and gave himself a little excited round of applause. The sweat stains in the armpits of his shirt were spreading, dark and damp. "The theme for the Secret Bogieman's Ball next year has been agreed and, oh this is just *lovely*, the theme is Under The Bridge? And lastly, if any of you are interested in getting involved with the Feminist Folklore book club, make sure you speak with Jenny Greenteeth, who, I believe, will be hanging out by the swamp round back after the Meeting if any of you want to catch her?" Dennis stopped speaking, seemed surprised that he'd run out of words, stared into the sea of indifferent eyes and stiffly walked away from the microphone.

Throughout all this, Perran had been trying to remember his speech, closing his eyes and mouthing the words silently, occasionally pulling a face and checking his hand-scrawled notes.

"You all right?" Trungle asked. "You having a stroke?"

"No," Perran hissed, "Shut *up*, I'm practising!"

At the front, Merlin adjusted his glasses, feeling vaguely sorry for Dennis the Troll, who really did try very hard. Most of the crowd were chatting amongst themselves again. Mab was pinching the bridge of her nose. Fat lot of good she'd done chairing this thing. Just like always, Merlin'd had to step up. Little John looked like he'd dozed off. The Storykeepers were fidgeting and repeatedly checking their watches. Robin Hood and Arthur were hurling sausage rolls at each other. The Dragon had the hiccups. Some of the Witches had already started to sneak off into the trees with barely disguised bottles of gin shoved up their sleeves.

He cleared his throat. "Well, I think that's just about everything for this year. Thanks awfully, all of you, for coming and..."

The crowd were already rippling, shifting, stretching, just waiting for the final word to allow them to make a break for it and get on with the more important aspects of the Meeting – getting drunk and eating too much, various high-stake poker games, weapons trades, that sort of thing.

"No!" a voice shouted across the clearing. Merlin peered into the crowd. Mab looked up. John opened his eyes. Even Finn McCool raised his head from his furious typing. "Not yet! We're not done yet!"

"There's always bloody one, isn't there?" Little John muttered. "Someone always has to ask a bloody question."

"Wait!" Perran was stumbling to the front, acutely aware that he was comprised mostly of oversized feet, as he tried to flatten his tatty looking piece of paper. "I'm meant to speak, I've got a timeslot, I'm on the agenda!"

Frank the Wisp flared in brilliant cerulean burst, rose up to float above the desk. "Let the boy speak!" he declared loudly, enunciating each word with relish. "He's *On The Agenda*!"

"Is he?" Mab flicked through her papers. "Who is he?"

"Looks like a Knocker," John offered. When Mab continued to look bemused, he added "Cornish lot. Miners."

Merlin's shoulders tensed and he turned to her, coughing loudly and mumbling ,"Ahem, hem, minersstrike, ahem."

"Oooooh of course." Mab smiled her very best executive smile. "You're the lad from the mines."

Perran shoved his helmet back on his head, and nodded. "Yes ma'am, majesty, um..."

"Just Mab." She wrinkled her nose at him. "What's your name, boy?"

He felt very flustered all of a sudden. "Uh, Perran..." He tried to place his notes on the lectern, realised the Troll had left it facing the wrong way, dropped his notes, tried to pick them up, dropped his pickaxe. Left the pickaxe on the floor, grabbed his notes. Stood up straight, pushed his helmet out of his eyes. Wanted to throw up.

"Well, Perran, have you had a good day? Had enough to eat?" Mab asked.

"Ye-yes, thank you, ma'am, Mab..." he shuffled nervously, turning the paper over and over in his hands, "Um, esteemed members of the Council, it's an honour to stand before you today, thank you for your time..."

"What time *is* it?" The Storykeeper without the glasses suddenly sat up. "I've got golf at four."

"It's three-forty," Little John said.

"Bugger that, I shan't be late, not for a supreme being of Alpha Centauri." He began to stand up.

"But, I've not finished yet!" Perran protested, knowing he had in fact, not even really managed to start.

"Of course, of course, you go ahead Pelan."

"Perran," Frank the Wisp corrected.

"Sorry?" Mab frowned at him.

"His name, your Majesty. It's Perran."

"Oh, I do apologise, Perran, do continue!"

Perran nodded, cleared his throat. "I would like to draw your attention today to the plight of the..."

"Is there any Battenberg?" the Storykeeper with the glasses asked, peering at the mostly decimated buffet table.

"Is it on an exploding boat?" asked the other, rising on tiptoes to look.

"To the plight..." Perran raised his voice, "of the Cornish miners –"

"Exploding boat?" Finn McCool pulled a face. "You scunners want me tae put that in tha minutes?"

The Storykeepers turned to face the giant and stared at him.

"You know," said the one without the glasses, "I've really no idea what he's saying."

Finn McCool pursed his lips, rising to his feet. "Ya bawbags talk tae me like ahm the fukken eejit here, and yer the ains got faces like dugs likken pish offa nettles!"

The Storykeepers watched his huge body rising above them. "Fascinating isn't it? It's *like* it's a language but... not a clue whatsoever."

Finn McCool roared, and Little John was trying to hold him back, "Leave it, Finn, they're not worth it!"

"The plight of the Cornish miners who have, of recent months, been forced to...!" Perran shouted.

"Exploding boats?" The Redcap General reappeared. "Exploding boats?! Bombs, is it? Let us at 'em, Sah! Point us at the Tommys or the Gerrys or the... the..."

"Oh, bugger this." Frank the Wisp threw his hands up in exasperation and disappeared in a small flash of blue light.

"Come an' fight me like a man!" Finn was jeering, as the Storykeepers backed away.

The Redcap's Goblin aide was crawling, commando style, across the grass in front of the desk, talking into his shoulder, "Red Fox Leader to Alpha Squadron One, we have a bogie, I repeat, a live bogie. Beware exploding cake..."

Behind them, the crowd were all already making their way out of the clearing. Robin and Arthur had resorted to firing cocktail sausages violently at each other. Perran stood clutching his speech, looking around at the utter chaos, saw Roz, with her very awesome hair and her lovely sympathetic smile waiting for him, and his stomach did that happy little warm thing. He looked back at Mab, who was pouring something from a hip flask into her mug, at the Giant who was being restrained by a Merry Man, at the two not-men in suits who looked, for the first time all afternoon, animated by the possibility of being sat on by the Giant, and the Wizard with the spectacles who was filming the mad Redcap and giggling.

"Fuck it." Perran threw his speech into the air, tossed off his stupid tin helmet, and went to see if Roz might like to go out with him.

As he strolled over to her, ducking out of the way of flying cocktail sausages, with his hands shoved into his pockets, Roz winced. "We did try to warn you. Trungle tried three times to talk to them about Dutch Elm disease in the back end of the 1800s..."

"Let me guess," Perran sidled up to her, "some mental Redcap tried to start a war with the trees?"

Roz laughed.

"Would you like to go for a walk with me?" he asked.

She sighed, contentedly, thinking she'd not done a bad job with helping this one find his courage. "Thought you'd never ask."

As they walked out of the clearing arm in arm, Old Jago leant on his walking stick and watched them. Then he bent and picked up the hand-written speech Perran had failed to start.

"All the miners want to do is talk," he said. "It's the humans, see. They've gone and privatised it all. The Knockers're worried they won't have a function anymore. Don't want to end up abandoned stories in the ether."

"Of course, of course, it's completely understandable." Merlin took the notes from Jago, glanced at them. "I'll be sure to make sure the right people see this, and get someone from the Union to pop along and have a chat."

Jago nodded as Merlin tucked the note into his robes.

"Pint?" the old Knocker suggested.

"Oh *hells* yes." Merlin sighed, his eyes fluttering shut. "Or twelve."

"Now, my magical matey," Jago winked, "You're talking!"

They walked out of the clearing together, leaving the Redcap General and his Goblin aide to carry out a controlled explosion of the Pavlova.

* * *

The stories, the really good ones, are the ones that hold a mirror up to all of existence and teach a fundamental truth through imagery and metaphor. Once upon a time, in the In-Between, at the Edge of Dreams, there was a Meeting, and nothing at all really happened even though there was an agenda. Because, in reality, it's usually easier to just send a sodding email.

* * *

The Man Who Went Up A Mountain And Came Down A Poet

I only went to hike, and see the world unfold below me like a soft map, all smoothed out soft creases and miles turned to inches beneath my feet. I only wanted to climb the Mountain. Cader Idris, they call it. The Giant's Seat.

They told me not to sleep, told me those that do wake up mad, or wake up a poet, or else don't wake up at all.

I don't recall sleep beckoning, only the vague notion of falling, and waking up cold, afraid, alone, untamed and untapped like a sap spring has been knocked into my bark.

I started to try and climb back down, and now I can't seem to help being a mess of metaphors and misplaced similes. There's something wrong with me.

There's a black lake nestled in the folds of the Mountain. They say it's bottomless. Maybe there's a lady that lives in there waiting to thrust a sword upon some other unsuspecting soul just out for a stroll... I can't shake these bloody rhymes off; they stick to my bootheels like well-worn Country songs with half-remembered lyrics.

I'm forgetting my name. It was... It was... something to do with letters strung together to signpost a person so we all know we're captains of our own little ships. I'm not so sure that's true anymore. I'm not so sure I'm me, and not you, or the sky, or the Mountain or the lake or...

Nothing is what it is; all things are like another, but never, maddeningly, the thing itself. Nothing is what it seems.

The Mountain is big and fits inside of me like a barely contained dream. It seems perhaps I just woke up mad, after all.

I wonder when the madness will stop trying to crawl from my hands in sprawling words and climb back to curl into the crawlspace of my mind.

I wonder, really, if there's much difference between the poet and the madman, when faced with so much sky

And rock and

The mountain is trying to leak out of my eyes.

It's too much.

The only thing I can do, staring at the shifting shades of light that flits from shadow to bright through rippling oceans of grass, is write.

I write it all, as I fall between the rock and the mad place.

The words are all I have.

* * *

ALICE EWENS

Ursilla's Coat

I am not a bit tamed – I too am untranslatable;
I sound my barbaric yawp over the roofs of the world...
(Walt Whitman – Song of Myself)

The ferry had definitely seen better days; there were circles of rust around the bilge holes like last nights' mascara, and it creaked and groaned as it moved. Ocean water spilled over the car deck and slooshed around vehicle wheels, then receded, as the ferry dipped and sipped at the North Sea – or was it the Norwegian Sea here? Sea spray lifted in the wind and splattered across the windscreen. Marie leant forward in the drivers' seat, crossed her arms over the top of the steering wheel to peer at the sky. She was restless. She wanted to get out, lean over the railing, like some of the other passengers, but – she glanced at Polly sleeping in the back seat, a sprawl of six-year-old wild abandon – she couldn't just wander off. So, she compromised and got out to brace herself on the car against the wind.

The island of Orkney had slid out of view and now it was grey water and big sky. Everything was so flat here. The water, the land. All these funny, flat, treeless islands barely poking up through the water, like bubbles in a pan on low heat. Some of the islands had cliffs, but the sky and sea were so vast that the land seemed dwarfed by it all. The cold sea spray was hitting her right in the face now; the grey forever sky, the wind, water and the birds all really making their point about how far she was from Chatham. She tilted her head back and watched the gulls overhead.

In less than ten minutes, she'd be rolling off the ferry on to Shapinsay and Spence would be waiting. At least, he better be, the sod. She wouldn't put it past him to be late, even living practically on top of the ferry port on an island with approximately four other people on it. Bloody Spence, swanning in without a care in the world, late, grinning, and getting away with it 'cause he was the golden boy and he always got away with everything. At least, he had 'til he'd come out, and then Dad got all weird. But, Spence had escaped into the world, made a life for himself and he seemed happy. Like, actually, genuinely happy and Marie was happy for him. Really, she was. The twinge of resentment annoyed her; she shoved it away and drummed her fingers impatiently on her arms, urging the ferry to move faster.

Kirkwall, the big town on Orkney, had been bustling and sweet, a postcard fishing town filled with folksy pubs and shops, but still quiet in comparison to the urban sprawl of the Medway Towns; to Chatham and its run-down concrete jungle of half closed-down high street. They called Kent the Garden of England and, if that was true, then the bit of Chatham she'd grow up in was that bit of overgrown rubble and half-collapsed **BBQ** at the back of the garden that you always meant to do something with and never did.

As the ferry turned across the headland of Kirkwall, she could see the town of Balfour on the neighbouring island of Shapinsay to her left. Orkney was quaint and folksy and Shapinsay looked bleak and windswept, a forgotten sister left to run mad on a moor. There was an odd grey castle, with turrets and everything, on the hill, and a stretch of red limestone buildings along the waterfront. From here, the rest of the island looked green and uninhabited. One of the waterfront buildings, a two-story perfectly symmetrical structure that looked like a doll's house complete with brick chimney right in the centre of the roof, stood slightly apart from the others, and was strung with white fairy lights. That must be it. That must be Georgie's Place. Spence had said he and Sam had wanted people to be able to see it from the ferries.

Polly made a sound like a disgruntled hippo in her sleep and Marie glanced through the partially open window to look at her. Mousey hair a fuzzy nest around her head, arms and legs out straight, head tossed back and mouth hanging open. Little snoring starfish clutching her purple elephant. She'd been so good. Two days of driving from Chatham, and one delightful little overnight stop outside Penrith in a Travelodge room that smelled like vomit. Polly had only wrinkled her nose at the Travelodge room, had entertained herself with Disney movies and YouTube videos on the tablet. She'd been good as gold. Patient. Far more patient than Marie had been. Far more understanding than Marie could've hoped. When Marie had buckled her into the car seat outside her Mum's house in Chatham and passed Polly the plush elephant, Polly had fixed those huge eyes on her and said,

"Daddy isn't coming."

It wasn't even a question, just a realisation of the truth.

"No, Squish, Daddy's not coming." Marie had sighed, waited for the barrage of questions to follow, but none came.

Polly studied the purple elephant, then her mother, then nodded quietly. "OK. Don't be sad, Mummy."

It had nearly broken Marie.

Barely a heartbeat ago, she'd been a girl herself, too much eyeliner and lip gloss, skirt too short, smirk too knowing, parading as an adult with this boy or that, desperate to be needed and wanted. Smoking round the back of the science labs gave way to clubs, too many shots, too many hangovers and the ache to be more than what she'd been assigned in life. She'd gone to college and got great A-levels, much to everyone's amazement. She got into all three universities she'd applied for, but her Dad had said it was a waste of time and money to rack up that much student debt and get no guarantee of a job at the end of it. So she took a sales job at BMW that paid pretty well. Spence had gone by then, off to London, then France, learning to be a chef in fancy restaurants, and Marie was resigning herself to a life lost in concrete suburbia, a life of same-ness. Work in the week, pissed on Fridays and Saturdays and sometimes on Sundays, shag if she was lucky, watching all her mates dissolve and blur into the same listless background. Then there was Steve.

She'd sold him a car and he'd offered to take her out to dinner in it. He'd been attractive in a local-lad-done-good sort of way. A bit rough round the edges but he'd had a good city job with a financial consultancy. He was older, but not by much. Her dad liked him which, in hindsight, should've been a warning sign. But at twenty, with a feeling of dread that her life was already mapped out and on rails, she'd latched on and held tight. He was the most exciting thing to have ever walked into her life and she let him have everything that she was. She blurred into the fabric of him. At first, she'd thought he was saving her. Later, when it all came undone, she realised he'd only been drowning and pulling her down with him.

The first few years had been good. They made an impression when they walked into a room together. He liked her to be made up, to wear the expensive watch he'd got her, and the heels. She'd liked to look nice for him. She'd liked the way he'd tell her no one else's' bird looked as well put-together as she was. They got a place behind Rochester High Street and would lay in bed on the weekends listening to the Cathedral bells ringing. Polly came along unexpectedly a couple of years later, but they'd both been thrilled – at least she'd thought they'd both been thrilled. He certainly acted the part at the time. But he hadn't been thrilled with her refusing to wear heels while pregnant, or that makeup and good hair slid down her list of important things. He'd sometimes have to work late or stay up in town for a few nights to get deals done or deadlines met, but he'd always call to say goodnight. And then after a while he didn't call to say goodnight anymore. He didn't like coming home to a messy home and baby crying. He didn't like the smell of baby sick that permeated Marie's skin. And then he was working later and longer, would come home angry and sulking if she asked too many questions. By the time Polly was four, he was hardly home. Bills started to go unpaid. She'd had to take up a second job pulling pints at the Man Of Kent three nights a week and get her mum to watch Polly.

Polly was silly, strange, so bloody confident and so smart; she'd stomp into a room full of strangers with her hands on her hips and declare "I'm Polly!" Polly loved dinosaurs and the stars and elephants and would reel off facts like she'd swallowed Google. She wanted to be either a garden gnome or a Christmas tree farmer. She was a weird girl and she was the best thing Marie had ever done with her life.

The arguments were never loud. They simmered and slithered under closed doors, punctuated with the bang of frustrated fists on countertops, the slamming of front doors, the chill of beds unslept in. She knew Steve was having an affair. Multiple, probably, but he never sat still long enough to confront. Three months ago, just after Polly's sixth birthday, she'd answered his phone while he'd been in the shower and got all the ammunition she needed. Turns out Steve was shagging approximately half of South London and racking up quite the cocaine debt. So she left. It had all come to a head with him standing in the street screaming up at her parents' place at two in the morning two weeks ago. Over the years, she'd felt disappointment, heartbreak, white rage, humiliation; had felt worthless and tossed aside like a snotty tissue but had never felt afraid of him until that night. Her mum had called the police. Marie had called her brother.

"Spence I gotta get out. I'm suffocating and he's mental. He's going to get himself killed or something. I can't have him around Polly when he's like this."

And Spence had said, "Come to the island, Mare. Don't tell him. Don't even tell Dad, just say you're coming to stay with me. They think I'm still in Edinburgh."

Sam had offered, in the background, to come down and get her, bless him, but she didn't want to wait, so she said she'd do the driving.

And here she was, at the start of the school summer holidays and three gorgeous weeks off work, the possibilities stretching ahead like the vast flat horizon. She was desperate to see her big brother again, desperate to feel the wind blowing through her soul, desperate to shed Steve's ghost that trailed over everything. Desperate to feel like her feet were on solid ground after being out of her depth her whole life.

* * *

Spencer wasn't late. He was right there, standing at the end of the jetty waiting with his mop of fair hair and lopsided easy grin, his hands shoved in his pockets. He was wearing chef's whites with black and white checked trousers and – she sniggered – a pair of grey Crocs. Despite the wind, his sleeves were rolled to his elbows and his cheeks were ruddy and round. He'd always looked a little like a Hobbit, despite being nearly six feet tall. If it weren't for the dusting of stubble and the broadness of his shoulders now, Marie could've sworn he was still seventeen and sitting on the end of her bed coyly telling her that he'd snogged David Rickshaw in the beer garden of the Tap 'n' Tin.

"Uncle Spence! Uncle Spence!" Polly was chanting.

"Squish Bean!" Spence yelled, throwing his hands up and performing a weird lolloping dance as Marie pulled in beside him. She was struggling to unbuckle her seat belt, then stumbling in a half-run, half-fall into her brothers' arms.

"All right, you skank?" He laughed, wrapping her in a bear hug and planting a kiss on her forehead.

"All right, minger!" She hugged him back.

"Get out of my way, let me get to the love of my life!" He shoved Marie aside and was lifting Polly out of the backseat into his arms with a satisfied '*oorrrgghh*' grunt.

"Hello Uncle Spence, I got an elephant called Osha!" Polly pushed the purple elephant into Spencer's face.

He took it in one hand, hitched Polly onto the opposite hip, and very seriously said, "Hello Squish Bean, and hello Osha." He threw his arm round Marie and pulled her close.

"How are ye, Spencer?!" a voice called from another car disembarking behind them.

Spencer waved. "Not too bad, Mac! Not too bad!"

The man Spence was calling to, in the Yaris, was white haired with a flat cap and broad smile.

"This is my sister Marie!" Spence continued, "And this," he shifted to indicate the little girl settled on his hip, "is Polly."

"I'm Polly!" Polly declared, throwing her hands up and waving.

The man in the car grinned wider and waved back with both hands. "Welcome to Shapinsay!"

Marie nestled against Spencer's shoulder, felt the wind pulling at her jumper and whipping her hair around them, and took a huge lungful of air like she was just coming up from underwater for a breath.

* * *

They drove the short distance from the ferry terminal to Georgie's Place with Spence in the passenger seat pointing things and people out.

"And that's Pauline, she does the post office on Tuesdays. And that's the shop, you can get your basics there but most things we get over on

221

Orkney or order in from the Mainland, and that's Tina who works at the gym…"

"There's a gym here?!" Marie laughed, shocked.

"Oh, aye," Spence adopted an impressively accurate Scottish accent, "'tis the very picture o' health here!"

They drove away from the village towards the castle.

"Is there a prince or a princess up there?" Polly pointed to it, grey and tucked in against the hill, surrounded by a small forest of squat trees. Up close, it was more stately home with turrets than ancient structure.

"Not these days." Spence shook his head. "It's owned by some foreign estate management company. Used to be a house, then a hotel and wedding venue, and now it's apparently a private home again, though it's empty. Owners live somewhere else and we lease our outbuilding off 'em for peanuts."

They were driving along a narrow lane towards the lone red brick building Marie had seen from the ferry, with Balfour Castle up on their right and the sea on their left on the other side of a low drystone wall. For an 'outbuilding' of the castle, it was pretty big. Suddenly an old woman clambered over the sea wall, almost stepping in front of the car.

"Shit!" Marie braked and swerved slightly but the woman simply stood, in a long greenish-brown wax coat, her mane of white curly hair billowing around her and did not move a muscle. She sank her hands into her coat pockets and simply watched the car pass her.

"Who the fuck is that?!" Marie wrenched the gearbox down a gear after nearly stalling.

"That would be Ursilla," Spence raised a hand and waved at the woman, "Shapinsay's resident sea witch."

"Swearing's bad, Mummy," Polly said, quietly.

"It is, love, sorry. That lady just surprised me!"

The solitary figure in the wax coat stood on the side of the lane and watched the car. Then she turned and strode off back towards the village.

The sudden near-miss and accompanying adrenaline filled the car with an odd ominous feeling, but it didn't last long, because they were pulling up in front of Georgie's Place, tires crunching in the gravel, and a round woman with a shock of pink hair and a bright turquoise kaftan was rushing out to meet them with her arms raised in welcome.

"And that," Spence said, grinning, "would be Georgie."

* * *

Georgie was Sam's Nanna and she was all belly laugh and dirty jokes as she ushered them all into the building. Inside, it was a cheerful and welcoming pub with tables spread out across the flagstone floor. The specials board hung over an open fireplace. The ceilings were exposed dark beams, but everything else was light and airy. Marie propped her suitcase against the wall and looked around, impressed. Everything, right down to the door fixings, the ornaments and art on the walls, the billiards table in the far corner, spoke cosy island life with a touch of class.

"Not bad, brother. Not bad at all..." She nodded her approval.

Polly ran into the bar, currently empty of any customers, and spun around, declaring loudly, "I like it!"

"I am extremely glad to hear it." Spence placed Polly's small green suitcase on the bar and balanced Osha the plush purple elephant on top of that. "We'll have a drink and a snack and then go explore your bedroom, eh?"

Marie could see a flight of stairs disappearing up behind the bar. She knew Spence, Sam and Georgie lived upstairs and that they had three guest rooms up there too, available to rent for tourists, touring bands during the Orkneys Folk Festival, or run-away sisters from the South-East of England.

"Make yourself at home, I'll grab us something to eat." Spence disappeared through a swing-door at the far end of the bar and Marie caught a glimpse of stainless steel and white tiles.

"We serve food from midday 'til nine. Tourists are usually gone before five and make up most of the lunchtime trade, but we do get a lot of the locals in for their supper of an evening." Georgie was pottering, shifting salt and pepper pots, aligning beermats on tables. "Spencer likes to call this a high-class gastro-pub." She grinned at Marie. "The locals love the fact they've got a Michelin-star chef right here on the island!"

"A summer working for Marco Pierre White isn't the same as having my own Michelin star, and you know it!" Spence yelled, from the kitchen.

"Oh hush, don't you burst my bubble," Georgie called back, and gave Marie a rueful grin. "Have a seat at the bar, pet. And you," she caught Polly round the waist as the girl ran past, "You can sit up here, with me!"

"Can I have banana marmite toast?" Polly allowed herself to be whisked up in Georgie's formidable arms and placed up on the bar.

Marie wrinkled her nose as she climbed onto a barstool, recalling that it had been Spence, three years back, who'd first made it for Polly on a rare visit south. "I don't think they do that here, Pol."

Spencer was clattering noisily in the kitchen.

"This place is fantastic!" Marie smiled. "Spence said it was an outbuilding of the castle or something?"

Georgie was pleased with Marie's compliment but tried to look modest. "The building has sat here as long as anyone can remember. It was some kind of communal island art space back in the 90s, good light from the sea I've been told, and empty after it. You'd no' believe the stuff the boys found in cupboards and in the attic when they leased the place. No one's sure what the building was first built for, maybe a caretaker's place or some such, but there's none on the island now that remember. Save possibly for Ursilla, who wouldn't tell you even if she knew."

"The sea witch lady," Polly chirped.

"Oh, you've met her, have ye?"

"More like nearly ran her over on the way here." Marie chuckled.

"Aye, she likes to pop up like a sea squall does our Ursilla. She's harmless, but the villagers like to say she's a mad witch. She knows the sea like an auld friend. Always on the shore and scavenging the rock pools, whatever the weather."

"Ursula was the sea witch in The Little Mermaid..." Polly pondered, "But *she* was a big squid lady. That woman earlier looked like just a woman."

"Most witches do." Georgie winked.

"I don't think that lady from earlier is a horrible witch like the one in The Little Mermaid though," Polly said after a pause, "that lady earlier just seemed a bit grumpy that Mummy drove the car a bit close to her..."

Marie rolled her eyes, wondering how long it'd take for Polly to get tired of telling people this one about Mummy's shit driving.

"She's been here longer'n anyone else I've met on the island." Georgie was polishing clean pint glasses with a white cloth, placing them, once wiped, onto the shelf above her.

"You're not from here?" Marie asked.

"Oh no, hen, I'm from Edinburgh, or close enough as makes any difference. Me 'n Sam lived there until your Spencer wandered into our lives and they found this place to make their own."

As if on cue, the front door was elbowed open with a bang by a tall, burly man with a mop of curling dark hair and beard, who clumped into the bar carrying a huge tray of fish. He wore a knitted sweater under bright yellow waterproof trousers and braces. He brought with him the smell of the sea, but not, Marie was pleased to realise, the smell of fish. The tray smelt only of fresh air and salt. The man saw the group of women sitting at the bar and grinned widely so Marie could see the resemblance to Georgie.

"You must be the sister!" the man said in a deep chestnut-y Scottish accent.

"I am the sister and you must be the... mister?" Marie laughed as she rose to her feet.

Sam swept towards her, slid the tray of fish and crabs on ice onto the bar, and ducked to press a whiskery sea-salt kiss to Marie's cheek. Polly gasped at the huge crabs and leant over to study them.

Spence and Sam had been together for nearly five years now but Marie had never met him. There were photos on Facebook and Instagram of course, and scribbled Christmas cards signed from them both, but that wasn't the same as meeting in person.

"This must be Polly the Squish Bean!" Sam whisked the girl off the counter and swung her around as if they'd been pals for years.

"Squish squash..." Polly giggled as Sam kissed her cheek too.

"How was your journey? Fair tired, I bet. Is Spence fixing you something tae eat?"

Marie couldn't get over how tall, broad and handsome her brother's partner was. She felt giddy on Spencer's behalf. "Ah I'm not too bad but I think we might be having an early night, eh, Squish?" Marie tucked stray hair behind her daughter's ear.

"No!" Polly protested, "I'm not very much tired."

"How are ye, Nanna? Good morning?" Sam carefully placed Polly back on the bar and hefted the tray of glistening fish again.

"Fine, fine. Sharon's eldest popped by to ask about shifts for Sunday and Spence says the pork loin from Clyde's needs collecting by tomorrow," Georgie told him.

"Right-oh then." Sam nodded and headed for the kitchen just as Spence re-emerged bearing a tray laden with sandwiches and mugs of tea and what looked like fruit scones. They did a funny two-step dance around each other as Sam ducked to kiss Spence, and they nudged each other out of the way, laughing.

Georgie raised Sam, Spence had said once, and never mentioned what the deal was with Sam's parents. Sam was kind and Georgie was the sort of woman who'd make a home out the contents of her handbag, so it didn't matter. They made Spence happy. Marie felt a pang of guilt and longing when she realised these people had filled a gap in Spence's heart. She and Spence had always been close; they still kept each other's secrets under pain of death, still called each other to gossip and spill hurts to, but these recent years it had been more of her hurts and more of him holding them for her. She knew their parents had let him down. She watched his life displayed here, the comfort and ease with which they all moved around each other; felt the warmth and love they all seemed to have for each other and how it seemed seeped into the walls of this place, and she felt lonely.

Spence brought them their feast of homemade snacks, and from under a tea cosy magicked two slices of Marmite on toast covered in mashed banana. Polly hooted and pumped her fists. Marie tried hard to stop the revulsion pulling her mouth into a grimace.

"Doesn't that look the absolute business?" Spence said with pride. "I might add it to the menu."

Personally, Marie thought it looked *and smelt* like something an unwell dog had done but she said nothing and made an 'mmm' face as she watched her daughter tuck into the toast, grateful to not be the one who had made it. Spence laughed at her. Sam returned a few moments later minus the yellow waterproofs and instead wearing faded jeans, leant himself against the bar and helped himself to a scone. They ate, laughed and chatted and, though Marie joined in, she couldn't help feeling outside of their cosy little bubble.

* * *

The next morning they'd been set to explore Shapinsay. It was only six miles long and there was a standing stone and an iron age broch, and a spooky graveyard and stories of giants, thieves and witches to play out and discover, according to the internet and Georgie's excellent tales... but of course, when they woke, it was foggy. Not just a bit misty, but a thick wall of impenetrable sea fog that had crawled out of the sea and settled over the whole island.

With too much energy to stay indoors, Marie took Polly along the short stretch of single-track lane they'd driven yesterday and climbed over the sea wall on to the rugged little strip of coastline that Polly insisted on calling the beach. The sea was calm; eerily so. Marie was wrapped in her big fuzzy grey cardigan, the one Steve had hated and always called the Yeti Coat. She sipped at the mug of coffee Spence had given her and watched Polly plodding along the shoreline in her lime-green wellington boots, prodding the rocks, seaweed and shingle with a stick of driftwood.

The thick fog suffocated the wind and smothered all sounds, so everything sounded too close and distorted. A car beeping its horn up on the far side of Balfour sounded like it was coming from the sea in front of them. The flat, too-close, too-clammy air agitated Marie. She wanted wild skies, blustery seas and big open spaces. It was as if the sea had seen her coming, felt her wanting and decided to pin her in with muffled close air, strange echoes and the weird lap-lapping of small waves on the shore.

There was a wooden rowing skiff tethered to the rocks with slimy rope gone green under all the seaweed and barnacles stuck to it. The skiff was rotten, listing to one side with a huge hole in its bottom. It didn't look like the little boat had hit something that had torn out the hole, but rather that it had been sat there waiting for so long that the dampness and time had just eaten into the wood until a chunk of it dissolved into nothing. Marie stared into the fog and wondered how low you had to have sunk to be able to relate so fully to a waterlogged, bottomless piece of old wood...

Steve had said she was pathetic, that she was nothing, just some stupid chav who got on her knees for any bloke that was nice to her, that she tied herself in a knot to anyone who'd give her direction. Steve had said a lot of things. But the stuff she remembered, the stuff that hurt the most, was the stuff that echoed the doubt she'd always felt deep in herself. Like maybe, even though he was a bastard, he could see her more clearly than anyone else ever had or would. The small waves lapped out of the nothing-fog.

"Mummy?"

Marie raked in a breath. "Yes, Squish?"

"What sea is this?" Polly was carefully plopping one stone after another into the shallows. "Is this the Channel? Or the Atlantic?"

Marie clenched her jaw against the mess of everything and pushed herself to her feet. "I think, up here, it's the North Sea, love. Maybe the Norwegian sea."

"How does the water know when it's stopped being one place and become another?" Polly contemplated the stone in her hand and launched it this time, seeing how far she could throw it. "Do you think the water knows when it's crossed some invisible line on a map made by humans and goes 'oh now I have to be Norwegian Sea water and stop being North Sea water'?"

Marie chuckled. "I don't think the water cares what we think it should be. It's all just water, all the time."

"Except when it's fog," said Polly, dropping another stone, *plonk*, "or icebergs."

"Yeah, except then." Marie placed her nearly-cold coffee in the shingle, and looked around for a flattish stone, plucked one up. It was cold, smooth and dark. "When I was little, Grandad would take me to Sheerness sometimes and we'd skim stones. I was pretty good..." Marie flung the stone with a flick of her wrist and it hopped and jumped across the listless water until it disappeared into the fog.

"Mummy!" Polly stared, mouth open. "That was seriously awesome!" She held out her hands full of stones to Marie. "Teach me?"

Marie inspected the stones being offered, selected another nice flat one. "It needs to be as flat as possible," she instructed, "then you hold it like this..." She demonstrated placing the stone between thumb and forefinger, with the other fingers curled out of the way beneath it. "You lean back, and... flick!" Marie released the stone and it skittered, hopped and danced across the water.

Polly cackled, jumped up and down. "Do it again!"

230

Marie grinned, glad to have some skill, no matter how small, that her daughter was impressed by. "Find us a good stone, then!"

Polly studied the pebbles still nestled in her cupped hands, plucked one from the pile. It was a pale greyish one, flat yes, but with a hole worn through it. Just like the skiff.

"Hag stone."

The voice was croaky as if it was used to a forty-a-day habit, or just wasn't used very often.

Marie jolted with surprise at the unexpected voice and turned. Though the voice had startled her, Marie wasn't entirely surprised to see it belonged to the white-haired woman she'd nearly run over yesterday.

Ursilla was stepping down from the low wall onto the mossy rocks behind them, her long kelp-green wax coat coming down to her shins. Marie could see knee-high rubber waders beneath that, maybe the flash of denim or faded cotton overalls. The woman's hair was big and wild, curled and hanging almost to her waist, mostly vivid white, and the bits that weren't were iron grey. Her face was carved with deep lines, her eyes were big, dark and deep set. The phrase 'like piss holes in the snow' rose in Marie's mind, inevitably in her dad's voice, and Marie tried her best to squash it down. Her dad's influence was a riptide. Her mum would've said 'boot button eyes'. So dark you couldn't tell pupil from iris.

"I'm sorry?" Marie made her face open, smiley and polite.

Oh shit, she braced herself for Mad Angry Scottish Lady, *here we go*.

"Hag stone," the elderly woman repeated in her creaky voice, stepping onto the shingle beside them. "Some reckon if ye hauld it up to yer eye you can see all the wee folk and the piskies and the goblins and the knockers and the like."

231

You don't often see old women with their hair long, Marie realised. Usually they have it set in little perms, or else short and messy like Georgie's. It was strange seeing such an old face with a mop of hair like this.

"Really?" Polly dropped all the other stones and studied the pale hag stone, then held it up to her eye and looked around, along the short stretch of shoreline they could see in the still-thick fog. Finally, Polly turned and looked up at the old woman, one eye screwed shut, the other peering through the hole in the stone.

"I only see you," Polly said.

Ursilla sucked on her teeth like there was a sherbet lemon tucked into her cheek. "Aye, well, I'm no piskie nor goblin."

"What are you then?" Polly demanded. "Are you a witch?"

"Polly!" Marie reached out and put her hand on Polly's head. "Be polite! I'm sorry, she's six..."

"But Uncle Spence said she was a witch!"

"Shhhh, *Polly!*" Marie laughed awkwardly, internally screaming and cringing.

"Ah well, if Uncle Spencer the great wizard of the kitchen says I am, then I suppose I must be, eh?" Ursilla stood with her arms braced behind her back, staring out to sea, but she flashed a wink at Polly, who looked delighted.

Marie was relieved that the woman didn't seem offended, nor mad or drunk or even all that scary. "You know my brother?"

Ursilla glanced sideways at her. "I know he's brought warmth and welcome to the island, aye. Him and his man, and long may it burn. There's no' enough honest love like that left in the world."

Marie exhaled, smiled, relaxed. "There's not many people of your generation as... open minded, I suppose. Even our dad was... well, Spence never brought Sam home to meet them. And... um, look, I'm sorry about yesterday, in the car. You just startled me."

Ursilla watched Marie with that unruffled, appraising dark stare and nodded once. She withdrew one hand from the pocket of her wax coat, and it was holding a mess of dark twine, possibly fishing line, maybe thick black cotton thread. There were a few small shells and a bubble-gum wrapper caught in the tangle which she plucked free with her other hand and pushed back into her deep pocket. She glanced down at the tangled black thread, raised it up to eye level and squinted at it, or perhaps through it at the shore. "Humans like to break the things that scare them. And 'different' scares 'em."

Then she began deftly unpicking the tangled line in her hands, turning and pulling bits here and there.

"Were you taking a walk?" Polly asked, attempting to skip a new stone across the water and failing.

Marie was mesmerised by Ursilla's bony fingers, callused, bent with age, shuttling back and forth in the black twine, unravelling but also seeming to re-knot and re-tangle pieces here and there.

"I walk all over the island, most days. See what gifts the sea has brought me. See what memories I need tae throw back."

Polly hefted a particularly large stone into the sea with a satisfying *thunk*. "What gifts did you find today?"

"You, bonnie lassie," Ursilla called back, not looking up from her hands. There was no sweetness in her words, just that harsh croaking bluntness, and yet it swelled Marie's chest with pride. Then, with a little tug and twist, Ursilla held up a pretty, knotted cord that was twisted in a tight little spiral like a strand of DNA.

"Here, lassie, pass me that hag stone ye've found."

"But I like it." Polly's fist tightened around it.

"And ye can keep it, I'll just make it extra special with ma magic witchy spells..." Ursilla flashed a wink again and held out a hand. Polly gravely placed the stone with the hole in it in Ursilla's rough-looking palm and the old woman slipped the hand-woven cord through the hole. With a quick tug and knot, it was a pendant, which she then held up for Polly to see.

"Ooooh!" Polly breathed, went to reach for it, hesitated, looked to Marie.

"You can take it," Marie nodded, "but what do you say?"

"Thank you!" Polly pulled the pendant over her head and spun to inspect some seaweed through the hole.

"Thank you for that, you didn't have to. You're very kind," Marie said.

"No I'm not," Ursilla replied flatly, with a scowl, "I'm a miserable auld woman. But ye bairn's a good sort who sees the truth o' things. So it's ma pleasure."

"Are you an artist?" Marie watched Polly parade up and down the shingle holding the pendant in both hands and peering through its hole. "I mean, do you sell jewellery?"

Ursilla made a scoffing sound immediately identifiable in any language as 'as if'.

"I make bits n' boabs n' jangles from the sea gifts but it'd take a month of buggering Sundays afore any o' them lot-" she gestured with a toss of her head towards the village, "would buy a thing from me."

Marie nodded. People don't like different do they, and there was no denying Ursilla was different. Ageless, with the face of a ninety-year-old and yet the smooth, unhindered movements of a woman much younger. She spoke her mind and didn't act like a little old lady. Swore too much. Stomped too much. Knew too much. Unquantifiable.

"Most of 'em think I'm mad. A weirdo or a drunk. 'Course that won't stop the ones whose families have been on the islands for generations, the ones who know the auld ways, from asking fo' baubles for the fishin' boats, or tae tie intae their windies for the good winds, or bring me a lock of their lassies or laddies hair so's they'll have sparks atween their legs."

Ursilla squinted at the fog and Marie frowned, not sure she understood.

"The sea's a fickle thing and I've known her for a lang, lang time," the old woman went on. "People here are more Viking than Scots. There's sea salt in the blood, mud and sand atween the soul and heart space. Auld superstitions, auld gods hang on every doorway, auld stories wrapped aroond every bedpost, though they'll do their prayers and bums up to the Virgin Mary and a' that on Sundays."

Ursilla sucked her teeth again and took a deep lungful of breath. "Ye go back lang enough and there's secrets in every trinket box on these islands." She spotted something in the waterline, some piece of sea-and-sand blasted glass made frosty and smooth, plucked it up like a bird and popped it into her deep pockets. "Aye..." She sighed. "That's the truth of it..."

And Ursilla the Possibly-Sea-Witch with the crazy hair and deep, dark eyes was striding away along the pebbled shoreline.

"Oh!" she stopped beside Polly. "If ye come doon here when the sun's oot and low, ye might see the seals. Sing 'em a song an' they'll save ye from drownin'."

Polly turned and threw a wide-eyed, enthralled look to Marie, but Ursilla kept on walking.

"Are you really a really real witch?" Polly called after the woman's departing back.

A short snorting laugh echoed back to them from within the fog bank. "I mebbe, at that. Away from haim for lang enough now that no soul'd remember me elseways."

Not even twenty minutes later, the fog lifted as if it had never been there and dazzling sunshine skittered across the bay.

* * *

Their time on the island was a crescendo of waves, wind and sunshine breaths caught on hilltops, hair caught in laughing mouths. Polly made friends with some of the local children, and an old bike was rustled up from somewhere for her to use, so she'd streak off down the lane with two or three friendly kids and be gone for hours, roaming the rocky beaches or flying kites. They never went out of sight of the houses and were always back by four. Sometimes they'd all come back to Georgie's Place in a gaggle of grubby knees and bike chains, and Spence would feed them if he wasn't too busy. Marie loved that all of the adults on the island, even the gruff farmers and fishermen, seemed to take a shared guardianship over the children and that Polly had so readily been included. Marie walked, thought, listened and read. And she made herself useful at Georgie's Place behind the bar, getting to know the locals, helping Spence with the social media for the pub, helping Sam haul in supplies from the van, even going out on the fishing boat with him a few times, gossiping and laughing with Georgie. Pretty soon, the bleak and windswept island engulfed them, the rock and peat yielding and surrounding them.

Sharon's eldest, one of their weekend waitresses, was off to Loughborough University in September and, on a dazzlingly bright Friday morning at the close of their second week, Georgie quietly tabled the suggestion that Marie and Polly stayed on the island indefinitely, as they cleaned glasses. She pointed out casually, without making eye contact, that there was a superb little primary school here on the island, that the older kids took the ferry over to Kirkwall for secondary school, and that there was a job here for Marie if she wanted it. It stirred something in Marie; an exhilarated rush of potential, and yet, also, it terrified her. She chewed her lip and retreated into herself. Sam and Spencer watched and exchanged looks but no more was said on it.

That night, after they'd said goodnight to the last of the customers, after the tables and the bar had been wiped down, after Marie had emptied the glass washer and Spence had turned off the hobs and the grill, and long after Sam had tucked Polly into bed with a story, Spence poured brandy for them all and they huddled round the bar. Marie's feet ached in that good sort of satisfied way that came from being useful and being able to see where she'd been. The subject of Ursilla came up when Sam said he'd seen her over the north side of the island carrying a sheep skull in one hand and a Ninja Turtles lunchbox in the other.

"Yeah but who *is* she? Did she grow up here?" Marie asked.

"Who knows." Spence had made sausage sandwiches for them and was trying to cram too much into his mouth. Onion gravy dripped down his chin. Sam watched him, amused yet disgusted, and tossed him a napkin.

"She said to me the villagers don't like her but that they ask her to *make them things?*" Marie picked at her own sandwich, tearing off slithers of bread and exposing the innards.

"Oh aye." Georgie nodded. Tonight, she was wearing a gold and red blouse and a huge statement necklace, her magenta hair spiked with wax.

When I grow up, I want to be just like her, thought Marie.

"They're reit superstitious they are, all of 'em. Any fishing town's the same. But here, they're fair quick to blame Ursilla for a poor catch or a lamb lost or when a sea mist comes up. Oh, make no mistake, she's *their* mad witch and they're proud to have one. But ye should see the way they avoid her on the high street, or if she pops intae the post office. You'd think she wis contagious." Georgie sniffed, swilled her brandy and took a slow sip. "But ah've seen 'em too, scurrying after her along the shore, askin' her for spells and whitnot to tie into the boy's rigging to keep their boats safe."

"You can't mean people actually believe she has any influence on the weather or other people?" Marie laughed. "She's an eccentric, artistic sure, a free thinker in a remote place, but she's just a woman." Marie chuckled and drank her brandy, but saw the look exchanged by the others. "Oh, come on!" She was incredulous. "Don't tell me you believe this bollocks?!"

Sure the island floated on the back of ancient history and the bones of dead Vikings but... to have these three, urbanites all of them until they moved here, go moon-eyed over Ursilla... she snorted.

"When we first came in to view this place," Spence placed his half-eaten sandwich down on the big wooden platter he'd laid out, "John Mac, the groundskeeper for the castle – you know, the guy who said hello when you were coming off the ferry?"

Marie recalled the white hair, the flat cap and the friendly welcome to the island.

"Well he let us in and showed us around, and he pointed Ursilla out down on the shingle by the lane, said she came with the island and would curse anyone that did her wrong. Said one year back in the 80s some kids were throwing stones at her over the sea wall up the other side of the island and then come the spring, every single lamb born to their dad's farms died. All of 'em."

"That could be anything, Spence..."

"Not here, it couldn't," Spence countered. "The sheep are their livelihood. They don't mess it up much."

"All right... but maybe Mac likes to exaggerate, give a bit of local colour to the boys looking to rent and do this place up?"

Spence inclined his head.

"Tell her," Georgie said quietly.

Marie looked at each of them in turn.

"She'll think we're insane..." Spence sighed.

I already bloody do. Marie kept the words behind her teeth but pulled a face into her brandy glass.

"Aye, but *we* know it's true." Sam propped his elbows on the bar. "We said we wanted this place. It was perfect. Everything we'd talked about. Despite the work it needed, and the junk left in all the nooks and crannies, it was perfect, and then Ursilla walked in, in her mac and wellies, like she knew we were in here. She looked at us like she could read us. Then she gave us that-" Sam pointed to a strange hanging mobile made of sea glass and shells suspended on fuzzy jute twine. There were weird knots and unpretty loops in the string, and it hung behind the bar. Marie had been working right underneath most evenings for a fortnight and not noticed it once. It looked lopsided, unbalanced. One good sneeze in its direction and it looked like it'd fall to pieces.

"Told us to hang it here and not to take it doon, so we'd always welcome in a good catch, a full house and a full purse."

"A nice, if fucking ugly and weird, housewarming gift, but..." Marie shook her head.

"Marie, we've been here two and a half years now," Spencer interrupted, "We're always in profit. There're always people booked in to eat. We never have any trouble. There's never been an evening when we haven't been busy. You think that's normal for a pub on an island off the coast of Orkney with three hundred people on it? An island that's completely shut off if the weather's bad? We get the shit weather and it's always on a day when we've already got guests booked in overnight, or there's a tour bus trapped on the island or when some bird watchers got caught in the fog and need a place to stay. We always get our deliveries on time. We're never stretched too far or left twiddling our thumbs."

"She blessed this place, and you boys, she did." Georgie nodded. "I swear it."

Marie shook her head in astonishment at their willingness to concede to the superstitions and folksy beliefs of these islands.

"None of the boats she made baubles for have ever gone doon or lost a man," Sam added, and sipped his drink. "She keeps 'em safe. Half the lads don't swim. But they'll avoid her and pretend they cannae see her like that might mean they have to accept whit she can dae."

"Why does she stay, then?" Marie swallowed down her brandy and thumped her glass on the bar triumphantly. "If she's this magical wise woman of the sea with her spells, why the fuck would she stay to let the people treat her like that?" She could feel the brandy glow across her cheeks, knew her voice was getting that fuzzy edge to it. "Look, don't get me wrong, I thought she was nice. Weird, but cool. She was nice to Polly. But she seems too smart to be stuck here if everyone seems to hate her and yet still tap her up for whatever gizmos they think'll stop their boats from sinking or get 'em pregnant or whatever."

"She's tied to the place, is what Mac says." Spence poured them all another brandy, was looking flushed himself now. "Says his great-granny told him a story about how she couldn't leave 'til she found something she'd lost."

"Something that'd been stolen," Sam added.

They fell to silence then, sipping their drinks, and the conversation flowed onto something else soon enough. It was only when Marie crawled into her big, puffy, comfortable bed after midnight, as she lay listening to Polly gently snoring in the fold-out bed across the room, that she realised what Sam had said. That John Mac's *great-granny* had told him a story about Ursilla. How old *was* Ursilla?

* * *

That night the mist rose and curled around the pub. Marie dreamt of being locked in a dark room she couldn't escape from. There were no windows, no doors and, like all good nightmares, the walls were slowly closing in on her. The room was slowly filling with thick fog, something cold and slimy was sneaking up her ankles, and no matter how hard she tried to scream, nothing came out of her mouth. She jolted awake to Spence leaning over her, shaking her by the shoulder, a half-entertained half-concerned expression on his face. She focussed on him, vaguely aware she had yelled something as she'd surfaced from the dream.

"What did I say?" She rubbed her face.

"You said 'let go of my toes, Piss-Flap'..."

Marie frowned, Spence's face split into a wide grin and Marie ended up giggling into the covers.

"Well then, Piss-Flap, what do you want? What time is it, anyway?"

"It's just gone seven."

Marie groaned, pulled the sheets over her face, hoping he'd get the idea and go away.

"I'm just letting you know I need to run over to see the bloke with the beef, Georgie got the early ferry over to Kirkwall to get her hair done, and Sam's taken Squish down to the beach to look at the seals."

Marie sighed, knowing more sleep wasn't going to be an option now, and pushed herself up into a seated position. She could still feel the cold dread of the dream clinging to her and the worrying niggling ache somewhere behind the eyes of an impending hangover. "The '*man with the beef*', eh? That a euphemism?"

"Of course." Spence drew back the curtains and straightened Polly's camp bed. "The band's on this afternoon so we need to stock up. I'll be gone about an hour I reckon, depending on how long it takes the beef man to load me up... oh you're *such* a child!" he said as Marie sniggered at him again, "I just didn't want you waking up to an empty building."

Marie nodded, dragged her heavy mane of blonde hair into a knot on top of her head and went over to stand beside her brother at the window. She leant her head on his shoulder. "You ever feel like you're just... stuck...?"

Spencer pressed a kiss into her hair. "I used to."

* * *

The sun hit the water at just the right angle to make everything too bright. Everything was silver. The brandy from the night before was creeping round her peripheral vision and Marie shielded her eyes as she picked her way over the low drystone wall and carefully across the rocks. She could hear Polly shrieking and laughing and could now see Sam's broad back silhouetted against the morning sun as he crouched on the shingle, pointing, one arm around Polly.

"Ah, ye see, there she goes now!"

There was a splash from the water.

They turned towards Marie as she picked her way towards them.

"Mummy!" Polly raced to her. The sun made a halo of Polly's wispy hair. Her cheeks were ruddy. The sea air was getting to that girl, Marie thought, flushing out the concrete and cars and the yelled swear words hurled from a cocaine-rattled Dad in the middle of a midnight street.

"Mummy look at the selkies!" Polly's small cold little hand wrapped around Marie's fingers and dragged her to the water's edge where the sea shushed back and forth on the pebbles and left frothy little bubbles.

"Selkies?" Marie squinted into the sun glaring off the water, could see vague shapes slipping and splashing just a way out, but nothing solid. More like ideas than anything else, forming and dissolving before she had the chance to focus.

"They're the seal-people, Mummy!"

"Ah it's just whit the islanders call 'em." Sam shrugged apologetically. "It's just silly stories..."

Marie put her hand on his arm reassuringly. "I love that you're telling her fairy tales."

"Not a *fairy* tale, Mummy, it's a folktale," Polly corrected.

Marie made a conciliatory face.

Sam chuckled. "The islanders say the seals here can turn intae people, when the conditions are right. Some reckon it's every seventh full moon, others say Midsummer's eve. Some even reckon it's every high tide. They say the selkies can slip oot their skins and be human for a spell. Even reckon they're quite the... uh...." Sam checked that Polly was far enough out of earshot, "bedroom dance partner, if ye ken whit I mean..."

Marie raised her eyebrows and smirked. "Oh! Well, if you see a lovely looking seal-man, send him over, eh?"

"I'll be sure tae, if he's no' lookin' for a rugged bit o' Scot's Pine, that is..." Sam waggled his eyebrows and Marie laughed.

Sam was a good lad. Funny. Kind. She wished she could find a Sam of her own. Big, brawny, *straight*... she smiled to herself. This place, this light and the tang of sea salt on everything, seemed to soften all the edges on things and people. The light shifted – a high veil of thin cloud or maybe her eyes had just become adjusted – and she could at last see the seals. She gasped spontaneously. They were glorious. There were five of them. Two were laying on a small rock a little way out, the other three flipping and slipping in and out of the water, over and under each other, seemingly solely for the purpose of delighting Polly, who was pointing, laughing and giggling. One of them came right up to the edge of the little rotten skiff and knocked the boat with a paw so that it rocked in the water. The seals were dark grey, mottled, shining and wet, with their long whiskers and puppy-like faces. They seemed cuddly and cute but there was an alertness, a deep intelligence in their faces. Their eyes were deep dark liquid pools that seemed to know eternity. Everything that had ever happened or ever would was in those eyes. Marie was utterly stunned by them. They watched her, all five of them growing suddenly still like they could see everything she had ever been or ever would be laid out in front of them. She felt naked, afraid and yet strangely at peace. Seen, completely. Understood. God dammit, her eyes were stinging with tears. Sam saw and she panicked he'd try to say something to fix it, but he didn't. He just quietly accepted her tears, squeezed her shoulder and gave her an understanding smile, then scooped up Polly and took her to the shoreline so Marie could have a moment to herself.

"It's no' a bad thing tae cry it oot..."

Marie glanced over her shoulder and Ursilla was sitting on the low wall, elbows on thighs, chin braced in cupped hands, knees spread like a man.

Marie dragged an arm across her eyes. "You do like to appear out of nowhere like a bloody sea fog, don't you?"

The woman had caught her unawares and that had made her snarky. She instantly regretted it but Ursilla gave her a rare roguish grin and all seemed to be forgiven.

"Is it a broken heart?" Ursilla asked, digging her toes into the shingle.

Marie took a deep breath, sighed, sat down beside Ursilla. Both women stared out to where the seals flipped and turned somersaults for Polly's pleasure. How to explain it? The dream, the urge to cry, the way the fog had made her feel the other week, the release then the terror she'd felt when Georgie had suggested she and Polly stay on the island.

"No. Not really. I mean, there was a bloke, Polly's dad, and he was a prick, but... it's more like I feel... trapped. Trapped in my own life. And I think maybe it's me that's doing the trapping. And there's this... this yearning in me, like I can feel it, right *here*," she balled her fist into her gut below the underwiring of her bra, "this ache to come away, but there's nothing stopping me except myself."

Ursilla sat beside her and said nothing.

"That doesn't make any sense," Marie finished, defeated, feeling that weird call rising in her again, this pull to climb and run and be high above everything else and breathe and scream into the wind. Marie looked at the woman beside her and was shocked to see a softness in the dark eyes, a bereft sadness.

"Tis a broken heart for sure, though not by the bairn's daddy," Ursilla said gently, "a broken heart from fear. A broken heart from being away from your haim for too lang."

Marie frowned. "My home's in Kent..."

"No," Ursilla snapped, reaching out and taking Marie's hands in her own urgently – her hands were rough and calloused and cool – "Your ain wild home. Your ain nature. Your soul's yearning for something it remembers, something older than here and now, older than Steve and Chatham and lip gloss and maths homework forgotten because some boy asked for a blowjob."

Marie was shaking her head, would have been saying *no, no, no, there's no way you can know that* if her voice hadn't shrivelled up somewhere in her chest.

"There's nae greater sorrow than a woman yearning to return to her wild." Ursilla squeezed Marie's hands for a moment then let them drop as she cast her eyes back to the sea where the seals watched, still and alert once more. Marie watched the seals watching Ursilla.

"There wis a man once," Ursilla said, quietly, almost as if to herself, "that promised me the moon. I wis a girl, younger than you are now, full and ripe and ready and wanting and he..." she closed her eyes, "he took me to his bed and stole my life away."

Marie felt the sadness welling in that cavern in her stomach, felt the tears once more, that comprehension of the female wound and pain. "I'm so sorry," she whispered.

"Oh it wisnae my body, no," Ursilla shook her head. "He was a handsome, bonnie man and I gave myself to him more than once and freely, happily. But he lied. I laid with him and he stole my home from me. Trapped me here. Hid away the piece of me that made me whole so that I would stay here with him. I believe he would've given it back in the end, when we'd grown bored of each other, but his wife... I didnae know he was bound to another... she found oot, and she found *it*, and she hid it away from both of us as punishment to him.

"The wife, she cast oot the man and he left the island for Norway or Scotland or wherever he had come here from... but I wis trapped here and couldnae leave. I begged and begged and *pleaded,* and I made her all the gifts of the sea to keep her farm well and her bairns safe but she wis poisoned with the jealousy and... she died without ever telling me where she'd hid it. And no other soul from then 'til now has ever known where she kept it. So, trapped am I. Like you. Barred from returning to my home. My wild."

The silence when she stopped speaking was a void. The waves and the sudden barking and honking of the seals, Polly's laugh and Sam's gentle voice poured into it and Marie was back, sitting on a cold damp uncomfortable wall looking up at this woman who looked just like a woman and yet was not, was something else. Something older. Something untamed...

"What did the wife hide from you?" The words were pulled out of Marie from that weird cavern in her stomach, the one that filled with the rising tide of yearning.

Ursilla cast one look down at Marie, with tears in her dark eyes, then one final look to the waiting seals. "My skin."

Then Ursilla was striding away up over the wall and along the lane back towards the village.

* * *

Ursilla's story clung to her. Or rather, the feeling of it magnified and mirrored the feeling in herself, reverberating around her skull. Ursilla's words had disturbed her at a level she couldn't articulate to her brother or Sam though they asked, though they were concerned. She busied herself, helping the lads get ready for the afternoon's event. She helped Spence prep potatoes for the chips and shred braised beef for burgers. She helped Sam drag tables to clear a 'stage' at the far end of the bar. She tested the fairy lights on the outside of the building with Polly's help. She kept her hands from trembling by filling them with things, by holding her daughter like a hurricane lamp.

The band arrived with most of their audience and with Georgie, hair freshly dyed, on the midday ferry. Because the ferries didn't run late into the night, the band was set to play from half past one in the afternoon until four, meaning any tourists could get the last ferry back over to Kirkwall at quarter to five. It appeared this was quite the happening, as many of the islanders had come along too.

The band were a four piece, three men and a woman. Marie was glad for the crowd and the sound that filled up her brain. Wines, whiskeys and pints were pulled, plates were shuttled back and forth from the kitchen, and Polly was an angel, keeping out from underfoot, making the customers smile, and delivering the odd bowl of chips to a table. There were drums, fiddles, pipes and a guitar, and the band all seemed to take it in turns to sing, or weave harmonies that made the hair on the back of Marie's neck stand on end. Truthfully she didn't have time to stop and really listen, but she was glad of it. And at four o'clock on the dot, the band stopped to raucous and rapturous applause.

"Thank you, Shapinsay! We've been Ha'penny Bit and you've been an absolute delight!"

Sam climbed onto a chair and yelled, over the excited voices all worked up over the music, "Ladies and gents, ye've got forty-five minutes to finish up and get back tae the ferry. The bar will now be closed to make sure none of ye try the 'oh sure I can drink a pint in half an hour' trick." The crowd laughed amiably. "Thank you for yer custom and we do hope ye come back to Georgie's Place again soon!"

The bar slowly began to empty, with brightly coloured anoraks and bags making a weaving crocodile back along the lane to the ferry port, until the pub seemed almost deserted. Maybe fifteen of the islanders remained, nursing their drinks quietly as Spence, Sam and Georgie cleared up. Spencer clocked who was left in the pub, peered along the lane at the ferry that had arrived and was in the process of boarding, and nodded at Marie.

"Bar's back on, my loves," she called, to a collective sigh and metaphorical loosening of ties. That's when the real party started.

The band refuelled with plenty of beer and a few burgers before picking up their instruments again. There was something different in the musicians and their music after that. As the evening fell into night and the sea and the village was lost in the darkness, the mood was lively and homely. Other islanders came in, bringing their own fiddles and bodhráns. This time round, the music was for themselves, not the tourists who needed them to repeat themselves slowly because they couldn't catch a thick Scots accent.

The music was rawer. The woman in the band, a strong lady with dyed black hair, tattoos and boots, disappeared out to their van and came back wheeling a bass drum that honestly looked like it was made from a beer barrel. She said they didn't usually play that drum indoors but, "whit the fuck, eh?!" One of the men swapped his flute for a set of bagpipes. The sound was huge, crashing over Marie like white-crested waves. The room clapped, stamped and banged their glasses. There was singing and there were shouts, whoops and howls.

The huge drum thundered through Marie; she could feel it in her chest and lower. The pipes wailed. The music called up all the ancient ones. People were dancing. Not the sweet soft kicks and steps of the ballet-like Highland dance, but a primal twirling and stomping. Marie moved from the hips, her feet pounding the flagstones in her worn-out trainers. Her hair slid from its bun and flew around her; Spence was spinning her around the floor, then Sam, then someone she didn't know and then she was dancing with no partner, bodies twisting in and around each other. The cavern inside her was filling with something like freedom.

Light-headed, with sweat dripping from her hair, she pushed out through the steam-streaked door and into the night, throwing her head and arms back to the inky sky and the pale globe of the moon. She wished she smoked. She wanted to pull something inside of her that wasn't a man. She could see the sea and she could feel wildness pulsing though her and she thought, finally, I'm home.

And then Spence was grabbing her by the shoulders, shaking her, his head matted with sweat, shouting something and she had to make herself quieten the roaring in her ears and focus on him.

"Mare, where's Polly?!" he was shouting, over the music. "Where is she? Where's Polly?!"

* * *

It was a slap, a bucket of ice water to the face, a shrinking, shrivelling, freezing moment of utter fear. She did not know where her daughter was. No one did, and suddenly she was the Worst Mother. No one remembered seeing Polly for maybe an hour. The band had stopped. The crowd had sobered. There were people looking all through Georgie's Place, in all the rooms, in the attic, the storerooms and the kitchen. There were people walking the lane calling Polly's name, and scouring the hill towards the castle. Someone called the police in Kirkwall, who'd called the coastguard because they had a chopper and a boat. How far could a six-year-old get on her own in the dark? Not far. The unspoken fear lapping around all their ankles wasn't of the island. It was of the sea. Polly had loved every second on the beach since they'd arrived. What if she'd wandered down there and tripped, slipped, banged her head? What if she'd not seen the water, got caught in an eddy or a riptide?

Marie was pinched, skin tight with dried sweat and worry, as she shone her phone's torch on the thin strip of beach. There was a white-noise buzzing in her ears as she scoured the shingle and the water's edge as she made herself carefully, slowly look along the shore. Don't miss anything. Were any of the shadows and odd shapes along the beach Polly? The water rippled and Marie's phone-torch beam snapped to where the sound had come from. What if there was a body floating face down and bloated? She nearly gagged as her light fell on the moving water... but it was just a seal, its head and eyes bobbing above the surface, staring at her. Just a seal. No body of a child. Just a seal. She steadied her breathing and matched the seal's stare, and from the same deep primal place that the music had touched, she whispered "Please... please..."

The seal blinked and then flipped beneath the surface again.

She was left staring at the black water, her mind blank, the panic threatening to spill upwards and outwards if she didn't think of something to do. The buzzing in her ears was immense. And then she realised it wasn't inside her head, the sound was out there over the sea, as the coastguard's helicopter erupted over the bay, low enough to whip Marie's hair and send waves across the water, its searchlight swinging back and forth. It wheeled overhead and back out again, and she could see a speedboat whizzing past out there too. She stumbled backwards away from the huge deafening darkness, picked her way back over the rocks and back towards the glow of Georgie's Place, all lit up like a Christmas tree. She banged in through the door and the people still inside looked up sharply. Spence came towards her with his arms out but she didn't want his comfort now.

"She's not on the stretch of beach down the lane. Not in the water... at least, not..." The end of that sentence hung like a threat.

"Sam's going to take the van, drive up through the village, he'll do a loop of the island." Georgie patted her on the arm as Sam bounded down the stairs and into the bar clutching his keys.

The front door opened again and it was the woman from the band, the one with the tattoos that had been playing the huge bass drum. She looked around, saw Marie. "We've got her. We've found her."

The drummer was followed in by Ursilla, unkempt and windswept as ever. At first Marie didn't understand, but then she saw – Ursilla was carrying Polly on her bag. Polly was asleep, cheek resting in Ursilla's wild hair, but as Marie's knees buckled and her hand was pressed to her mouth trying to contain the relieved sobs that wrought their way free, Polly opened her eyes and Ursilla let the child slither down to the ground.

Polly ran towards Marie, who knelt on the floor sobbing uncontrollably, with her arms thrown wide.

"Mummy!"

"Oh come here you little... angel... you little *shit*... you... where *were* you?"

Spence dropped to his knees beside them, hugging them both, and Sam was laughing, relieved, and Georgie sat down heavily on a bar stool with her eyes closed and someone said they'd call the coastguard off. Marie didn't care. She held on to Polly, her anchor, her albatross.

"She was in the orangery, up at the castle..." Ursilla said quietly. "She'd gotten herself in through a broken window, industrious little mite, but couldn't get back out the same way."

"The *castle*?!" Marie looked from Ursilla back to Polly. "Squish, what were you doing *inside* the castle?"

"I was just looking..." Polly's voice was petulant.

"That's a private place, and it's dangerous! What if you'd gotten badly hurt? And you know better than to run off like that!"

"I'm sorry..." Polly mumbled, her bottom lip wobbling. "I'm sorry... I was only trying to help."

"Ah, lassie," Ursilla shook her head, "it's ma fault she wandered off. She thought to help me. I didna ken until it wis too late..."

Marie looked at the older woman sharply, but Polly's eyes glistened as huge tears welled up and spilt down her cheeks and her bottom lip trembled. "Don't be angry with Ursilla, Mummy, it's me. She didn't do anything except find me when I got stuck."

Marie held her tightly. "It's OK, it's OK, I was just really, really scared. It's OK." She smoothed the girl's hair and rocked the child and honestly, at that point, she was soothing herself just as much.

"Well then." Ursilla sighed, pulled her coat about her tightly and disappeared back into the strange darkness.

* * *

Tucked up in bed later that night, when all had settled and gone quiet, Polly's small hands and cold feet were pressed against Marie as mother and daughter held onto each other. They whispered into the soft folds of the bed covers, the purple plush elephant caught between them. Marie was propped on one elbow.

"Earlier, you said you were trying to help when you'd gone up to the castle. What did you mean?"

Polly was twirling a strand of Marie's hair around her fingers and, for a moment, Marie thought her daughter might ignore her. But then Polly looked up at her.

"I was just looking for the coat."

Marie frowned. "What coat?"

"The one that got stolen from Ursilla."

Marie stroked the child's soft cheek. "Did she tell you that story, too?"

"No, it wasn't her, I promise. The seals told me. They told me to use the magic seeing rock to find it." Polly reached into the neck of her dinosaur pyjamas, pulled out the hag stone, still on its black woven cord and held it out for Marie to see. Marie remembered the story and the seals and the way Ursilla had known things she couldn't have known, how the old woman had gone up to the castle in the darkness and brought back her daughter without anyone having told the woman Polly was missing. So she didn't question her daughter's truth. There seemed little point anymore.

"...did the seals tell you it was at the castle?"

"No..." Polly thought hard for a bit. "Just that it was locked up in a cranny in a box. What's a cranny?"

Marie kissed the girl's sweet-smelling head. "It's a dark little hidden corner where forgotten things get left."

"Did you get left in a cranny? Is that why you've been sad?"

Marie shifted and lay her head on the pillow beside Polly. "Yeah, maybe. I think I found myself tucked away all forgotten and dusty earlier. But then..."

"Then I was naughty and I ran off without saying," Polly finished.

"Hmmm." Marie smiled. "I think maybe we both did a bit of running off without saying today. But we won't do it again, eh? No more helicopters and search parties, OK?"

Polly nodded, "OK." She was still holding the hag stone, turning it over in her small palms and held it up to squint at Marie through the hole. "Goodnight Mummy. I'm sorry and I love you."

"I'm sorry and I love you too, Squish Bean. Sleep tight."

They snuggled down and closed their eyes, Marie's hair still wound around the small fingers of her daughter. But when Marie woke in the ghost light of morning, Polly was gone again.

* * *

"Polly?!" Marie sat up, stared around the room, visually checking the fold-out bed – which was empty, with the purple stuffed elephant now neatly placed on the pillow – and the window. The room was empty. She felt the panic stirring in her stomach again and was dragging on her yeti cardigan over her big Smashing Pumpkins T-shirt that she slept in when the door opened quietly and there was Polly standing in the doorway with one hand on the doorknob. She was still in her pyjamas but wearing her wellington boots. Her hair was a fluffy slept-in mess. Marie rolled her eyes, slumped back into the bed.

"What did we say last night? No running off without saying!"

Polly simply stared at her from the doorway. "Sorry," she muttered absently, "I did say. Maybe you were still sleeping..." She looked distracted, deep in thought.

"Squish? You OK?"

Polly's eyes focussed on hers. "I think I found it, Mummy... but it's stuck..."

Marie stared at Polly, saw the hag stone hanging around her neck, saw dust and cobwebs and smears on her pyjama knees, saw the serious, urgent look in her daughter's eyes and knew. She just knew. Marie flung back the covers, pulled on her baggy sweatpants and shoved her feet into her trainers without socks, even though that usually made her squirm and feel gross, and piled her hair up off her face into a messy knot. Polly held out a hand; she took it and Polly was pulling her along the corridor past the closed bedrooms, to a weird little nook at the very end of the hall up a funny little uneven step. There was another door here with a metal latch, that Polly had left open; the door to the attic.

"Up there?" Marie peered into the gloom. Polly nodded gravely, holding the hag stone in one hand. Marie nodded. "Show me, sweetheart."

The attic stairs were uneven and wooden and they creaked. Polly went first, taking each step one at a time, carefully, holding Marie's hand. She seemed so much smaller then, so much younger, the way she climbed like a toddler. But when Marie nearly tripped in the half-light, she understood. Polly was guiding her and Polly was being careful on her account. The attic was huge and filled with stuff – boxes and things covered in dust sheets. There was a vague order to it all, and Marie guessed Spence and Sam had been trying to organise it but given up. It felt like they could keep walking and round a stack and disappear into Narnia. But Polly led her to a dark corner beneath the eaves, hung with swathes of cobwebs.

"This is a cranny, right?" Polly let go of Marie's hand and pushed her hair out of her face then put her hands on her hips. There was a stack of boxes and sacks piled in the dark corner.

"It is, babe, yeah,"

"Then I think... um... the thing... the *coat* is in that one." Polly pointed to a heavy-looking black trunk at the bottom of the pile.

"Yeah?"

Polly held up the hag stone in front of her eye and peered at the trunk. "Pretty sure."

"What does it look like?" Marie covered her face with an arm and used the other to hook away some of the hanging cobwebs. Polly took the pendant from around her neck and offered it to Marie. Marie took it, turned it over in her hand, held it up to her eye and closed the other. Nothing looked any different. She peered around the room, at the pale light streaking in through the single window within the beams and slant of the roof, then back at the trunk Polly had pointed to.

"It just looks like a... a trunk to me...?"

Polly tutted and sighed audibly. "Well of course it does, to you!"

Marie puffed her cheeks. Of course. She realised she felt out of place in this adventure, like the Mum was never meant to come along on these sorts of things.

"Mummy, *please*! Focus!" Polly stamped her little green-booted foot in frustration. "I can't move this on my own, it's too big and I'm too small and there's no one else to help. But... it's so close now, and it wants to be found. It's been in here ever such a long time, all forgotten and lost and smelly."

Polly's eyes were big and serious and threatening to spill tears again. Marie didn't need to be asked twice. She didn't need to see the 'wee folk' or the sparkles that danced around the trunk or hear the seals speaking to her or whatever the hell Polly saw and heard. If Polly said so, now, after everything, after the wild tide had risen in her chest yesterday, that was good enough. Marie cleared the top of the trunk. It was locked. Marie dragged it out of the corner, inspected it, twisted it round to see the lock better in what little light there was. She set her body weight against the flat lid and it would not budge. She slid down to sit on the floor, contemplating the trunk. Polly hovered at her elbow.

"Should I go find Uncle Spence or Uncle Sam?"

"No," Marie shook her head, "I just need to break it open with something."

Polly sat down beside her, the two of them in the dust in their pyjamas with their legs outstretched, dishevelled and grimy, their hair matching haystacks, with the same partly-annoyed, partly 'puzzle-solving' expressions on their faces.

"...like a crowbar..." Polly muttered.

Marie swivelled her head slowly to look at the girl with that same puzzled expression. They locked gazes for a beat and then were scrambling to their feet and running back to the stairs, down through the building like a cyclone.

"Keys!" Polly yelled, snatching up the bunch from where Sam had left them, on the low shelf below the bar, and tossing them smoothly.

"Keys!" Marie acknowledged, turning to scoop them from the air, and unlocking the front door. The alarm beeped at them until she punched in the code, and they spilled into the gravel car park where the van sat waiting for them to unlock it.

Marie's feet almost lifted from the ground as she leant into the back and heaved the tool kit towards her across the bed of the boys' van. It was a small transit van, tall enough to stack crates of fish, meat or veg into, and small enough to wind round the lanes on the island without annoying any of the residents or getting stuck on a bend. She flung open the lid to the tool box, rattled and rooted around in it, flung aside a couple of socket wrenches and spanners and yes, thank you Spence and Sam for not skimping on the handyman DIY shit, she pulled free a hefty metal pipe and lifted it exaltingly. Polly cheered. Marie slammed everything shut and turned to see her brother in his dressing gown, in the doorway, bemused. Marie grinned, waved the crowbar triumphantly, and pushed back past them into the bar.

The members of the band that had stayed overnight now sat in the bar around a table as Sam and Georgie were setting up for breakfast around them. They all looked up as Marie careened into the room. She slid to a stop, Polly slamming into her, and Marie cleared her throat, lowered the crowbar, hitched her cardigan back onto her shoulder, very much aware of how she looked right then. She took Polly's hand.

"Morning," Polly chimed, beaming widely at everyone, "Try the marmalade, it's lovely."

Marie felt the giggle bubble up in her throat and escape before she could stop it, so she threw a salute to the room with her crowbar for good measure before quick-stepping across the bar, dragging Polly alongside, and diving back up the stairs. Spencer hovered for a beat, threw an apologetic shrug at Sam, and followed his sister.

Spence appeared in the attic as Marie was stripping off her cardigan. She caught his expression, but ignored it, instead passing him the garment. His confused and slightly annoyed look deepened, but he still reached out and took it from her.

Marie slotted the pronged end of the crowbar under the edge of the lid of the trunk and leaned on it. There was a promising creak but it didn't move. She tried again and was rewarded with a cracking sound.

"What are you doing? *What's she doing?*" Spence grew more confused, more annoyed, more convinced that his sister had gone entirely round the bend and possibly taken a detour via 'Drunk Before Breakfast'.

Marie paused, looked up at him, huffed her hair from her face. "It's pretty bloody obvious, Spence, I'm cracking open this trunk with your crowbar."

Spence went to snap back, caught his breath, thought better of it, as Marie shifted the crowbar and levered it again.

"...why?" Spence directed his question to Polly, believing the six-year-old to have a better handle on reality right now.

"It's got Ursilla's sealskin in it," Polly replied.

Spencer's expression mirrored the series of thoughts and emotions cycling through his brain. Maybe it was the matter-of-fact tone of Polly's voice, or the way Marie glowed like a fire had been lit under her. Maybe it was when he remembered the sea glass and string mobile hanging behind the bar and that they'd never had a bad day's business since Ursilla had given it to him. Maybe it was the way Ursilla had delivered Polly home last night without waiting for so much as a thanks. Whatever it was, Spence settled on, "Want me to do it?"

Marie paused, sweat-streaked, and glared at him. "*No.* Piss off."

He held his hands up apologetically, but she wiped her face and considered him. "But you can help, if you like."

They stood side by side, brother and sister, both old enough to know better than to believe in fairy tales, or *folktales* or whatever this was, and smart enough to know there were just some things you didn't question, and they heaved on the crowbar. They both grunted with the effort, the heavy lid cracked and, finally, splintered open. Marie staggered, Spencer caught her by the elbow, and pulled away the broken pieces of the trunk lid. There was a foul smell, like rotted eggs and seaweed and damp, musty Oxfam shops.

Spence heaved, "Oh God that's hideous," and covered his nose and mouth with the crook of his arm.

Marie grimaced, but Polly was reaching into the chest, which was big enough to swallow her whole, and standing back up with a heavy, matted, pale mottled grey thing in her arms. It was big, it looked heavy, it had a slight sheen to it, and it stank.

"This is it!" Polly cried, "This is it! We've found it! Mummy this is it!" She was gathering the pelt up, but it kept slipping, sliding and pooling around her feet.

Marie was breathless and was surprised to realise she felt close to tears. She shoved the shattered trunk out of the way and helped Polly to scoop up the sealskin. "Shall we take it down to her?"

Polly nodded and heaped the folds of hide up into Marie's arms. Spencer watched them like he was trying to surface from a dream, then bent and cleared a path back to the stairs so Marie didn't trip.

The three of them spilled back down both flights of stairs, back into the bar. The band had gone – left already, or gone back to their rooms to pack up, Marie didn't know – but Sam and Georgie were still there, sipping tea and eating toast with, Marie almost laughed again, marmalade.

"Can't really stop, sorry for looking like a psychopath earlier..." Marie stumbled through the bar, peering over the bundle in her arms, as Polly guided her to the front door and out into the daylight.

They went to the slither of shoreline down the lane. Marie was trying not to trip, her T-shirt was slipping off her shoulders and her sweatpants were sliding down her hips. She didn't care.

"What should we do, Squish?" Marie looked around, squinting in the light.

Polly was peering through the hag stone at the sea, then she crouched down at the water's edge and splashed her hand.

"Leave it here. On the shore. She'll find it. They'll call her."

Marie was out of breath, a little disappointed. She was finally, finally, alive. Finally, she'd come home to herself. She wanted more than to leave this oily, smelly bundle of sealskin in an abandoned pile on the rocks and for that to be the end of it.

"Are you sure?" Marie sighed, placing the skin on the largest rock, the one that the rotten wooden skiff was tethered to, pushing her hair out of her face.

"Yep," Polly stood back, hands on hips, "that's what they say."

Marie looked from Polly out to the water, where the five seals were hovering, heads bobbing up and down like they were waiting. Which, of course, they were. Marie smiled, nodded. Then looked down at the slime and algae and barnacle-covered rope that tied the weathered, worn and half-sunken little skiff to the shore, reached down and yanked it free. The rope squelched in her hand and she let it drop and disappear into the water. Then she yelled. It wasn't a scream, no. A yell. A bellow. A feral yawp from the sea cave inside of her that was now filled with campfire, stars and the beating of beer-barrel drums. Of course it was symbolic. That didn't matter. She felt amazing. She looked insane. Mad women often do. But 'mad women' often just meant women who'd found their wild.

"Shall we stay?" Marie asked. "Are we home?"

Polly ran around in circles with her arms out wide like a footballer that had just scored the winning goal. Marie watched her funny, odd, witchy daughter, who hadn't yet learnt to lose her wild, and copied her. They spun around, howling and whooping and circling, then raced back to Georgie's Place. Spence had made them huge mountains of buttery toast with lovely marmalade. The radio was playing and Sam was singing. Georgie was laughing.

Yes, the sun was shining, and out there, in the wind and the salt spray, the woman who'd been trapped for so long found what had been taken from her and she wept, and she was free. She was alive and slipping out of her coat and into her skin and sliding through the waves. Finally, after so long. Six beautiful seals swam out of the bay. And some stories end exactly as you think they should.

* * *

Lamp Light, Marsh Light

It's dark outside and it's gotten late, but we're comfy and dry in here. Wiggsy brought his Nintendo Switch with him and we'd been taking it in turns playing Smash Bros, but then we got a bit bored, so we've been lying in our sleeping bags talking. The music from the other tent went off an hour or so back. I can't see their light on, either. I can hear Mr. Cooper snoring somewhere off in his tent by the van. He snores like a cartoon character. Shrimpo's got this elastic thing round his head with a light on it, but he keeps looking right at me as we chat and nearly blinding me. He thinks it's funny, but it's kind of giving me a headache. I don't tell him, though, or he'll only do it more – he'd probably climb over here and shine it right in my eyes. So I lay in my sleeping bag with an arm over my face. Wiggsy's looking for the crisps; they're in the nylon Sainsbury's bag for life his mum packed us off with, but he's decided I'm lying, or an idiot, and that they're definitely in his backpack, so he's emptying everything over the floor of the tent as he looks. No use me trying to tell him again, he'll only get in a piss.

The tent's meant for four, but it only just fits us three in it. It's not bad though; it's got these little compartments that zip up around a middle bit, so we've all got our own little room. Kind of. It's better than waking up with Shrimpo spread out like a starfish on top of me, like when we went to Leeds festival last year.

"I can't find 'em!" Wiggsy is moaning, "I'm starving!"

"That's 'cause they're in the Sainsbury's bag..." I sigh.

"No, they're not... I know they're not 'cause I remember putting 'em in here!"

Right. Fine. 'Course. You carry on, son.

It seemed like a laugh, camping with these two, but now I'm stuck in a tent with them in the bum-end of nowhere in Norfolk, with Shrimpo being a git and Wiggsy being... Wiggsy... I'm kind of wishing I was doing History and not Geography. Then I'd be in France for my field trip instead. Chloe's on that trip. I could've gone with her, helped her with her research, maybe. I could've been sitting round a campfire with her right now, or in some cafe ordering her a glass of wine or alright, maybe a coffee, but still... that would be better than this.

Shrimpo farts and, after a moment, laughs loudly and gives himself a round of applause.

"Christ almighty, Shrim, that is... urgh... something's died up your bum!"

I could've been in France.

Wiggsy's got the giggles now, but he leans across all of his stuff and unzips the front to let in some fresh air. I can't help but laugh too, even if it does smell like death.

"Light a match or something!" I'm spluttering.

Shrimpo finds his lighter in his pocket and flicks it alight, wafts it around a bit to try and burn off the methane. He's wiping his eyes, whether from laughter or his noxious fumes, I have no idea, and sits up. "I'm having a smoke. Who's got the tin?"

"You can't!" Wiggsy turns on him, "Mr. Cooper's just down there!"

"Mr. Cooper is sawing logs, tucked up in his jammies with his ear plugs in." Shrim's pulling on a hoodie. "Trust, bruv, he's out for the count. It's nearly three in the morning!"

"What if he's not though, *Liam*," Wiggsy's got his worried mum voice on, "what if he wakes up and smells it? You'll get us booted home." He's got that pinched look on his face, those little spots of pink on his cheeks he gets when he's angry or nervous. Mostly he gets angry to cover his nerves.

"You think Mr. Cooper is going to take seven A-Level lads camping in the Fens and not expect someone to smoke a biff? Nah, fam, he'll be glad we're not all getting wasted and puking in the canals." He finds the tin in his hoodie pocket, starts rolling a joint.

Wiggsy's freaking out, silently now, picking things up, shoving them in his bag.

"Wiggs... it's all good mate." I try to placate him, but he's ignoring me. "Oi, Stuart?" I sit up. Wiggsy glances at me, awkward, annoyed. "If Cooper *does* wake up, and if he *does* smell it, it'll be Shrimpo that'll get done, not us. All right? Shrimpo's a dickhead but he sticks to the code."

"Dickhead's code!" Shrimp hoots, and plays an imaginary trombone. Then he rolls out of his little 'room' of the tent in his boxers, hoodie and socks.

"Don't worry yourself my little Wiggums, I solemnly swear that, if it comes to it, I will tell Coop that you almost cried, begging me not to throw my youth away on this dirty mind-altering substance." He slaps Wiggsy on the back and Wiggs does actually look grateful.

As Shrimpo shoves his feet into his DCs, joint hanging from his lips, he reaches into the Sainsbury's bag, plucks out the bag of Doritos and throws them at Wiggs. I grin.

Then all six feet of Liam 'Shrimpo' Jones is climbing over Wiggs and pushing his way out into the night. I see the flare of the lighter, see the silhouette of thick smoke in the light of his stupid head lamp, smell that good smell. Fuck it. It'll help me sleep, anyways. I scramble into my jacket, pull on my wellies, still slightly slimy from our wading expedition earlier, and climb out to join him. I can feel Wiggsy's eyes on my back. If it weren't for the threat of Mr. Cooper, he'd be out here, getting more toasted than either of us. But he's scared of messing up his exams. I can't really blame him, but he is like some old man's old woman sometimes, the way he nags.

The night air is crisp and cold. Shrimpo's bouncing on the balls of his feet, wincing against the smoke and the cold air on his face. Bet he wishes he's put his jeans back on. He passes me the joint without me asking and we smoke in silence for a bit. There's more sky than anything else here, but it's cloudy tonight. Bet the stars would look good if you could see 'em. There's some trees, but they're mostly short and dark against the horizon. There's a mist sliding around the grass and reeds, and lots of croaks and rustles coming from the water bank. I can just make out Dan and Mark and the others' tent maybe two-hundred metres away, and Mr. Cooper's over to the left, by the hulking shape of the school mini-van.

"What's that?" Shrimpo says into the dark, quietly.

"What?" I look at him and then in the direction he's pointing.

"There's a light..." he mutters.

I squint, but smoke gets in my eye and I cough. And once I start coughing, I can't stop, and my eyes are streaming and I feel a bit dizzy so I hold the joint out to him and crouch down.

From inside the tent, right on cue, Wiggsy says "Shitey whitey!" like he's dead pleased with himself that karma's about to smack me round the head for daring to partake.

But I've got it under control and tell Wiggsy to fuck off. He throws a crisp at me through the opening in the tent. I throw back a clod of grass.

"There!" Shrimpo says again, urgently. "Look, there's a fucking light out on the water. In the mist."

I crane my neck to look, but honestly, I can't see anything. "You're toasted..." I mutter in reply.

266

Then he drops down to his knees beside me at the tent entrance, the joint falling ignored to the ground beside us. He's got this look on his face. He's terrified, and that's weird.

"There's someone out there," he whispers.

"Fuck, it's Cooper!" I hiss back, stubbing out the joint in the damp grass, wafting the air around us.

"Shit! *Shit!* I knew it, get back in the tent... just pretend we're asleep!" Wiggsy is grabbing at the back of Shrimpo's hoodie, trying to drag him in. Shrimpo swats him away.

"Not Cooper." He looks dead at me.

"Dan, or one of them lot gone for a piss?" I suggest.

He contemplates the possibility, but shakes his head. "Nah, bruv, it weren't none of them, it was..."

There's a splashing sound. A slopping, sloshing wet sound that carries through the mist and reeds to us, and we all hear it. We all freeze. I reach up and turn off Shrimpo's headlamp and we're plunged into darkness.

If someone's trying to sneak up on us to play a prank, I am not going to be caught off guard. I am ready. I am prepared. I almost start giggling at Shrimpo's ridiculous scared expression, but I hold it together and slowly climb to my feet. I'm peering into the dark. I can still hear Mr. Cooper snoring. The flap to the other tent is still shut. I step into the long grass at the side of the tent, careful not to step in the mud or miss the bank and step straight into the canal. There's definitely something moving out there, but it's late and it's dark and there are plenty of things that go hop in the night. Something flickers out of the corner of my eye. I turn, try to focus and find it. Then there's a flash, but not bright, more like someone striking a match or checking their phone, out over the water. It's an odd sort of flickering, shifting, glowing light, and there's still that sound of something moving in the water.

It's a man. I see him.

A man, with a wide brimmed hat, holding a pole, with a lantern on the end of it. It's the lantern I could see bobbing on the end of his pole. He's got a long coat on, I think, though it's hard to see. And I'm gripped with the complete certainty that he cannot see me; that he must not see me. I also cannot move. Like, my feet are just stuck. My body is stuck. I'm so scared. Everything just feels so wrong. A pair of hands grab my shoulders and yank me backwards and down, back into the grass by the tent. It's Wiggsy.

I look at him and know he saw the man with the lantern too. We all have. Wiggsy doesn't say anything, just indicates with a little flick of his hand that we should get back into the tent. Shrimpo's in there already, his head poking out of the flap, beckoning us furiously. I edge myself backwards, willing silence in every movement, wincing at the rustle of the plastic tent sheet. Wiggsy's right behind me and he's trying to zip the tent shut as quietly as he can. We're all breathing hard and shallow and Shrimpo has to lean round me to help close the tent, but finally we're in. We're cocooned in the plastic canvas. I don't even know what I'm feeling right now, other than that repeating mantra of *"Stay quiet, stay quiet, stay quiet."*

My phone lights up, on my sleeping bag where I left it, and makes a loud buzzing sound, followed by a ping. It's a message, but the screen is all lit up and illuminating the tent and we're all staring at it and each other, and there's splashing outside, rushing towards us, getting closer. I fling myself across the tent and bundle the phone into my jacket, switching it to silent, glad to have it in my hand in case... in case what? I don't even know what I'm afraid of. Some random man wading in the river?

That's when we hear it. The whistling.

It's a shrill sound, these long drawn out notes. It's not even really a melody. Just... varying pitches of sound echoing in the dark. We huddle closer together and I can feel Shrimpo shaking. The whistling stops. The splashing stops. I feel like my chest is going to explode.

There's that light, that strange flickering glowing light, and it's outside the tent. The lantern man is outside the tent. We can see his shadow against the tent wall. He's moving slowly, the lantern swaying on its pole, the weird not-quite-blue, not-quite-yellow light dipping and flaring. The shadow stops. He's *right outside the tent.* He whistles again. Almost like he's calling us. I feel the sound in me, like I want to be sick and my eyes are going to pop out of my skull. Wiggsy's breathing so loud beside me, he's almost whimpering, so I put my hand over his mouth and his breath is hot and wet on my palm. Instinctively, we sink down, lowering ourselves, making ourselves small, holding our breaths. I screw my eyes shut. I want to go home. I can still see that glowing, ghostly light imprinted on my eyeballs, I can still see it dancing.

I can't bear it. *I can't bear this.* He's still out there. It's almost like he's calling me. I want to go to it. I wonder if I should...

* * *

Between A Rock And A Hard Place

Now

It's a Tuesday mid-morning in London. Cam is in on the way back from the gallery, idly scrolling through Twitter when Tom messages to remind her about the phone interview with Anna Martinez from Style Out at eleven. Cam checks the time, responds to Tom that she's on it, then, after a moment's thought, asks him to reschedule the Just This interview to later in the week because of the lunch with Dustin Cornell. Tom replies immediately, saying he's already done it, rescheduled for 11 a.m. on Thursday. Cam flicks through her calendar. He has! He's even highlighted it for her, and added a reminder for Dad's birthday with a couple of suggested gift ideas.

Jesus Tom, she raises an eyebrow, *you're good.*

He's a little too young and trendy, a bit too much of the 'I'm your best pal and biggest fan even though you're my boss *air kisses'* thing for her liking, but he has made life easier over the last eighteen months. If Tom wasn't careful, people were going to start thinking Cameron Newbank was organised.

"You want to stop off for coffee, or are you good?" Lou asks from the driver's seat.

She glances out of the window at the sun-flooded city. Bricks, tarmac, Hackney Carriages and people in their early summer dresses and short sleeves dodging between the traffic. Shoreditch wears its June morning well. Before the students and hipsters have fallen out of bed and after the rush-hour queues. There's something incredibly tempting about the idea of grabbing an overpriced flat white and sitting in a sun-lit window to watch a city breathe and unfold around her. But she doesn't have time today. A week before the exhibition and she barely has time to catch her breath.

270

"No, thanks Lou, just straight home is fine."

Lou glances at her in the rear-view mirror and nods.

She sighs at the promise of the day being shut up in its box and slid onto a shelf away from her, and slumps back into the leather seat. The car passes Spitalfields Market and turns towards Clerkenwell.

The flat is cool, dark and quiet. Cam likes the exposed brick, even if it does make her exactly the type of person Dustin Cornell, darling of the Sunday morning brunch show, described as the 'storyteller for a Millennial post-influencer world'. Whatever the hell that meant. She suspects it probably involves not wearing socks with her shoes and drinking gin infused with nettles cultivated in dog piss or something. She slips out of her suit jacket, drapes it over the tall back of the chair in the corner, and stretches her arms above her head until her shoulders pop. The wall behind the armchair is a storage display installation that came with the apartment. It's both industrial and rustic, made of dark wood and copper pipes. It's full of books, a lot of pot plants, some of her favourite prints, and the Mamiya rb67 medium format camera that Samuel Hayland personally sent as a gift when she sold out her first solo exhibition back in 2009. She glances around the apartment, chewing her lip. She's out of place here, in this life, in this world of press releases, Personal Assistants, interviews, lunch with T.V hosts, money, fame. These clothes, even. The dove grey suit just oversized enough to be on trend, the pale-yellow silk camisole top, even the fresh 'buzzed at the sides and platinum on top' haircut that she could have done herself in the bathroom except that Tom had booked her in to some fashionable salon in Hoxton... it's all *'her'*. Sort of. She likes it all. But it's in the same way you like the beautiful and well-maintained garden of someone else – to walk through, to admire, but from afar. It wasn't meant to be yours.

At ten forty-five, she goes into her office with her coffee, sits behind her huge banker's desk, flicks through the last edition of Style Out, Googles

271

the journalist Anna Martinez (a freckled girl with a mass of dark curls who barely looked done with puberty), fires off a few replies to Tom, to Judy at the studio, to Rupert at the events management place about the exhibition opening, and swirls the spoon absently in her cup. At ten fifty-five, Anna Martinez sends a typed message via Skype to check Cam is,

'doing good, having a great morning and all ready for our catch up?'.

Christ. More *let's pretend to be best friends, though this is a purely professional transaction* bullshit. Cam rolls her eyes and types back,

'Sure thing! Got my coffee, all ready this end!'

Then she grits her teeth, and waits.

At ten-fifty-seven and thirty seconds, Anna Martinez video-calls her.

The interview is just as predictable as Cam had suspected it would be. All the usual 'insights', where they throw around words like 'strong narrative', 'contemporary', 'confrontational', and yep, even 'brave'. The same questions about Cam's upcoming show – an editorial collection she's calling Urban Fairy Tale, documenting the shifting landscape of the East End, the people, the gentrification. It had been a real vanity project but she knows, undoubtedly, that it will sell. Cam's work always sells.

Anna Martinez asks her about her time working for Hex Magazine, about having her shot of Henry Davidson on the cover of Forbes, about her parents and childhood. It's almost a copy-paste of every interview she's done in the run up to the exhibition, from Time Out to The Big Issue. Everyone has wanted to interview her. No one can think of original questions.

"This is your fourth exhibition with Hayland Gallery, the first in over five years. How do you think your work and style now compares to that of your first show, when you exploded into the art world from relative obscurity?"

272

Here it comes, Cam thinks, and leans back in her seat, watching Anna Martinez's amiable face.

"Do you think it captures that same... fervour, that same gritty honesty of Boy, Anachronism?"

There it is. Cam nearly applauds. A decade later, everyone still, eventually, asks about Boy, Anachronism.

"It'd be foolish of anyone to think their art wouldn't evolve over time. I was nineteen when I shot Boy, Anachronism. I turned thirty in April. Are you the same person you were eleven years ago?" Cam smiles broadly to show she's being playful, not difficult.

Anna grins back, although the smile doesn't quite reach her eyes. "Right. Sure. And what about the model in that now-iconic image? Would you ever consider working with him again?"

Cam blinks. She's made it very clear many, *many* times that the Boy, Anachronism shot isn't a subject up for discussion. "It was a long time ago."

"It's an incredible story, almost legendary now, the Boy On The Rock in Cam Newbank's first shoot, the photograph that propelled you to stardom, and how he has never modelled since."

Cam squares her jaw, smiles thinly. "It *is* a great story, isn't it?" and says nothing more.

She sees the acknowledgement and disappointment in Anna's eyes and knows the point has been made. Anna diverts the questions back to the exhibition, the fact that Cam has already sold three of the pieces before it opens. Cam even manages to throw in a few pithy lines she knows the magazine, and the gallery, will love. Nothing sells a show, or a brand, these days like a few Instagrammable quotes. She could already see, "I'm interested in the people. The people are the stories," overlaid on one of her gritty urban shots of teens drinking under railway arches. She manages to wrap up the interview by midday.

In the silence that follows her hanging up, in the seam of sunlight and dust falling across the office, Cam Newbank leans her elbows on the desk, steeples her index fingers and rests her face against her hands. She stares into the blank, dark laptop screen. She's frowning. It's not the first time someone has asked about Boy, Anachronism. It happens all the time. The shot is on postcards, birthday cards and T-shirts in Urban Outfitters. Normally, these days she can dodge it, brush it off, wrap it up in something else and deflect. She's not usually this rattled anymore. But something about today. Maybe it's the way Anna Martinez looked at her. Maybe it was the gallery meeting this morning, the car stuck in traffic and the endless hours of press, socials and moving through this life as an intruder.

Right after she'd taken the shot, when she was still just an art student that no one had heard of, all she wanted to do was talk about it. These days, she refuses to discuss it. How do you talk about something, some *one* that only exists in a single photograph now? No one believed the truth back then, so she'd stopped telling the truth almost as soon as her work got discovered. Cam pushes herself to her feet. She wants to see the photo. It's been years since she last looked at the original. She needs to look at what started it all. But she needs a drink first.

The tumbler of scotch and soda with ice clinks satisfyingly. It's an understated sound. No pop of champagne corks for Cam, no. She hitches up her expensive suit trousers and squats, knowing she'll have dust all over the turn ups, knowing she really should've changed into something else before digging around in here, but stays on her haunches anyway. She places the tumbler between her knees and contemplates the cardboard box. The spare room is mostly used to house stuff that doesn't neatly slot into the rest of the apartment. A lot of it *is* work related – old posters, prints, portfolios. A ton of paperwork before everything got digitised.

Some old sketchbooks. Journals. This corner, between the wall and the large bureau, is a jungle of tall brown document tubes that all want to fall in different directions as soon as Cam looks at them. There's a few smaller boxes and tins of old negatives, alternative shots that got as far as an options layout but never made the final cut, and this cardboard box. She pulls the box towards her and tentatively, as if it might rear up and bark at her, places a hand on the top of the stack in it. These are all photos from before. Before Boy, Anachronism. Or at least, up to and including it. She takes a gulp of her scotch, then rifles through the box until she finds the acid-free wax paper sleeve, pulls it from the box and slides the print out of it. She balances it flat on her fingertips. It sends a tremor up her spine and every hair on her arms stands on end. She remembers when she got this back from the printers, when it landed on the doormat of her parents' place, when she'd torn open the envelope, slid out the print, felt that exact same tremor, the same as when she'd seen the image on the digital screen of the camera, same as when she'd opened the SD card and seen the single file there.

The photograph is black and white. It's of a young, handsome man with brown skin. He's wearing white cyber-punk PVC clothing complete with white-blonde dreadlocks and draped hood. His mouth and chin are covered with a cowl-like collar, but his piercing eyes and chiselled cheekbones are striking. It's an outdoor shot. The young man crouches upon a megalithic stone chamber, on a flattish capstone balanced across the top of three other standing stones. The photo is at an angle taken up, so the clumpy white rave boot of his right foot is in the foreground, closest to the camera. He's staring defiantly down the lens, chin lifted. The pose and angle give a strange sensation that he's about to climb out of the print. His hyper-futuristic clothes and pose against the bleak, ancient rock structure and timeless Dartmoor sky behind him create a strange juxtaposition of time. Boy, Anachronism. She'd come up with the name while shooting him, inspired by a Dresden Dolls song. Zana. The boy who never existed. Cam stands, taking the print and her glass, and heads back to her office.

Then

In 2008, Cam had been in her second year of a Bachelor of Arts in photography at the Plymouth College of Arts. She was an OK student. Enthusiastic, but nothing special. Not really. She was one of a sea of strange kids with odd haircuts and interesting fashion choices who really wanted their art to *mean* something. They were all fiercely earnest about the importance of the pursuit and creation of Art with a capital A and terrified that it might actually not mean anything at all. Cam blended in. She was likeable, easy going, took part if she had to, went to parties to hide in kitchens and play with cats, dated occasionally. But. Cam Newbank knew at nineteen that she was average and it killed her. She hated that she knew truly, deep inside, she didn't have anything unique to say; that she was beige, bland, afraid and just another waste of breath trying to carve out a space for herself. She knew, at nineteen, that she'd never amount to anything. She tried hard, really, but there were always others that were just... better. More creative, more talented. She just sort of faded into the background – at College, and in life. Even her friends seemed more alive somehow, more vital. Like they'd managed to tap into something that lit them up from inside. Kelly never seemed to be sitting still, even while at work. The two of them worked weekends in Atomic Vintage, a second-hand shop. Kelly was always working on some project or idea, moving forward under some strange steam.

"You just got to find your groove, babes," Kelly said to her once while straightening clothes on rails, "it's like you're afraid that if something, or God forbid *someone*, lights you up, you'll get burnt up into nothing."

"Icarus was a lesson in precaution," Cam replied, trailing after her, absently re-touching the stock Kelly had just set out.

"But God, at least he *flew!*" Kelly grinned. That day Kelly had been wearing metallic green lipstick.

In the second term of 2008, between Easter and Summer, Cam was handed a coursework assignment based around the concept of 'New versus Old'. She was to research the theme then devise and shoot a final image that illustrated this concept. Her coursework sketchbook and the final piece would account for a percentage of her degree. She looked at the assignment sheet and her mind was blank. Around her, other students – the ones with the bold haircuts and colourful clothes – were already talking animatedly about ideas, concepts, different ways they could interpret the theme. A queer twist on an Edwardian gentleman; a futuristic space drag queen in platform space boots stomping through a mossy and misty graveyard; staging war correspondent-type shots of kids in ruined buildings; changes in technology or transport. Cam felt a rock clang hollowly into the depths of her belly as she realised, already, she was at risk of being left on the starting blocks. She couldn't mess this up. She refused to. She needed to nail this, to prove she could, that she was good enough. She needed to come up with something that would carve out her space and let everyone see her. Old versus new. She turned the phrase over and over, tasting it, exploring it the way you push your tongue against a painful tooth. She needed to find her groove. She needed to fly. She flipped open her notebook and scribbled, in large thick letters, ANACHRONISM. Then she underlined it several times. Then she scooped up her belongings and headed to the library.

The following weeks were full of research, of sketching ideas, of mind maps and scribbled notes. But despite her efforts, despite her resolution to create something unique and captivating, she could not pin down a strong-enough idea. Until, in the middle of a strange Wikipedia vortex of clicking through tenuously linked articles, she found Kits Coty.

She'd been looking up burial rites, thinking perhaps she could build her project into something goth and dark about changing death rituals. Kits Coty was a megalithic stone chamber. Three huge slabs of rock with a flat table on the top. Some kind of entrance, apparently, to a burial mound, or gateway to the underworld. Druidic. It was located in the middle of Dartmoor less than an hour away, on a small hill in the centre of a strange, stunted oak forest called Wistman's Wood. Something about the name and the single badly-focussed photograph, captured her attention. She opened a new browser tab and searched specifically for Kits Coty and finally found it listed on a crappy slow-loading website called A Pictorial History of the Dorset and Devon Countryside. There was a better photo, mystical and archaic. She read the accompanying text and an idea, a thought, began to climb its way out of her skull like an oil-slicked seagull dragging itself onto a shore. Could she not place something so out of place and hyper-futuristic in that landscape and create her anachronism?

The image of those stones, with the twisted oak trees and the wind-blasted hills beyond, and the words she read about it – druidic rites and ghostly haunted trees – all climbed inside her, took hold. Grew roots. She knew she *had* to shoot there. The idea was like a fever. She started to find she was imagining the mound and the stones when she was supposed to be working, or reading, or eating. She started, after a while, to dream about it. It didn't concern her, not really. She was fired up for the first time; she had an idea and it was a good one. Why should it worry her that a place she had never seen, never heard of even, was reaching into her dreamscapes?

In June, Kelly invited her to a club night she had organised with a bunch of their mutual friends; some kind of alternative art house dance music night. She went because Kelly was probably her best friend, and she hadn't gone out for so long. She had really tried with her outfit and makeup but when she walked into the club and saw that it was filled with all manner of

278

strange and curious people, with a lot of leather and bare skin, she knew once again that she was beige. She accepted the fact by slotting herself into a quiet corner, on a stool, with her bag strap across her body like a barrier. She sipped her drink through its straw and wondered when it might be acceptable to go home again. She wasn't sure about the music – it was loud, and thumping – but the people were fascinating. Everyone was a piece of art. Everyone was weird and fine with it. She wished she could be like them. She pulled out her slim digital camera and snapped a few shots. She wondered about asking Kelly if she could be the official event photographer for their next club night. That way she would have a purpose, wouldn't have to talk to anyone, and would get to document it all. The idea thrilled her. It was 'out there' and brave, for her. She watched a group of gorgeously pale goths move past her like smoke and lightning storms; one of them met her gaze and his eyes were... wrong somehow, too bright, luminous and captivating, and something whispered in the back of her mind that, if she wanted to, she could follow them...

Kelly bounced across the bar at her, collected her into a cuddle. Today her lipstick was a dark blackberry red.

"I'm so glad you're here!" She grinned. "There's someone I think you should meet."

"Oh?" Cam was startled, ruffled, feeling out of her depth and glad that Kelly was holding on to her, else she might slip into some horrific introverted whirlpool and never surface.

"Remember you were telling me all about that idea for your final piece? Your Anachro-whatsit shot? How you were looking for someone to photograph?" Kelly was moving them across the club, weaving them around people, shouting into Cam's ears.

Cam nodded.

"Well," Kelly turned her by the shoulders, "this is Zana."

279

And there he was. Tall, brown-skinned, dressed in ripped black trousers and black T-shirt, but with that shock of white dreadlocks trailing down his back. His eyes were strikingly blue. She wondered if he was wearing coloured contacts. He was with a group of other people, some of whom Cam recognised from College. They greeted her with smiles and waves. Zana appraised her coolly.

"He's a cyber punk!" Kelly added, in the same way a pushy mother might introduce their daughter to a prospective husband with 'he's a *lawyer*'.

"Only on the weekends," Zana said quietly, with a hint of a smirk. "You're the photographer?"

Cam had never been The Photographer, like she was the only one, like she was something, like she'd been the topic of conversation. It made her feel a strange sort of hunger. She nodded and he nodded back, a cool little gesture that was more a lifting of his chin and a faint smile at her, an acceptance.

"Zana Mahoud." He shook her hand.

He was beautiful and, if she'd been into that kind of thing, she might have blushed. Instead, she felt relieved. Her wild, ancient landscape, the stones, they knew he was the one. She could see him already in the shot, in her mind. He was perfect.

Zana, it turned out, lived down the road from Cam's parents' place. Both his parents worked at the dockyard. They were Iranian but Zana preferred to tell people he was Persian because he liked the cats, the rugs and the fact that it sounded so much more exotic. He was a DJ and a student at Plymouth University. He was studying advanced mathematics and physics, partly because he was good at it and partly, he said, because people looked at him and didn't expect him to be smart. He liked to mess with people's expectations. Cam liked him. He didn't seem to care that she was awkward and shy. He didn't seem to think her idea was weird. He nodded and said, "Cool" a lot. She talked more to him in that loud club than she ever spoke to anyone. It was like the words were being pulled out of her. She offered him a hundred pounds for his time, if he was OK to provide the costumes. He was, and they agreed she'd pick him up from his parents' place at 9 a.m. next Wednesday. She left the club that night strong and focussed, like she might have finally figured out how to tap into that glow she'd been longing for.

This was how Cam came to be walking along a trail high up on Dartmoor towards an old oak forest on a bright morning in June, following the tall and slender back of a man dressed in white PVC. He had his shirt with the draping cowl hood tied around his waist and walked in a white cotton vest. His slouchy soft leather boots, also white, strode ahead effortlessly.

"I'm sorry if you get your stuff muddy..." Cam called, realising too late that an outdoor shoot dressed entirely in white was unlikely to be practical.

"It's fine, I bought wipes. All this gear wipes clean," he paused, "which has its benefits."

She could hear his chuckle. He was carrying the reflector disc in its cover, slung over his shoulder. She carried her camera bag and light gun. They'd parked in the car park of a picturesque hotel at the start of the walking trail to the woods and popped in to use their toilets. Zana had gotten changed and applied a little shimmer across his cheekbones. He was so cool and effortless. He'd sworn he didn't model, only that he liked to dress up nice for the clubs. Makeup, he'd said, was the dry ice smoke screen of the illusion. He'd also sworn he was only twenty-three, but he moved and spoke like he'd been on the earth for thousands of years. He really was an anachronism, born in the wrong time. The world wasn't ready for him yet. Nothing fazed him. Not even the entire reception area of the hotel staring at him as he walked decisively back out to meet Cam.

Everything he did was decisive, she realised. He just smiled that little half smile and presented himself to Cam, held out his arms.

"Hyper-futuristic enough?"

She shrugged. "I mean, you could be a little less dazzling and fabulous, you know..."

He laughed.

"You look perfect. This is going to be awesome."

Wistman's Wood, the internet said, was only about a mile down the track from the hotel and they could see it hugging the side of the valley as they marched towards it. It was reeling them in, and Cam felt more energised the closer she got to it. It was a beautiful morning, bright, not too hot and not too cold. There was a high thin but solid cover of cloud, so the lighting was as perfect as Cam could hope for. No weird shadows or shifting light to try and combat. She was ready. She was exhilarated. Zana's easy-going calmness buoyed her as they entered the woods.

It wasn't like any other forest or wood that Cam had ever been in. The oak trees were twisted like something from a Grimm's tale, but short and squat. The internet had also said this was because of the altitude. Zana was able to reach up and touch the branches easily, which he did often. The trees grew, arthritic and reaching, from between huge boulders and slabs of granite. Everything was covered in moss. Tendrils of lichen clung to the low branches like hag's hair. Anywhere they placed a hand was spongy and velvety. They knew the mound and Kits Coty were in the centre of the wood, and the wood was only a narrow slither on the valley-side, so they kept walking without turning, in the direction the track had pointed them. The wood was small; only 400 meters long and 100 wide at its widest, on an incline, which meant they had to climb a little here and there. It shouldn't take them long to find the mound. As they walked, they could see the open moors through the trees on either side. They walked. They chatted sporadically, pointing out interesting rocks and moss to one another, commenting on the shapes that the oak branches made. Cam paused to take photos as they walked. There were so many interesting shapes and patterns of light and shade. They walked. After a while, they stopped talking. They walked and the light changed. They walked and the sun arced overhead. They walked and they did not turn and yet they did not find the mound or the stones.

Zana stopped, braced his hands on his hips and stared intently at a moss-covered boulder in front of him. Cam stopped behind him, her breathing heavy. They seemed to have been moving steadily uphill.

"We're going in circles." He pursed his lips and looked up at the sky through the boughs.

"That's not possible. It's too narrow. We can't..." Cam was looking around them, frowning.

"We've been walking for two hours." Zana turned and fixed his gaze on her. His boots were streaked with green and brown.

She opened her mouth, closed it again, let out an exasperated sigh. "We can't be lost. It's not big enough to get lost in." She knew they were in the right place. She knew the mound and the stones were nearby; she could *feel* them. They hadn't turned, they hadn't backtracked. Zana stepped to his left and she could see what he'd been looking at so intently. The boulder was, like all the others, covered in moss, but there were bare tracks in the moss, a spiral with a large blob at its centre.

"We've been going in circles," Zana repeated, and leant himself against the rock.

Cam frowned and turned to look back at the way they'd come. She could still see the sky through the branches, the open moorland either side of the wood and yet something was stopping them from finding the mound; the mound that had been weaving through her dreams and pulling her here.

She huffed, annoyed, and jiggled her foot as she thought. Zana stood quietly and watched her.

"This is weird, right?" she said, finally.

"Yep." Zana answered flatly, still cool and unfazed despite everything.

"This wood is weird. It's old. It's..."

"Alive?" he finished. She met his gaze again and nodded slowly.

"They do say it's a haunted Druid's wood..." Cam laughed at the absurdity. "Maybe we need to ask the spirits' permission to see the stones?"

Zana shrugged, hauled himself on top of the boulder with the spiral moss markings, cupped his hands to his mouth and shouted, "Can we come in, please?!"

His voice echoed into silence as Cam stared up at him. "What the hell was that?" she asked, eventually.

He looked down at her, slid back down from the boulder. "Just asking politely."

"You are *weird*," she told him. He grinned.

They continued to walk and hadn't gone more than a few yards when the trees thinned and opened to a clearing; the grassy slope of the mound and the stones.

Zana was creeped out, trying to hide it. "We must have just... missed it earlier? Got turned around?"

Cam shook her head and shrugged at Zana. "I guess you asked nicely enough!"

He glanced at her and his unease dissipated, replaced with that easy-going smile. "Right. While we've still got light." He dropped his bag on the floor, slipped the synthetic cowl-necked hooded shirt from his waist and over his head, arranged the hood and his dreadlocks so they spilled over his shoulders, took out the packet of wipes and cleaned off his boots. "Where do you want me?"

It wasn't a big mound and the stone chamber wasn't huge. From the photo Cam had first seen of it, from what she'd been imagining and seeing in her dreams, she'd expected something bigger. Maybe something like the mound of Glastonbury Tor. This was a grassy hillock rising out of a clearing amidst the trees, with something a little like a stone garden shed on the top of it. But she felt giddy, a little seasick. She *knew* she was here to get the shot because the stones wanted her to be. So she pulled her camera free from its case, swapped in a new battery, shoved the two filters she'd brought along just in case into her back pocket. "Let's get the fuck to work, then."

She shot and he posed. She didn't need to give him much direction, he seemed to instinctively know how to stand, how to angle his face, the sort of defiant gaze she wanted him to wear. They moved like it was choreographed, like it was ballet. They barely spoke. Step, click flash, crouch, click flash, shift, click flash. It was dream-like and somehow urgent. And then, Zana looked at the stones and swung himself up onto the capstone. Cam moved around the mound looking at him through the viewfinder, searching for the perfect moment, for the image, peeling away everything unnecessary, all the negative space, searching for the composition. She walked the mound three times. He crouched, posed, and she took the shot. She knew as soon as her finger released the shutter that this was it. She could taste electricity and copper in her mouth, like blood. Zana seemed to know it too, because he relaxed and sank onto his rear, his head dropped forward as if he'd just run a marathon.

"Boy, Anachronism," Cam muttered. "That's the title."

"Hey," Zana was reaching into a hollow in the rock between his legs, "look at this." He held out a fistful of large rusted iron nails. "These must've been here for years!"

He tossed them down into her waiting hand and she inspected them. They were heavier than she expected.

Gifts like these often were.

She was still inspecting them, mesmerized, feeling the Universe shifting around her and those rusted nails, as Zana jumped down from the stones, as Zana said something with a chuckle that she didn't quite catch, as Zana peered inside the stone chamber and stepped inside, as the Universe shifted with an almost audible snap.

Cam blinked and licked her lips. She was thirsty. She should have bought a bottle of water.

"I reckon we're done!" she called. She pocketed the nails, and raised her camera, viewed that last image on the screen. She felt a crawling sensation over her skin, an excitement, an awake-ness. This was definitely it. "That's the shot, right there! Come have a look!"

She was already excited to see it printed. She was thinking black and white. Moody. Atmospheric. All the stark contrasts adding to that anachronism feel.

"Zana?"

She looked up at the mound, at the stone chamber. It was empty. Zana was gone.

She yelled his name until her voice was hoarse. She called his phone number and was told the number could not be identified. A group of walkers heard her yelling and came to help, but could find no sign of him

286

either. Someone called the police for her. Statements were taken. A few officers combed the woods in case he'd fallen and hurt himself or knocked himself unconscious. The woods were empty. They took her back to the hotel where her car was still parked. They interviewed the hotel reception staff. None of them had any recollection of seeing Zana though they remembered Cam. She told them she didn't believe them.

The hotel's CCTV footage clearly showed Cam walking into the hotel lobby, using the toilet, and then leaving again, *alone*. Cam saw the expressions of the police officers shift from concerned to sceptical and weary. Eyes rolled and phrases like, "Waste of police time" were muttered. She was threatened with a fine.

"No, you're not listening to me, he was here. Zana Mahoud. He's missing! Look, see, I was taking his photograph all day!" she showed them her camera gear, grabbed her camera, clicked to the review mode and...

There was one single photograph on the SD card. Just one. After an entire day of shooting. Not even any of the shots of the moss and the trees. Just that last shot of Zana crouched on top of the stones.

"And that's your camera, is it? You didn't find it or take it from somewhere?" The police officers were impatient.

It was only the fact that you could clearly see her carrying the camera equipment on the hotel's CCTV that stopped them accusing her of theft. One single photograph of a boy she claimed had vanished, could have been abducted, could be hurt. She gave the police his name, his age, his address, what course he was studying, and she sat in the hotel lobby in shock, disorientated. The iron nails were still in her pocket, digging into her thigh. She scooped them out and held them in the curve of her palm, feeling their strange and extraordinary weight. That strange sensation of the shifting, of vertigo. When the polite but evidently annoyed police officer came back to find her, Cam wasn't entirely surprised to be told they could find absolutely no record of Zana Mahoud anywhere. Not at the address she'd given, nor at the University.

He didn't even really disappear. He ceased to have existed at all. There were no legal records of him. No one knew him. Cam visited his parents' house herself, the place she had picked him up from. They were sweet but wary. Just as they'd told the policeman who'd visited, they said, they had no son. Only a daughter called Naisha, who was sixteen. They showed her pictures. Not even Kelly recalled him, assured her that Cam must've been talking to someone else at the club, that Kelly had introduced her to a group of people, but that she didn't know the boy in the photograph. Kelly had that same disturbed and confused look on her face that everyone got when Cam tried to talk about how Zana had disappeared, that the only proof she had that he had ever existed at all was this single photograph. And that was the other entirely strange and unexplainable thing. The photograph.

It had such a strong effect on everyone that saw it. It was a good shot, sure, but people looked at it like it was the ceiling of the Sistine Chapel, or the Mona Lisa, like it changed something in them. She got it printed, that lone image on the SD card, mostly to see it larger, to see Zana's face, to show people and say "See, *that's* him!"

Everyone that saw it agreed it was a fantastic shot, though no-one knew the model. They all said they couldn't articulate the feeling it evoked; something visceral and primal and raw. Her lecturer fell silent for almost twenty minutes while studying it and then said he needed to call some people.

And that was how Cameron Newbank became famous at nineteen. A single photograph of a boy the Universe wrote out of existence that somehow captivated everyone. It was the lynchpin of her first show. In 2013 the wall-sized print of Boy Anachronism, which had famously hung in the foyer of the Plymouth Arts College, sold for £23,000 at Christies to some foreign banker. Cam didn't recall their name. Sometime during that same year, a man came forward saying he was the model. Of course, it wasn't Zana. Cam didn't even have to disprove it. The guy did it himself by having too much of a traceable past. He had never been in the UK in 2008.

Now

Cam finishes her glass of scotch. The photograph, that first original print out, sits on the mahogany desk. She stands, goes back to the spare room and to the cardboard box full of the before things, from her before life. Tucked right in the bottom, out of sight and out of mind, is a small Old Holborn tobacco tin. It rattles as she removes the lid. Inside sit the six rusted square-tipped nails Zana had pulled from the hollow in Kits Coty's roof. They were horseshoe nails. Iron. Iron to bring luck. Iron to shoe your horse and take you where you need to go. A gift, unasked for. The granting of a wish she'd never wished.

Except.

She had, hadn't she?

In that darkest corner of her dusty heart, she had. She'd needed something to carve out her space and let her shine, so she could show them all. So she could be somebody. She'd read the story of the Kits Coty on that website: Ask for something. Want it with everything you are. Ask the woods to let you in. Place something on the roof of the chamber – an offering. Walk the mound three times. If the stones like what you've offered, they'll take it and shoe your horse for you.

She'd read it, and not really believed, but she had hoped. She had wanted. And then she'd had to make sure. And he was really gone.

A gift granted. A life altered. But there is always a price, and the price was the boy. Zana had gone willingly, dressed in white to the Druids place. He'd even asked permission.

She's out of place in this world. She does not belong. Not really. She can never truly relax and own her new life. She does not know if the stones will take it back from her.

But she will cling to it while it lasts.

She replaces the lid and buries the tin, the nails, the promise that the stones made her in return for the sacrifice, back in the bottom of the box.

She stands and brushes the dust from her very expensive suit trousers and kicks the box into the darkness beneath the bureau.

Cam Newbank has an exhibition to sell out.

* * *

The Dreamer awakes,
The shadow goes by,
The tale I have told you, that tale is a lie.
But listen to me, bright maiden, proud youth,
The tale is a lie; what it tells is the truth.

(Traditional folktale ending)

About the Author

Alice is an over-thinker, worrier, dreamer, storyteller, and story collector.

Born in Medway, in the South-East of the UK in the late 80s, she briefly attended Bath Spa University to study creative writing. After dropping out and taking a job as a trainee technician with an engineering consultancy (something that is exactly as exciting as you think it is), she took up writing again.

She now lives in Bristol, in the South-West of the UK, with a husband and a cat. She is an avid tea-drinker and fan of a well-placed swear word, but she had to let the consulting engineer life go after 10 years – it was just too much crazy fun for her to manage...

Alice's work is often confessional and maximalist, peeling back the layers of society to peer at the goings on beneath. She hopes you won't hold this against her.

This is her first collection of short stories and she asks that you treat them nicely. Maybe leave out the odd crust or bowl of milk for them. They might decide they like you and stay.

293

Printed in Poland
by Amazon Fulfillment
Poland Sp. z o.o., Wrocław